HIGH DRUID OF
SHANNARA

TANEQUIL

POCKET
BOOKS

LONDON • SYDNEY • NEW YORK • TORONTO

HIGH DRUID
OF
SHANNARA

TANEQUIL

TERRY
BROOKS

First published in the United States by Random House,
Inc., 2004
First published in Great Britain by Simon & Schuster UK
Ltd, 2004
This edition first published by Pocket Books, 2005
An imprint of Simon & Schuster UK Ltd
A Viacom company

1 3 5 7 9 10 8 6 4 2

Simon & Schuster UK Ltd
Africa House
64-78 Kingsway
London WC2B 6AH

www.simonsays.co.uk

Simon & Schuster Australia
Sydney

A CIP catalogue record for this book is available from the
British Library

ISBN 0-7434-1498-5
EAN 9780743414982

Printed and bound in Great Britain by
Bookmarque Ltd, Croydon, Surrey

To the Big Island Book Bunch—
Abby, Amanda, Beth, Brian, Eric, Gerard, Judine, Kathy,
Kevin, Lloyd, Nan, Paul, Russell, Val, and Yvette—
who still believe that a good book
is the best entertainment of all.

HIGH DRUID OF SHANNARA

SHANNARA

TANEQUIL

ONE

Sen Dunsidan, Prime Minister of the Federation, paused to look back over his shoulder as he reached his sleeping chambers.

There was no one there who shouldn't be. His personal guard at the bedroom doorway, the sentries on watch at both ends of the hallway—no one else. There never was. But that didn't stop him from checking every night. His eyes scanned the torchlit corridor carefully. It didn't hurt to make certain. It only made sense to be careful.

He entered and closed the door softly behind him. The warm glow and sweet candle smells that greeted him were reassuring. He was the most powerful man in the Southland, but not the most popular. That hadn't bothered him before the coming of the Ilse Witch, but it hadn't stopped bothering him since. Even though she was finally gone, banished to a realm of dark madness and bloodlust from which no one had ever escaped, he did not feel safe.

He stood for a moment and regarded his reflection in the full-length mirror that was backed against the wall opposite his bed. The mirror had been placed there for other reasons: for a witnessing of satisfactions and indulgences that might as well have happened in another lifetime, so distant did they seem to him now. He could have them still, of course, but he knew they would give him no pleasure. Hardly anything pleasured him these days. His life had become an exercise conducted with equal measures of grim determination and iron will. Political practicalities and expediencies motivated everything he did. Every act, every word had ramifications that reached beyond the immediate. There was no time or place for anything else. In truth, there was no need.

His reflection stared back at him, and he was mildly shocked to see how old he had become. When had that happened? He was in the prime of his life, sound of mind and body, at the apex of his career, arguably the most important man in the Four Lands. Yet look what he had become. His hair had gone almost white. His face, once smooth and handsome, was lined and careworn. There were shadows in places where his worries had gathered like stains. He stood slightly stooped, where once he had stood erect. Nothing about him reflected confidence or strength. He seemed to himself a shell from which the contents of life had been drained.

He turned away. Fear and self-loathing would do that. He had never recovered from what the Morgawr had put him through the night he had drained the lives from all those Free-born captives brought out of the Federation prisons. He had never forgotten what it had felt like to watch them become the living dead, creatures for which life had no meaning beyond that assigned by the warlock. Even after the Morgawr had been destroyed, the memory of that night lingered, a whisper of the madness waiting to consume him if he strayed too far from the safety of the pretense and dissembling that kept him sane.

Becoming Prime Minister had imbued him with a certain measure of respect from those he led, but it was less willingly bestowed these days than it had been in the beginning, when his people still had hope that he might accomplish something. That hope had long since vanished into the rocks and earth of the Prekkendorran, where so many had shed their blood and lost their lives. It had vanished with his failure not only to end the war that had consumed the Four Lands for the better part of three decades, but even to bring it closer to a meaningful conclusion. It had vanished in his failure to enhance the prestige of the Federation in the eyes of those for whom the Southland mattered, leaving bitterness and disappointment as the only legacy he could expect should he die on the morrow.

He walked to his bed and sat down, reached automatically for the goblet that had been placed on his bedside table, and filled it from the pitcher of wine that accompanied it. He took a long drink, thinking that at least he had managed to rid himself of the intolerable presence of Grianne Ohmsford. The hated Ilse Witch was gone at last. With Shadea a'Ru as his ally, even as treacherous as she was, he had a reasonable chance of ending the stalemates that had confronted him at every turn for the last twenty years. Theirs was a shared vision of the world's future, one in which Federation and Druids controlled the destinies and dictated the fates of all the Races. Together, they would find a way to bring an end to the Free-born–Federation war and a beginning to Southland dominance.

Although it hadn't happened yet, and nothing he could point to suggested it would happen anytime soon. Shadea's failure to bring the Druid Council into line was particularly galling. He was beginning to wonder if their alliance was one-sided. She had the benefit of his open support and he, as yet, had nothing.

Thus, he was forced to look over his shoulder still, because doubt lingered and resistance to his leadership grew.

He had just emptied his goblet and was thinking of filling it anew when a knock sounded at his door. He jumped in spite of himself. Once, an unexpected silence would have startled him. Those he feared most, the Ilse Witch and the Morgawr, would not have bothered to knock. Now every little sound caused the iron bands that wrapped his chest and heart to tighten further. He gave them a moment to loosen, then stood, setting the empty goblet carefully on the table beside him.

"Who is it?"

"Apologies, Prime Minister," came the voice of his Captain of the Guard. "A visitor wishes a word with you, one of your engineers. He insists it is most urgent, and from the look of him, I would judge it to be so." A pause. "He is unarmed and alone."

Dunsidan straightened. An engineer? At this time of night? He had a number of them working on his airships, all of them assigned to find ways to make the component pieces of his fleet work more efficiently. But few, if any, would presume to try to talk to him directly, especially so late at night. He was immediately suspicious, but reconsidered as he realized that an attempt to see him under these conditions indicated a certain amount of desperation. He was intrigued. He put aside his reservations and irritation and stepped to the door.

"Enter."

The engineer slid through the doorway in the manner of a ferret to its hole. He was a small man who lacked any distinguishing physical characteristics. The way he held himself as he faced Sen Dunsidan suggested that he was a man who recognized that it was important not to overstep. "Prime Minister," he said, bowing low and waiting.

"You have something urgent to speak to me about?"

"Yes, Prime Minister. My name is Orek. Etan Orek. I have served as an airship engineer for more than twenty years. I am your most loyal servant and admirer, Prime Minister, and so I knew that I must come directly to you when I made my discovery."

He was still bent over, not presuming to address Sen Dunsidan as an equal. There was a cringing quality to his posture that bothered the Prime Minister, but he forced himself to ignore it. "Stand up and look at me."

Etan Orek did so, though his effort at meeting Sen Dunsidan's practiced gaze failed, his eyes preferring to fix on the other's belt buckle. "I apologize for disturbing you."

"What sort of discovery have you made, Engineer Orek? I gather this has something to do with your work on my airships?"

The other nodded quickly. "Oh, yes, Prime Minister, it

does. I have been working on diapson crystals, trying to find ways to enhance their performance as converters of ambient light to energy. That has been my task for the better part of the past five years."

"And so?"

Orek hesitated. "My lord," he said, switching to the more formal and deferential title, "I think it best if I show you rather than tell you. I think you will better understand." He brushed at his mop of unruly dark hair and rubbed his hands together nervously. "Would it be too much of an imposition to ask you to come with me to my work station? I know it is late, but I think you will not be disappointed."

For a moment, Sen Dunsidan considered the possibility that this might be an assassination attempt. But he dismissed the idea. His enemies would surely come up with a better plan than this if they were serious about eliminating him. This little man was too fearful to be the instrument of a Prime Minister's death. His presence was the result of something else, and much as he hated to admit it, Sen Dunsidan was increasingly interested in finding out what it was.

"You realize that if this is a waste of my time, there will be unpleasant consequences," he said softly.

Etan Orek's eyes snapped up to meet his, suddenly bold. "I am hoping that a reward will be more in order than a punishment, Prime Minister."

Dunsidan smiled in spite of himself. The little man was greedy, a quality he appreciated in those who sought his favor. Fair enough. He would give him his chance at fame and fortune. "Lead the way, Engineer. Let us see what you have discovered."

They went out the door of the bedchamber and into the hallway beyond. Instantly, Sen Dunsidan's personal guard fell into step behind them, warding his back against attack, lending him fresh confidence just by their presence. There had never been an assassination attempt against him, although he had uncovered a few plots that might have led to one. Each time, those involved had been made to disappear, always with an explanation passed quietly by word of mouth. The message to everyone was made clear: Even talk of removing the Prime Minister from office would be regarded as treason and dealt with accordingly.

Still, Sen Dunsidan was not so complacent as to think that an attempt would not be made eventually. He would be a fool to think otherwise, given the restless state of his government and the discontent of his people. If an assassination attempt were successful, those responsible would not be condemned for their acts. Those who took his place would reward them.

It was a narrow, twisting path he trod, and he was aware of the dangers it held. A healthy measure of caution was always advisable.

Yet that night he did not feel such caution necessary. He couldn't explain his conclusion, other than to tell himself that his instincts did not require it, and his instincts were almost always correct. This little man he followed, this Etan Orek, was after something other than the removal of the Prime Minister. He had come forward very deliberately when few others would have dared to do so, and for him to do that, he had to have very specific plans and, in all likelihood, a very specific goal. It would be interesting to discover both, even if it proved necessary to kill him afterwards.

They passed through the Prime Minister's residential halls to the front entry, where another set of black-cloaked guards stood waiting, backs straight, pikes gleaming in the torchlight.

"Bring the coach around," Sen Dunsidan ordered.

He stood waiting just inside the door with Etan Orek, watching as the other shifted anxiously from foot to foot and cast his eyes everywhere but on his host. Every so often, it appeared he might speak, but then he apparently thought better of it. Just as well. What would they talk about, after all? It wasn't as if they were friends. After tonight, they would probably never speak again. One of them might even be dead.

By the time the coach rolled into the courtyard beyond the ironbound entry doors, Sen Dunsidan was growing impatient with the entire business. It was taking a lot of effort to do what his engineer had asked, and there was no reason in the world to think the trouble would be worthwhile. But he had come this far, and there was no point in dismissing the matter until he knew for certain that it merited dismissal. Stranger things had happened over the years. He would wait before passing final judgment.

They boarded the coach, his guards taking up positions on the running board to either side and on the front and rear seats outside the cab. The horses snorted in response to the driver's commands, and the coach lurched ahead through the darkness. The compound was quiet, and only the lights that burned in a scattering of windows indicated the presence of the other ministers of the Coalition Council and their families. Outside the compound walls, the streets roughened, smells sharpened, and sounds rose as a result of the greater numbers housed there. Overhead, the moon was a bright, unclouded orb in the firmament, shining down on Arishaig with such intensity that the city lay clearly revealed.

On nights like this, the Prime Minister thought darkly, magic often happened. The trick was in recognizing if such magic was good or bad.

At the airship field, on the north edge of the city, Etan Orek directed them to one of the smaller buildings, a block-shaped affair that sat beyond the others and clearly was not used to house anything so grand as a flying vessel. A sentry on watch came out to greet them. Clearly confused and intimidated by the unexpected appearance of the Prime Minister, he nevertheless hastened ahead of the entourage to unlock the doors to the building.

Once there, the engineer led the way, indicating a long corridor barely lit by lamps at each end, the spaces between dark stains and shadowed indentations. Two of Sen Dunsidan's guards moved ahead, taking note of each place in which an assassin might hide, close on the heels of an impatient Etan Orek.

Halfway down a second corridor, the engineer stopped before a small door and gestured. "In here, Prime Minister."

He opened the door and let the guards enter first, their bulky forms disappearing at once into shadow. Inside, they fired torches set in wall brackets, and by the time Sen Dunsidan entered, the room was brightly lit.

The Prime Minister looked around doubtfully. The room was a maze of tables and workbenches piled high with pieces of equipment and materials. Racks of tools hung from the walls, and shards of metal of all sizes and shapes littered the floor. He saw several crates of diapson crystals, the lids pried open, the crystals' faceted surfaces winking in the flicker of the torchlight. Everything in the room seemed to have been scattered about in haphazard fashion and with little concern for what it might take to find it later.

Sen Dunsidan looked at Etan Orek. "Well, Engineer Orek?"

"My lord," the other replied, bowing his way forward until he stood very close—too close for the Prime Minister's comfort. "It would be better if you saw this alone," he whispered.

Sen Dunsidan leaned forward slightly. "Send my guards away, you mean? Isn't that asking a little bit more than you should?"

The little man nodded. "I swear to you, Prime Minister, you will be perfectly safe." The sharp eyes glanced up quickly. "I swear."

Sen Dunsidan said nothing.

"Keep them with you, if you feel the need," the other continued quickly, then paused. "But you may have to kill them later, if you do."

Dunsidan stared at him. "Nothing you could show me would merit such treatment of the men in whose hands I daily place my life. You presume too much, Engineer."

Again, the little man nodded. "I implore you. Send them

away. Just outside the door will do. Just so they don't see what I have to show you." His breathing had quickened. "You will still have them within call. They can be at your side in a moment, should you feel you need them. But they will also be safely away, should you decide you don't."

For a long moment, Sen Dunsidan held the other's gaze without speaking, then nodded. "As you wish, little man. But don't be fooled into thinking I have no way to defend myself should you try to play me false. If I even think you are trying to betray me, I will strike you dead before you can blink."

Etan Orek nodded. An unmistakable mix of fear and anticipation glittered in his eyes. Whatever it was, this business was important to him. He was willing to risk everything to see it through. Such passion worried Sen Dunsidan, but he refused to let it rule him. "Guards," he called. "Leave us. Close the door. Wait just outside, where you can hear me if I summon you."

The guards did as they were told. Once, there would have been hesitation at such a request. Now, after having survived a handful of unpleasant examples resulting from such hesitation, they obeyed without question. It was the way Sen Dunsidan preferred them.

When the door was closed, he turned again to Etan Orek. "This had best be worth my time, Engineer. My patience is growing short."

The little man nodded vigorously, running his hand through his dark hair as he led the way to the far end of the room and a long table piled high with debris. Grinning conspiratorially, he began to clean away the debris, revealing a long black box sectioned into three pieces.

"I have been careful to keep my work hidden from everyone," he explained quickly. "I was afraid they might steal it. Or worse, sell it to the enemy. You never know."

He finished clearing the table of everything but the box, then faced Sen Dunsidan once more. "My assigned task for the past three years has been to seek new and better ways in which to convert ambient light into energy. The purpose, as I am sure you are aware, is to increase the thrust of the vessels in combat conditions, so that they might better outmaneuver their attackers. All my efforts to readapt a single crystal failed. The conversion is a function of the crystal's composition, its shaping and its placement in the parse tube. A single crystal has a finite capability for conversion of light into energy, and there is nothing I have found that will alter that."

He nodded, as if to reassure himself that he was right about this. "So I abandoned that approach and began to experiment with multiple crystals. You see, Prime Minister, I reasoned that if one crystal will produce a certain amount of energy, then two working together might double that figure. The trick, of course, is in finding how to channel the ambient light from one crystal to the next without losing power."

Sen Dunsidan nodded, suddenly interested. He thought he understood now why Etan Orek had been so anxious to bring him there. Somehow, the engineer had solved the dilemma that had plagued the Federation for years. He had found a way to increase the power generated by the diapson crystals used in his airships.

"At first," the other went on, "all of my attempts failed.

The crystals, when I found a way to place them so that their facets transferred their converted energy from one to the other, simply exploded in the tubes. The additional power was too much for any one of them to handle. So then I began working to combine more than two, attempting to find a different way to channel their energy in a manner that was not so direct and less likely to incur damage."

"You were successful?" Sen Dunsidan could not contain himself. Etan Orek's insistence on dragging out this business was wearing on him. "You found a way to increase the amount of thrust?"

The little man shook his head and smiled. "I found something else. Something better."

He walked over to the torches and extinguished them one by one until only those by the door were still burning. Then he moved to the box and raised its hinged lid, revealing a series of diapson crystals of varying sizes and shapes that were nested in metal cradles throughout the three sections of the box. The crystals had been arranged in sequence from small to large and in lines, but each one was blocked front and back by a shield carefully cut to its individual size. Narrow rods that crisscrossed the chambers like spiderwebs connected all the shields.

Orek stepped aside so that Sen Dunsidan could peer inside. The Prime Minister did so, but could make no sense of what he was seeing. "This is what you brought me to see?" he snapped.

"No, Prime Minister," the other replied. "I brought you to see this."

He pointed to the far end of the room, where a piece of

heavy metal armor was fixed to the wall. Then he pointed down again toward the very rear of the box, where dark canvas draped an object Sen Dunsidan had overlooked.

Etan Orek smiled. "Watch, my lord."

He lifted away the canvas to reveal a diapson crystal that looked something like a multifaceted pyramid. The instant the canvas was removed, the pyramid began to glow a dull orange. "You see?" Orek pressed. "It begins to gather ambient light. Now, watch!"

Seconds later, he fastened his fingers about the crisscrossed rods and snatched away the network of shields.

Instantly, light erupted from the pyramid crystal and ricocheted through all the other crystals in the box, brightening them one by one with the same dull orange glow. Swiftly the light built, traveling down the length of the box from crystal to crystal, gathering power.

Then, with an audible explosion, the light shot through a narrow aperture at the front of the box in a thin ribbon of fire that struck the piece of armor at the far end of the room. The metal erupted in a shower of sparks and flames and then began to melt as the light burned a fist-size hole right through its center and into the wall beyond.

Swiftly, Etan Orek pulled on a rod attached to the cradle in which the rear crystal rested, taking it out of line in the sequence. At once, the other crystals began to lose their power and their light began to fail. The engineer waited a few moments, then dropped the connecting shields back into place and re-covered the rear crystal with the canvas.

He turned to Sen Dunsidan and did not miss the look of

shock on the Prime Minister's face. "You see?" he repeated eagerly. "You see what it is?"

"A weapon," Dunsidan whispered, still not quite believing what he had witnessed. At the far end of the room, the piece of target metal was still red-hot and smoking. As he stared at it, he envisioned a Free-born airship in its place. "A weapon," he repeated.

Etan Orek stepped close. "I have told no one else. Only you, my lord. I knew you would want it that way."

Sen Dunsidan nodded quickly, recovering his composure. "You did well. You will have your reward and your recognition." He looked at the engineer. "How many of these do we have?"

The engineer looked pained. "Only the one, Prime Minister. I have not been able to build another yet. It takes time to calculate the proper angle and refraction needed. No two crystals are exactly alike, so each of these boxes will have to be built separately."

He paused. "But one may be more than enough to do what is needed. Consider. To power the crystals in this box, I used only the torchlight by the doorway, a small and feeble source. Think of the power that you will have at your command when the crystals are exposed to bright sunlight. Think of the range and sweep when you increase the field of fire. Did you notice? The light does not burn the aperture at the front of the box. That is because it is glass-fused, and the light does not burn the glass as it does the metal. It heats it, singes it, but does not destroy it. We control the power of our weapon accordingly."

Sen Dunsidan was barely listening, his thoughts racing

ahead to what the discovery meant, to its vast possibilities, to the certainty he felt that in one bold stroke he could change the course of history. He was breathing hard, and it required an effort for him to calm himself enough to address his immediate concerns.

"You will tell no one of this, Etan Orek," he instructed. "I will give you space and materials and a guard to allow you to work undisturbed. If you require help, you shall have it. You will report your progress to me and to me alone. Your superiors will be instructed that you have been assigned to a project of a personal nature. I want you to build me as many of these weapons as you can. Swiftly. If one is all you can manage, then one will have to do. But others would be most desirable and would enhance your reputation even further."

He placed his hand on the engineer's narrow shoulder. "I see greatness in you. I see a life of fame and fortune. I see a position of responsibility that shall transcend anything you have ever dreamed about. Believe me, the importance of what you have accomplished is impossible to exaggerate."

Etan Orek actually blushed. "Thank you, Prime Minister. Thank you, indeed!"

Sen Dunsidan patted his shoulder reassuringly and departed the room. His waiting guards fell into step as he passed. Two he left stationed at the workroom door with strict orders to allow no one but himself to enter or leave. The engineer was to be kept under lock and key. He was to take his meals in his workroom. He was to sleep there as well. He was to be allowed to come out once a day for an hour when everyone else had gone home, but at no other time.

He was in his coach and riding back toward his bed-chamber when he decided he would not have Etan Orek killed right away. He would keep him alive until he had constructed at least a handful of these marvelous weapons. He would keep him alive until after the Free-born army had been smashed and the Prekkendorran reclaimed.

Six weeks ought to be just long enough.

TWO

Dawn's faint silver tinge was creeping over the eastern horizon in a dull wash when Shadea a'Ru heard the tinkle of the bell. She was already awake, sitting at the desk in the chambers reserved for the Ard Rhys of the Druid Council, the chambers that had once belonged to Grianne Ohmsford but now belonged to her. She was already awake because she could not sleep, preoccupied by her ever-shifting plans for the order and troubled by her inability to bring them to pass.

Her lack of success wasn't entirely unexpected, of course. Even though the Ilse Witch had been enormously unpopular with the Druids in general, Shadea was not much better liked. She had alienated almost as many members of the order as her predecessor, using her superior talents and physical prowess to intimidate and bully when she would have been better advised to use more subtle means. Now it was taking all of her efforts to persuade her followers that she had changed her ways and would be for them the understanding, concerned leader they all foolishly believed they needed.

In the meantime, the order languished. She had secured her hold on the office of the High Druid through the aid of her allies, especially Traunt Rowan and Pyson Wence, either of whom was better suited to the role of diplomat than she was and who together had worked tirelessly to bring as many Druids into line as they could manage. But the effectiveness of the Druid Council continued to be limited, its shadow no more intimidating or impressive than it had been with Grianne Ohmsford at its head. Still regarding the order with distrust and disdain in equal measures, none of the nations or their governments spent a moment to consider the position of the Druids on any of the issues affecting the Four Lands. The sole exception was the Federation—but that was only because she had made Sen Dunsidan her ally early on, giving him the promise of the order's backing to put a favorable end to the war on the Prekkendorran. Even the Prime Minister was in scant evidence these days, however, the leader of the powerful Federation having retired to Arishaig with scarcely a word of communication since his announcement of support for her as acting Ard Rhys.

That was not out of character for Sen Dunsidan, of course. His history as leader of the Coalition Council was notable for his behind-the-scenes manipulations and judicious absences. Long had he coveted his position; it was no secret. He had gotten it because his rivals had died mysteriously, both on the same day, a coincidence too obvious to ignore. But in the years since he had realized his goal, he seemed less satisfied. Once a very public man, he now appeared rarely and only when it was unavoidable. She had endured his sly and condescending attitude on more than one occasion. But he seemed less sure of himself these days, less driven, and she thought that his secrets were beginning to erode his once unshakable confidence.

Nevertheless, he was a valuable ally. If he chose to hide out in Arishaig, it was of no matter so long as his support of her was made open and obvious to all. The trick was in finding a way to persuade him to accommodate her.

For now, there was the matter of the bell and what it signified. She rose from her desk and walked to the alcove window that opened north. On the ledge just outside the frame, she had constructed a platform and secured a wire cage for her carrier birds, the same species that Grianne Ohmsford had used when the chambers had been hers. The sound of the bell meant that the one she was expecting had finally returned.

She opened the window and peered inside the wire enclosure. The fierce, dark face of the arrow swift peered back at her, its sleek, swept-back wings folded into the sides of its distinctively narrow body, its right leg bound with the tiny message tube. She reached into the cage and stroked the bird familiarly, speaking soothingly, calming it. The birds imprinted on their owners early and never shifted their allegiance. She had been forced to destroy all her predecessor's birds because they were useless to her. Their loyalty was legendary, and like creatures that mate for life, they would not accept a new master.

After a moment, she slipped the tube from the swift's leg and brought it into the light. Unfastening the tip, she

pulled out the tiny piece of paper inside and carefully un-
rolled it.

The familiar block printing confirmed what she had suspected for days:

GALAPHILE DESTROYED. TEREK MOLT AND
AHREN ELESSEDIL DEAD. I TRACK THE BOY.

The scrye waters had told them already of the destruction of the *Galaphile*, and she had assumed that Terek Molt
was gone, as well, especially since there had been no word
from him since. That Ahren Elessedil was dead was the first
positive piece of news she had received on the matter. She
was more than pleased to have Grianne Ohmsford's
strongest ally out of the way.

I track the boy.

She felt a shiver of excitement at the words. Aphasia
Wye still hunted Penderrin Ohmsford. The boy was
doomed. Once Aphasia began to hunt, there was no escape. It was only a matter of time. She had feared the assassin had perished in the conflagration that had consumed
the *Galaphile*, and after days with no communication, she
had dispatched the arrow swift to seek him out. It did not
matter to her how he had survived, only that he had.

She carried the tiny message back to her writing table
and fed it into the flame of the candle. The paper blackened and curled and turned to ash. She bore the charred
fragments back to the window, blew them into dust, and
watched them drift away on the wind.

Aphasia Wye.

She had found him quite by accident, an outcast and re-
cluse living at the edge of the teeming, squalid hovels that
encircled the city of Dechtera. She had been in the last
year of her service with the Federation, a big, strong
woman with little fear and a burning ambition. Her intro-
duction to Aphasia Wye came about because she was looking for a certain deserter from the army, a man she knew
well enough to dislike and stay clear of in other circumstances. But a rumor of his presence in the tenement sections of the city having surfaced, she was assigned to find
and bring him back. She was given no choice in the matter.

Aphasia Wye, however, had found him first. A street
child of unknown origins, Aphasia had grown up as something of a legend to those who populated the dark under-
surface of Dechtera. At some point in his early life, he had
been badly disfigured, but not before he had been so se-
verely mistreated that the damage to his physical appearance could not begin to approach the damage to his
psyche. Emotionally and psychologically, he dwelled in a
realm few others had ever occupied, dark and soulless and
empty of feeling. If he had a code of conduct, Shadea had
never been able to figure out what it was. That it involved
killing as a ritual cleansing was something she learned
when she went looking for the deserter. That it was
quixotic and arbitrary became clear when she discovered
that Aphasia felt an unexpected connection to her.

His attraction to her might have had something to do
with their similar backgrounds as orphans and children of
the street, outcasts who had been forced to make their own
way in the world. It might have had something to do with

their mutual acceptance of violence as a way of life. When she found out what he had done to the deserter, her only response had been to ask for a piece of the man to prove that he was dead. She had not sought an explanation of the circumstances. She had neither approved nor disapproved of the act. That might have impressed him.

Then again, he might have recognized that she was drawn to him, finding his disfigurement, both external and internal, oddly attractive, as if surviving such damage was proof of his resiliency, of his worth. That he was repulsive to look upon, all crook-limbed and spiderlike, did not matter to her. Nor did his penchant for mutilating and eviscerating his victims, which might well have reflected his own lack of self-esteem. In the world of the Federation army, strength of heart and body counted for more than strength of character or physical appearance. Judgments were passed daily on the former and seldom on the latter. She found Aphasia Wye admirable for his talents and cared nothing for the package in which those talents came wrapped. Killing was an art, and this man, this odd creature of the streets and darkness, had elevated it to a special form.

She visited with him regularly after that, talking of death and dying, of killing and surviving, and their conversations confirmed that they were more alike than might appear to be the case on the face of things. He spoke in short, halting sentences, his voice the sound of crushed glass and dry leaves, intense and tinged with bitterness. He had no time for words with most people yet found them pleasant when shared with her. He didn't say so, but she could feel it. He

lacked friends, lacked a home, lacked anything approaching a normal existence, gnawing at the edges of civilization
the way a rodent would a garbage pit.

At first, she couldn't determine anything about his way
of life. What did he do to stay alive? How did he spend his
time? He wouldn't reveal such things, and she knew better
than to press. It wasn't until he was sure of her, until he felt
the connection between them to be strong enough, that he
told her. He was a weapon for those who needed one and
could afford to pay. He was a poison so lethal that no one
he touched lived beyond that moment. Those who needed
him found him through word of mouth spread on the
streets. He came to them when he chose; they were never
allowed to find him.

He was an assassin, although he didn't call himself that
yet.

Two years later, after she had decided to leave the Federation and pursue her ambitions elsewhere, she had been
drugged and violated by a handful of men who wanted to
make an example of her. Left for dead, she had recovered,
tracked them down, and killed them all. Aphasia Wye had
helped her find them, though he knew better than to de-
prive her of the pleasure she took in watching them die. Afterwards, she had fled Dechtera and the Southland for the
protective isolation of Grimpen Ward and the Wilderun.
Deep in the Westland, she had continued her study of
magic in preparation for her journey to Paranor, where she
intended to become one of the new Druids.

Within two months of her arrival, Aphasia Wye appeared in Grimpen Ward, as well. How he found her was a

mystery she never solved; nor did it matter. In truth, she was glad to see him. He had followed her, he said, because he wanted to see what she was going to do. It was an odd way of putting things, but she understood. He wanted to share in the violence and upheaval in which she almost certainly intended to immerse herself. He understood her as well as she understood herself. There would be killing and death in her life no matter where she went or what she did. It was in her nature. It was in his, as well.

He did not live with her, or anywhere that would suggest they shared a relationship. He stayed on the periphery of her existence, surfacing only when she put out word for him or when he sensed, as he was capable of doing, her need for him. When she met Iridia, Aphasia Wye was the first person she introduced to the Elven sorceress. It was a test of sorts. If Iridia was disturbed by Wye, she would be of little use in more repellent situations. Iridia barely gave the assassin a second glance. She was made of the same stuff as Shadea and driven by the same relentless hunger.

So the three of them had coexisted in Grimpen Ward until Shadea had come east to Paranor, bringing Iridia with her. Aphasia Wye had been left behind very deliberately so as not to complicate her induction into the Druid Council. Later, when she was firmly established and there was need, she had sent for him. The others who had joined her conspiracy against the Ard Rhys—Terek Molt, Pyson Wence, and Traunt Rowan—instinctively disliked and mistrusted her dangerous friend. Molt called him a monster from the first. Wence called him worse. Rowan, who had heard of him during his time in the Southland, kept his thoughts to himself. But when mention of Aphasia Wye was made in his presence, his face betrayed him every time.

All in all, it made Shadea a'Ru very happy to find them so unsettled by a man who answered only to her.

She turned from the window of her sleeping chamber and walked back to her desk. There was a great deal she did not know about Aphasia Wye. In truth, he unsettled her, as well, at times. There was something subhuman about him, something so primal that it was irreconcilable with human nature. It was his gift to be so, a gift she was quick to take advantage of when confronted with difficult situations. Remorseless and inexorable, he never failed. She would have used him against the Ard Rhys had she not believed Grianne Ohmsford the more dangerous of the two and the one person besides herself who would be a match for him.

But against the boy . . .

She bent down to blow out the candles.

It was late in the day, the assignment of duties given out and the members of the Druid Council dismissed to their rooms, when Traunt Rowan and Pyson Wence appeared at the door to her chambers. She had not seen them since that morning, when she had advised them of the message from Aphasia Wye. Their response had been guarded—perhaps out of a sense of resignation that the unpleasant task of capturing the young boy was going to be carried out after all; perhaps out of a sense of futility they felt regarding the whole business. Neither had been overly supportive of the endeavor. It was as if they believed that eliminating Grianne Ohmsford was all that mattered, that beyond her removal lay green pastures and blue skies. *They lack the fire of old,* she thought, *the passion that brought them into my circle of influence.* But she didn't worry. They were still committed enough to do what was needed and not likely to disappear in a pointless rage as Iridia had done.

Besides, she was already making plans for new alliances that would eliminate the necessity of maintaining the old.

"A message just reached us, Shadea," Traunt Rowan began as soon as he had closed the door behind them. "We have found the boy's parents."

She felt a surge of elation. Everything was finally falling into place. Once they had the parents under their control, they could rest easy. There was no one else who would pursue the matter of the Ard Rhys' disappearance, no one who cared enough to become involved. Kermadec might still be out there, or Tagwen, but neither possessed the magic of Bek Ohmsford. He was the one who was dangerous.

"Where?" she asked.

"In the Eastland. We have been searching that area ever since Molt discovered from the boy that his parents were on an expedition in the Anar. But no one had seen or heard anything until a week ago. Then a trader working the supply route along the Pass of Jade on the lower edge of Darklin Reach sold some goods to a man and woman piloting an airship named *Swift Sure.* They are the ones we seek."

"A week ago?" Shadea frowned.

"Ah, but here is the thing," Pyson Wence interrupted

eagerly. "All this time we have been searching for them in the Wolfsktaag Mountains, because that is where we assumed they were going. But that isn't where they have been! They have been exploring the Ravenshorn, farther east and so deep into the Anar that no word has reached them of our search. We are fortunate, Shadea, that they still have no idea of what has happened to their son or we would have lost them for sure."

"Have they no idea now?"

Wence shook his head. "None. We learned of it by accident, our spies making inquiries everywhere until they found the trader. He, of course, had no idea of the value of his information and gave it willingly to those who did. So now we have their location. What do we do?"

She walked to her window and stood looking out, thinking it through. She must be careful; unlike the boy, Bek Ohmsford possessed enough magic to incinerate anyone foolish enough to give him reason to do so. He would not be easily disposed of. He must be brought to Paranor if it was to be done properly.

She turned back to them and gestured at Traunt Rowan. "Take the *Athabasca* and go east. Find our spies and get what additional information you can. Then find the boy's parents."

"Am I to kill them for you?" the other asked, not quite managing to keep the disdain from his voice.

She walked over to him and stood close. "Do you lack the stomach for it, Traunt? Are you too weak to see this matter through?"

There was a long pause as she held his gaze. To his

credit, he did not look away. He was conflicted perhaps, but determined, too.

"I have never pretended to support what you are doing, Shadea," he said carefully. "I would not have bothered with either the boy or his parents, but the decision was not given to me to make. Now that we are committed, I will do what is needed. But I won't pretend that it makes me happy."

She nodded, satisfied. "This is what you do then. Tell them that the Ard Rhys has disappeared and we are seeking her. Tell them that their son has gone looking for her, and we are seeking him, too. If they come with you to Paranor, perhaps they can help find both. None of this is a lie, and in this instance the truth is preferable. No one is to die outside these walls if we can help it."

Traunt Rowan nodded slowly. "You will keep them alive just long enough to help you do . . . what?"

"To help us find the boy, if it becomes necessary, and perhaps to help us make certain that Grianne Ohmsford is safely locked away within the Forbidding. If we can trick Bek Ohmsford into using his magic to seek them out, we can be assured that our efforts to eliminate the Ohmsford threat will succeed."

"I think we should kill him and be done with it," Pyson Wence declared, brushing her suggestion aside. "He is too dangerous."

She laughed. "Are you such a coward, Pyson? We have eliminated our greatest enemy, our most dangerous foe. What do we care for someone as unskilled as her brother? He isn't even a Druid! He doesn't practice his magic. He chooses to ignore it entirely. I don't think we need spare too much concern for his abilities. We are Druids of some power ourselves, as I recall."

The small man flushed at the rebuke but, like Traunt Rowan before him, did not look away. "You take too many chances, Shadea. We are not as powerful as you pretend. Look at how things stand with the Council. We barely control it. Our grip is so tenuous that it could slip entirely upon a single misstep. Instead of hunting down Grianne Ohmsford's relatives and playing games with them, we should be consolidating our power and strengthening our hold on the Council. With Molt dead and Iridia gone off on her own, we need more allies. There are allies to be had, of that I am certain. But they won't come without persuasion and enticement."

"I am aware of this," she replied evenly, keeping her anger in check. He was such a fool. "But watching our backs is our first order of business just now. We mustn't let any of those who have strong feelings for the former Ard Rhys become a threat."

There was a strained silence as they faced each other. Then Pyson Wence shrugged. "As you wish, Shadea. You are our leader. But remember—we are your conscience, Traunt and I. Don't be too quick to dismiss us."

I will do worse than that soon enough, little rat, she thought. "I would never dismiss you without first listening carefully to what you have to say, Pyson," she said. "Your advice is always welcome. I depend on you to offer it freely." She smiled. "Are we done?"

* * *

She waited until they had closed the door behind them before sitting down to write the note. Traunt Rowan would depart Paranor for the Ravenshorn at first light, both he and Pyson Wence having agreed to accept her decision on the fate of the Ohmsfords. In truth, they didn't care one way or the other about the Ohmsford family, so long as they could feel they had put some distance between themselves and any bloodletting. They were strong enough when it came to manipulation and deceit, but not so good when it came to killing. That was her province—hers and Aphasia Wye's.

She sometimes thought how much easier her life would have been if she had never come to Paranor. Perhaps that would have been the wiser move. She would not be Ard Rhys of the order, but neither would she be forced to bear the burden of its members' confusion and indecision. She could have practiced her magic alone, or even with Iridia as her partner, and accomplished much. But she had been desirous of more than that, greedy for the unmatchable power that came from leading those who could most affect the destiny of the Four Lands. Sen Dunsidan might think that the Federation was the future of the world, but she knew differently.

Nevertheless, there were times when she wished she could simply eliminate all the Druids and do everything herself. Things would be accomplished more quickly and efficiently. Events would progress with less conflict and argument. She was tired of shouldering the responsibility while being questioned at every turn by those she depended on to support her. They were a burden she would gladly shed when the time was right for it.

She wrote the note swiftly, having already decided on
its contents while listening to the prattling of Pyson
Wence. The time for hesitation was through. If they
weren't strong enough to do what was needed, she would
be strong enough for them.

When the note was finished, she read it back to herself.

WHEN YOU FIND THE BOY, DON'T BOTHER
WITH BRINGING HIM BACK.
KILL HIM AT ONCE.

She rolled up the paper and placed it into the tube she
had retrieved from the arrow swift earlier in the day. Walking over to the window, she reached into the bird's cage
and refastened the tube to its leg. The sharp-beaked face
turned toward her as she did so, the bright eyes fixing on
her. *Yes, little warrior,* she thought, *you are a far better friend to me
than those who just left. Too bad you can't replace them.*

When the tube was securely fastened, she withdrew the
swift from its cage and tossed it into the air. It was gone
from sight in moments, winging its way north into the twilight. It would fly all night and all the next day, a hardy,
dependable courier. Wherever Aphasia Wye was, the
arrow swift would find him.

She took a moment to think about what she had done.
She had imposed a death sentence on the boy. That had
not been her original intent, but her thinking about the
Ohmsfords had changed since she had begun her search
for them. She needed to simplify things, and the simplest
way of dealing with the Ohmsfords was to kill them all and

be done with it. She might tell Traunt Rowan and Pyson Wence otherwise, might suggest there was another way, but she knew differently. She wanted all doors that might lead to Grianne Ohmsford permanently locked and sealed.

By this time next week, that job would be done.

THREE

Tagwen crossed his arms, tucked his bearded chin into his chest, and gave a frustrated growl.   "If this isn't the most ill-considered idea I have ever come across, I can't think what is!" He was losing what little remained of his patience. "Why do we think there's even the possibility of making it work? How long have we been at it now? Three hours, Penderrin! And we still haven't a clue about what to do."

The boy listened to him wearily, admitted to himself that Tagwen was right, and promptly continued talking it through.

"Khyber is right about not relying on the Elfstones. We can't do that unless we're certain that this creature has the use of magic, as well, magic that the Elfstones can react to. I haven't seen anything that suggests it does. It might not be human, but that doesn't mean it relies on magic. If it does, and we find that out, then Khyber can use the Elfstones to disable it. But otherwise, we need to find a different way to gain an advantage."

"Well, we have seen how fast it can move," the Elven girl said. "It's much quicker and more agile than we are, so we can't expect to gain an advantage there."

"What if we could find a way to slow it down?"

The Dwarf grunted disdainfully. "Now, there is a brilliant idea! Maybe we could hobble it with ropes or chains. Maybe we could drop it into quicksand or mud. Maybe we could lure it into a bottomless pit or off a cliff. There must be dozens of each in these mountains. All we need do is catch it napping and take it prisoner!"

"Stop, Tagwen," Khyber said quietly. "This isn't helping."

They stared at each other in uneasy silence, brows furrowed in a mix of concentration and frustration, a little more of the latter revealed on Tagwen's bluff face than on the those of the other two. The night before, the *Skatelow* had appeared in the sky above the foothills west of the Charnals. Twelve hours had passed since the horrifying discovery that the creature from Anatcherae had commandeered the airship, killed Gar Hatch and his Rovers, and taken Cinnaminson prisoner. No one had slept since, though they had pretended at it. Now that daylight had returned, they were sitting in the sunshine on a mountainside trying to decide what to do next. Mostly, they were arguing about how best to help Cinnaminson. Pen might have persuaded his companions that they should not abandon her, but that didn't mean he'd persuaded them there was a way to save her.

"It would be less mobile if we could lead it into a confined space," Khyber suggested.

"Or force it to climb a tree or a cliff face," Pen added, "where it couldn't use its speed or agility."

"A ledge or defile, narrow and slippery."

"Why don't we find a way to force it to swim out to us!" Tagwen snapped irritably. "It probably doesn't swim very well. Then we could drown it when it got close. Bash it over the head with an oar or something. Where's the nearest big lake?" He blew out his breath in a huff. "Haven't we covered this ground already? What are the chances of making this happen? What in the world is going to persuade this creature to go anywhere we want it to go!"

"We have to find a way to lure it off the ship," Pen declared, looking from the Dwarf to the Elf and back again. "Off the ship and away from Cinnaminson. We have to separate them if we are to free her."

"Oh, that shouldn't be so hard," Tagwen mumbled. "All we need is the right bait."

His face changed instantly as he realized the territory he had mistakenly entered. "I didn't mean that! I didn't! Don't even think about it, Penderrin. Whatever else happens, you have to keep safe. If anything happens to you, the Ard Rhys has no chance of being saved. I know how you feel about this girl, but you should feel more strongly still about what you have been sent to do. You can't risk yourself!"

"Tagwen, calm down," the boy told him. "Who said anything about risking myself? I'm just looking for a way to tip the balance in our favor long enough to free Cinnaminson and make an escape. In order to do the former, we need to separate her from her captor. In order to do the latter, we need to get control of the ship."

"Get him off the ship and away from Cinnaminson, then get us on the ship and safely away," Khyber summarized.

She stared at him. "That doesn't seem like something that is likely to happen in the ordinary course of events."

"Well then, we will change the course of events," Pen declared. "This thing might be faster and stronger than we are, but it isn't necessarily smarter. We can outthink it. We can find a way to trick it into making a mistake."

Tagwen got to his feet, making a rude noise that left no doubt about his opinion of this proclamation. "I've had enough of this. I need to take a walk, young Penderrin, young Khyber. I need to leave this conversation behind and clear my head. I was secretary and personal assistant to the Ard Rhys when we began this odyssey, and I haven't left that life far enough behind to feel comfortable with this one. I applaud your efforts in trying to save Cinnaminson, but I cannot think how they will lead to anything. If, while I am gone, you come up with the solution to this dilemma, I will be happy to hear all about it on my return."

He gave them a perfunctory bow, one stiff with impatience and dismay, and walked away.

They watched him go in silence, and it wasn't until he was well out of sight and hearing that Khyber said, "He may be looking at this with clearer eyes than we are."

Pen bristled instantly. "I suppose you think we should give up, too? Just leave her to that monster and go on our way?"

The Elven girl shook her head. "I don't think that at all. When I told you I would help, I meant it. But I'm beginning to wonder what sort of help we can provide. Maybe we would be smarter to continue on to Taupo Rough and ask help from Kermadec and his Trolls. Whatever this thing is, the Rock Trolls are likely a better match for it than we are."

"You might be right," Pen agreed. "But in order to find out, we have to go all the way to Taupo Rough, then persuade Kermadec to help, then come back this way again and find the *Skatelow*, which is flying while we're on the ground. I don't much care for our chances there, either. If we don't do something right now, it will probably be too late. This creature won't bother keeping Cinnaminson around if it's not to its own advantage."

He was remembering how Cinnaminson, blind but privy to a sort of inner mind-vision that sighted people did not possess, had deliberately led her captor away from the spot where Pen and his companions were hiding in the rocks. He could not be certain that she had known he was there, but Pen felt in his heart that she had. Her courage astonished him, and he was terrified that it might have cost her life.

"All right." Khyber straightened and leaned forward. "Let's try it again. We know what we need to do. We need to get this thing off the *Skatelow* and away from Cinnaminson. We need to keep it off long enough to take over the airship, get airborne, and escape. How much time would that take if you were piloting?"

Pen thought, running his hand through his red hair. "A few minutes, no more, if the power lines haven't been disconnected. Even then, not long. A reconnect from any draw to any parse tube would be enough to get off the ground. Cut the ropes, engage the thrusters, open the draws, and you're away. We wouldn't have to worry about Cinnaminson until after we were airborne."

"All we need to figure out, then, is what it will take to get our cloaked friend off the ship." She considered. "Besides you."

"But I am exactly what it *will* take, Khyber," he said quietly. "You know that. I'm what it's after. We know that much from Anatcherae. We don't know the reason, but we know I'm what it's come for." He took a deep breath. "Don't look at me that way. I know what I told Tagwen."

"Good. That means you know as well that you are talking nonsense. Tagwen was right to warn you against latching on to any plan that exposed you to risk. That isn't why you came on this journey, Pen. You are the reason for everything that's happened, and you don't have the right to put yourself in a position where you could be killed."

"That isn't what I'm suggesting!" He couldn't keep the irritation from his voice. "The trick is to make sure that by becoming bait, I can still get away when I need to. The trick is in getting the monster off the *Skatelow* and me on, all at the same time. But I don't see any other way of making that happen if we can't deceive this thing into thinking it has a chance to get its hands on me."

Khyber sighed. "You assume that getting its hands on you is its goal. What if it simply wants to kill you? It came close to doing that in Anatcherae."

Pen looked down and rubbed his eyes. "I've been thinking about that. I don't think it *was* trying to kill me. I think it was trying to scare me. I think it was hoping I would freeze in place and it would be on me before anyone could help. It wants me for its prisoner, to take me to whoever sent it."

He saw the look of doubt that crossed her face and went on hurriedly. "All right, maybe it was trying to injure me or slow me down. It's possible."

She shook her head. "What's possible is that you are no longer in touch with reality. Your feelings for this girl have muddled your thinking. You're starting to invent possibilities that have no basis in fact or common sense. You have to stop this, Pen."

He suppressed the sharp reply that struggled to break free and looked off across the mountainside. They were wasting time, going nowhere, and it was his fault. What they were supposed to be doing was traveling to Taupo Rough to find Kermadec, so that he could reach the ruins of Stridegate and the island of the tanequil, gain possession of a limb from the tree, fashion it into a darkwand, return to Paranor, get through the Forbidding, and somehow rescue his aunt, Grianne Ohmsford, the Ard Rhys! Even without speaking the words aloud, he was left breathless—and left with a feeling of urgency for getting on with what he was supposed to do.

Yet here he was, doing none of it. Instead, he was insisting on rescuing Cinnaminson, and it was admittedly for selfish reasons. He looked up at the clear blue sky, then down at the foothills that banked and leveled to the shores of the Rabb. He felt a momentary stab of panic as he realized that Khyber was right in her analysis; he *was* grasping at straws.

But he couldn't bear to think of leaving Cinnaminson in the hands of that spidery creature, not feeling as he did about her.

There has to be a way.

Why couldn't he think of what it was?

Why couldn't he think of *something*?

Shouldn't his magic be able to help him? He had been chosen for this journey expressly because his magic would give him a way to communicate with the tanequil. If it would allow him to do that, shouldn't he be able to find a way to use it here? It had possibilities he had never dreamed of; the King of the Silver River had revealed as much. One of those possibilities ought to be available for use here. If he could think of it. If he could get past the feeling that his magic was small and insignificant, no matter what anyone said—spirit creature or human. If he could persuade himself that it was good for something more than drawing the interest of moor cats like Bandit and reading the danger signs in the flight of cliff birds. If he could just do that, he ought to be able to use it to help Cinnaminson.

He was looking for a place to restart the conversation with Khyber when Tagwen walked back out of the rocks, brushing off his hands and looking less owlish than earlier.

"You can't imagine what I just found," he said. Pen and Khyber exchanged a quizzical glance. "Broad-leaf rampion. Hardly ever find it in low country. Prefers higher elevations, cooler climates. No snow, mind you, but a hint of frost seems to favor it."

Both the boy and the Elf girl stared at him. He looked quickly from one to the other. "Never heard of it? It's a plant. Not very big, but fibrous. It secretes a sticky resin from splits in its skin. You break off stalks, crush them up, fire the whole mess to release the resin, separate it from the plant material, mix it with wort moss and albus root, cook it all until it thickens, and you know what you get?"

He grinned through his beard with such glee that it was almost frightening. "Tar, my young friends. Very sticky tar."

So now they had a means, of sorts, of gaining an advantage over their enemy. If they could manage to lure it into a patch of that tar, everything it touched would stick to it, including the ground itself, and it would quickly become so bogged down with debris that it would have great difficulty functioning. Better still, if they could find a way to bring it into contact with something as immovable as a tree, it wouldn't be able to function at all.

They spent the remainder of the morning distilling resin from the plant and turning it into a small batch of tar. They were able to find the albus root and wort moss needed to make the mix, and they cooked it over a smokeless fire using an indented stone for a bowl. When it was ready, they formed it into a ball, allowed it to cool, and wrapped it in young broad leaves tied together with strips of leather. The tar smelled awful, and they had to consider the problem of disguising its presence as well as tricking the creature on the *Skatelow* into stepping into it.

"This won't work," Khyber declared, wrinkling her nose against the stench as the three of them stared down at the steaming pouch. "The creature will spot this in a heartbeat and go right around it."

Pen was inclined to agree, but he didn't say so. At least the leaf-wrap was holding together, although it didn't look any too secure.

"If it's distracted, it might not notice the smell," he said.

"There's not very much of it to work with, either," the Elven girl continued doubtfully. "Not enough to cover more than maybe two square feet, and that's stretching it. How are we going to get it to step into a space that small?"

"Why worry about it?" Tagwen asked, throwing up his hands. "We don't know how to find this thing anyway, so the matter of applying the tar unobtrusively and in sufficient amounts to render the creature helpless is of very little consequence!"

"We'll find it," Pen declared grimly.

They started walking north, the direction the *Skatelow* had flown. Pen reasoned that the creature knew Cinnaminson's talent was most effective in the dark. It probably preferred to hunt at night anyway, since that was the only time they had ever seen it. They had been keeping watch for the *Skatelow* since sunrise, but hadn't seen anything other than birds and clouds. Pen felt pretty certain that the airship wouldn't reappear until nightfall.

As they traveled, they discussed how they were going to lure their hunter into the tar once they found it and attracted its attention. There were all sorts of problems about accomplishing this. In order to get it into the tar, they would have to spread the tar around, then lead the creature to it and hope it stepped blindly in. It didn't seem too likely that this would happen; the thing hunting them was smart enough to avoid such an obvious trap. More to the point, one of them was going to have to act as bait, and the only one who would do was Pen. But neither Khyber nor Tagwen would hear of that, so another way had to be found.

It was midafternoon, and they were high on the slopes

leading up to the Charnals, when they finally began to put
a workable plan together. By then they were beginning to
think about food again, remembering how good the rabbit
Pen had caught two days before had tasted and wishing
they had saved a bit of it. They had water from the mountain streams and had found roots and berries to chew on,
but none of it was as satisfying as that rabbit.

"We can build a fire," Khyber said. "That will attract attention from a long distance. The creature on the *Skatelow*
won't miss it. But we won't be there. We'll bundle up some
sticks and leaves to look like sleepers, but we'll be hiding
back in the rocks."

Pen nodded. "We need to find the right place, one
where the creature will have to land in a certain spot and
approach in a certain way. It has to seem to the creature
that we think we are protected but really aren't. It has to
think it's smarter than we are."

"That shouldn't be too hard," Tagwen declared with a
snort. "It *is* smarter than we are."

"An open space leading to a gap in the rocks would be
ideal," Pen went on, ignoring him. "We can coat the ground
and rock sides with the tar. Even if it just brushes up against
it, that would help." He looked over at Tagwen. "Does this
stuff stay sticky when it gets cold?"

The Dwarf shook his head. "It stiffens up. We have to
keep it warm. Frost is a problem, too. If it frosts, the tar will
harden and lose its stickiness."

There were so many variables in the plan that it was
tough to keep them all straight, and Pen was growing increasingly worried that he was going to miss at least one of

them. But there was nothing he could do about it except to continue talking the scheme over with Khyber and Tagwen, hoping that, together, they could keep everything straight.

The afternoon slipped away, and the shadows were beginning to lengthen when Khyber suddenly gripped Pen's arm and said, "There! That's what we're looking for."

She was pointing across a sparsely wooded valley to a meadow that fronted a heavy cluster of rocks leading up into the mountains. The rocks were threaded by a tangle of passages that gave the cluster the look of a complicated maze. The maze lifted toward the base of a cliff face that dropped sharply for several hundred feet from a high plateau.

"You're right," Pen agreed. "Let's have a closer look before it gets dark."

They went down through the valley, into the trees, and along a series of ravines and gullies that rains and snowmelt had carved into the slope, watching the sun slide steadily lower on the horizon. East, the sky was already dark behind the mountains, and a three-quarter moon was on the rise. Night birds were winging through the growing gloom, and night sounds were beginning to surface. A wind had picked up, bitter and chill as it blew down out of the higher elevations.

They were almost through the trees when Pen drew up short and pointed back the way they had come. "Did you see something move just then?" he asked.

The Dwarf and the girl peered through the dark wall of trunks and the pooling shadows. "I didn't see anything," Khyber said.

Tagwen shook his head as well. "Shadows, maybe. The wind."

Pen nodded. "Maybe."

They went on quickly and were out of the trees and across the meadow in moments, heading for the rocks. Pen saw at once that it was exactly what they had hoped to find. The meadow sloped gently upward into a jumble of boulders too high and too deep to see over. There were passages leading into the rocks, but most of them ended within a dozen yards. Only one led all the way through, traversing small clearings in which sparse stands of evergreens and scrub blocked clear passage. It was possible to get through, but not without maneuvering over and around various obstacles and making the correct choices from among the narrow defiles. Best of all, one of the choices led to an outcropping at the edge of the woods they had just come through—and it was elevated enough to allow them to see over the rim of the maze to the meadow below.

"We build our fire in one of these clearings, make our sleeping dummies, and hide out here." Pen had it all worked out. "An airship can spot our fire if she comes anywhere within miles, but we can spot the airship, too. We can tell if she's the *Skatelow*. We can see her land, we can watch what happens. Once the creature comes into the rocks, we slip down off the outcropping, skirt the trees, and come at the ship from outside. It's perfect."

Neither the girl nor the Dwarf cared to comment on that bold declaration, so it was left hanging in the stillness of the twilight, where, even to Pen, it sounded a bit ridiculous.

They went back through the maze to a clearing where the opening from the meadow was so narrow it was necessary to turn sideways to squeeze through. Pen looked around speculatively, then found what he was looking for. On the other side of the clearing, deeper in, was a rocky alcove where someone could hide and watch the opening.

"One of us will hide here," he said, facing them. "When our friend from the *Skatelow* comes through that opening, the tar gets thrown at it. The leaves will split on impact, so the tar will go all over. It will take the creature a moment or two at least to figure out what happened. By then, we'll be heading for the airship."

Tagwen actually laughed. "That is a terrible plan, young Penderrin. I suppose you believe that you should be the one who throws the tar, don't you?"

"Tagwen has a point," Khyber agreed quickly. "Your plan won't work."

Pen glowered at her. "Why not? What's wrong with it?"

The Elven girl held his angry gaze. "In the first place, we have already established that you are the one individual who is indispensable to the success of the search for the Ard Rhys. So you can't be put at risk. In the second place, you are the only one who can fly the airship. So you have to get aboard if we're to fly out of here. In the third place, we still don't know what this thing is. We don't know if it's human or not. We don't know if it has the use of magic. That's too many variables for you to deal with. I'm the one who has the Elfstones. I also have a modicum of magic I can call upon if I need to. I'm faster than you are on foot. I'm expendable. I have to be the one who confronts it."

"If you miss," Tagwen said darkly, "you had better be fast indeed."

"All the more reason why you and Pen have to be moving toward the *Skatelow* the moment it enters the rocks. You have to be airborne before it can recover and decide it has been tricked, whatever the result of my efforts. If it gets back through that maze and out into the meadow before you board and cut the lines, we're dead."

There was a long silence as they considered the chances of this happening. Pen shook his head. "What if it brings Cinnaminson into the rocks with it?"

Khyber stared at him without answering. She didn't need to tell him what he already knew.

"I don't like it," Tagwen growled. "I don't like any of it."

But the matter was decided.

FOUR

Night descended across the rugged slopes of the Charnals like a silky black curtain pricked by a thousand silver needles. The clarity of the sky was stunning, a brilliant wash of light that gave visibility for miles from where Khyber Elessedil sat staring northward in the company of Penderrin and Tagwen. The purity of the mountain air was in sharp contrast to the murkiness of Anatcherae on the Lazareen or even to Syioned's storm-washed isolation on the Innisbore. There was a hushed quality to the darkness, the sounds of the world left far below on the hilltops and grasslands, unable to rise so high or penetrate so deeply. Here, she felt soothed and comforted. Here, rebirth of the sort that the world always needed was possible.

They had done what they could to prepare for the *Skatelow*'s appearance. They had built their fire, a bright flicker of orange just below where they sat hiding, feeding it sufficient wood so that it would burn for hours before it needed replenishing. They had placed the tar ball close enough to protect it from the cold so that it would stay sticky inside its leafy wrapping. They had built their straw men, scarecrows made of debris and covered with their cloaks. They had spent time working on the look of them, on the setting of positions, placing them just far enough away so as not to be immediately recognizable for what they really were, but close enough to suggest the possibility of sleeping travelers. They had done this before the sun had disappeared into the hills west, before twilight faded and darkness arrived. They had studied all the possible routes of approach and escape, marked well the path from where they hid to where the fire burned and from where they hid to where the tree line would lead them back to the meadow.

They were as ready, she supposed, as they were ever going to be. She wished they could do more, but they had done all they could think to do and would have to be content with that.

The plan was unchanged save for one aspect. Instead of hiding down in the rocks ahead of time, she was waiting with Pen and Tagwen until the *Skatelow* made her approach. That way she would know better when to make ready. Her plan was simple—wait for the creature to appear, toss the tar from her hiding place in the rocks, and run. By then, Pen and Tagwen would already be aboard the *Skatelow* and flying to meet her. If they were unable to land again, they would simply drop her a line and whisk her away.

It all sounded simple, but she was already having her doubts. For one thing, the tar ball was heavy and unwieldy. It was going to take a mighty throw to get it to fly more than twenty feet. That meant letting their hunter get awfully close. And it was going to be difficult to be accurate. The tar was squishy and crudely formed; it wasn't going to be like throwing a rock or a wooden ball. She was also thinking back to how fast the creature had moved along the rooftops of Anatcherae, and she didn't think she could outrun it if the tar didn't slow it down.

Of course, she would use her Druid skills to help in the effort, an implementation of a little magic to help with speed and direction and control. But her skills were untested for the most part and never in circumstances as dire as these. She would have to get everything right.

She sighed wearily. It didn't do much good to think about those things because she knew she couldn't change any of them. Most plans involved an element of luck. She was going to have to hope she had a lot of it with this one.

She listened to the breathing of her companions in the stillness, to the soft scrape of their boots on the rocks as they shifted position. Pen was lying down, and Tagwen was sitting with his head between his knees. Both were dozing. She didn't blame them. It was nearing midnight, and there had been no sign of the airship. She was beginning to think that it had gone another way, even though Pen insisted the creature would return to search the only area they could reasonably be expected to cover on foot. Cinnaminson might attempt to steer it away from them, but it would know approximately where to look no matter what she said. So far it hadn't appeared, however, and Khyber was growing impatient.

And cold. Without her cloak to keep warm, she was

shivering. This whole journey had been a disaster as far as she was concerned. But she was the one who had encouraged it, insisting that Uncle Ahren take them all under his Druid's wing and bring them in search of the tree that would give Pen entrance into the Forbidding. She was the one who had said they had an obligation to help the Ard Rhys.

She felt her throat tighten, and her eyes filled with tears as she thought of Ahren Elessedil, dead in the Slags. Her mentor, her surrogate father, her best friend—gone, killed by another Druid. Druids at war with Druids—it was an abomination. She had wanted so badly to be one of them, but now she wasn't sure. Ahren was dead, Grianne Ohmsford was locked in the Forbidding, and the very order she had so desperately wanted to join was responsible for all of it. She had learned a little of how to employ elemental magic, but so far it hadn't proved very useful. She carried the Elfstones, but they weren't really hers. In plain language, she was a rank amateur, a thief, and a runaway, and she was risking her life to achieve something she wasn't sure she believed in.

She gave vent to her disappointment and despair, crying silently, keeping her face turned away from the other two so as not to wake them. She stopped after a few moments, deciding she had been self-indulgent enough, and composed herself. She could not afford to waste time. The decision had been made, the journey had been undertaken, and there was no turning back. She had believed rescuing the Ard Rhys was the right thing to do when she had started out, and nothing had changed. The loss of her uncle was staggering, but she knew that if he were there he would tell her not to give up, to remember what was at stake, to be brave and to trust in what her instincts and common sense told her was true. He had come through worse on the voyage of the *Jerle Shannara*. He had found strength in recognition of his own failures and his ability to confront them. A boy younger than she was now, he had remade himself into a man. She must do no less for herself, if she was to be deserving of his trust.

Absorbed in her thoughts, she very nearly missed seeing the sleek, dark shape of the *Skatelow* as it appeared on the horizon and turned toward them.

"Pen!" she hissed frantically. "Tagwen!"

They jerked awake, the Dwarf starting so violently that he nearly rolled off his perch. She seized his shoulder to steady him, then pointed out to where the airship sailed through the starlit sky like a dark phantom. "That's her," Pen whispered.

"I'm going down," Khyber announced, climbing to her feet. "Don't forget. Once you see that thing leave the airship, move into the trees. Even if it brings Cinnaminson into the rocks, Pen. No matter what."

She didn't hear his response, if he gave one, and she didn't look back at him. She couldn't worry about him anymore. He was going to have to do his part, just as she was going to have to do hers, and that meant he was going to have to put all thoughts of Cinnaminson behind him. She wasn't sure he could do that, but it was out of her control.

Her heart was beating rapidly and her face felt flushed as she hurried through the maze toward the fire, blood singing through her veins. She forced herself to focus on the task ahead, picturing herself flinging the tar ball at the creature, imagining it coated in black goo. She glanced skyward once or twice, but she was too deep in the rocks to see what was happening with the *Skatelow*. The creature hunting them had to have seen the fire. Patience, she told herself. It was coming.

She reached the clearing and retrieved the tar ball from beside the fire. The tar was warm and pliable through its leafy wrapping, in perfect condition for its intended use. She turned back to her hiding place and stepped inside. The crevice was deeply shadowed and slightly elevated from the fire and the three cloaked forms stretched out around it. She could see everything that might happen and not be seen herself. Moon and stars lit the open space, revealing the opening to the passageway through which the creature would enter the clearing. But the angle of the moon left her own hiding place in the rocks shadowed and dark.

She hefted the tar in her hands and settled back to wait.

If she had been a little more proficient with her magic, she might have floated the tar out over the entry point, as Ahren had taught her to do with a leaf, dropping it on the creature when it appeared. But that required skill and timing she did not yet possess, and she could not afford to miss on her one opportunity. Thinking of her inability to use her magic made her wish she had studied longer and harder when she'd had the chance, when Ahren was still there to teach her. Who would teach her now? There was only so much she could do for herself, and now no one in the Druid ranks whom she could turn to.

If she even got the chance to try.

The minutes passed. The darkness was deep and silent, a sweeping shroud lying soft and gentle across the world. Nothing moved. The clearing remained empty.

The longer she stood there waiting, the more certain she became that the whole plan was doomed to fail. The thing that hunted them was quick and agile. Her chances of actually hitting it were poor, and her chances of escaping afterwards were poorer still. She began to think of ways in which she could use her small magic to slow it down— something, anything she could do to get far enough ahead of it that it couldn't catch her. A cold certainty began to creep through her that she didn't possess the necessary tools. She was just learning magic, just beginning to make the sort of progress that would lead her to a command of real power.

Maybe she could use the Elfstones. Maybe the thing was possessed of magic, after all. They had been referring to it as *creature* rather than *human being* all along. It certainly looked to be so from the brief glimpses they had caught of it in Anatcherae. So maybe the Stones would work against it.

Or she could try summoning the wind that she had used to sweep it off the deck of the *Skatelow*. The wind had worked once. There wasn't any reason it shouldn't work again. That was a magic she could safely command. That was a weapon she could put to use.

She waited some more. The minutes dragged by. The creature did not appear.

Something was wrong. It had been too long. It should

have been here by now, if it was coming. She hated that she couldn't see what was happening beyond the clearing. It left her blind and helpless to do anything but stand there and hope they had guessed right about what the creature would do. But what if they hadn't?

Her eyes scanned the clearing, probing the passage opening at the far side. Still nothing moved.

Then a soft scrape sounded right above her hiding place, and a small shower of dust descended in a tiny cloud.

Her breath caught in her throat. It was right above her.

She froze, caught off guard completely. *Right above me.* Did it know she was there? She waited, trying to regain control of her muscles, listening to the silence, anticipating so many bad possibilities that she wanted to scream to relieve the tension.

Then she saw it, creeping along the rim of the rocks to her right, circling the clearing like a big spider, cloaked and hooded, as silent as the dark into which it had blended so easily. She realized at once the mistake they had made. They had assumed it would come at them on the ground because that's what they would have done in its place. But the thing wasn't like them. In Anatcherae, it had used the rooftops. Aboard the *Skatelow*, it had hung from the rigging. It liked the advantage of height. It had used it here, coming into the maze not through the twisting passageways, but over the tops of the boulders, leaping and crawling like the insect it resembled.

Do something!

It was still moving, slowly and just a few yards at a time, studying the fire and the bundled forms. It might have sensed something was wrong or it might simply have been making sure it wasn't missing anything. Whatever the case, if she was going to use the tar, she had to do it while the thing was still within striking distance. It would see her the moment she moved, of course. She would have to step out from her hiding place, and it would see her.

She realized suddenly that this wasn't going to work. She wouldn't be fast or accurate enough. It could drop down in those rocks much faster than she could move. It was looking for a trap, and it would spot her the moment she left the shadows.

What else can I do?

The question echoed in her mind in a hopeless wail of despair.

Then all at once the creature wheeled about, looking off to the south, toward the trees below the meadow, toward the path that Pen and Tagwen were already surely taking to reach the *Skatelow*. It froze in place, tensed and staring. A second later it was gone, bounding over the rocks and out of view, moving so swiftly that it seemed simply to disappear.

She stood staring after it for a second, realizing what it intended, immobilized by her sense of failure and helplessness to prevent it from succeeding. She was too far away to reach them, too far away to get back to where they were.

There was only one chance. Breaking from her hiding place in a rush, she raced across the clearing and through the passageway that led out to the meadow and the airship.

* * *

After Khyber Elessedil disappeared into the rocks, Pen sat with Tagwen and watched as the *Skatelow* moved steadily closer to their hiding place and then finally started to descend toward the meadow. Even with the bright moon and stars to aid him, he could not make out what was happening aboard the airship. As the vessel landed, he searched for Cinnaminson and her captor without success. A cold premonition began to seep through him that it was too late for her; that the thing that had taken her prisoner had decided she was not worth the trouble. His premonition was not eased when he saw the shadowy form of the creature slide over the side of the vessel to tie her off and then start toward the rocks in a skittering crawl.

"We have to go, Penderrin." Tagwen nudged him.

He took a moment longer to scan the decks of the *Skatelow* for any sign of the girl, but all he could make out were the desiccated forms of Gar Hatch and his crew, still hung from the rigging. He swallowed and forced himself to look away.

She'll be all right, he told himself. *It won't have done anything to her yet, not this quickly.* But his words sounded hollow and false.

They descended from their hiding place in a crouch, staying back from the light and any view from the meadow. Pen glanced through the rocks only once to make certain the creature was still heading toward the fire, caught a glimpse of its dark, skittering form, and turned his concentration to the task at hand. It took them a few minutes to get through the back end of the maze and down to the forest edge, where they could begin to make their way out to the meadow.

They moved swiftly then, anxious to reach the airship and take control of her. The moonlight brightened their way, and they made good progress skirting the tree line, but their path was circuitous and it took them longer than Pen had thought it would. The minutes seemed to fly by and still they hadn't reached the opening between the trees and rocks that would get them out onto the flats.

"Do you hear anything?" he whispered to Tagwen at one point, but the Dwarf only shook his head.

Finally, the meadow came into view ahead of them, its grasses silver-tipped and spiky in the moonlight. They began to move away from the maze, but still Pen couldn't see the *Skatelow*. He glanced toward the rocks, catching a quick glimpse of the fire's orange glow rising from their midst, dull and smoky against the darkness. The creature must be all the way in by now, but he still hadn't heard anything. Any minute, Khyber would throw the tar into its face. They had to move faster. They had to get to Cinnaminson.

"Tagwen," he whispered again, looking back to catch the other's eye, beckoning him to hurry.

He was just turning away again when he caught sight of a spidery shape leaping across the boulder tops and coming toward them with frantic purpose. At first he didn't comprehend what he was seeing. Then he let out a gasp of recognition.

"Tagwen!" he shouted. "Run!"

They bolted ahead, galvanized by the boy's frantic cry, the Dwarf not yet fully understanding what had happened but accepting that it was not good. They tore down along the tree line and into a vale that fronted the meadow. In the distance the *Skatelow* was visible, silhouetted against the skyline, dark and silent. Pen turned toward it, taking a quick glance sideways into the rocks as he did so. The creature was still coming for them, moving swiftly across the crest of the maze, leaping smoothly and easily from boulder to boulder, closing the distance between them with frightening ease.

It's too close, Pen thought in horror. *It's coming too fast!*

"Faster, Tagwen!" he cried.

The Dwarf had seen the creature as well and was running as fast as his stout legs could manage, but he was woefully slow and already falling behind. Pen glanced back, saw his companion dropping away, and slowed. He wouldn't leave Tagwen, not even to save himself. He reached for his knife, readying himself.

Where is Khyber?

Its cloak billowing behind it like a sail, the creature leapt from the edge of the rocks to the open ground, landing in a crouch that only barely slowed it as it came at the boy and the Dwarf on all fours. Crooked limbs akimbo, head lowered within its concealing hood, it rushed them in a scuttling sideways charge.

"Pen!" Khyber screamed in warning, appearing abruptly out of the maze, rushing into the meadow and turning toward them.

Then a huge, dark form catapulted out of the trees behind them, a blur of gray and black that rippled and surged like the darkest ocean wave. Hugging the ground in a long, lean shadowy flow, it intercepted the creature so quickly that it was on top of it before the other knew what was happening. With shrieks that caused the hair on the back of Pen's neck to stand straight up, the two collided and went tumbling head over hindquarters through the long grass. Roars and snarls and a terrible, high-pitched keening followed as both scrambled up, clots of earth and grass flying in all directions.

"Bandit!" Pen breathed in disbelief, the name catching in his throat as the massive moor cat's masked face wheeled into the light, muzzle drawn back, dagger teeth gleaming.

The creature was up as well, and moonlight flashed off a strange knife held in one gnarled hand, its blade as silver as the crest of waves caught in sunlight, its edges smooth and deadly. In the glow of moon and stars, Pen could see it clearly, and he knew at once from its unnatural brilliance that it was a thing of magic.

Bandit never hesitated. Enraged by whatever animal instincts the creature had provoked, determined to see the thing torn apart before backing away, it closed on its enemy with a scream that froze Pen's blood. In a knot of rippling fur and billowing cloak, the antagonists tumbled through the grass once more, locked in a death grip that neither would release.

"Bandit!" Pen cried out frantically, seeing the knife flash as it rose and fell in short, choppy thrusts.

"Run, Penderrin!" Tagwen shouted at him, pulling on his arm for emphasis. "We can't wait!"

The boy obeyed, knowing there was nothing he could do to affect the battle between the creature and the moor cat. Remembering Cinnaminson, he tore his eyes away from the struggle. With Tagwen panting next to him, he raced for the *Skatelow*. Bandit had been following them all this time, he thought in wonder. Had the moor cat come into the high country solely because of their chance meeting and his few halting attempts at communication? He couldn't believe it.

Behind him, he heard grunts and gasps, snarls and spitting, sounds of damage inflicted and damage received.

They were almost to the airship when he forced himself to look back again. The creature was staggering after them, coming as swiftly as its damaged limbs could manage, its cloak shredded. Bandit lay stretched on the ground behind it, unmoving. Damp, glistening patches of blood coated its still body. Tears filled his eyes, and the boy made himself run even faster.

Khyber was already aboard the airship, hacking at the anchor ropes with her long knife, freeing the vessel of her moorings. Pen climbed the ladder so fast he couldn't remember later whether his feet had even touched the rungs. His eyes searched everywhere. There was no sign of Cinnaminson.

"Get us out of here!" Khyber screamed at him. "It's coming!"

Pen leapt into the pilot box, fingers flying over the controls. He unhooded the diapson crystals as an exhausted Tagwen tumbled onto the deck, gasping for breath. Khyber cut away the last of the anchoring lines. On the plains below, their pursuer was closing on the ship in a terrible, hobbling rush, the bloodied knife lifted into the moonlight, a low wail that sounded like a dog in pain rising from the dark opening of its hood. Pen threw the thruster levers forward, feeding power to the parse tubes, and the *Skatelow* lurched and began to rise.

They were too slow. The creature caught the low end of the rope ladder with one hand and held on, lifting away with the airship.

"Tagwen!" Pen cried out frantically.

The Dwarf heaved to his knees, looked over the side, and saw the dark thing below, one hand gripping the ladder, the other the strange knife. Grunting with the effort, he began yanking on the brace of wooden pins that held the ladder in place. Below, the creature swayed in the wind, got a better grip on the rope, and began to climb. One of the pins came free, and Tagwen threw it aside. The ladder dropped to an unnatural angle, and the creature spit out something so terrifying that for a moment the Dwarf froze in place.

"Tagwen, the other pin!" Khyber howled at him, crawling across the listing deck.

The creature had both hands back in place now and was climbing swiftly. At what might have been the last possible moment, the Elven girl shouted out something in Elfish and flung out both hands in a warding gesture. The last pin erupted from its seating in an explosion of wooden splinters and flew off into the night.

The rope ladder and the creature fell away without a sound.

Tagwen and Khyber peered over the side, searching. The landscape below had turned to forest and hills that were dark and shadowy. There was no sign of the creature.

In the meadow farther back, Bandit's still form was a dark stain on the silvery grasses.

As soon as they were safely airborne and the airship was flying at a steady rate of speed, Pen asked Tagwen to take over the controls. "Just keep her sailing as she is and you won't have any trouble. I have to take a look below."

Tagwen nodded without comment. "I can go with you," Khyber offered quickly. "It might be better—"

Pen held up his hand to stop her from saying any more. "No, Khyber. I need to do this by myself."

Without looking at her, he climbed out of the pilot box and walked to the rear hatchway. The door was open, and moonlight brightened the stairs leading down into the shadowed corridor below. All he could see in his mind was Bandit's bloodstained body, an indelible image that dominated every possibility he could imagine for Cinnaminson's fate. He purposely had not looked again on the corpses of Gar Hatch and his crewmen, trying to hold himself together against what he might find.

He paused at the top of the stairs, listened to the silence, then took a deep breath and started down.

At the bottom of the steps he stopped again, peering ahead into the gloom. Nothing moved. No sound reached his ears. He fought back against the panic rising inside, determined not to give way to it. He moved ahead cautiously, the sound of his own breathing so loud that it felt as if every other possible sound was blocked away. At each door, he paused long enough to look inside before continuing on. There was no one in the storerooms or sleeping chambers that the members of the little company had occupied on their journey out of Syioned.

The door to the Captain's quarters stood ajar at the end of the corridor. It was the only place left to look. Pen couldn't decide at this point if he wanted to do so or not. He couldn't decide which was worse—knowing or not knowing.

He pushed the door open and stepped through. Shadows cloaked the chamber in layers of blackness, concealing and disguising in equal measure. Pen stared around blindly, searching the inky gloom.

Then he saw her. She lay stretched on the bed, bound hand and foot with ropes and chained to the wall. Her face was turned away, and her pale blond hair spilled across the bedding like scattered silk.

"Cinnaminson," he whispered.

He went to her quickly, turned her over, and took away the gag that covered her mouth. "Cinnaminson," he repeated, more urgently this time.

Her milky eyes opened, and she exhaled softly. "I knew you would come," she whispered.

On deck, Khyber stood next to Tagwen in the pilot box. She had thought to take down the bodies of the Rovers, then decided to leave that job for later. The night air was cool and clear, and it felt good on her face as the airship sailed the feather-soft skies.

"You should go see if he's all right," Tagwen said.

She shook her head, brushing away strands of her dark hair. "I should stay right where I am."

"I don't hear anything. Do you?"

She shook her head a second time. "Nothing."

They were silent again for a moment, then Tagwen said, "Did you see what happened back there in the meadow?"

She nodded. "I saw. I don't understand it, though. That cat must have tracked us all the way out of the Slags. Why would it do that? Moor cats don't like high country like this. They don't ever come up here. But that one did. Because of Pen, I think. Because of the way he spoke to it back there, or how he connected to it, or something."

Tagwen snorted. "That's not the strangest part. It's what happened afterwards, when it attacked that creature. It gave up its life to save the boy. To save all of us. Why would it do that?"

She touched the controls lightly, fingering without adjusting, needing to make contact with the metal. "I don't know." She glanced over at him. "Maybe Pen's magic does more than he realizes. If it moved that cat the way it seems to have, it isn't just a way of communicating or of reading behavior."

"Doesn't seem so."

Again they fell silent. Ahead, stars filled the horizon with diamondlike brilliance, myriads spread across the dark firmament, numbers beyond imagining.

"I don't think we killed it," she said finally.

Tagwen nodded slowly. "I don't think so, either."

"It will come after us. It won't give up."

"I don't suppose it will."

She looked out into the night. "It's probably already tracking us."

Tagwen snorted and rubbed at his beard irritably. "I hope it has a long walk ahead of it."

Pen could feel Cinnaminson trembling as she told him the story. "They caught us coming back across the Slags. They were in a Druid ship, the *Galaphile*, and they snared us with grappling hooks and came aboard. One of them was a Dwarf; I could tell by his voice and movements. He wanted to know where you were, what we had done with you. Papa was terrified. I could feel it. I knew from what had happened in the swamp how frightened he was of them. He didn't even try to lie. He told them he had abandoned you after finding out who you really were. He gave them your descriptions and identities. I couldn't do anything about it."

She took a deep breath and pressed him closer. "I couldn't do anything about any of it!" she whispered and began to cry again.

He had freed her hands and feet, and he was sitting with her on the bed, holding her, stroking her hair, waiting for her to stop shaking. He let her cry now, knowing she needed the release, that it would help to calm her. She seemed to be all right physically, but emotionally she was close to collapse.

"They left as soon as they got directions from my father on where to find you. The other one must have come aboard while this was happening. We never saw it until they left, and then all of a sudden it was there. It didn't say anything and we couldn't see who it was, wrapped in that cloak and hood. It didn't look or move like a human, but I think it is. It spoke to me a few times, a strange voice, hoarse and rough, like someone talking through heavy cloth. I don't know its name; it never gave it."

He touched her face. "We dropped whoever it was over the side of the *Skatelow* as she was rising. We tricked it off, and it was trying to get back aboard, but we managed to cut the ladder loose as it was climbing up. I think it might be dead."

She shook her head at once, her face rigid with terror. "It isn't dead. It isn't. I would know. I would feel it! You haven't spent three days with it like I did, Penderrin. You haven't felt it touch you. You haven't heard that voice. You haven't been through what I've been through. You don't know!"

He pressed her close again. "Tell me, then. Tell me everything."

"It made us prisoners. I don't know how it managed, but I never heard anything. No one even had a chance to struggle. I was locked away below, but I heard everything. It tortured Papa and the others and then it killed them. It took a long time. I could hear them screaming, could hear the sounds of—"

She broke off, gasping. "I'll never forget. Never. I can still hear it." Her fingers were digging into Pen's arms. She took a deep breath. "When it was over, the . . . thing came for me. I thought I was next. But it knew about my sight, about how I could see things in my mind. That was what it wanted. It told me to find you. I was so afraid that I did what I was told because I didn't want to die. I did everything right up until I found you, and then I turned us another way. I don't know why. I don't know how I found the courage. I thought I was dead, then."

"We saw you lead it away," Pen whispered. "We knew what you had done. So we came after you."

"If you hadn't . . ."

She shuddered once and began to cry again. "I can't believe Papa is gone."

Pen thought of Gar Hatch and his cousins hanging from the rigging like scarecrows, food for scavengers. He'd have to cut them down and dispose of them before she was allowed on deck. Maybe she couldn't see with her eyes, but she could see in other ways. He didn't want that to happen.

"Tell me what this is all about," she whispered. "Please, Pen. I need to know why Papa's gone."

Pen told her, starting at the beginning with the disappearance of the Ard Rhys, detailing his own flight west to find Ahren Elessedil and their journey before they had found Gar Hatch and the *Skatelow*. He told her how he had come to be in this situation, what he was expected to do and why, and where they were heading now. He confided his doubts and fears to her, admitted his sense of inadequacy, and revealed his reasons for continuing on nevertheless. As he spoke, she stopped shaking and grew quiet in his arms. Her horror of what had happened seemed to drain away, and the calmness he had been awaiting settled over her.

When he was finished, she lifted her head from his shoulder. "You are much braver than I am," she said. "I am ashamed of myself."

He didn't know what to say. "I think we take our courage from each other."

She nodded and closed her eyes. "I want to sleep awhile, Pen. I haven't slept in three days. Would it be all right if I did?"

He covered her with blankets, kissed her on the forehead, and waited for her to fall asleep. It only took a few minutes. He stood looking down at her afterwards, thinking that finding her alive was the most precious gift he had ever received and he must find a way to protect it. He had lost her once; he would not do so again.

His resolve on that point would be tested at some time, he knew. What would he do when that happened? Would he give up his life for her as Bandit had for him? Did he love her enough to do that? There was no way to know until he was faced with the choice. He could tell himself anything, make any promise he wished, but promises were only words until more than words were required.

He paused at the doorway and stared into space. He knew how much she would depend on him. She would need him to be there for her. But that worked both ways. Because of how he felt about her, he depended on her to be there for him, too. He might be only a boy and she even younger than Khyber, but that didn't change the truth of things.

They would need to be strong for each other if they were to keep each other safe.

He closed the door softly behind him as he went out.

FIVE

The day's heat still clung to the foothills below the Ravenshorn, sultry and thick in the waning of the afternoon light, when Rue Meridian said in a surprised voice, "That looks like an airship coming toward us."

Bek Ohmsford turned and caught sight of the black dot out on the western horizon, backlit by the deep glow of the setting sun. Even though he wasn't sure what he was looking at, he took her at her word. Her eyes had always been better than his.

He glanced at her admiringly. He couldn't help himself. He still loved her as much now as he had when he had met her some twenty years earlier. He had been just an impressionable boy back then, and she, older by several years and a good deal of life experience, a woman. Circumstances and events had contrived to make falling in love the inevitable result of their meeting, and all these years later that surprised him still.

She remained strong and beautiful, undiminished in any way by time's passing, a rare and impossibly wondrous treasure. Blessed with dark red hair and bright green eyes, a tall rangy body, and a personality that was famously mercurial, she constantly surprised him with her contradictions. Born a Rover girl, she had flown airships with her brother, fought on the Prekkendorran, journeyed to the then unknown continent of Parkasia, and returned to marry and stay with a man whose world was so different from hers that he could not begin to measure the gap between them. She might have chosen another way, something closer to the life she had abandoned for him, but she had not done so, nor voiced a moment's regret. As wild and free as her life had been, it seemed impossible to him that she had given it up, but she had done so in a heartbeat.

Together, they had settled in Patch Run and started their airship exploration business. They had wanted a son, and one had been born to them within the first year. Penderrin to her, Pen to him, Little Red to his footloose Rover uncle, Redden Alt Mer, he was everything they had hoped for. Having Pen in her life changed Rue noticeably, and all for the good. She became more grounded and settled. She found greater pleasure in her home and its comforts. Always ready to sail away, she nevertheless wanted time with her baby, her son, to prepare him to face the larger world. She taught him, played with him, and loved him better than anyone or anything but Bek. As a consequence, Bek loved her better, as well.

She caught him looking at her and smiled. "I love you, too," she said.

Bound to each other initially by the experiences they had shared during their journey aboard the *Jerle Shannara*, they discovered that they also shared an important similarity in their otherwise disparate backgrounds: Both had lost their parents young. Bek had been raised by Coran and Liria Leah, Quentin's parents, and Rue by her brother. It was their mutual decision that Pen would know his parents better than they had known theirs. From the beginning it was their intention that he should share in all aspects of their life together, including their business. He became a part of it early, learning to fly airships, to maintain and repair them, to understand their components and the functions they served. Pen was a quick study, and it was no stretch for him to master the intricacies of navigation and aerodynamics. By the time he was twelve, he was already designing airships as a hobby. By the time he was fourteen, he had built his first vessel.

He wanted to fly with them on their trips, of course, but he was not yet ready for that. It was a source of great disappointment to him. But he was young, and disappointments didn't last.

Bek shaded his eyes with his hand to cut the glare of the setting sun. He was of medium height, not as tall as she was, but broader through the shoulders, his hair and eyes dark and his skin browned by the sun. Always quick and agile, he was nevertheless beginning to feel the inevitable effects of sliding into his middle years. His less-than-perfect eyesight, he thought, was the first indication of what lay ahead.

"I think that's a Druid ship," Rue said quietly.

He peered at what was now definitely identifiable as an airship, but he still couldn't tell what sort it was. "What would a Druid airship be doing out here?"

She glanced at him, and he could tell that whatever she was thinking, it wasn't good. They were miles into the Central Anar, in wilderness that few ventured into who weren't in the trapping, trading, or exploration business. The Ravenshorn Mountains were mostly unsettled and infrequently traveled other than by the Gnome tribes that called them home. A Druid airship so far out would be coming for a very definite purpose and on business that couldn't wait.

Bek looked at their passengers, who were sitting around a map, talking about where they wanted to go next. Two from the Borderlands, three from the deep Southland, and a Dwarf—all had signed on to see country that they had only heard about. They were five weeks out of Patch Run, where Bek and Rue had begun a series of stops to pick up their customers and take on supplies. They had three weeks left in the Eastland before they started back.

"Your sister?" Rue suggested, nodding toward the airship.

He shook his head. "I don't know. Maybe."

He didn't want to voice what worried him most. One of the reasons a Druid airship would come for them was that something had happened to Pen. Word would reach Grianne, and she would come to tell him herself. But he wouldn't let himself think like that, not just yet. This probably had something to do with the Ard Rhys or the state of the Four Lands.

They kept watch as the airship sailed toward them through the fading afternoon sunlight, moving unerringly toward their campsite. How it had located them was a mystery, since few knew of their intended destination. A Druid could find them with help, but only Bek's sister possessed sufficient magic to track them with no help at all. He could see now that it was indeed a Druid airship that approached, so he began to suspect that she was aboard.

The other members of the expedition had seen the ship and come over to stand with their guides. A few asked what she was doing there, but Bek just shrugged and said he had no idea. Then he asked them to move back into the campsite and closer to where *Swift Sure* was anchored, a precaution he would have taken in any event.

"Are you expecting trouble?" Rue asked him, cocking one eyebrow.

"No. I just want to be ready."

"We're always ready," she said.

"You are, at least."

She smiled. "That's why you were attracted to me. Don't you remember?"

The big airship eased out of the sky to the grassy shelf that fronted the encampment and overlooked the woodland country west. Anchor lines were dropped fore and aft, and a rope ladder was thrown over the side. Bek recognized the *Athabasca*, one of four ships-of-the-line in the Druid fleet, capable of great speed and power. He was impressed by her look. But not even a Druid ship could match the speed of *Swift Sure*.

A Druid began to climb down the ladder, dark-robed and hooded, swaying unsteadily as he carefully placed one foot below the other. A big man, Bek saw, powerfully built and strong, but unfamiliar with airships and flying. He stepped off the ladder, pulled back his hood to reveal his face, and started toward them. Bek had never seen him before, but then most of the Druids at Paranor were unfamiliar to him. Except for his sister and Ahren Elessedil, who was no longer at Paranor, he had met only one or two others over the years, and those he barely remembered. The Druid life was his sister's life, not his, and he had kept himself deliberately apart from it. Sometimes he felt badly that he was not doing more to help her in her work, but it was not work he had ever cared to involve himself in and so he thought it better not to pretend he did.

The man who approached was younger than they were, though not by much, and his careworn face suggested he might be aging in other ways. Their lives filled with secrets, their work clandestine and often unknowable, Druids always troubled Bek. It was a role that fit his sister well, the clothes of her life as the Ilse Witch, where she had perfected the art of subterfuge and dissembling. Such skills were necessary in the world of the Druids, even though intended for good and not for evil. Druids were not well liked in the Four Lands. It was not a prejudice he shared, understanding them as he did, but it was a fact of life. Power fostered fear, and fear mistrust. The Druid order was for many the genesis of all three.

"Aren't those Gnome Hunters crewing the *Athabasca?*" Rue asked suddenly. "Where are the Trolls?"

It was too late for speculation. "Bek Ohmsford?" the Druid asked as he came up to them. He held out his hand without waiting for a reply. "My name is Traunt Rowan."

He shook Bek's hand, then took Rue's as well. His grip

was firm and reassuring. He spoke in even, measured tones that radiated sincerity and concern.

"I was sent by the Druid Council to bring you back with me to Paranor," he continued, looking at them in turn. "The Ard Rhys has disappeared. We don't know what happened to her, but she's gone, and we haven't been able to find out why."

Bek nodded. His sister had disappeared before, many times. She was known for going off without warning on undertakings she wished to keep secret. "You must have reason to be worried about her beyond what you've told me. She has gone her own way without advising others many times in her life. Why is this time any different?"

"Her personal assistant, Tagwen, always knows where she is. Or at least he knows when she is leaving. This time, he didn't know anything about what happened. Nor did the Troll guard. No one did. This is where matters become a bit more complicated. Tagwen was concerned enough that he sought out Ahren Elessedil to help search for her. Together, they traveled to Patch Run to find you. But they found you gone and spoke with your son instead. When they left, they took him with them. Now we can't find any of them."

Bek felt a stab of fear. Rue's fingers reached out to find his and tightened sharply. "How did you find all this out? You haven't received any messages, have you?"

The Druid shook his head. "None. We found out what we did by asking those who knew bits and pieces of the truth. Tagwen left word where he was going. We followed him to the Westland village of Emberen. We discovered that he spoke with Ahren Elessedil and that they left together. From there, we tracked them to Patch Run. But we don't know what happened after that. We only know that your son is gone, as well."

He grimaced. "I'm embarrassed we don't know more. We have been searching for them for days. We have been searching for you, too. We think that the disappearance of the Ard Rhys might indicate that her entire family is in danger. There is some indication of this being so. She has many enemies, and everyone knows you are close to her and are possessed of the Shannara magic, as well. Some of those enemies might consider you as dangerous to them as she is."

"Penderrin would never go off with anyone, even Ahren Elessedil, without leaving word for us," Rue broke in suddenly. "Did you look for a message?"

"We did," Traunt Rowan said. "We looked everywhere. But we didn't find one."

You searched our house, Bek thought. *That was bold. Why did you feel the need?*

"If Pen failed to leave a message, it was because he didn't have enough time to do so." Rue was sliding into her protective mother role, and Bek could see the anger in her eyes. "Why wasn't he offered your protection earlier?"

A flicker of irritation appeared on Traunt Rowan's handsome face and then quickly disappeared. "We did what we thought best at the time. We were a little disorganized, confused. We didn't know what had happened at that point."

"You still don't, it seems," she snapped.

The Druid turned to Bek. "If you will return with me to

Paranor, perhaps we can find them together. We know you have a strong connection to your sister, that you share the use of her magic. We were hoping that you might find a way to apply your talents to help us with our search. If we can find either your sister or your son, we have a chance of finding both."

He hesitated. "I admit that we are growing desperate. We need a fresh approach. We need any help that we can get."

He sounded sincere and his plea had merit, but something troubled Bek. He couldn't put his finger on what it was, but he couldn't quite make himself dismiss it, either.

"What of the expedition?" he asked, trying to think it through.

"I will see that everything is taken care of. Another ship, paid for by the order, will fulfill your obligation to your passengers. With your permission, I will fly back with you aboard your airship to Paranor. The *Athabasca* can continue her search. We have all of our airships out looking, crisscrossing the Four Lands. I don't want to take any of them out of service until this matter is settled." He paused. "We are doing everything we can to find your son."

He directed this last comment at Rue in what was surely an effort to reassure her, but Bek was pretty certain it was too late for that.

"We have to find him, Bek," Rue said quickly. "We have to do whatever it takes."

She was right, of course. But that didn't mitigate his sense of uneasiness. Why would Pen, who was always so dependable, disappear without a word to anyone? Where would

Ahren Elessedil have taken him that required such secrecy? Looking at it from every conceivable angle, he kept coming back to the same two possibilities—that his son had been forced to flee or that Traunt Rowan was lying.

"Let me talk with our passengers and tell them what's happening," he said to the Druid. "Then we'll come with you."

He took Rue's hand and led her over to where the six who had hired them were standing in the shadow of *Swift Sure*. Quickly, he told them a version of the truth—that an emergency had arisen that required them to leave immediately for home, that another airship with another Captain and crew familiar with expedition work would come to allow them to complete their outing. There were a few disappointed looks, but everyone took it well. None of them asked for their money back. They shook hands and wished one another well.

After giving a wave of reassurance to Traunt Rowan, Bek walked over to the crates of supplies stacked on the ground at the airship's stern and began checking through them. Rue, who had hesitated before following him over, bent close. "What are you doing?"

"Pretending that I'm doing something useful," he said. "Gaining us a little space and time so that we can think."

She joined him in poking through the crates, her eyes never leaving his face. "You don't trust him, either."

He glanced back at the Druid, who was leading their passengers over to the *Athabasca* in preparation for boarding. "Why do you think Tagwen felt the need to seek out Ahren Elessedil when there are more than a hundred other

Druids at Paranor whom he could have turned to? Why would he choose to seek help outside Paranor's walls? That doesn't feel right."

"No," she agreed, "it doesn't."

"But let's assume he had a good reason for traveling all the way to Emberen to find Ahren. Why did Traunt Rowan and the other Druids suddenly feel a need to follow him? If they were worried about our family, why wouldn't they go straight to Patch Run to warn us? They've thrown Pen into the mix as a reason for their search, but they didn't know anything about a connection to us before they started looking for the other two."

Rue's mouth tightened. "He said Pen might be in danger, that we all might. But he never said from whom, did he?"

"I take your point. Whatever the case, I don't think we are being told the truth."

She straightened abruptly. "Then why are we going back to Paranor? If this is some sort of a trap, we shouldn't be so quick to step into it."

He shook his head. "They want something from us. If they didn't, they would have taken a different approach. Besides, if we don't go to Paranor, we lose our best chance of finding out what is really going on."

She brushed back loose strands of her long red hair and looked off into the distance. "I could make him tell us everything in about ten minutes if you left me alone with him."

Bek smiled in spite of himself. "He's a Druid, Rue. He's too powerful to play games with. Anyway, if we scare him, he won't be so eager to tell us anything. Even when he lies, he gives us small glimpses of the truth. Let's make use of that for now. We can skin him and hang him out to dry later."

She reached over and took his hand. "I want Penderrin safe, Bek. If this involves your sister, it probably involves her enemies, and her enemies are too dangerous for a boy to deal with." She glanced over at the Druid airship. "I hate it that we've become involved in her life again."

He straightened and took her in his arms. She let him do so, but her body remained stiff and angry as he held her. "Don't be too quick to blame this on Grianne," he whispered. "We don't know anything for sure yet. We don't even know that Pen is missing. All we know is what we've been told, and we can't really trust that."

She nodded and inclined her head into his shoulder. "What if he's telling the truth? We can't dismiss that possibility, either. Just because he hasn't told his story well doesn't mean it isn't true. We can't take chances with Pen's safety."

He pressed her against him reassuringly. "Nothing will happen to Pen. Remember who raised him. He isn't without resources or skills. If he's disappeared, it may be because he wants it that way. What we need to do is to discover the reason. But we have to go to Paranor to do that. Are you willing to take the chance?"

She backed out of his embrace, and he saw the familiar resolve reflected in her green eyes. "What do you think?"

SIX

§

Shadea a'Ru walked alone down the lower west corridor of the Druid's Keep, listening beyond the soft scrape of her footfalls for other sounds. The air was warm and stultifying outside the walls of the Keep, but cool and resonant inside. A barely audible whisper of faraway voices reverberated off the stone walls like motes of dust dancing in the light.

She listened to those voices carefully, but only to make certain they did not follow her.

They would be serving the noon meal now, and a period of rest would follow for those who cared to take advantage of it. Few would. The Druids she led knew there were consequences for any failure to complete their work. She kept them guessing as to what those consequences might be or when to expect them. She let them work without supervision or deadlines because her unpredictability was all the incentive they required. A little uncertainty and a few object lessons were strong motivators.

She did not visit acts of reprisal on those who disappointed her; she knew better than to do that. She did not use her office to punish outright. She had learned a long time ago that consequences must be administered in more subtle ways. A few well-chosen examples set the tone. She provided them early on, within days after gaining the position of Ard Rhys, a clear indication of her expectations. She chose two younger Druids, ones lacking in broad support, ones whose presence would not be missed. She called them into her office and simply dismissed them. She sent them home without offering them even the smallest clue as to how or why they had failed. They might apply for reinstatement, she advised, once they had determined the nature of their shortcomings. It was a fair and just approach to the strict demands of the order's disciplines, and no one could find fault with how she had handled things.

Yet the underlying message was unmistakable. If one failed, whether one understood how or why—one paid the price. The best way to avoid such consequences was to work hard and not make trouble.

Of course, the more powerful of the Druids were not so easily intimidated. Their dismissal would result in confrontations of the sort she was trying to avoid. Yet she was determined that they all be brought into line, that they be made to accept her leadership and her control. She did not require that they make a public display of their loyalty; she needed only to know it was understood that she was Ard Rhys in more than name.

Hence, this clandestine meeting with the most powerful of those whose support she required. If Gerand Cera would agree to back her openly, if she could gain his support for her efforts, then the rest would be easier to persuade. The problem was that Cera hated her almost as much as he had hated Grianne Ohmsford. If she was to have any success in gaining his support, she must first find a way to change his feelings.

She paused at the entry to a rotunda that served as a hub for a series of connecting corridors. Light from narrow slits cut high up in the circular walls reflected off the stone blocks, measuring sticks for the single stairway that led upward to the west watchtower and its parapets. She had chosen this remote and private spot to test Cera's resolve. If he feared to meet her there, alone and unprotected by his followers, he was not the ally she needed. If he appeared, it would reinforce her belief that he would serve the purpose she had set for him.

She needed a fresh ally. Terek Molt was dead, Iridia Eleri had abandoned Paranor, and Traunt Rowan and Pyson Wence were beginning to show signs of vacillation. Though the latter two did her bidding, they failed to command the respect and fear of the Dwarf and the sorceress. She was incensed about Iridia, who had simply disappeared after the death of her beloved Ahren Elessedil, but there was nothing Shadea could do about it. Searching for Iridia would consume time and resources. Worse, it would demonstrate weakness. Better to deal with her later.

She thought fleetingly of Traunt Rowan, who should by then have been deep in the Eastland and close to making contact with Bek Ohmsford and his wife. If he succeeded in bringing them to Paranor, she would have new leverage in her search for the boy and his companions should the unthinkable happen and Aphasia Wye fail. She would also have a means for reconfirming that Grianne Ohmsford was safely imprisoned within the Forbidding, where she could cause no further harm. The brother's magic could be put to that use. It was dangerous to use him that way, but it was a risk she felt she had to take. When she was done with him, when she had hunted down the boy and verified that his aunt was dead and gone, it would be easy enough to dispose of the entire Ohmsford family.

But first things first. She must concentrate on the task at hand, the manipulation of Gerand Cera. She glanced around the rotunda, their appointed meeting place. There was no sign of him.

"I am here, Shadea," he said from the shadows behind her.

She turned with a start. Tall and menacing in his black robes, he was standing just inside the same hallway she had come down. He must have followed her all the way to their meeting place, and she had not heard him do so. It was a clear demonstration of his skill, given so that she would not mistake his coming as an indication of weakness. It was typical of him; he had survived over the years by making certain no one ever misjudged what he was capable of doing.

"Gerand Cera," she greeted him, holding her ground.

He came up to her, lean and hatchet-faced, his nose and cheekbones narrow and chiseled, his mouth a thin line of disapproval. His expression was unreadable, as if his mind had emptied of thought and his heart of emotion. He was a formidable opponent, and there were few at Paranor who would dare to challenge him.

"Are we alone?" he asked.

He would already know the answer to that question, she thought. He only wanted to let her think he trusted her not to lie to him. "Of course. What I have to say to you is not meant for other ears."

"I didn't think so." He glanced around, as if come for the first time to a new place. "No one is likely to pass down these corridors, I suspect. Nevertheless, we are too much exposed to suit my taste. We should not be seen meeting like this, even by accident."

She nodded. "Come this way."

She led him into another of the passageways and from there into an unmanned guardroom fronting the outer wall.

"Here?" she asked. He nodded, and she closed the door behind them. "This should serve our needs."

He walked over to a bench set against the far wall and sat down. "Let me save you some time and effort, Shadea. You have summoned me because you require my help. Your own allies seem to be disappearing rather more rapidly than I think you anticipated in the wake of what's happened. Some won't be returning, I suspect. You are Ard Rhys in name, but your grip on the title is tenuous. Allies are necessary. I would be the one whose support you covet most. Am I right?"

She was angered by his presumptions, but kept her feelings in check. He was right, of course. That was one of his strengths—the ability to analyze a situation quickly and accurately. "Your support would be welcome," she acknowledged.

His sharp features tightened. "Why should I give it to you?"

"I could suggest the obvious—that it would be safer for you to have me as a friend than an enemy."

His smile was bitter. "You could never be a friend to me, Shadea. You could never be a friend to anyone you viewed as a potential rival. I accept that. I don't want you as a friend, in any case. As well, I don't want you as an enemy. Your successful elimination of Grianne Ohmsford demonstrates sufficient reason for that. Such an impressive piece of work. So unexpected. No one knows how you did it. Gone almost as if she never existed. Care to explain how you managed it?"

She shrugged. "As you said, you don't want me as your enemy."

"So, then, I can have you as neither friend nor enemy. Perhaps there is some middle ground?"

"Perhaps. Why don't we try to find it?" She walked over and sat down beside him, taking away the advantage of height to put them on an equal footing. "I do have need of your help. You have read the situation accurately. I have lost old allies; I need new ones. The Council follows me for now, but it may shift allegiance when the opportunity arises. I can do nothing to further the Druid cause until the problem is safely eliminated. Think what you want of me, but my goal in all of this is to make the order stronger and more effective. Under Grianne, we were wallowing in discontent and ineffectiveness. That has changed already, even in the few days she has been gone."

Gerand Cera arched one eyebrow. "How so?"

"I have gained the unqualified support of Sen Dunsidan and the Federation. That support goes beyond his openly professed acceptance of my stewardship of the order. A deeper understanding has been forged, one that will eventually give us control over him."

He nodded slowly. "He will crush the Free-born, and you will have the order stand by and let it happen. But how will you then gain control of him?"

She smiled. "What you need to know is that I do not intend to let things proceed in the disorderly fashion allowed by my predecessor. I intend to take action and to take it now. I will change the course of history, and I will make the Druid order the spearhead for that change."

"How ambitious of you," he said softly.

"I won't deny it. I am ambitious for both the order and myself. You can join me in this effort or you can continue to oppose me. If you join me, I will give you fresh standing in the order, a chance to advance at my side, equal in almost everything."

He laughed. "Until you no longer have need of me."

She held his gaze. "Or you of me?"

They stared at each other in silent appraisal, each measuring the other's hidden intent against the possibility of truth contained in the words already spoken. The silence lengthened and Shadea caught a hint of uncertainty in the other's black gaze.

"An alliance, then?" he said.

"A very close alliance. Personal as well as professional."

He stared at her. "You don't mean for us to become joined in *that* way, do you?" he asked softly.

She nodded slowly. "Oh, but I do. Why not? Don't tell me it hasn't crossed your mind. It crosses every man's mind, sooner or later. I see how they look at me. I know how they think. I am offering myself to you. I understand the risk of doing so, of course. But there are always risks. What I seek is an open and obvious alliance that no one in the order will dare to challenge."

"Well," he said, pursing his thin lips. "I didn't expect this. Do you find me so attractive?"

She shrugged. "Not in the way you might think. Attractive in a different way. Women and men don't always think alike about these things. Accept my offer, and I might even explain it to you one day."

He stared at her without answering, looking directly into her eyes and searching for what she was hiding. She let him hold her gaze, patient and unflinching. "You could move into my quarters, of course," she said. "You could sleep with me or not, as you choose. What matters is that others see us as a couple. We would be seen as joined in all things, not necessarily by proclamation, but otherwise openly so. I am Ard Rhys, but you would be my shadow half. Your word would be mine. We would advance the cause of the order together."

He let his eyes drop to her body, then rose and walked away and stood looking at the wall. "I will not say I am not tempted. You understand me well enough to know I am. We both crave power in all its forms. Your submission would be immensely satisfying. But where does this lead? How does it end?"

She laughed openly. "Do you need to know in order to

be persuaded, Gerand Cera? Aren't you excited by the idea that neither of us can know how this will end, that it is a gamble we must accept? Life is risk! What is the point otherwise?"

He turned back to face her. "What of your other allies? How will they view this change of plans?"

She shrugged. "They will accept it. They haven't any choice. I am the one they answer to." She reached up to touch his cheek. "And now to you, as well, if you accept my offer."

He shook his head. "You would dispose of me in an instant, discard me with not a second thought."

"You would do the same with me," she countered. "We do not fool each other in any way about this arrangement. We make use of it until it no longer suits us, and then we see how things stand. It does not necessarily have to end in killing. It can end in any number of other ways. Are you so committed to my death that you cannot imagine any other possibility? Do I appear no different to you than Grianne Ohmsford did?"

He smiled. "You are different in more ways than I can count. I do not mistake you for her. But I do not mistake you for anything different from what you are, either. I would have to watch my back constantly were I to accept your proposal."

She put her hands on his narrow shoulders and drew him a step closer. "Oh, come now. What would be the purpose of making this offer if all I wanted was to see you dead? There are much less complicated ways to achieve that end. Once I have joined with you openly, it immediately becomes more difficult for me to dispose of you, doesn't it? Besides, what would be the reason? I need you alive and at my side if I am to achieve what I seek. You can see that, can't you?"

His lean features showed nothing, impassive and unrevealing as she pressed herself close and kissed him on the mouth. "Can't you?"

Then he was kissing her back, and she knew she had him.

Later that night, when the Druids of Paranor were asleep or at work in quarters kept open for that purpose, the night fallen in a thick black veil through skies so clouded that neither moon nor stars could penetrate, she slipped from her bed to walk the empty corridors and think. She spared only a single glance back at the sleeping and sated Gerand Cera before closing the door on him. Her seduction of her most dangerous enemy had been a success. It had even been enjoyable. She had not lied to him. She found him attractive enough. His menacing look and poisonous mind drew her much the way she thought the Ilse Witch must have felt drawn to snakes. They were treacherous by instinct and unpredictable by nature and one could not trust what they would do because they frequently did not know themselves. But they were fascinating, as well. She flushed with heat and passion imagining how it would feel to hold one close to her breast and feel its deceptively silky skin sliding against her own.

She slipped down the empty corridor outside her room,

hugging the shadows as she moved to the stairwell that led upward into the central tower and the parapets that ringed it. She wore her nightgown and nothing more, disdainful of clothing, of armor and weapons, of trappings that hampered and slowed. She feared nothing in this world, so why should she care how she appeared or what she revealed? Convention and conformity were for others. She would be what she liked.

For now, Gerand Cera was hers. She knew he thought otherwise. He had taken her body and would think he had taken her mind in the bargain. He had allied himself with her so that he could gain a toehold on the steps of the office she warded. He was probably already planning how he would dispose of her. But she had known all that going in, had understood that he would accept her proposition only to get what he coveted most—the position she held. He would stay close to her so that he could more easily eliminate her.

But that was a blade that cut both ways. Keeping him close allowed her the same opportunities. His plans for her were no different than hers for him. Yet the bargain favored her. She was the one who would be seen to have united the Druids, to have pulled the two central factions together, so that there would no longer be bickering and dissatisfaction. She was the one who would be seen to have allowed common sense to prevail over pride. She was the one who would be seen as the real leader of the order, and Gerand Cera, though he might claim otherwise, would be only the consort of the Ard Rhys.

A consort, she had already decided, whose usefulness at Paranor would quickly run its course.

She climbed to the tower and walked out onto the parapet. A wind blew chilly and brisk out of the west, but anxious to feel something cold against her skin, she let it wash over her without shivering. She closed her eyes and breathed in the night, listening to its faint sounds, to its soft voice. She was at peace there, alone on the top of the Druid's Keep, her fortress, her world. She had won it, and she would keep it. Those who could help her might do so, but they had better know their place.

In the morning, Gerand Cera would address the Council. Ostensibly, he was to speak to the state of the Four Lands and the role of the Druids in monitoring its vicissitudes. But the true purpose of his speaking was to make clear that he was now allied with her, had become her consort, her shadow self. He would do so thinking to impress upon the listening Druids that he had gained control of her. None would believe it. It didn't matter what he said or did. None would believe.

If they did, they had better not let her find out.

SEVEN

It was late in the day when *Swift Sure* sailed out of the shadows enfolding the Dragon's Teeth toward the brightly lit towers of Paranor, sharp-edged and spiraling against a horizon colored crimson and gold by the setting sun. Bek worked the rigging and sails in preparation for their arrival, while Rue stood in the pilot box, easing the big ship into position. It was a still, windless day, and sailing her required little in the way of skill, her steady progress reliant mostly on the power fed out of the diapson crystals. The journey had taken barely forty-eight hours, the weather clear and uncomplicated, the voyage made by flying day and night, the senior Ohmsfords taking turns at catching a few quick hours of sleep when needed. It was a schedule they were used to, having followed it on numerous occasions when there were weather reasons to do so. They might have anchored and slept in this instance, but both were anxious to get to their destination and find out the truth about Pen.

Of one thing they were quite certain. Traunt Rowan was

holding something back, and whatever it was, it had everything to do with why they had been summoned.

Bek glanced over to where the Druid sat on a viewing
bench with his back against the foremast and his safety line
cinched tightly about his waist. He was not comfortable in
the air, so he had spent much of his time in that position.
He was friendly, though. He was more than willing to talk
whenever they approached, always amenable to a discussion of the facts surrounding the disappearances of Grianne
and Pen, seemingly anxious to help them find their family.
Yet as Bek had observed at the start of this journey, it was
what Traunt Rowan didn't say as much as what he did that
kept giving him away. There was no mention still of why
the Druids had decided to go in search of Tagwen after his
departure from Paranor or why that pursuit had led them to
Pen. There was no mention of what had become of the
Troll guard that had served his sister so faithfully from the
beginning of her term as Ard Rhys. Most important of all,
he offered no suggestion as to what might have happened
to Grianne.

Bek was aware that he might be overreacting to omissions that were nothing more than oversights on the part of
a distraught messenger, omissions easily explained once
broached. But Bek had always trusted his instincts on such
things, and his instincts in this case warned him that something was not right. Because Rue felt the same way, he was
inclined to keep his concerns to himself and to watch his
back until he had a better understanding of what had happened.

As *Swift Sure* settled down inside the broad west court,

where the Druid airships were anchored when not flying, it occurred to him that he had been to Paranor only twice before in his life. It was a shock to realize that he had not come more often than that, given that Grianne had been Ard Rhys for almost twenty years. But he understood the reason for it. Both times he had visited, he had been anxious to leave. The walls of the Keep closed in on him, shut him away and gave him a trapped and helpless feeling. The stone passageways reminded him of the underground lair of the Antrax. The dark forms of the Druids reminded him of the Morgawr and his Mwellrets. His time in Parkasia still haunted him, its memories unpleasantly vivid and troubling.

His sister had been anxious to explain what it was she was trying to achieve with the order, how she envisioned it serving the Four Lands. It was Walker Boh's dream she was seeking to fulfill, and she had dedicated her life to making it come true. But it was her vision she was following, not Bek's, and he had trouble finding reasons to believe in it as she did. He did not share Walker's belief in the importance of the Druids to the Races; he did not accept that a Druid Council would function any more effectively or wisely than the governments already established. He trusted his sister and believed her to be capable and committed. But she was still only one person, and however powerful she might think herself, she was diminished measurably by how she had lived her life as the Ilse Witch. Her exposure to the truth of who and what she was through contact with the Sword of Shannara had caused her psyche to suffer great damage. She might have woken from the coma into which she had fallen as a result of having faced up to that truth, but he wasn't sure she had come back from it whole.

Her responsibilities were so overwhelming and the response of those she sought to help so disdainful that he found himself wondering whether she might revert to the dark creature she had been before he found her. He hated himself for thinking that way, but he understood the pressure she was under and the weight of the task she had given herself. It was one thing to reestablish the Druid order; it was another to lead it. He wanted to tell her to let go, to come away with him. Even while she was explaining what it was she was trying to do, he wanted to urge her to stop. But, in the end, he said nothing. It was her life, not his. It was her decision.

Standing on the foredeck of *Swift Sure* as Rue set the big airship down on Druid soil, he found himself wondering if he would ever see Grianne again. His concerns had all been for Pen, but it was Grianne who had disappeared first and been gone longest. Because she had a history of such disappearances and because she had always returned from them, he had given little thought to what the most recent one might mean. But it was possible, even for an Ard Rhys, to venture too far into unfriendly territory and not be able to find a way out again. It was possible, even for Grianne, not to return.

He turned his attention to dropping the anchor lines then, as the airship touched the ground, climbing down the rope ladder to secure them. The air within the Druid walls felt hot and still. He smelled the dust and the dryness; he could breathe them in. Already, he was wishing he were somewhere else. Taking a deep breath to calm himself, he waited for Rue and Traunt Rowan to descend. It was pointless to dwell on his discomfort. He was here, and here he would remain until he found what he had come looking for.

With Rue beside him, he followed the Druid toward a pair of massive double-entry doors at one end of the court. But before they reached them, the doors opened and a small group of black-cloaked figures emerged into the fading light. As they moved into the courtyard, their long shadows played against the earth like wraiths, faceless and bodiless within their coverings. A chill went up Bek's spine, a warning to be careful. He had formidable magic at his command, but his skills and experience were not the equal of these.

As the contingent approached them, Traunt Rowan turned back to Bek and Rue. "Your arrival is much anticipated," he said with a deferential nod.

There were three of them, two leading the third, one of the two a broad-shouldered woman of some size and obvious strength. She pulled back her hood as she reached him, and he knew instinctively from the strong features and military bearing that she was the leader. "Bek Ohmsford," she said, extending her hand. "I am Shadea a'Ru, Ard Rhys in your sister's absence."

She shook his hand quickly, took Rue's in turn, then nodded to her companions. "My First of Order, Gerand Cera, and my assistant, Pyson Wence."

Bek nodded to them in turn, the first tall, thin, and sharp-featured, the second physically unintimidating, but with eyes that reminded him of a hunting bird's. Deferring to the woman, neither spoke on being introduced.

"What have you learned of our son?" Rue asked at once. "Have you found him?"

"We haven't." Shadea met her gaze without flinching, something a lot of men couldn't do. "We continue to search, of course, for both your son and the Ard Rhys, but we have run out of places to look. If you come with me, I will explain."

Without waiting for their agreement, she turned and started back toward the Keep, her two companions and Traunt Rowan falling quickly into step behind her. Bek glanced at Rue, shrugged, and they followed as well. He was trying to remember if his sister had ever said anything about any of these Druids, but nothing came to mind. Aside from Ahren Elessedil, Tagwen was the only one he could remember her speaking about and the only one he could remember meeting. He wished now that he had paid better attention.

Inside the Keep, Shadea beckoned them forward to walk with her, and the other three Druids gave way as they moved ahead.

"The Ard Rhys disappeared after retiring to her chamber several weeks ago. She went into her room and never came out. There was no sign of a struggle when we found her missing. The Trolls on watch said she had not come out during the night and that they had heard nothing. I dismissed them anyway, simply as a precaution. We have many enemies, and they have many reasons to want us gone. The Trolls might have been subverted."

That was one explanation, Bek thought, though it didn't feel right. "I recall my sister saying more than once how much she depended on them, how reliable they were."

Shadea's sun-browned face turned his way sharply, and she brushed the short-cropped blond hair from her forehead. "She may have made a mistake by trusting them. We don't know."

"No one has seen her since? No one has sent any word of her?"

"None. Tagwen seemed to have an idea about what might have happened, but then he disappeared as well. We tracked him to Emberen and to Ahren Elessedil. Then we tracked them both to Patch Run. Apparently, when they left, they took your son with them. That was the last thing we discovered that's worth talking about. We still don't know why the Ard Rhys disappeared or where she might have gone. We don't know where your son, Tagwen, and Ahren Elessedil have gone, either. Our airships continue to search, but time slips away, and that doesn't favor our efforts. I am hopeful that by coming to Paranor, you can change things."

Bek felt Rue's hand tighten in his own. "How can I help you? I don't know anything about this."

Shadea a'Ru nodded. "It is no secret that you are extraordinarily close to your sister. The story of how you found each other twenty years ago is common knowledge. Your inherited magic drew you in ways that nothing else could. It binds you irrevocably. I think we can make use of that in finding her and very likely your son, as well. I'll show you how."

They passed down the shadowed corridor and ascended a series of stairs to the upper levels. In a broad, high-ceilinged hall that ran down the center of the Keep, they encountered other Druids moving about in small groups,

carrying books and papers and conversing with one another. A few looked them over as they passed, taking note
of the two who were clearly not of their order. But no one
looked for very long, turning quickly away when they
caught sight of Shadea.

They are afraid of her, Bek thought.

He remembered that it had been the same when he had
come to visit his sister—the same looks, the same quick
averting of faces when she passed. Nothing had changed in
her absence. It made him wonder if it was the nature of the
position or of the candidates drawn to occupy it. It made
him wonder why anyone would want it.

As they turned down a secondary passageway, one nar-
rower and less heavily traveled, a young Druid rushed into
their midst, colliding with Bek in a flurry of confusion and
knocking him to the floor.

"Sorry," he apologized quickly, reaching down to help
Bek up again. The papers he had dropped lay scattered
everywhere about them. "I didn't see you. I was in a hurry.
My mistake. Are you all right? Well, then. Again, sorry."

Their hands clasped, and Bek felt a tiny piece of paper
pressed into his palm. "There, no harm done," the young
Druid declared, his eyes meeting Bek's quickly before looking
away. He apologized again, this time to Shadea, and bent to
retrieve his papers from the floor. The big woman gave him a
withering look and walked right on past, beckoning the others to follow. Bek glanced down briefly at the young Druid as
he passed him. The other man did not look up.

As they continued on, Bek slid the piece of paper into
his pocket. He had never seen the young Druid before. He

glanced over at Rue, but she didn't seem to have noticed anything.

They climbed several sets of stairs and traversed several more corridors before coming to a room set high in the Keep. Gnome Hunters stood watch without, and the door was locked and barred. The Gnomes moved aside quickly as Shadea stepped up and manipulated the locks. When the door was open, the Druids ushered the Ohmsfords inside.

Bek glanced around. The room was empty except for a huge basin of water that sat at its center. The basin bowl was shallow and broad, and the waters it contained were a very deep green. There were lines and markings drawn on the surface of the basin below the waters, bumps and ridges, as well. It was a map, he realized, moving over to get a closer look, a map of the Four Lands.

"This is where you can help us, Bek," Shadea a'Ru announced, moving up beside him. Rue had already taken up a position on his other side, and he could feel the anticipation radiating from her like body heat. "This room is called the cold chamber. The stone walls insulate the basin. The scrye waters in the basin monitor the lines of power that bind the earth. They reflect disturbances in those lines when a powerful magic is used. We study them in an effort to discover where magic is being used outside the purview of the order."

She turned to him. "We had thought to use the scrye waters to track your sister's movements after she disappeared, but there have been no disturbances that would indicate the use of her magic. Still, the waters will track such magic, even its most minuscule application, if their power to interpret is enhanced. If you were to apply the magic of the wishsong to that end, we might be able to discover where she is. I know you possess the power to control its effect on things. Will you use it here?"

Bek held her gaze a moment, trying to read what was behind it. She was asking him to do something very straightforward, but he was suspicious of her motives. Traunt Rowan's omissions and shadings still troubled him; his uneasiness about the circumstances surrounding the disappearances of his sister and son hadn't lessened. He was tired from lack of sleep and worry, and he didn't trust that he was thinking clearly.

"I know you want me to do this right away," he told her. "I want that, too. But I don't know that I can help you effectively until I am better rested. Application of the magic of the wishsong requires a steady concentration that I don't feel I can bring to bear just now. What I would like to do is eat something and get some sleep, then try in the morning, when I'm fresh."

"Bek!" Rue exploded angrily, gripping his shoulder so hard it hurt. "This is our son and your sister we are trying to help! What do you mean, you need to rest? You can rest later!"

Her words made him flinch, but he looked directly at her. "I'm worried for them, too. But I don't want to make a mistake. I'm just not sure I'm recovered enough from that fever to focus the way I need to. Not without a little food and rest first."

He turned away from the surprise and confusion that flashed sharply in her eyes. "Tomorrow, then?"

Clearly unhappy with the delay, Shadea a'Ru took a moment to consider. Reluctantly, she nodded. "Tomorrow will be fine. Traunt Rowan will see you to your sleeping chambers and arrange for food to be brought. Rest well."

She swept out of the room without sparing him another glance, a hint of disgust reflected on her strong features. The taller of the two Druids who went with her turned briefly to study him, and Bek did not care for what he saw in the dark eyes. Then they were gone, and Traunt Rowan was saying something about arrangements for the night. Bek didn't hear all of it; his attention was back on Rue, who was looking at him in what he hoped was a less judgmental way.

"Come with me," the Druid ordered, his own face dark and troubled.

It took them only a few minutes to reach their sleeping chambers, which consisted of two rooms with a bed, a few furnishings, a single door, high windows, and a pair of unfriendly looking Gnome Hunters already positioned at the doors.

"To keep you safe," Traunt Rowan explained quickly. "We are taking no chances with your family, even here. Until we find out what has happened to the Ard Rhys and your son, we intend to keep close watch over all of you. I will have dinner sent right up."

When he was gone and the door securely closed behind him, Bek put a finger to his lips before Rue could say anything, shaking his head in warning. He motioned about the room, to the walls and ceiling, to the vents and doors and windows, where other ears might be listening. When she nodded her understanding, he took her in his arms and put his lips close to her ear.

"Are you all right?"

He felt her nod into his shoulder. Her mouth pressed against his ear. "What was all that about a fever? You haven't had a fever in months."

"An excuse to keep Shadea at bay," he whispered. "Something about all this isn't right. I need to think about what she's asking me to do."

Another nod. "I don't trust her, either. I don't trust any of them. They're lying about something."

"That young Druid who bumped into me in the hallway? That wasn't an accident. He gave me a note; I have it in my pocket. He pressed it into my hand while he was helping me get up. He didn't want Shadea and the others to see what he was doing. He took a big chance."

"Do you know him? Is he Grianne's friend?"

"I don't know who is or isn't her friend at this point."

"Have you looked at the note?"

He shook his head. "I was waiting until we got away from the others. I didn't want to take a chance that they might see me looking at it." He paused, looking past her to the stone walls. "Walk with me over to the window. Stand close so we can shield what we're doing."

He felt her hand press against his back. "Do you think they might be watching as well as listening? Here?"

He shook his head. He didn't know. But he wasn't about to chance it. The safety of his sister and his son were at stake, and some among the Druids might not have their best interests at heart, no matter what they said.

They moved over to the window. The sun was setting on the horizon, a bloodred orb hung against a cerulean sky. Shadows had lengthened into dark pools, and the moon was just visible along the northeast horizon. The air outside felt cool and fresh on their faces as they leaned out, resting their arms on the stone sill, hunched close together with their backs to the room.

Bek slipped the scrap of paper from its hiding place and laid it in front of them, keeping his hands cupped about it. They bent close. Four words were printed on it in block letters.

DO NOT TRUST THEM.

That was all. Bek studied the note a moment more, glanced at Rue, then pocketed it anew. When he had a chance to do so, he would destroy it. But he would have to be careful how he handled it. Druids could reconstruct messages from nothing more than ashes.

"Clearly, not everyone is in agreement about what has happened to my sister," he said. "The young Druid, for one."

"Maybe others, as well."

He laid his hand on her arm. "We can't trust anyone."

She nodded, her eyes shifting to find his. "What are we going to do?"

He smiled. "I was hoping you could tell me." He leaned over and kissed her forehead gently. "I really was."

* * *

In bed that night, wrapped in each other's arms, comforted by the darkness and the silence, they talked about it.

"Do you think they are listening still?" She said it with an edge to her voice that suggested what she might do to them if she discovered they were.

He stroked her hair. "I think they have better things to do."

"I hope they weren't watching when we bathed. That makes my skin crawl. But I can imagine that ferret-faced Druid doing it."

"No one watched us bathe."

She was silent a moment, pressed up against him. "At least the meal they gave us was decent. They didn't try to poison us."

"They have other plans for us. Poison doesn't figure into things until we've served our purpose."

He felt her face turn toward his own in the dark. "Which is? You have a hunch, don't you?"

His voice was already a whisper, but he lowered it further. "I've been thinking about it. Grianne disappeared for no discernible reason, but Tagwen went outside the order to find help. That suggests he didn't know who to trust among these Druids any more than we do. He knew he could trust Ahren, though. So he traveled to Emberen to ask for his help. Ahren would have given it willingly. That much I feel pretty certain about."

"Me, too."

"But then they went to Patch Run. Maybe they did so to look for us, but they found Pen, instead. So they asked Pen where we were. He probably told them and wanted to go with them. Somehow, he persuaded them that it was a good idea."

"Or they had to take him because they thought he was in danger."

"Right. But what happened then? Did they come looking for us? If they did, why didn't they find us? Pen would have been able to track us down. He would have known how. Ahren would have helped him, using Druid magic. Anyway, something happened to prevent that. So now these Druids who've brought us here are looking for them. And, ostensibly at least, for Grianne, as well. But they can't find them."

"They want us to find them," Rue whispered. "They want us to do their work for them. But maybe not to help. Maybe to do harm."

It made sense. While the Druids might profess that their intentions were honorable, there was good reason to think otherwise.

They were silent again for a time, pondering their fresh insight, trying to think through what they should do about it. Bek felt his wife tighten her grip on him. "We can't help them. We can't put Penderrin in any more danger than he is already in."

"I know."

"I hate it that he's become involved in this, in your sister's life, in Druid intrigues and gamesmanship."

"Don't underestimate Pen. He is smart and capable, and he has some experience in the world. He might not have magic to protect him, but he has his wits. Besides, if he's with Ahren, he's as protected as he would be with us."

"I wouldn't agree with that. Anyway, he shouldn't have to be protected in the first place."

He felt her anger building. "Rue, listen to me. We can't change what's happened. We don't even know for sure what that is. That's what we came to find out. Maybe we will, once we have a chance to talk with that young Druid. In the meantime, it doesn't do us any good to get too angry to think."

"What makes you think I'm angry?"

"Well—"

"Don't you think I have a right to be angry?"

"Well—"

"Are you suggesting I can't be angry and think at the same time?"

He hesitated, uncertain of his reply, then felt her begin to shake with suppressed laughter. "Very funny," he whispered.

She poked him in the ribs. "I thought so."

They lay quietly, listening to each other breathe. Bek ran his hands along his wife's ribs and down her legs. He could feel the ridges where scar tissue had formed over wounds she had suffered twenty years earlier aboard the *Jerle Shannara*. They were a testimony to her strength and resiliency, a reminder of how hard her early life had been. He had always believed her to be stronger than he was, tougher of mind and body both. He had never stopped thinking of her that way. Others might think that because he possessed the use of the wishsong's magic, he was the stronger. Some might even think that being the male in their partnership made him the stronger. But he knew better.

"I won't get angry until after I get Penderrin back," she said suddenly, her words so soft he could barely hear them. "I don't make any promises after that."

"I wouldn't expect it."

"We will get him back, Bek. I don't care what it takes."

"We'll get him back."

"How?"

"You asked me that earlier."

"You didn't answer."

"I was thinking. I'm still thinking."

"Well, hurry up. I'm worried."

He smiled at her insistence, but was glad she couldn't see him doing so. She was scared for her son, and he would not want her to mistake how he was treating the matter. He was worried, too. But he understood that what was needed was a calm, measured approach to untangling the puzzle surrounding Pen's and Grianne's disappearances. Rue's strength might lie in her determination, but his lay in keeping his wits.

"I'll hurry," he promised.

"I would appreciate that."

"I know."

"I love you."

"I love you, too."

Minutes later, they were asleep.

EIGHT

Bek and Rue were awake early, troubled enough by the challenges that lay ahead that the first inklings of light in the east were sufficient to bring them out of their fitful sleep. They washed and dressed and found breakfast waiting outside the door in the form of bread, cheese, fruit, and cold ale. When they retrieved the food tray, the hallway was deserted save for the Gnome Hunters, who were stationed across the hallway. Bek nodded agreeably but got no response.

"I don't think we are guests in the usual sense of the word," he told Rue as he closed the door.

Within an hour, Traunt Rowan was knocking, his eyes bright with anticipation. "Are you ready to try now, Bek?" he asked.

Bek was. He had a plan, although he hadn't confided it to Rue. He told her when they woke that he knew what to do, but that it was better if he kept it to himself. Her own response should not seem forced or planned. She must trust him even if it looked like he was doing something he should not. He understood what was needed. No one at Paranor could be trusted with Pen's or Grianne's whereabouts. If he was lucky enough to discover that information, it belonged to them and them alone.

He had explained it all in a whisper as they lay together in the deep gloom of early dawn, still wary of who might be listening, determined to make no mistake that would reveal their true intentions.

They left the sleeping chamber behind Traunt Rowan, who led them back down the hall and up the stairs to the cold chamber and the scrye waters. Bek held Rue's hand in his own, a reassurance that transcended physical presence and touched on emotional support. He could read her feelings in her touch, in the strength of her grip. He took his cue from those. He spoke with the Druid conversationally, asking if there was any news, if the airships searching for his sister and son had returned, if the day seemed a good one. He told Traunt Rowan that their sleeping arrangements were more than adequate, better than they had been used to over the past few weeks. He praised the food. He talked to put the other at ease. He talked to calm himself.

"Shadea is ready," Traunt Rowan advised him as they reached their destination, and Bek understood it to be a warning that he should be ready, as well.

The cold chamber felt frigid in the wake of the night's recent departure, the chill of the darkness still present. Bek shivered involuntarily as he entered the room, hunching his shoulders against the sudden change in temperature. Shadea a'Ru stood to one side, looking out the window at the sunrise, her broad shoulders wrapped in a scarlet cloak that fell all the way to the floor. When she turned, he saw that the clasp that fastened it bore the crest of the Druid order, the instantly recognizable emblem of the Eilt Druin. It flashed brightly as the light caught it momentarily, and Bek thought he caught a reflection of that hard brightness in Shadea's eyes as well.

"We are anxious to begin, Bek," she said perfunctorily, nodding to Rue, but not speaking to her. "Are you sufficiently rested now?"

"I am," Bek assured her. "Let's begin."

She beckoned him to stand with her at the basin. Bek moved over to peer down into the swirl of deep green waters, seeing fluctuations on their surface that seemed to have no discernible origin. He studied them for a moment, then glanced at Shadea expectantly. As he did so, he caught sight of Gerand Cera, who was standing back and to one side of him in the shadows. He wondered how many more were in hiding somewhere in that room. He wondered if he was going to be able to fool them all.

"You already understand what it is the scrye waters do," Shadea said. "If you can use your magic to connect with their impulses, you should be able to reach beyond what is visible for a more comprehensive reading. I am hopeful that your reach will extend to the magic that resides in your sister or perhaps your son. Any little trace, any clue revealed by doing so may prove helpful."

Helpful to whom? he thought. But he said nothing, only nodding in response.

"Would you move back from me a little?" he asked.

All of them, Rue included, stepped away from the basin

to give him the space he needed. He took a deep breath and closed his eyes in concentration. He calmed himself, centered himself, and then lost himself in the deep silence that settled over the room. He would have only one chance, and if he wasn't convincing enough, he would be in the worst trouble of his life. These were Druids, he reminded himself for what must have been the hundredth time. Druids weren't easily fooled when it came to the use of magic.

On the other hand, none of them possessed or truly understood the magic of the wishsong. That was his edge, if he had any.

He waited until he could hear himself breathing in the stillness, then summoned the magic. He began with a low humming, a sound that mirrored a wind's whisper as it passed through the branches of the trees, soft and silky. He brought it out of its resting place and let it fill him with warmth. The cold of the room lessened and then disappeared. His concentration was so complete that the people around him disappeared as well. He was alone, lost in himself and in his magic.

When he opened his eyes again, he saw only the basin in front of him. He reached out with his hands and let them hover just above the deep green waters, so close he could almost feel the strange ripples that disturbed the otherwise placid surface. He moved his hands slowly, taking his time, not rushing the flow of the magic from his body. He watched the waters respond as he let the first tendrils stroke their surface. He felt them shudder at the intrusion.

He worked more swiftly then, enveloping the scrye wa-

ters in a broad swath intended to detect any obvious sign of
Grianne or Pen. The former's presence would reveal itself
immediately, so strong was the connection between them.
Shadea had been right about that; their shared use of magic
was a powerful link. But nothing showed itself; no sign of
his sister surfaced. He kept searching, sending the wishsong's magic deep into the scrye waters, into the gridwork
of the lines of power that crisscrossed the Four Lands, sifting and probing. He moved his hands in a slow, circular
motion that took him in all directions, toward all of the
possible places she might have gone.

Still nothing.

He was beginning to think that his efforts were a waste
of time, a result he did not like to contemplate, when
abruptly he touched on something. The surface of the
scrye waters rippled in response, and he moved his focus
away immediately so Shadea would not see. He continued
his search in other areas, taking his time, trying to give an
appearance of thoroughness. He must seem to be working
hard at making the magic connect; he must not appear du-
plicitous. But it was harder now, because his instincts were
to return to the place on the gridwork where he had found
what he was looking for.

Time slipped away. Nothing further revealed itself. He
let his hands sweep back to the point of connection, a testing of his previous discovery. Once again, the scrye waters
rippled, and he felt the presence of wishsong magic. Moving his hands away, he marked the place in his mind, knowing now where to go and what to look for.

Then, preoccupied with his discovery and ready to

break this off, he let his hands settle over the place on the gridwork that marked Paranor's solitary spires.

Instantly, the scrye waters boiled and steamed, then exploded in a massive geyser. Magic ripped through Bek, breaking down his defenses and his connection with the basin waters. He was caught completely unprepared, and the next thing he knew he was flat on his back on the floor, his clothing steaming and his hair singed.

"Bek!" Rue was at his side, cradling his head in her hands, bent close to his face. He blinked hard, trying to dispel the dizziness that was making the room spin and her voice echo. Had he lost consciousness? How long had he been lying there? "Look at me!" she said. "Can you see me? Can you hear what I'm saying?"

He nodded wordlessly. Their Druid hosts were gathered around him as well, crouched like vultures, faces a mix of hunger and expectation. He had planned to deceive them by creating a diversion with the wishsong's magic. He hadn't planned on it happening this way. His entire body throbbed and his head ached as if he had taken a physical beating.

"What did you see?" Shadea demanded of him, her eyes narrowed. "You must have seen something, felt something."

He shook his head. His tongue felt thick in his mouth, and his teeth were gritted against the pain. "Nothing," he mumbled as he worked his jaw muscles, trying to make them relax. "I don't know what happened. I was working the magic, just a general search. My hands passed over Paranor's location on the map. Then this."

He saw recognition in her eyes, a glint of satisfaction

and exultation, a response that suggested she had found what she had been looking for and that it was not something she would ever reveal to him.

Then a veiled, guarded look took its place, and she smiled. "You came in contact with the magic that wards the Druid's Keep, Bek. It was a backlash of the protections we set in place for ourselves. Paranor was defending us. I should have warned you. Are you all right?"

"I'll need to rest myself a bit before I try again. I'm not done yet with my search."

"You shall have all the rest you need." She stood up, glancing at the other two. "He has done well, for his first attempt. He'll do even better next time. Traunt, take our guests back to their rooms. See that they have everything they need while Bek recovers. Food and drink and fresh clothing, perhaps a walk in the gardens later. On the morrow, Bek, we will try again."

She was gone from the room so quickly that he had no further chance to question her odd response. Still woozy, he drew himself up into a sitting position and hung his head between his knees.

"That was dramatic," Rue whispered as she placed his arm over her shoulders and helped him to stand. Traunt Rowan had moved ahead to open the door for them and was looking down the hallway after Shadea and Gerand Cera. "Did you intend to hurt yourself like that?"

"I didn't intend to hurt myself at all, if things had gone the way they were supposed to," he whispered back. He saw the look of surprise in her eyes and managed a tired smile. "I didn't plan any of that."

"What happened, then?"

"I don't know. Something I didn't expect. But it wasn't wasted effort, anyway."

She leaned close. "Penderrin?"

He nodded. "I think I found him."

He fell asleep almost immediately after reaching their bedchamber, too exhausted even to remove his clothes. He slept soundly until Rue woke him to make him eat something, and then he fell right back asleep. He dreamed, but his dreams were disjointed and strange, a collection of images from his past life and from other lives entirely, all connected in a way that made them surreal and unfathomable. He thought he was aware of Rue speaking to him more than once, but it wasn't enough to bring him out of the dreams.

When he woke again, the sun was setting. He was alone in the room, a tray of food sitting on the table by his bed. He ate, then washed and moved over to sit by the window and watch the sun disappear and the moon come up. Stars began to appear in the darkening sky north.

It was another half hour before Rue reappeared.

"You're awake," she said as she came through the doorway and saw him. "How do you feel?"

"As if I've been thrown off a cliff. But better than I felt earlier. The dizziness is gone; the aching isn't so bad. I expect I'll live. Where were you?"

"Traunt Rowan took me for a walk in the Druid gardens." She smiled. "They really are beautiful, and I would have loved to see more of them. But the walk turned into an inquisition. I spent most of my time fending off questions about Pen. The Druids don't know much about our son, but they seem awfully eager to learn. Too eager."

She kept her voice low, moving over to sit beside him on the bench. "On the other hand, I got a good look around. I have a better idea of how to get around than I did before. I thought we might want to know where all the doors and windows are, in case we end up having to get out of here quickly."

She put her arm around him. "You scared me this morning. Are you sure you're all right?"

He leaned over and kissed her, then put his lips against her ear. "I've been thinking while you were out," he whispered. "Thinking about this morning and what happened in the cold chamber. I have some ideas that might be worth considering."

"Tell me about Penderrin first," she insisted, putting her arms around him and drawing him close, her voice a whisper as well. "I've been waiting all day for you to be coherent enough to talk to me. You said you found him?"

He nodded into her shoulder. "In the Charnal Mountains. It happened too quickly for me to be sure exactly where he is; I couldn't take the time to find out without giving away what I was doing. But it was definitely him."

"Why would he be all the way up there?"

"I don't know." He took a deep breath. "Here's what I do know. I was doing a general search through the scrye waters for any sign of Pen or Grianne. I found Pen in the Charnals, like I said, but I moved away from the contact before Shadea or one of the others could tell what I was doing. Maybe they wouldn't have known anyway, but I didn't want to chance it. I purposely didn't search Paranor on the grid; after all, that was where Grianne was supposed to have disappeared. What was the point?"

"A question you might have answered differently if you had stopped to think about it," she said quietly.

He nodded. "True enough. Anyway, I worked my way back to Pen to make certain he was in the Charnals, that I hadn't made a mistake. Then I moved my hands away again, trying to decide what to do next. I let my concentration lapse, and my hands drifted back down over Paranor. That was when the scrye waters exploded and threw me away from the basin. Shadea claimed that Paranor's warding magic responded to my intrusion, defending the Keep. But I wasn't trying to intrude. I wasn't doing anything threatening. What I was doing was searching for Pen and Grianne, and I think the magic that wards Paranor reacted to that. I think it reacted because I found something it was trying to hide."

She was silent a moment. "But it wasn't Penderrin because he is somewhere in the Charnals. So it has to be Grianne."

"I think so. When she disappeared, Tagwen left Paranor without confiding in any of the Druids who might have helped him. I think the key to discovering what happened to my sister lies here, and that these Druids who claim to be her friends are covering it up."

"But you were brought here to find her. Why would they do that if they are trying to hide where she is?"

"I think we were brought here to find Pen and found Grianne by accident. Did you see Shadea's face when I explained what I was doing when the magic threw me back from the scrye waters? She was elated! I think it confirmed something she already knew about Grianne. It's Pen she's looking for, but she had to tell me to look for my sister, too, because it would have seemed odd not to."

Bek felt her shake her head slowly against his own. "I still don't understand what Penderrin has to do with all this. I still don't see why he's up in the Charnal Mountains, miles from everything."

He didn't make an immediate response. He didn't have the answers to those questions. His instincts told him that Pen was running away, that he had fled Patch Run to avoid capture, perhaps from these Druids, perhaps from someone else. What troubled him was that Pen would have come looking for them if he had been able to do so. He wouldn't have run off blindly, and he certainly wouldn't have gone into the Charnals without a very good reason.

He stared off into the growing dark. Pen was level-headed and capable, but that didn't stop Bek from being frightened for his son. Pen was just a boy, and he lacked the life experience necessary to deal with this sort of danger. If he was being chased, there was always the possibility that he would panic.

"Bek, I just thought of something," Rue whispered. She moved so that they could see each other, her face so close to his that they were almost touching. "If Shadea knows the wishsong's magic exposed Grianne, she will expect it to expose Penderrin as well. You won't be able to pretend otherwise for long."

He nodded. "I thought of that."

"We can't allow that to happen. How are we going to prevent it?"

He leaned forward and kissed her on the mouth. "While they're sleeping, we're going to use the scrye waters and find him ourselves."

NINE

N ight had fallen across the Four Lands, and Arishaig was bright with the light of torches and candles when Sen Dunsidan made his way back from dinner to his sleeping chambers. The day had been productive. An address before the Coalition Council had produced a standing ovation following his carefully worded promise that he had found a way to resolve the war on the Prekkendorran quickly and favorably. Even those who would have liked to see his role in the Federation government diminished congratulated him afterwards for his courage and commitment. They were counting on him to fail, of course, but he was confident that he wouldn't.

This was due in part to an earlier visit to Etan Orek, who had completed all work on the first of what he was now calling his "fire launchers." He had mounted it on a swivel that allowed it to swing left and right at a ninety-degree firing angle and was equipped with a sighting system and recoil springs to keep it from disrupting the flight of an airship, once it was in place and operating. It was also equipped with controls to manipulate the amount of energy fed through the crystals and released from the mouth of the firing tube.

When Sen Dunsidan had tested it this time, the scope of its destructive capabilities had left him breathless with anticipation.

His excitement was only marginally diminished by news that no other weapons were yet complete. But after long hours of experimentation using different combinations of crystals, Orek was close to duplicating his first effort and expected to complete a second launcher before the week was out.

At the construction site for Federation airships, mercenary Rover designers and builders were at work on a huge new flagship, the *Dechtera*, which would carry Sen Dunsidan's secret weapon into battle when she was completed. He inspected their work and was satisfied with their progress. For the first time in a very long time, he could imagine a world dominated by the Federation.

His bedchamber was lit with candles, but deeply shadowed in its corners and alcoves when he entered, and he might not have seen her at all had she not immediately moved out into the light to greet him. His heart went directly to his throat in that instant, freezing his muscles and his voice so that he was rendered completely helpless. Then he recognized her, and he gave a quick, sharp sigh.

"Iridia," he said. He straightened himself, his composure recovered and his irritation fanned. "What are you doing here?"

"Waiting for you."

Iridia Eleri stepped forward, her slender body and white skin giving her an almost ethereal look. She was wrapped in a lightweight traveling cloak that hung open to the floor, and her dark hair fell in loose waves about her shoulders. He was captivated, as always, by her impossible beauty. He had not seen her in weeks, not since she had given him the liquid night that he, in turn, had given to Shadea a'Ru to eliminate Grianne Ohmsford and seize control of Paranor. She had been his spy within the Druid's Keep for some time, but it was not until she had provided the potion that she had proved her real value.

"Waiting for me for what reason?" he demanded. "It was our agreement that you would remain at Paranor and monitor the activities of our new Ard Rhys, so that I might have eyes and ears inside the Keep. It was our agreement that you would never come here."

The Elven sorceress shrugged. "The agreement has been changed."

He had never trusted her, never felt comfortable with what she was doing for him. He was more than willing to accept her offer of help and make use of her services as a spy. But she had been close to Shadea for too long for him to feel comfortable with the idea that she was ready to switch loyalties to him. It was one thing to betray Grianne Ohmsford, whom they all hated. It was another to betray a friend. Not that someone like Iridia would ever be bound too closely by friendship. But her machinations confused him. She would not tell him where she had gotten the liquid night. She would not tell him why she had chosen to pass it to Shadea through him rather than to give it to her friend directly. She would not explain her need for secrecy in working with him. Try as he might, he could not figure out what she would gain from all this. That sort of thing tended to bother a man whose life was built around understanding the nature of manipulations.

"You look tired, Sen Dunsidan," she said. "Are you tired?"

He shook his head. "I am irritated, Iridia. I don't like surprises and I don't like people who second-guess my decisions without speaking to me about it first. Why has our agreement been changed?"

She moved to one of the chairs flanking the windows looking out over the city and sat down. He could barely see her in the dim light, but he was aware suddenly that something was different about her.

"I have had a falling-out with Shadea," she said. "The damage cannot be repaired. She will no longer consult with me on things of any importance. She will seek to diminish me and ultimately to eliminate me completely. As a result, I cannot be effective as your spy."

"A falling-out?" he repeated.

"Of a sort that has nothing to do with our agreement. She does not know about you and me. She does not even suspect. What has caused the breach between us has to do with someone I once cared for deeply."

He had heard rumors about her involvement with another Druid, of a love affair that Grianne Ohmsford had put a stop to. Could this be whom she was talking about? But Shadea had not had anything to do with that business. He couldn't see the connection.

"So I came here," she finished, reaching for a goblet and pouring wine from the decanter that sat next to it.

"You came here to do what?" He moved forward a couple of steps to see her face better in the dim light, still trying to decide what was different about her.

She drank deeply of the wine, then set the goblet down and looked at him. "I came here to be your personal adviser. If I cannot be effective within the order, then I shall be effective from without. Our agreement still stands, Prime Minister. It has simply been altered. My usefulness must take another form. Since I can no longer spy on the Druid order, I shall advise you regarding it. I shall give you the kind of advice that no one else will, advice gained from having lived among them, of knowing how they think, of understanding what they will do. No one else can provide this."

He hesitated, finding her argument persuasive, but not quite trusting her motives.

"You need me to tell you what to expect from them," she said. "No one knows Shadea a'Ru better than I do. You have an alliance with her and with the order through her, but you need to know how to make use of it. I know how far she will allow herself to be pushed and in what directions. I know what will persuade her when persuasion is needed. I know her weaknesses far better than you do."

"I know her well enough to keep her at bay," he said.

She laughed softly. "You know her well enough to get yourself killed. If you think she will honor your agreement once she has no further use for it, you are a fool. She made it to gain credibility for the order and for herself.

She will use you to see the Free-born smashed and the balance of power shifted, and then she will use you to gain control of the Federation, as well. Surely, you accept that this is so."

In fact, he did. He had known as much all along, although he didn't like thinking about it. He had accepted it as a necessary consequence of his alliance with her because he needed that alliance in order to end the stalemate on the Prekkendorran. Even with his new weapon, he was wary of the Druids, of their power as wielders of magic. What Iridia was telling him was nothing new, but it was making him take a fresh look at the realities.

"Your intent is to act as my adviser?" he repeated, trying to get used to the idea.

"Your Druid adviser. Your *personal* Druid adviser. No one else in all the Four Lands will have one, save you. That will give you a measure of respect that you could gain in no other way. It will give you stature for what needs doing."

"You would leave the order?"

She laughed again, and the sound sent a chill up his spine. It wasn't the laugh itself; it was the emptiness it suggested. "I have already left the order. Better to be your adviser in Arishaig than a whipping boy in Paranor. Understand me, Sen Dunsidan. I am a sorceress of great power. I was born with it; I was trained to use it. I am the equal of Shadea, though she might not think so. I might have been the equal of Grianne Ohmsford. I want for myself what you want—recognition and power. Yours will come with the Federation's victory over the Free-born. Mine will come when I have replaced Shadea as Ard Rhys.

Together, we can make both happen more easily. Accept my offer."

He studied her without speaking. Could she have turned against him and become Shadea's spy? Could this be an elaborate charade, part of a plan to eliminate him? But, no, if Shadea wanted him dead, it would be easy enough to make him so. It would not require such a complicated approach. Besides, what use was he to Shadea if he was dead? Another from the Council would simply take his place, and she would risk losing her alliance with the Federation. He could think of no reason she would want that to happen.

He folded his arms across his chest. "Very well, Iridia. I accept. Your advice would be most welcome." He held up one finger. "But I hope this isn't a game you play with me. If I find that it is, I will have you killed without another thought. You might be a Druid, but you are still only made of flesh and blood."

Her pale face tilted slightly, as if she were seeing a strange animal. "Who was it who offered her services to you as your spy in the Druid camp? Who was it who told you of a way to dispose of Grianne Ohmsford without casting suspicion on yourself? Who brought you the liquid night? Who has stood by you every step of the way? Name another, besides me."

There was a coldness to the challenge that warned him against any answer but one. "Your point is well taken." He felt dangerously close to the edge of something he neither understood nor could control. What was it about her that was suddenly so troubling?

"I shall arrange rooms for you in my home," he added quickly, realizing that he was staring.

She didn't seem to notice. She rose and walked to the bedroom door. "Do not bother. I will look after myself. I am used to doing so." Then she turned. "When you have need of me, I shall be there."

She drew her cloak close about her and was gone.

Guards were stationed at the chamber doors and servants were at work farther down the hallway of the Prime Minister's residence, so the Moric waited until it was safely alone in an empty room at the back of the house before shedding its clothing and skin. It hated the stench of both and was anxious to return to the sewers, where it had been in hiding for several days while spying on the human Dunsidan. When the clothes and skin were removed, it folded them up and stuffed them into a bag under its cloak, strapping the bag over its sleek body. It would not wear them again until the next meeting. By then, it would be better able to bear the smell.

Relieved of its disguise and free to depart, it went out the window. It was three stories up, but since it had come in by climbing the wall, it had no difficulty leaving the same way. Using its claws to grip the stones, it went down like a lizard, crawling and skittering until it was back on the ground. From there, it scurried across the grounds and through the shadows to the edge of the compound, went over the wall, and faded into the night.

It had been in the city for the better part of a week,

making itself familiar with its new surroundings. After coming out of the Forbidding, it had acted quickly to eliminate the human who had facilitated its crossing, absorbing it as a sponge would water, consuming flesh and bones and blood, but assimilating its memories and traits and keeping the skin to disguise itself. The Moric was a demon, but it was a changeling, as well. While most changelings could only pretend at being other creatures, however, the Moric could actually devour and become them. It was a useful ability, particularly here, in this world, where it would have been quickly noticed otherwise.

The woman's death had assured its secrecy, and her skin had given it a way out of the Druid safehold. Too many magic users resided there for the Moric to feel comfortable. It was powerful, but no match for large numbers. Besides, it had taken what it needed from the Druids. Misguided and corrupt, they had yielded to the temptations offered them and unwittingly opened the door that imprisoned it. So desperate were they to indulge their own greed that they had never stopped to think what it was they were really doing. How easily manipulated they had been! First the woman whose skin it inhabited, then those who shared her hatred of the one human it feared. Had she not been betrayed and sent into the Forbidding to take its place, it would still be locked away in the world of the Jarka Ruus. But the cunning and deception of the Straken Lord had deceived them all, and so for the first time in centuries, a demon was free.

Still, it would all be for nothing if the Moric did not accomplish what it had been sent to do. The human Dunsidan was the key. The Moric hadn't known as much when it had come to this city, its plans not yet fully formed, its intent for the most part to find a way to make use of its human disguise.

But yesterday it had discovered the project the human Dunsidan had sought to keep secret. It had learned of the weapon he had built and the hopes he harbored of using it against other humans. The Moric had watched as the man in charge played with the crystals. It had watched as Dunsidan used the weapon, burning through thick metal, twisting and destroying entire slabs in seconds. There was something of interest. The human thought to use the weapon as a tool of war. The Moric was not so shortsighted.

The city was sleeping, and the Moric was able to pass freely down its streets and alleyways. The few humans it encountered never saw it. It climbed the walls or hid in the darkness and waited for them to pass. It could have killed them easily and would have enjoyed doing so, but it was there for a different purpose and would not allow itself to be distracted. Its value lay not only in its adaptability, but also in its single-minded determination. There would be plenty of time for killing humans later, when its task was complete.

When it reached the entrance to its hiding place, it glanced around to be certain it was alone before going down through the grates. The smells of the sewer were sweet and welcome, and it hastened to reach the cold, dark catacombs through which they tunneled. It was the one place in that wretched world that reminded it of its own. It

could feel at peace there. It could find comfort. One day, it
promised, everything would be just like that.

The darkness was thick and deep beneath the earth,
within the tunnels, and the Moric found a shelf submerged
in several inches of fetid water and sewage and settled
down to sleep.

T E N

§

They were still miles away when Grianne saw the fortress for the first time. It sat on a plateau that fell away hundreds of feet from a huge mountainside. Silhouetted against the empty horizon, black and stark within a swirling mix of gray mist and low-hung clouds, the fortresses' towers and parapets jutted sharp and hard-edged from the mottled rock as if they had blossomed like a cancer.

It was a huge, sprawling complex. She stared at it from the bed of straw on which she lay, her chains clanking softly as she rolled and swayed with the pitch of the wagon in which she was caged. They were moving in the direction of the fortress, and she felt certain that it was their destination. Whoever had made her a prisoner would be waiting there. She contemplated what that might mean as the strange caravan rolled on, the bull beasts snorting and huffing from their exertions, the wolves surging past in flashes of gray ruff and snarling muzzles, the creaking of ironbound wheels and leather harness mingling with the staccato snapping of whips and the odd croaking of wagon drivers she could not see. Dust filled the air, thick and choking, and she smelled its dryness and age. It made her choke, and she buried her face in her shoulder to breathe. Her body ached from being shackled, and her head throbbed from the ingestion of grit and the stench of the animals.

Once, when she was looking in the right direction, she saw the strange creature that seemed in charge of the little procession, its oddly elongated face peering in at her, topknot of coarse black hair swaying with its steps, bearded face intense and bright-eyed with interest. It did not speak to her as it had the first time it had approached, merely studied her a moment before moving on.

Exhausted and sick at heart, she dozed for a time, and when she woke again they were climbing a long, winding ramp that led to the fortress. It looked even bigger by then, looming up in a cluster of peaked roofs and crenellated walls, blacker than the soot of a wet fire and sharper-edged than a throwing knife. She sat up, bracing herself against the pitch and roll of the wagon, looking up the rampway to where a pair of massive, ironbound gates had opened to admit them. Creatures that reminded her of Weka Dart in the way they carried themselves scurried about on the tops of the walls and along the ramp itself, the metal of their weapons and armor glinting dully. The fortress was heavily defended, whoever its lord, and the only approach seemed to be up the fully exposed ramp.

She was reminded suddenly of Tyrsis, Callahorn's great fortress in the Four Lands. This keep could be a mirror of that one, and she suspected that it was situated on the same

plateau in this world as Tyrsis was in her own. The similar-
ities surprised her, and yet she knew that in the divergence
of separate histories, some things would work out much the
same. The use of geography in choosing natural positions
of defense would surely be one.

The gates swallowed them up and closed behind them
with a booming sound. Then there were faces all around
her, sharp-featured and hungry looking, fringed in coarse
hair and dominated by flat noses and pointed ears. Goblins,
she realized, though she had never seen one. They had
been banished into the Forbidding in the time of Faerie, she
had read in the Druid Histories. Some of them grinned unpleasantly, revealing sharp, pointed teeth and black gums.
They reached through the bars to touch her. The wolves
snarled and snapped angrily at them, as if protecting a meal
they would soon enjoy. The drivers she couldn't see flicked
their whips and croaked. The air was filled with raucous
sounds and fetid smells and, even inside the walls of the
keep, clouds of dust.

The caravan rolled to a halt at a central tower, one
ringed with walls that were spiked and barbed atop their
parapets and through which the mouths of spear launchers
protruded like serpent tongues. A flurry of activity announced their arrival as dozens more of the Goblins surrounded the wagons, some bearing lengths of rope and
chain attached to slip-nooses and clamps and some bearing
weapons. Grianne could no longer hear the snarls of the
wolves; presumably the huge beasts had been locked outside the last wall they had passed through, their task as
herders complete.

The creature with the topknot reappeared, coming out of the Goblin throng to unlock and open the door to her cage. She stood quietly as her keeper entered, thinking that if it got close enough, she might break its neck. But it kept its distance once inside, staying just out of her reach, working instead on the chains that held her fast, releasing them one at a time from the cage walls and passing the ends over to groups of Goblins waiting to receive them. It all seemed well rehearsed and smoothly accomplished, and she was given no opportunity to resist.

So she remained calm and let them do what they chose. She could wait. Her gag was left in place and her irons kept locked as she was led down out of the wagon. She was aware that her jailers held the chains taut so that she could be yanked over quickly if she tried to make a sudden move. It seemed clear to her that any effort at reaching for the gag in her mouth would trigger such a response. She couldn't know if they were aware of the wishsong's power and so were keeping her gagged because of it or if they were simply warding against the possibility of her employing any combination of utterances and gestures that might trigger an onslaught of magic.

She glanced once at the drivers of the wagons and found them to be creatures that resembled huge toads, perched on their seats with their hind legs tucked under them, short forearms gripping the reins to the bull beasts, wide-mouthed heads hunched forward, lidded eyes fixed and staring. They made no move to climb down off the seats. They gave no indication that they had any interest at all in what was happening around them.

She saw that the cages ahead of and behind her were empty. She was the only object of transport.

The creature with the topknot appeared directly in front of her, its strange face blank and its flat eyes staring. It beckoned for her to follow, and she was assisted by the Goblins, who tugged none too gently on her chains to let her know what was required, allowing her to move but keeping her just the other side of being off balance. She straddle-walked after and through them, doing what was required of her, biding her time because that was all she could do.

Ahead of her, massive doors opened to the outer wall of the tower they had drawn up to, and she was led inside. The wall was several feet thick, and its doors were crossbraced with massive timbers and iron bars. Inside, the courtyard was barren and empty of life, a killing ground between the first wall and a second of equally imposing girth. Murder holes overlooked the entryway from walls and gatehouses on both sides. Topknot walked ahead, moving toward a second set of doors. The Goblins followed, halfdragging her with them.

The second set of doors opened into a large room ablaze with torchlight. A single stairway wound down out of the darkness ahead; it was the only other entry into the room. The air was cool and damp, and slicks of water shimmered on the floor and stained the walls. Chains hung from iron rings all about the room; at its center sat a chair similarly equipped. A torture room, Grianne decided, and she shivered involuntarily. At Topknot's direction, the Goblins moved her over to one wall, spread her legs, and fastened her ankle irons to rings embedded in the stone. Then a heavy leather belt was cinched tightly about her waist, and her wrists were chained to rings in the belt so that she could not lift her arms more than a few inches on either side.

Her mind raced. Had they brought her all this way just to kill her? Did they plan to torture her for information? She closed her eyes momentarily, and when she opened them again, the Goblins were on their knees, Topknot had gone into a deep bow, and the lord of the keep was coming down the stairway.

She knew it for a demon right away, though not one she recognized. It was big, taller than she was, and broad through the shoulders. It walked upright like a man and in general was proportioned as one, though the resemblance ended there. Its skin was black and spiky, with clusters of spines sticking out everywhere except its face, which was flat and devoid of expression, its features buried so completely that at first glance it seemed possessed only of cold blue eyes that fixed on her with glittering intensity. It wore no clothes, but an assortment of bladed weapons was strapped about its body, some shaped in ways she had never seen. In one hand it carried a strange collar.

When it got to within ten feet, it stopped and held out the collar. Topknot appeared as if by magic to take it, walked over to Grianne, and fastened it securely about her neck. Once it was in place, the angular creature looked back at its master.

"What you wear is called a conjure collar," said the demon that had brought it. To her surprise, it spoke in a language she recognized. "If you attempt to use your magic, it will cause you sufficient pain to make you wish you hadn't. If you disobey me in any way, it will punish you. Nod if you understand me."

She nodded. Topknot removed the gag. She coughed and spit to rid herself of the dryness and dust that were in her throat. Topknot studied her thoughtfully, then released the ankle chains as well.

"Get down on your knees and bow to me," the demon said.

She wasn't sure she had heard right and she stared in disbelief. The expressionless face looked away, and one clawed hand gestured languidly. Excruciating pain exploded all through her, radiating out from the collar like strands of barbed wire into her throat, her body, and her limbs. She screamed at the assault, unable to stop. Clutching herself, she dropped to her knees and lowered her head toward the demon.

"You will speak only when told to," it said. "Nod if you understand."

She nodded at once. The conjure collar no longer tore at her, but the pain lingered in small waves that rose and fell with every breath she took. She gasped with the effort required to endure it.

"When you speak to me, you will address me as *Master*. Nod if you understand."

She nodded.

"Would you like some water? You may answer."

Her jaw clenched in fury. "Yes, Master."

"Give her water, Hobstull." The demon's mouth was a thin, lipless opening on the lower half of its flat, empty face. Its voice was raw and hoarse, suggestive of damage sustained by its vocal cords. There was no tonal inflection or hint of emotion.

Topknot brought her a cup filled with water that tasted of metal and smelled of swamp, but she drank it anyway. When she was finished, he backed away at once. She looked around. The Goblins had faded away. She was alone with Hobstull and the master of the keep.

"Do you know where you are?" the latter asked. "You may answer."

She nodded. The demon waved dismissively, and pain ratcheted through her once more, dropping her into a fetal position, where she lay moaning and sobbing. The demon studied her impassively, then came forward a step.

"Answer me as you have been taught. I want to hear you speak the words you were told to speak."

She squeezed her eyes shut against her humiliation and rage, fighting to keep from breaking down completely. "Yes, Master," she whispered.

"Do you know where you are? You may answer."

"Inside the Forbidding, Master." She opened her eyes again and looked up.

"Inside the world of the Jarka Ruus," the demon corrected softly. "Where I brought you to live."

She barely heard it; her head was buzzing with the aftereffects of the conjure collar's pain. The demon beckoned to Hobstull, who moved to fill the water cup once more, then hauled her to her knees so that she could drink again of the foul-tasting water. She accepted his gift wordlessly.

"You may thank me," the demon said.

She took a deep breath. "Thank you, Master."

The demon nodded. "Hobstull is not pleased with you. You made him work much harder than he intended when he left here three days ago. You made him feel inadequate. He is my Catcher, my finder and keeper of specimens. He is the one you must rely on for food and drink, so you don't want to upset him."

She looked briefly at Hobstull, who stared back at her with the same inquisitive look he had displayed earlier.

"Hobstull uses traps meant to lure his quarry by sounds, sights, and smells that speak to their deepest needs. He is very good at it. I have acquired many specimens as a result of his cleverness and perseverance. You are the latest and perhaps the most important. But you are still only a specimen. Do you understand?"

A specimen. She kept the anger from her face and voice with an effort. "Yes, Master."

"Good." The blue eyes glittered. "I am Tael Riverine, Straken Lord of Kraal Reach. I rule here. I rule everything from the Dragon Line north to the Quince south, from Huka Flats west to Brockenthrog Weir east. I rule you. Learn to accept this. I am your master, now and forever."

A pause. "Do you understand, Grianne Ohmsford, once Ard Rhys of the Druids?"

She felt her heart sink. She had been hoping desperately that her capture was by chance and not by design, that she would have a chance to gain her freedom after her captor's interest in her waned. But if the demon knew who she was, she was there because it had intended to bring her there, and there was no longer any chance of being set free.

"Yes, Master," she managed.

It saw the look on her face. "You didn't listen closely enough to what I said earlier, did you? You weren't paying attention."

She cringed in spite of herself, anticipating another rush of pain.

"I said that you are inside the world of the Jarka Ruus, that I brought you here to live. You are here because of me. You are here because I wished it to be so. Think back to your own world, to your visit to the ruins of the Skull Kingdom, where once the Warlock Lord ruled. Think back to the fires that ignited and burned without reason. Think back to the face you saw in those fires when you tried to probe them with your magic."

She knew at once what the demon was telling her. She remembered it all, especially the face that had appeared in the flames, coming out of hiding just long enough for her to see its features clearly.

It was this face. It was the face of the Straken Lord.

"You remember now, don't you?" the demon said. "Good." It gestured. "Get on your knees again and bow to me."

She did so, a chill settling through her as she realized how deeply in trouble she was.

"Take her, Hobstull," the Straken Lord ordered.

Without bothering to wait, the demon turned away and disappeared up the stairs into the gloom.

Hobstull walked over to where she knelt, clipped a fresh chain to a ring on the belt about her waist, and pulled her back to her feet. His eyes studied her for a moment, and then he tugged on the chain to indicate she was to follow. Moving to a heavy iron door concealed under the stairs, Hobstull led her through the opening and down a flight of worn, water-stained stone steps that lay beyond. She followed docilely, intent on conserving what was left of her strength for a time when she could put it to better use. She was thinking about her predicament. What she had been told by the shade of the Warlock Lord was confirmed. She was inside the Forbidding because the Straken Lord had arranged for a handful of Druids who hated her to be swayed into using magic that would put her here. Mostly, she was there because by being there something else had been set free. The Straken Lord hadn't admitted to it, but she was certain from what the shade of Brona had told her that it was so.

Yet it wasn't the Straken Lord that had crossed over into her world in response to the magic that had brought her here, but another demon, one she still knew nothing about.

Why hadn't the Straken Lord gone itself? Was the real purpose of the exchange to bring her in or to send the other demon out? The key to understanding everything was buried in the answer to that question.

At the bottom of the stairs, Hobstull turned back along a row of thick wooden doors into which tiny eye slits had been cut. As they passed those slits, she heard sounds emanating from within. Once or twice, blackened digits poked out tentatively, as if sampling her taste on the air she stirred in passing. Torches burned on the walls, creating a thick, smoky haze all along the corridor. Fresh air wafted down stone vents from somewhere above, but not enough to dispel the haze. The flames flickered and sputtered from the pitch-coated heads of the torches, casting her shadow against the stone walls as she passed. *Not a place from which many escape*, she thought.

She looked down at the chains she wore and saw herself as her captors did—an animal on a leash, a creature for display, a pet to amuse them, a curious specimen. In her own eyes, she had been reduced to the lowest level of existence possible, but in the eyes of her captors she was being treated exactly as she deserved. Men were less than animals in the world of the Jarka Ruus. Demons and demonkind were at the top of the food chain; Men were little more than an oddity. It was funny, but she had never thought about it before. She had never thought much about the Forbidding at all. It was a fact of life, but one so far removed from her day-to-day existence that it barely merited consideration.

Until now. Until it was all that mattered.

Hobstull stopped before one of the doors, inserted a key into the lock, and opened it. Leading her inside by the chain at her waist, he turned her about, unfastened the chain, and backed out the door. He looked at her again for a moment in that now-familiar way, then closed the door and locked it behind him.

Grianne Ohmsford, Ard Rhys of the Druid order, stared helplessly into the darkness that closed about her.

ELEVEN

Rigid with indecision, paralyzed by a sense of helplessness and loss, she stood without moving for a long time. The darkness and solitude of her prison only seemed to emphasize how desperate her circumstances had become. All that was familiar and dependable had been stripped away—her friends and family, her home and possessions, her entire world. The pain and humiliation she had been forced to suffer at the hands of the Straken Lord had shattered her confidence. Everything she had relied upon to sustain her, even her sense of how things worked, had vanished so completely that it seemed impossible in the wake of its passing to imagine ever getting it back again.

Finally, she sank to her knees on the stone floor of the cell and cried. She hadn't cried in a long time, and she wouldn't have cried now if she could have prevented it. Someone might hear and by hearing come to understand just how devastated she was. She had spent years learning how to keep any sense of weakness carefully hidden—first as the Ilse Witch and later as Ard Rhys. Since she had been a tiny child, she had fought to protect herself by hiding her feelings. But that method of self-protection, along with all the others she had been able to rely upon, had vanished.

When she was cried out, she rubbed her face against her shoulder to dry her eyes then stared blankly into the darkness. The slit in the heavy cell door admitted a small amount of light, and after a time her eyes adjusted to it sufficiently that she was able to see a little of her surroundings. Her cell was approximately ten feet square with a single bed covered with straw, a slop bucket, and a drain in the center of the room. There was nothing to eat and no water to drink. There were no covers for her bed. There was no place other than the bed to sit.

She tested the shackles that bound her wrists to the leather belt about her waist, then pulled on the belt as well. Both were tough and unyielding. She rolled her head to get a sense of the thickness of the conjure collar, but without being able to see it or put her hands on it, there was little she could determine. The clasps to both were behind her, where she could neither see nor reach them. Nothing in the cell would reflect their images. She took a deep, steadying breath and exhaled. There was no help anywhere.

She got to her feet again and walked to the door, peering through the slit into the corridor beyond. She could see parts of cell doors set into the far wall. Torchlight flickered and cast a mix of shadows and light, but there was no discernible pattern. She could hear faint sounds of movement and talking, but could not make out the sources of either. Smells permeated the air, and none of them was pleasant.

What am I going to do?

She turned away from the door and stared back into the darkness of her cell. No one who mattered knew where she was. The boy who was coming to rescue her—a boy!—had no idea where to look for her. Not that she thought it mattered. A boy wasn't going to make a difference anyway. No one was. Perhaps Weka Dart might have been able to help once upon a time; it was difficult to tell. But he certainly wouldn't be able to help now. The Ulk Bog had warned her against going back, almost as if he had known what would happen. The idea stopped her in midthought, a dark and suspicious voice in her subconscious. But she dismissed it quickly. It wasn't as if he had sent her to her doom. She had chosen her own way, and he had chosen his. She had done this to herself. Now any help from him was improbable at best. He was safely away and would stay so.

Questions nagged at her. What was she doing here? Why wasn't she already dead? The Straken Lord had brought her into the Forbidding, and it knew who she was. When she had been the Ilse Witch, she had disposed of her enemies swiftly and without hesitation, once they were in her power. A live enemy was always dangerous. So why was the demon keeping her imprisoned? Was there something about the transfer of its ally into the Four Lands in exchange for her that required it to keep her alive? She had not considered the possibility. Maybe the magic that had facilitated the transfer failed if either of them died in the other world. But did they both die in that situation? If so, then the Straken Lord had a vested interest in protecting her until its ally was ready to return.

She thought awhile about how that return might happen, but it was impossible to figure out without knowing what her counterpart had crossed over to accomplish.

Her thoughts drifted to other things, to the turmoil in the Four Lands, to the betrayal by her own Druids, and to concerns for her family. It was possible that those enemies who had dispatched her here would try to eliminate Bek, as well. Once he found out she was missing, her brother would come looking for her. Her enemies might try to stop him. It wouldn't be the first time that an enemy had come after members of the Ohmsford family with that idea in mind. The fact that she was Ard Rhys made the current generation of Ohmsfords targets in a way they hadn't been since the time of Shea Ohmsford and the Warlock Lord.

The longer she spent thinking about the ramifications of what had happened to her, the more determined she became. Her sense of indecision and confusion disappeared. Her fear turned to anger. She began to pull herself together, to regain the shattered pieces of her confidence. She no longer accepted her imprisonment as a condition about which she could do nothing. No one had ever imprisoned her and kept her so. She had not gotten so far in the world by giving in to her weaker emotions. She had not survived by giving up in seemingly impossible situations.

She tested the strength of the chains and belt again, this time trying to move the belt around her waist so that the buckle was more to the front. She was able to do this by sucking in her breath and jerking her hands all the way to the right. This brought the buckle around to her left side far enough that she could see how it was made. What she saw gave her hope. If she could find something to hook it on, she might be able to pull the leather tongue free of the metal clasp and then loosen it from the catch, as well.

A search of her cell walls, stone block by stone block, turned up nothing. What protuberances she discovered were too smooth or flat to be useful. She turned her attention to the door. The handle was a smooth metal grip fastened to the door at both ends. No help there. But on making a careful check of the hinges, she found a metal nail head on the lower hasp that had worked free from the wall just far enough to offer a possible hook.

She spent the next hour working the leather of the belt tongue, where it passed through the buckle, around the nail head and pulling it loose, inch by inch. All the while, she listened for the sounds of her jailers, for the soft scrape of boots on stone, for the tiniest creak of a door opening. She heard nothing.

At the end of the hour, she had freed tongue from buckle and was working on the catch. This was harder because the leather had to be pulled back much farther and with greater force. She struggled with it until she had exhausted herself, then tried again. Somewhere along the way her strength gave out and she fell asleep.

She woke to the sound of her cell door being opened. Hobstull appeared, blank-faced and empty-eyed, his topknot bobbing gently with his unhurried movements. He carried a tray on which rested a cup of water and some unidentifiable food. He set it by the door, glanced over at her perfunctorily, and went out again without speaking, closing and locking the door behind him.

When he was gone, she got to her feet and went over to the food. Because her hands were still chained to her waist, she could not use them to feed herself. She was forced to kneel and eat and drink like an animal. Her rage burned with a white-hot fury, but she made herself consume everything. She would need her strength for what lay ahead, and what lay ahead was freedom.

She began work again on the buckle as soon as she was done. She was stronger now, both physically and emotionally, and she stuck with the endeavor long after common sense told her it wasn't working. She did so because she couldn't think of anything better to do or any other plan to try. There were times, she knew from experience, when it was best just to continue on rather than to shift directions, even when it didn't seem as if you were getting anywhere. Your chances of success weren't always something you could measure accurately. Perseverance in the face of failure counted for something.

In the end, she was rewarded. Long hours later, the tongue at last pulled free of the troublesome catch, and the belt fell away from her waist. She held it in her hands, staring at it for a moment in shock, relief and fierce satisfaction surging through her. Her wrists were still bound by its chains, so she could not rid herself of it entirely, but she had a more complete range of motion than before and could lift her hands to her throat and the hated conjure collar.

But even as she started to search for the clasp that would open it, she hesitated. It was possible that any effort at trying to take off the collar would trigger a response of the sort that had laid her out earlier. It was also possible that the Straken Lord would be alerted to the fact that she had tampered with it. She could not afford for either to happen until she was safely away from the fortress. But if she left the collar in place, she could not use her magic to protect herself or to aid in making her escape. She would be imposing a severe handicap on herself before she even found a way out of her cell.

It was asking a lot. Maybe it was asking too much.

Reluctantly, she lowered her hands. She would leave the collar in place for the time being and take her chances.

She went back to working on the clasps and chains that bound her wrists to the belt. The iron from which they were made would not be easily bent, and she lacked the tools to do the job in any case. She would have to get out of the cell before she could do anything more.

Then, suddenly, she heard the rough scrape of boots outside her door.

Immediately, she stepped to one side, fastening her hands about the heavy belt and drawing it close against her chest. A key turned, and the lock released with a soft snicking sound. Then the door opened, letting in a sudden flood of torchlight. A Goblin stepped through, already bending down to retrieve the food tray that Hobstull had left for her. Summoning every last ounce of strength she possessed, she hit it in the face with the belt, and it dropped without a sound. She thought she might have killed it, but she couldn't stop to worry about that. She dragged the Goblin to one side, where it wouldn't be seen from the doorway. Seizing the keys it carried, she peered through the door and found the corridor deserted.

Gripping the belt firmly, cradling it to her chest once more to mask the rattle of the chains that bound her to it, she went down the hallway in a controlled rush, taking just a moment to close the door behind her. She didn't know how soon her captors would find out she was free, but she didn't think she should count on it taking very long. By the time they did, she had to be outside the walls of the keep if she was to have any chance at all.

She reached the stairs and started up. She could hear the soft rustlings of other prisoners below, muted by the heavy wooden doors and thick stone walls. If they saw her, they might cry out. She moved quickly up the stairs, glancing behind as well as ahead, her heart hammering. She reached the landing at the top of the stairs and stopped. She couldn't hear anything. She pressed her ear against the door. Still nothing.

There was no help for it. She had to go out.

She turned the handle slowly. To her surprise, it gave way, and the latch clicked open. She peered cautiously through the open door to see what lay beyond. She could hardly believe her good fortune. The chamber was empty.

She slipped through the door and into the darkened space under the stairway. She was back in the room in which the Straken Lord had confronted her. She glanced around furtively, stepping out far enough to peer up into the darkness of the stairwell into which the demon had ascended. She couldn't see anything.

Across the room, the door leading out into the courtyard stood closed.

For the first time, she was at a loss as to what to do. If she went out the courtyard door, she would be completely exposed to the denizens of the fortress. Kraal Reach was crawling with demons and Goblins, and the chances of her getting through all the surrounding walls and gates to the outside were slim at best. She needed to find another way.

A disguise would help, she thought suddenly.

She glanced around the room, but there was nothing in sight. No cloaks or armor or anything to conceal who she was. There were no other doors besides the one she had come through and the one leading out. Her choices were clear. She could either take the stairs the Straken Lord had climbed or retrace her steps into the cells.

She felt a rising panic and quickly forced it down. She could not make herself go back. She would go up.

She began to climb the stairs.

She was halfway to the top when the door leading in from the courtyard opened and Hobstull appeared. She froze on the stairs, pressed against the wall, hoping the shadows were sufficiently deep to hide her. Hobstull closed the door and walked to the stairs leading down to the cells. Without glancing up, the Catcher went through the doorway and disappeared.

In minutes he would discover that she was gone.

Abandoning caution, she raced up the stairs to a dark corridor. She glanced all about for signs of the Straken Lord, but saw nothing. Slipping down the corridor as fast as she could manage while still keeping silent, she reached a rack on which hung a series of black cloaks. She snatched one off and flung it about her, then hurried on. She turned several corners as the corridor wound its way back into the tower, listening all the while for sounds of an alarm. But no alarm was given.

Finally, she arrived at a door that opened onto a walk-way overlooking the fortress. She could see all of the keep's walls now, five concentric rings that enclosed increasingly larger courtyards and broader buildings the farther out she looked. The Pashanon was a hazy gray emptiness that spread away below the bluff, but the fortress itself teemed with life. She saw how completely trapped she was, how far she must go to reach safety, and she despaired. Without her magic to aid her and her hands free of the constricting chains, she could not hope to get away. Even a disguise would not be enough with so many demons and check-points to pass through.

She had to find a way to even the odds.

She glanced around furiously and found what she was looking for. Iron spikes protruded from slots in the battle-ments, a defense against intruders seeking to climb in. She walked to a cluster set far enough back that they weren't immediately visible to those passing below. Hooking the metal ring that bound the chain to the clasp on her right wrist about the closest spike, she began to twist it against its fastening. The clasp cut into her wrist until she was bleeding, but she continued to apply pressure, gritting her teeth against the pain.

At last, the ring snapped apart, and the chain and clasp fell away.

It took her even less time to free the left wrist, but cost her about the same amount of blood. Hugging her dam-aged wrists to her chest, letting the blood seep into her clothing, she searched for a way down. Finding nothing, she began to follow the walkway around the tower. There was still no alarm, something she found odd. Perhaps Hobstull hadn't gone to her cell after all. Perhaps the Catcher had gone into the cells for something else. She couldn't know.

She found a watchtower with a trapdoor and ladder leading down to the next floor. She climbed down quickly, found another trapdoor and another ladder, and climbed down that one, as well. From the courtyard below, she heard the chatter of the Goblins and, from somewhere beyond, the growls and snarls of the demonwolves. Too many enemies lay between her and safety. She hadn't a hope of getting past them all.

Her mind raced. Could there be a way underground, tunnels used by the defenders of the keep to move from wall to wall without exposing themselves, just as there was in Tyrsis, in her own world?

She went down the rest of the way, to the floor of the tower. There was nowhere else to go from there except outside or back into the main structure. Wrapping the cloak tightly about her body, she went out the door and into the courtyard. A scattering of Goblins was at work, but none of them even bothered to glance over at her. She walked swiftly across the open ground to the nearest door, opened it, and ducked inside.

Now she was in a building backed up against the next wall leading out, a storeroom for weapons and armor, and she passed through it to a door on the other side and down the corridor beyond. The corridor twisted and turned through the building as she followed it, and soon she was hopelessly lost. She kept searching for a stairway leading underground, but found none. Her plan of escape was rapidly coming apart.

Finally, she found a door that opened into the next courtyard. But there were demonwolves everywhere, prowling the grounds and lying in the shade, dozens of them, huge gray beasts with thick ruffs about their necks and jaws strong enough to snap a spear handle. She glanced at them just long enough to measure the danger before shutting the door. If she had the use of her magic, she wouldn't have worried. Without it, she was no match for them.

But she had to get across the courtyard if she was to escape. There wasn't any other way.

She opened the door and looked out again, searching for an overhead walkway that would connect the two walls. There wasn't one, or at least one that she could see. Nor was there any indication of any other way across.

She closed the door again and stood there, trying to think what she could do.

In the next instant, the cry of alarm she had been dreading rose from behind her, the thunder of a drum followed by the deep moan of a horn. She didn't mistake it for anything other than what it was, and without another thought, she went out the door and started across the courtyard for the far wall. Instantly, the demonwolves glanced over at her, but she didn't look back at them, keeping her eyes directed straight ahead, trying to act as if she belonged, moving for the closest escape.

Just a few minutes were all she needed.

Behind her, the warning continued to sound, and now Goblins were appearing all along the battlements atop the walls on either side, turning this way and that, searching. She kept moving, trying not to let her panic take control of her, trying to stay calm.

She reached the door and grasped the handle to open it. The door was locked.

Without pausing, she turned toward the next door down, walking quickly to reach it. But by then the demon-wolves were moving, their suspicions aroused. Heads lowered, ruffs standing up like bunched quills, muzzles drawing back to reveal the rows of teeth concealed behind, they advanced on her. The first low growls and snarls came from their throats. Alerted by the sounds, a pair of Goblins on the wall behind her stopped to look down into the courtyard.

A huge wolf positioned itself directly in front of the door she was trying to reach and turned to face her. She stopped at once, a mistake. The wolf snarled defiantly, sensing that she was either afraid or intimidated. She turned back the other way, but more wolves were closing in, blocking her passage, and trapping her. On the walls, other Goblins were gathering, staring down at her.

She was finished, she knew, unless she used her magic.

She reached quickly for the conjure collar to release its clasp, but couldn't find the catch. Frantically, she searched its length for a buckle, for any telltale bit of metal. Nothing. The wolves drew closer, openly menacing now, teeth showing as they stalked her. The closest was no more than ten yards away. She had no choice. Even with the conjure collar in place, she would have to use her magic to defend herself.

"Haahhh!" she growled at the wolves, making a quick warding gesture that caused them to fall back.

She advanced on them as if she meant to punish them and, uncertain as to what she might do, they gave way to her. They were creatures of the Straken Lord, after all, and it had trained them to do its bidding. At some point, punishment had been a part of that training. As fierce as they were, they couldn't completely ignore the responses that had been conditioned in them.

Her audacity froze them in place, but only for a moment. It was enough. By then she was back at the first door she had tried, her one chance at escape. She was discovered, and if she couldn't get through the door, her captors would be on her in moments. She quit looking at the walls and the wolves. She ignored the shouts and growls that rose behind her. She quit thinking about anything but the door. Bracing herself, she summoned the magic of the wishsong to break free of her prison.

But the minute the first strains of the magic rose within her, the conjure collar reacted with blinding pain that seized her throat in a paralyzing grip and froze her vocal cords. The pain was instantaneous, and it rushed through her with relentless purpose, knocking her backwards with its force, sapping her strength and numbing her mind. Caught in the terrible grip of the collar's magic, she stiffened and screamed soundlessly, unable to help herself in any way.

She went down in a heap in the dusty courtyard, tumbling into blackness, lost to everything but the pain and an unmistakable sense of failure that trailed after her through the gathering dark like a death shroud.

TWELVE

Pen Ohmsford and his companions sailed the *Skatelow* through the northeast skies over the foothills fronting the Charnal Mountains in search of the village of Taupo Rough and Kermadec. Finding the former would provide them with a temporary haven; the latter, with the guide they needed to reach Stridegate. As Maturen of the Taupo Rough Rock Trolls, it was within Kermadec's power to give them the aid they required in their search for the Ard Rhys. The Trolls might be reluctant to help outlanders in most situations, but where it concerned Grianne Ohmsford, Kermadec would see that an exception was made.

It took them the remainder of the night, but they were sailing at quarter speed, slow enough that they could track movement on the ground and watch the horizon for shadows that didn't belong. Caution was needed, for there were things hunting them besides the Druids, and they were all too aware of how desperate their circumstances had become. They were lucky to have escaped the crea-

ture that had killed Gar Hatch and his Rovers and taken
Cinnaminson as prisoner, and they were reasonably sure it
was not done tracking them. But even if they avoided that
particular monster, there was nothing to say that others
hadn't been sent to hunt them, as well. At flight from a
world in which all the safety nets they had once relied on
had been taken down, they could not afford to make a mistake.

The boy came back on deck after Cinnaminson was
asleep and, with Khyber's help, took down the bodies of
Gar Hatch and his Rover cousins, wrapped them in sheet-
ing, and stowed them belowdecks for burial at a later
time. Then he relieved Tagwen at the helm. While he
checked the *Skatelow*'s course and speed, he repeated to
the Dwarf and the Elven girl what Cinnaminson had told
him. For a while afterwards, no one said much of anything. Tagwen offered to take the wheel back so that Pen
could get some sleep, but the boy insisted on staying at
the helm through the night, just in case his flying experience might be needed for evasive action. Having gotten
Cinnaminson back in one piece, he was not about to
chance losing her again to carelessness of his own
making.

So Khyber and Tagwen slept instead, and Pen was still
at the helm when dawn broke in a slow brightening of the
skies through gaps in a wall of massive peaks that rose before them. The stars and moon had gone, and the darkness
was receding west, the new day a promise of the possibility, at least, of something better and safer. Pen's eyes were
gritty and blurred by then, and his need for sleep was acute.

When Tagwen appeared with a simple breakfast of bread and cheese he had scavenged from the supply room below, the boy was so grateful he could barely speak. He ate ravenously and, after looking in on Cinnaminson to be sure she was all right, went off to bed.

He awoke near midday when Khyber shook his shoulder and told him to come on deck. "I think we've found Taupo Rough," she announced with a grin. "Come see."

He rose and went topside, finding Cinnaminson there, as well, come awake a few hours earlier to join the Elven girl and the Dwarf in the pilot box. Looking out over the ship's bow to the landscape below, he saw a cluster of dark stone buildings and walls stacked in close proximity to one another on a low bluff and backed up against a cliff face that was riddled with caves connected by ladders and walkways. His initial impression was of a warren that probably ran as deep into the mountain as it extended out from it. Trolls of all sizes and shapes were moving about, but there seemed to be little interest in the *Skatelow*'s approach. No defensive maneuvers were being undertaken, and from what Pen could make out, there were few guards of any sort.

The boy knew almost nothing about Trolls. He had seen a few in his life, some of them had come to Patch Run to employ his parents. But his travels had not taken him into the deep Northland, where the tribes made their homes, and Trolls by and large did not venture south of their traditional homelands. He thought that he had heard his mother speak in the Troll tongue once or twice, but he couldn't be sure.

"Can we communicate with them?" he asked impulsively.

"I can speak a little of their language," Tagwen ventured. He shrugged. "It won't matter, once we find Kermadec."

If this is Taupo Rough and if Kermadec is here, Pen thought without saying so.

As he brought the ship slowly around toward the village, he called to memory what little he knew about the inhabitants. Trolls were nomadic by tradition, and frequently resettled themselves when their safety was compromised or their dissatisfaction with local conditions grew sufficiently strong. But because they were tribal, as well, they established territorial boundaries within the regions they traveled, and one tribe would never think of invading another's domain. Of such trespasses had the worst of the Troll Wars been born, wars that had died out years ago in the wake of the establishment of the First Druid Council. Galaphile and his Druids had made it their first priority to stabilize relations within the Races. They had accomplished that by setting themselves up as arbitrators and peacekeepers, developing a reputation for being fair-minded and nonjudgmental. The Trolls, who were the most fierce and warlike of the Races in those days, had accepted the Druids as mediators with surprising enthusiasm, anxious perhaps to find a way to put an end to the tribal bloodshed that had plagued them for so long. Trolls were creatures of habit, Pen's father had told him once. They embraced order and obedience within the tribal structure as good and necessary, and self-discipline was the highest quality to which a Troll could aspire.

There was more than one species of Troll living in the Northland, but by far the most numerous of the tribes were Rock Trolls. Physically larger and historically more warlike than the other tribes, they were found principally in the Charnals and the Kensrowe, preferring mountainous terrain with caves and tunnels rather than open encampments as safeholds. The Forest and River Trolls were smaller in size and numbers, and they were not nomadic in the way of Rock Trolls. The differences went on from there, but Pen couldn't remember them all. What he mostly remembered was that Rock Trolls reputedly made the finest weapons and armor in the Four Lands, and they knew how to use both when provoked.

"Someone's noticed us now," Khyber announced, nodding toward a handful of Troll warriors walking out to meet them.

Pen let the airship settle to the earth in an open space at one end of the plateau, well away from the village and its fortifications. Whatever happened, he did not want to give an impression of hostility. He shut down the thrusters, closed off the parse tubes, walked to the railing, tossed out the rope ladder, and climbed down to set the anchors. The others followed, with Tagwen in the lead, looking bluff and officious.

The Trolls came up to them, huge and forbidding giants, their barklike skin looking like armor beneath their clothing, their strange, flat-featured faces devoid of expression, but their eyes sharp and watchful.

One of them spoke to Tagwen in deep, guttural tones, a query of some sort, Pen thought. The Dwarf stared at the speaker blankly, then glanced hurriedly at Pen. The boy shook his head. "You're the one who says he speaks the language. Say something back to him."

Tagwen gave it a valiant try, but it came out sounding a little as if his last meal hadn't quite agreed with him. The Trolls looked at one another in confusion.

"Just use whatever Troll-speak you possess and ask him if Kermadec is here," snapped Khyber, impatient with the whole business. "Ask if this is Taupo Rough."

The Dwarf did so, or at least appeared to do so. Pen caught the words *Kermadec* and *Taupo Rough* amid all the garble, and the reception committee seemed to do the same. One of them nodded, beckoned for them to follow, and turned back toward the village. The other three fell into place about them like a stockade.

"I hope we haven't made another mistake," Khyber muttered to Pen as she glanced about uneasily.

Pen took Cinnaminson's hand and held it firmly in his own. The Rover girl did not pull away, but moved closer to him. "It doesn't look it, but this village is heavily defended," she whispered to him. "We can't see most of it. Most of it is hidden inside the mountains. I can feel the heat of furnaces and forges. I can feel movement in the earth radiating out from the rock."

The boy exhaled sharply. "Are these Trolls enemies?" he asked. "Are we in danger?"

She shook her head. "I can't tell. But they are prepared to do battle with something, and whatever it is, they mean to see it destroyed if it tries to attack them."

Pen nodded. "If we have to flee, I will stay right beside you."

She said nothing in reply, but squeezed his hand tightly.

They moved through the heavy stone walls that formed the outer fortifications into the village itself. Trolls turned to look at them, Trolls of all sizes and shapes, but their gazes were brief and didn't linger. A few young Trolls, barely five feet tall yet—though big when compared to Tagwen, who was not much more than that himself—fell into step beside them, casting interested glances at the outlanders. No one tried to speak to them, and no one did anything threatening. Pen studied the buildings as he walked, comparing them with those of Southland villages. The biggest difference was in the construction, which was almost entirely of rock and suggested that every building provided its own defense. Each unit had heavy ironbound wooden doors and shutters, and weapons ports had been cut into the walls for use by the defenders. It had taken a lot of work to build the homes, and it seemed in direct contradiction to the nomadic tradition of the people who occupied them.

"We didn't do anything to protect the airship," Khyber whispered to him suddenly, a frown crossing her dark features.

Pen nodded. "I know. But what could we have done?"

"Sent Tagwen on ahead alone until we knew what to expect," she replied. "We aren't being very smart about this."

Pen didn't respond. "I don't sense any hostility," Cinnaminson said quietly. "We aren't threatened."

Khyber rolled her eyes as if to suggest that a blind Rover girl might not be the best judge but didn't pursue the matter.

They had just rounded the corner of a massive building that looked to be a storehouse rather than a home when a huge Rock Troll appeared in front of them, arms outstretched and voice booming out in familiar Dwarfish.

"Bristle Beard, you've found your way!" the Troll shouted, reaching down to pick up Tagwen and hold him out at arm's length as if he were no more than a toy. "It's good to see you safe and sound, little man!"

Tagwen was incensed. "Put me down at once, Kermadec. What are you thinking? A little decorum would be appreciated!"

The big Troll set him down at once, drawing back. "Oh, well then, sorry to have distressed you. I was only expressing my great joy at finding you in good health. It hasn't been a good time at Paranor, Tagwen."

"This does not come as news to me!" the Dwarf snapped. He cleared his throat officiously. "Here, let me introduce the others."

He did so, giving a quick explanation of who his companions were without yet getting into why they had all come together. Kermadec nodded to each at the mention of their names, his flat features somehow reflecting the pleasure he took in meeting them. There was an exuberance and expansiveness to the big man that transcended what Pen had heard of the Troll character, and he found himself liking their host right away.

"Penderrin," Kermadec said, taking the boy's hand in his own. It was like shaking hands with a rough piece of wood. "Your aunt and I are great friends, friends from as far back as the coming together of the Druid order, and I regret what has happened deeply. Your presence indicates that you intend to join me in doing something about it. You are most welcome."

He turned to Tagwen. "Now you must tell me all about what has happened since our parting at Paranor, and I will do the same. Come with me to my home, and we will have something to eat and drink while we talk. Is that an airship you flew in on, Bristle Beard? I thought you hated airships!"

Dismissing the Trolls who had guided them in from the *Skatelow*, Kermadec led them on through the village until they were almost to the cliff face against which it was backed. At that distance, Pen could see clearly the sophisticated network of walkways and ladders connecting the village to the caves and tunnels that riddled the cliff. He could also hear, for the first time, the sounds of hammers striking anvils and smell the fires of the furnaces that serviced them.

What was odd was that he couldn't see any smoke or ash.

He asked Kermadec about that, and the Troll pointed skyward. "The residue of the furnace fires goes into a vent system that carries it out the other side of the near peaks. It helps keep the air we breathe out here in the village clean. It also helps disguise what we do. You can't be sure where we keep the furnaces until you get this close. The furnaces are our lifeblood. Without the furnaces, we can't make the weapons and metal tools we trade to the other Races for the goods we need. Without the furnaces, we would revert to what we once were—raiders and worse. If anything happens to them, we are left without a way to make a living."

"What do you do with the furnaces when you move to another site?" the boy pressed. "You don't take them with you, do you?"

Kermadec laughed. "That would be a neat trick, young Penderrin. The furnaces are built right into the rock of the mountain. No, we shut them down, cool them off, and conceal them. We close off the entrances that lead to them, as well. And we set traps to discourage the uninvited. As long as I can remember, no one has ever bothered our furnaces."

"And there are those who would, I can promise you," Tagwen declared grimly.

Kermadec clapped him on the shoulder so hard he almost knocked him off his feet. "If they could, Bristle Beard. If they could."

"So you have other furnaces in other places?" Pen pressed.

"Half a dozen that have been constructed over the years, more if you count the ones we have abandoned as unsafe. We are a mobile people, but our villages are well established. We simply move back and forth among them, choosing the one that seems most advantageous with each migration. Just now, we are concerned about uninvited guests and so have chosen this village, with its superior defensive positioning."

Khyber glanced about. "You don't look all that ready to go to ground if you are attacked. No guards, no sign of anything out of the ordinary. We just sailed right in on the *Skatelow*."

"Only because we saw you coming from five miles off

and identified your sloop as harmless." The dark eyes swept back to her and away again. "Don't mistake what you see, Khyber Elessedil. We keep close watch in all directions. We won't be easily surprised. If we are threatened, we can disappear into the caves behind the village in a matter of minutes, much quicker than an enemy can reach them. Once inside, we can survive for months on the provisions stored. Or we can escape through any number of back doors. And there are extensive fortifications inside the caves as well, in case an attack is pressed. Believe me, things are not entirely as they seem."

Which was in keeping with most of what they had encountered on their journey to reach Taupo Rough, so his guests decided to take him at his word.

A few minutes later, they were settled inside the big Troll's home, a sprawling affair occupied by his brothers, sisters, parents, and grandparents, as well as a child or two somehow connected with the rest. Kermadec explained, on completing introductions, that Trolls tended to house together in families, often living that way the whole of their lives. The house his family occupied had once belonged to another family, but that family had lost enough members over the years that they no longer needed anything quite so large. Since Kermadec's family had grown, they were offered the other family's home in exchange for their smaller one.

It was an odd approach to determining living conditions, but one that the Trolls seemed quite used to. Homes didn't seem to belong to any one person or family, but to the entire community. Pen thought that perhaps because Rock Trolls moved so often, they weren't quite so attached to their possessions, homes included, and were therefore able to share more freely.

Still, he was curious about all those people living together under one roof, and after being served a cold drink of black tea and herbs, he asked what determined if any member of the family moved away. Or didn't they? This produced an even odder and more complicated explanation of the Troll lifestyle. Trolls, Kermadec offered, did not maintain family units in the same way as the other Races. Trolls started out life as children in one family, but often ended up as children or even adults in another. When sickness or death rendered parents unable to raise their children, other parents stepped in. When a child or adult grew dissatisfied with a family situation, he or she could petition to move elsewhere, and frequently the move was allowed. It was thought better to accommodate that individual and try to ease the source of dissatisfaction than to allow the problem to fester. The move didn't happen until a thorough effort had been made to resolve the conflict.

Moreover, Troll parents did not regard their children as the exclusive property of the family and were not possessive of the responsibility for raising them. The care, nurturing, teaching, and disciplining of children was the responsibility of the entire village, and everyone was involved in the rearing process. Successes and failures were always shared; decisions and pronouncements were never left to one person. A Troll child started out life as the result of the union of two people, but reached adulthood as the result of the efforts of many.

"Well, that's enough for now about the social structure of Rock Trolls, young Penderrin," Kermadec declared, seating himself across from the boy and the others. "Tell me everything that's happened. Bristle Beard, you begin. Right from the time I left you at Paranor. Tell it all."

So they did, each of them speaking in turn, each of them adding a piece to the larger puzzle. Tagwen told of coming to find Pen's parents at Patch Run and finding only Pen. The boy related the details of their escape from Terek Molt, the subsequent encounter with the King of the Silver River, and the task he had been given—to travel to the ruins of the ancient city of Stridegate and the forest island of the tanequil. Tagwen then picked up the story once more to tell of their decision to seek help at Emberen from Ahren Elessedil. Much of it was difficult, especially Khyber's recitation of the events surrounding her uncle's death in the Slags. When it came Cinnaminson's turn to speak of the creature that had killed her father and her cousins aboard the *Skatelow*, she was forced to stop and compose herself several times. But both Elf and Rover made it through their tales, through the dark and terrible hurt they had experienced, to emerge, Pen thought, a little stronger than when they had started out.

Kermadec listened carefully and, when they had finished, shook his head in a mix of disgust and disbelief. "I knew our Grianne had placed too much faith in her ability to keep those Druid sorceresses from reverting to kind,

Tagwen. Even an Ard Rhys can do only so much with black hearts and foul schemes."

He sighed. "But losing Ahren Elessedil? I never thought I would live to see that. I never thought anything could happen to him, as much as he had survived already. He was the best of them, Khyber, your uncle. The best of them all."

She nodded in acknowledgment of the kindness of his words. "I appreciate hearing that."

"And Cinnaminson." He turned to the Rover girl. "I am sorry for the death of your father, whatever the circumstances that brought it about. Your father is an irreplaceable loss. You have shown great courage and presence of mind in surviving the madness that consumed him. I will send my Trolls to see that he and his cousins are given burial."

He leaned forward. "Now, then. You have told me your tale; let me tell you mine. Maybe we can make some sense of this business once I do."

After leaving Tagwen at the Druid's Keep, Kermadec had traveled north on foot out of Paranor and across the Streleheim to the ruins of the kingdom of the Warlock Lord. He did not want to do this, but he had no better idea of where to begin his search for Grianne Ohmsford. Days earlier, he had accompanied the Ard Rhys to investigate rumors of apparitions and strange fires within those ruins and had encountered an impossibly dark and evil presence. The Maturen felt certain that there was a connection between that presence and the disappearance of the Ard Rhys, and he was hopeful that by taking a closer look at the site where the presence had revealed itself, he might discover something useful.

It was a long shot at best, and as Kermadec had made clear to Tagwen, the Troll people did not go into the Skull Kingdom for any but the best of reasons. Kermadec was brave, and there were few dangers that could turn him aside, but that was one of them. Rock Trolls had an inbred fear and distrust of the land where the Warlock Lord had ruled and been destroyed. Rock Trolls, in that time and place, had served the Warlock Lord, slaves and soldiers to help in the conquest and subjugation of the Four Lands. It had taken many years for the Trolls to recover from those monstrous times, years for them to be accepted again by the other Races. Grianne Ohmsford had done much to make that possible. If a journey to the forbidden land was what it would take to help her in turn, then so be it.

Nevertheless, he had determined that he would not go back there alone.

So he traveled first to a Gnome village situated below the River Lethe on the western borders of the Knife Edge, seeking a man he believed would know better how to protect against the danger he expected to encounter in the ruins. The man's name was Achen Wuhl, and he was a Gnome shaman of some repute in the tribe to which he belonged. He was old, perhaps ninety, and he had been a shaman the whole of his life, living with the Warst, a tribe that migrated across the Streleheim between the Kensrowe and the Charnals.

Kermadec had met Achen Wuhl twenty years before on an outing that had brought a company of his Trolls in contact with the Warst while the latter were under attack from Mutens. In most circumstances, Rock Trolls would have nothing to do with Gnomes because the two Races were traditionally at odds over territorial rights and migratory routes. But the Trolls hated Mutens worse than anything. Voiceless, soulless remnants of the Warlock Lord's dark magic, the Mutens survived in the Knife Edge in much the same way as the Werebeasts did within Olden Moor—by preying on the Gnomes who worshiped them as sacred spirits.

So Kermadec had broken the unwritten rule that forbids Trolls from interfering with the lives of Gnomes, and his company had come to the aid of those unfortunates who were being butchered by the Mutens because they had ventured too close to the monsters in a misguided effort to appease them. Among those rescued were women and children and the shaman, Achen Wuhl, who accepted the gift of his life from the Trolls with a promise that some day he would repay the favor. Kermadec had not claimed that promise before. He chose to claim it now.

With Achen Wuhl in tow, he journeyed back through the Knife Edge, carefully avoiding the caves of the Mutens, until he was back within the ruins of the Skull Kingdom at the site where Grianne Ohmsford and he had encountered the strange fires and the apparition. Without revealing the involvement of the Ard Rhys, he recounted to Wuhl the events of his earlier visit, suggesting that the apparition had appeared unbidden and that he was searching for its source. Together, they combed the ground surrounding the cold and blackened fire pit that had given birth to the presence, looking for something that would reveal its source. They found nothing. As nightfall approached, Kermadec suggested they leave and come back in the morning. But Achen Wuhl insisted that they stay. Once it was dark, the shaman would try to summon the apparition himself.

Kermadec felt that was a dangerous undertaking and that he should put a stop to it. But he was desperate to discover what had become of the Ard Rhys, and the shaman was still the only chance he had to unlock the secret. Achen Wuhl was a skilled conjurer and an experienced shaman. He would not be careless in his efforts. He might accomplish what Kermadec could not: find a link between the apparition and the Ard Rhys. Ignoring his instincts, which were screaming at him to get out of there, Kermadec convinced himself that the risk was necessary.

So they sat together in the growing dark, the old Gnome and the Troll Maturen, watching and waiting for something to happen. Darkness fell, and nothing did. Midnight came and went. The mountains were still and deep and seemingly empty of life.

Finally, with the moon down and the stars layered across the black firmament like scattered grains of brilliant white sand, the shaman rose from his place in the rocks. Motioning for Kermadec to remain where he was, he moved forward to where the fires had appeared last.

"I had a bad feeling about it right away, but I kept still," the big Troll told Pen and his companions. "I could still remember how that apparition made me feel, how dark and terrible was its visage, and I thought it would be better if we didn't see it again, ever. But the little man was determined; he had courage. So I let him go. I was thinking that this was the way I would reach your aunt, Pen. I was thinking that this was how I would discover where she was."

He shook his head at the memory. "Achen Wuhl brought up the fires right away, as if all he had to do was reach down to wherever they were hidden and summon them up. The fires flared and hissed right in front of him, bright flames burning with such intensity I could feel the heat from where I was sitting a dozen yards away. I heard the shaman muttering, saw the movement of his hands. I peered through the darkness to the flames, watching. *This is what I've been hoping for*, I kept thinking. *I'm going to find her, after all.*

"But then all of a sudden the flames just exploded. It was as if they found a fresh source of fuel, though there wasn't anything but the darkness for them to feed on. They shot upward a hundred feet, maybe more, all brilliant orange and yellow-tipped, crackling and hissing. It surprised me so, I almost fell over. But here's the odd thing. There wasn't any new heat. The fire burned with the same intensity, at the same temperature as before. Like magic."

He exhaled softly. "Something reached out of the flames and wrapped itself about the old man. I don't know what it was. A part of the fire itself, I guess. It snatched him up and it pulled him in. He was gone in an instant, so fast I barely saw it happen. He never made a sound. He just disappeared. The flames consumed him. There was nothing left.

"Then I saw that face, the one the Ard Rhys and I had seen days earlier. I saw it in the fire, just for an instant. It was a dark and twisted thing, its eyes like a cat's, only blue and freezing cold. Those eyes were searching the darkness beyond the fire, hunting. I stumbled over myself trying to hide from them. I flattened myself against the rocks the best way I could. I never thought to do anything else. It was instinct that drove me, that warned me that if the eyes found me, I would go the way of the old man.

"So I hid. The face was there, the eyes searching for a moment more, and then both were gone. A second later, the flames were gone, too, collapsed into a black smear of ash burned into the stone of the pit. The heat died with the flames, and the night turned still and empty again.

"I stayed where I was for a few minutes more, then came out to look around. In the starlight, I could see what was left. Nothing. Nothing at all."

His voice trailed off and his gaze dropped to where his big hands knotted in his lap. In the silence, Pen could hear himself breathe.

"It was a trap," Kermadec said quietly. "It was a trap set to snare anyone who dared to search for the Ard Rhys. It got the old man. It could have gotten me just as easily. I came back to Taupo Rough alone. I will never go back to that place again."

"Does this mean you won't help us?" Pen asked him, impatient to know where Kermadec stood on the matter.

"Did I say that?" the Rock Troll exclaimed. "Did I say I wouldn't help you find this tree so that you can fashion

your darkwand? Did I say I wouldn't help you reach the Ard
Rhys and bring her out of the Forbidding? Shades, young
Penderrin! Of course, I will help you! If I have to carry you
to Stridegate and back again on my own shoulders, I will do
so! All the Rock Trolls of Taupo Rough will carry you, if
that's what's needed. We owe more than a little to your
aunt for bringing us back into the mainstream of the Four
Lands. She gave us trust and recognition when no other
would, and we won't let that gift be for nothing. Whatever
those black hearts at Paranor might pretend, we are still the
Ard Rhys' protectors, and we will see her safe again or
know the reason why!"

He stood up suddenly. "But I need to think on this a bit.
The country into which you must go is dangerous—not
that the rest of the Four Lands isn't, so long as Shadea a'Ru
is acting Ard Rhys. But it's treacherous country all on its
own, made more so by the presence of Urdas and some
other things that have no name. We must make certain we
keep you safe in your travels, those of you who decide to
go."

He glanced sideways at Cinnaminson. "But there will be
time for that later. For now, eat and rest. I'll set sentries to
keep watch for the dark things tracking you, and I'll start
the process of outfitting an expedition. But how will we
travel? It's safest if we go on foot. Airships have difficulty
getting through these mountains. The winds are unpredictable; they can send airships into the rocks as if they
were pesky insects. But time is important, too, and travel
afoot is slow."

He shook his head worriedly and went toward the door.

"I'll think it through. Just ask, if you need something. There's plenty who speak the Dwarf tongue here. We'll celebrate your safe arrival tonight."

Then he was out the door and gone.

"I don't want you to leave me behind, Pen," Cinnaminson told him as soon as they were alone.

They had eaten, and Khyber and Tagwen had gone out to look around the village. The boy and the girl sat together in Kermadec's home, the other members of the big Troll's extended family coming and going silently about them, engaged in tasks of their own. It was after midday, and Pen was feeling the need to sleep again. But he couldn't sleep until this conversation was finished.

"I can't be responsible for putting you in any further danger," he replied, deliberately keeping his voice down so as not to attract attention.

Her face was anguished. "The thing that killed Papa still tracks us. It didn't die back there in that meadow. It will come after us. If it finds me, it will use me to find you—just like before. How can that be any less dangerous than what you might find where you are going?"

"You will be safe here," he insisted. "Kermadec's people are too well armed and this village too well fortified for anything to get to you. Even that thing we escaped. Besides, you don't know that it's still coming."

She kept her empty eyes fixed on the sound of his voice, as if she could actually see him speaking. "Yes, I do. It's coming."

He rose and walked to the open doorway of the room, stood there thinking, then came back to sit beside her.

"I'll have you sent home aboard the *Skatelow*. Someone in this village must know how to fly an airship. They will take you back into the Westland, to wherever you need to go. Kermadec will arrange it. I'll ask him to see that you are protected."

She stared at him for a long time, as if perhaps she hadn't heard right, then shook her head slowly. "Do you wish to be rid of me, Pen? Do you no longer need me in your life? I thought you said you cared about me. No, don't speak. Listen to me. You cannot send me home. I don't have a home to go back to. My home was with Papa, aboard the *Skatelow*. There isn't anyone else who matters now. Only you. My home is with you."

He looked down at his hands. "It's too dangerous."

She reached over and touched his cheek. "I know you are afraid for me. But you don't need to be. I'm blind, but I'm not helpless. You've seen that for yourself. You don't have to make me your responsibility. You only have to let me come with you."

"If I let you come with me, I make you my responsibility whether I like it or not!" he snapped. "Can't you see that?"

"What I see is that I can be of use to you." Her voice was desperate, almost pleading. "You need me! I can guide you where you are going in the same way I guided you across the Lazareen and through the Slags. No one else can see in the dark the way I can. No one else has my sight. I can help, Penderrin. Please! Don't leave me behind!"

"Of course, you're coming," Khyber Elessedil said quietly.

The Elven girl was standing in the doorway, watching them. They had been so wrapped up in their conversation, they hadn't heard her come back in.

"Khyber, you're not helping—"

"Don't lecture me, Pen. We don't need lectures, she and I. We share something that puts us in a better position to see what is needed here than you do. We've both lost someone important to us on this journey. We've lost a part of our family and, therefore, a part of ourselves. We could be diminished by this, but we won't let that happen, will we, Cinnaminson? We will use it to make us stronger. Neither of us would consider for a moment being left behind. If you think that I am better equipped to handle what lies ahead because I have the use of the Elfstones or that Cinnaminson is less able because her talent lies only in her mind-sight, then you need to think again!"

She was so vehement that Pen was left speechless. Of all the people he had expected to agree with him on the matter, Khyber was at the top of the list.

"Get out of here, Pen," the Elf girl ordered, gesturing toward the door. "Go find something to do. Cinnaminson and I need to talk. While we do, you think about what I just said. You think about whether what you are asking of her is reasonable or not. You think about everything that's happened while you're at it. Use your brain, if you can find a way to it through all your wrongheaded opinions."

She was angry, her face flushed and her gestures curt and threatening. Pen stood up slowly and glanced down at Cinnaminson. She was staring straight ahead; tears were leaking from the corners of her eyes, streaking her smooth face. He started to say something, then stopped himself.

As he left the room, he felt Khyber Elessedil glaring at him. He walked through the house, past the surreptitious glances of the Trolls, his gaze directed straight ahead. When he was outside again, he stopped and stared into space, wondering exactly what had just happened.

THIRTEEN

§

Darkness had fallen over Paranor, deep and smothering, and the Druid's Keep was wrapped in silence. Within the fortress halls, the Druids came and went like wraiths; cloaked in black and hooded, they passed down halls that echoed softly with the scrape of slippers and the rustle of robes. Some cradled books and loose-leaf writings in their arms. Some carried materials for the tasks they had been given in the cause of the Druid order.

One carried nothing but a second cloak, neatly folded over one arm, so preoccupied that not a glance was spared for those it passed.

Bek Ohmsford looked up as the cloaked figure entered the room, and it took him a moment to realize it wasn't a Druid at all, but his wife. Rue Meridian came over to where he lay looking hot and feverish beneath his covers and laid the cloak at his feet.

She bent close to keep her voice a whisper. "I hope you don't feel as bad as you look."

He smiled. He was hot and sticky, and beads of sweat dotted his forehead. "I look terrible, don't I? That root you gave me really works. Traunt Rowan was here earlier to see how I was doing. I told him the fever had come back worse than before and was highly contagious. He was in and out of the room in seconds. No one has been back since. You found the robes, I see. No one saw you?"

She sat beside him, leaned over, and kissed his forehead. "Have a little faith, Bek. I am resourceful enough when it's needed. I just asked for them. I told the Druid I stopped that we would feel more comfortable being here if we were dressed as they were. Besides, it isn't me they're interested in. They watch me from around corners and through cracks in doors, but they don't pay close attention. You are the one who matters. So long as they think you intend to do what you were brought here to do, we won't have any trouble."

Bek nodded. "After tonight, we'll be more trouble than they thought possible. Hand me a cold cloth and towel."

She rose and did what he had asked. He sat up in the bed and began wiping himself down, washing away the sweat and grit, then drying off. The room was streaked with shadows, and the candles he had lit at sunset did little to chase the gloom. All the better, he thought, for what they had in mind.

"Did you have a chance to check out *Swift Sure*?"

She sat next to him again, keeping her voice low. There was still reason to worry that they were being listened to. "They cut loose the aft radian draws and locked down the thruster lever. I didn't see anything else. I pretended not to notice even that. I thought it better for them to think us unaware of their efforts. It might take us three minutes to make the necessary repairs. We can get away easily enough when we need to."

He finished cleaning himself, rose, and began to dress. He moved quickly and quietly, glancing over at the door every so often, listening to the silence that surrounded them. It was infectious, that silence. Everything about the Druid's Keep was measured in layers of silence, as if sound were an unwelcome intrusion. Perhaps it was, where power resided in such quantity and struggles to control it were all done through secret machinations and subtle deceits.

"I won't be sorry to be gone from here," she said. "Everything about this place is oppressive. How your sister stands it is a mystery to me. I wish her well, once we have her safely back from wherever she's gone, but mostly I wish her the wisdom to choose, then, to be somewhere else."

"I know." He glanced around. "I wish I had a weapon."

She reached beneath her robes, brought out a long knife, and handed it to him. "I retrieved it from the ship. I have my throwing knives, as well. But I don't think weapons are going to do us much good if we have to stand and fight."

"They might against those Gnome Hunters." He tucked the long knife into his belt, then reached for the other Druid robe. "Any sign of the young Druid?"

She shook her head. "Nothing."

They hadn't so much as caught a glimpse of him since he had slipped Bek the warning note on that first day. Bek had burned the note and had Rue scatter the ashes from one end of the Keep to the other, but he still didn't know who had tried to warn them or why. Clearly, the young Druid knew something about what was going on. He might know something about Pen, as well. But it was too risky to try to find out who he was. The best they could do was to keep watch for him, and so far he hadn't reappeared.

"You would think he would try to make further contact." Bek tightened the sash that bound the robe. "If he went to the trouble to contact us in the first place, he must want to help. He must be on my sister's side in all this."

"Maybe, but that doesn't mean he knows where she is or what's happened to her. He might not know anything other than what he's told us—that Shadea and the others are responsible. Maybe warning us was all he ever intended to do. It was enough to put us on guard."

Bek finished with his preparations and walked over to put his hands on her shoulders and draw her close. "You could wait for me aboard *Swift Sure*," he said. "I can do this alone."

"I think we had this discussion about twenty years ago, didn't we?" She leaned into him and kissed his mouth. "Let's just go."

They moved to the door and stood there for a moment listening. The Gnome Hunters assigned to the task of keeping watch were still stationed across the hallway, but they had been there for three days, and they were bored. It wouldn't take much effort to get past them.

Bek looked at his wife. "Ready?"

She nodded, pulling up the hood to her cloak. He did the same, then opened the door and stepped through. Already, he had the wishsong's magic working, a soft low hum that carried no farther than the ears of the guards. It whispered purposefully to form images in their minds. It told them that the cloaked figures leaving the room were Druids, easily recognizable as such by their robes, that they needn't bother with them and could look away.

By the time the guards looked back again, of course, the hallway was empty.

Bek and Rue moved swiftly to the stairs leading up to the cold chamber, turning into the stairwell before they could be seen. They had been fortunate in not encountering a single Druid on their way. If the Gnome Hunters at their sleeping room door didn't realize they had been duped, they stood a good chance of reaching their destination unnoticed.

They climbed the stone stairs to the next floor, sliding through shadows and pools of light as soundless and stealthy as foxes at hunt. This was a dangerous business, and they knew it. If they were discovered, their duplicity would be revealed and there would no longer be any chance of using the Druid's magic to find Pen. Worse, they probably would have to fight their way out of Paranor, and Bek wasn't sure they were up to it. It was one thing to have survived while traveling aboard the *Jerle Shannara*, while they were still young. It was another to test themselves when they hadn't fought a real battle in twenty years. Now was a poor time to find out if the magic of the wishsong could save them from the dangerous and experienced Shadea a'Ru.

In short, it would be best not to get caught.

At the top of the stairs, they stopped again while Bek

peered around the corner and down the hallway. Nothing moved. The floor seemed deserted. There were no sleeping chambers on this floor, but a little farther on was the stairway that led to the north tower, which housed the quarters of the Ard Rhys. Shadea a'Ru would be there.

After a moment, they started down the corridor for the cold chamber. The biggest danger they faced was that someone else would already be in the room when they got there. That would not only prevent them from carrying out their plan, but would require them to explain why they were there, unescorted and uninvited. It would be a difficult situation. At best, they would probably be forced to flee from the Keep.

But luck was with them. When they opened the door, they found the cold chamber empty. Rue took a moment to scan the corridor once more, making sure no one had seen them, then nodded to Bek to close the door. They stood inside in silence, the chilly air penetrating even the heavy fabric of the Druid robes. Rue shivered. Bek made a quick survey of the room, glancing toward the deep shadows, peering into the gathered gloom. No candles or torches were lit there, and they wouldn't risk lighting any. But a faint wash of light from moon and stars spilled through the high windows and reflected off the scrye waters in the stone basin, letting them see well enough to do their work.

Their plan wasn't complicated and didn't require much time. Bek had sensed Pen's presence in the Charnals during his initial effort to make contact, but he had lacked time and opportunity to pinpoint his son's location. Now, alone and undisturbed, he would use his magic on the waters to discover exactly where Pen was. Once he had accomplished that, they would slip back down through the Keep to *Swift Sure* and be on their way to retrieve him. The Druids might discover what had happened and try to follow, but their vessels were no match for *Swift Sure*, which was the fastest ship in the sky.

With Rue standing watch at the door, Bek moved to the basin and stood looking down at the scrye waters and the map of the Four Lands drawn on the surface of the bowl. The waters were still and untroubled, at rest save for where the faint pulse of the earth's magic crisscrossed the surface along the earth's lines of power. Bek studied their movements for a moment, then fixed his gaze on the Charnals and called up the wishsong. He did it quickly and quietly, directing the magic toward the area of the waters where he had sensed Pen to be the day before. He kept his concentration focused as he worked the magic deep into the basin, searching.

It took him only moments. His connection with his son was strong, born of his own history as a member of a family that had been connected by magic for centuries, and he found him almost instantly. He peered close, tightening down his search, marked the spot in his mind, and pulled the magic back again.

He went still, watching the scrye waters quiet and smooth once more, silver in the moonlight. He stepped away from the basin and turned back to Rue, nodding.

Together, they went out the doorway and back down the empty corridor toward the stairs. Neither spoke, unwilling to break the deep silence, to risk exposing themselves in any way. They would talk when they were aboard *Swift Sure* and safely away from this place.

On cat's paws, they descended the ancient stone stairs toward the torchlit corridor below, listening and watching.

They had just emerged from the stairwell into the corridor when the heavy metal-laced nets dropped over them, pinning them to the floor, and dozens of Gnome Hunters appeared all around them, crossbows notched and ready.

Pen had explored the Rock Troll village for what remained of the day. He'd been so tired he could barely keep his eyes open but was unable to sleep because of what had happened in Kermadec's home between himself and Cinnaminson. But Khyber's scathing attack on him, an attack he still didn't understand, really troubled him. Once or twice in his wanderings, he thought to return to the house and confront her, but he just couldn't make himself do it. He was embarrassed and hurt, in part because he didn't understand it, but mostly because it had happened in front of Cinnaminson.

So he forced himself to stay away until the evening celebration began, the welcome arranged for them by the members of the village, a feast with music and singing, neither of which he had ever associated with Trolls. But the music, consisting of pipes, drums, and a curious stringed instrument called a fiol, and the dancing, which was energetic and robust, brought him out of his mood sufficiently that by the time he had eaten two plates of rather wonderful food and drunk several pints of very strong ale, he was feeling pretty good again.

He even participated in the dancing, urged on by Kermadec and buttressed by the effects of the ale. He danced with whoever was nearest—men, women, and children alike—as there seemed to be little partnering in the Troll forms of dance, and he found himself thoroughly light-headed and happy by the time he was done.

Cinnaminson appeared with the others of his little group, and she sat with him during dinner and even danced with him briefly, but he couldn't find the right words to say to her, and so they didn't talk much. Tagwen was as taciturn as ever at first, though after a little of the ale he began to open up and pontificate endlessly on the virtues of hard work. Khyber smiled and clapped and spoke pleasantly to Pen, acting as if their earlier confrontation had never happened.

It was only when the evening was growing late, and his eyes were so heavy he was afraid he might fall over if he didn't sleep soon, that the Elven girl came over to sit beside him. He was alone at that point, sipping at his ale, listening to the music, and watching the Trolls dance in the firelight with what appeared to him to be boundless energy.

"I was too hard on you earlier," she said, putting her hand over his. "I didn't mean to scold. At the time, I was so mad, I just lashed out. I assumed you understood the problem, but thinking it through later, I realized you didn't."

He looked at her. "What problem?"

"If I tell you this, you must promise to keep it to yourself. Do you promise?"

He nodded. "All right."

"When I heard you tell Cinnaminson she couldn't come with us, all I could think about was how insensitive you were being to her situation. You saw it as common sense: If she came, she would be placed in danger again, and you wanted to keep her safe. I saw it through her eyes: You were casting her off as damaged and useless, no longer worthy of being a part of your life. She's in love with you, Penderrin. I warned you about this, but you paid no attention to me. You brought this on yourself, giving her so much of your time aboard ship, telling her how wonderful she was."

He bristled instantly. "I didn't say anything I didn't mean! Anyway, I don't see—"

She held up one hand in warning. "Don't say anything more until you hear me out. You *don't* see, indeed. If you did, we wouldn't be having this conversation. Now, listen. What do you think happened to her after that monster killed her father and the other two? Do you think she was left alone? Do you think that all that happened was that she was used to track you? It was bad enough that she had to lie trussed up and helpless belowdecks and listen to the cries of her father and cousins as they died; that was damage enough for an entire lifetime. But that wasn't the end of it."

He went cold. "What are you saying?"

Her dark eyes fixed on him. "I'm saying that she endured three days alone with that monster, and it wasn't satisfied with using her gift for night sight. It used her for other things, too. She told me. You didn't ask her if she had been abused physically, did you? It never even occurred to you that she might have been violated in other ways. This thing, this creature that took her, doesn't have any qualms about watching others suffer. It likes it. It enjoys inflicting pain. All kinds of pain."

He stared at her. He tried to say something, but the words lodged in his throat. A wave of nausea washed through him.

"So now she views herself as despicable." Khyber held his gaze. "When you tell her she can't go with you anymore, she sees it as an affirmation of what she already believes to be true about herself—that she is worthless, that no one could love her. It doesn't matter that you don't know the truth because she has kept it to herself. It's enough that *she* knows."

Pen looked off into the darkness, filled with sudden rage, filled with a need to exact revenge for what had happened, but impotent to do anything but sit and fume. The images that filled his mind were so terrible that he couldn't bear them. "I didn't realize what I was doing by telling her she couldn't come," he said quietly. "I didn't know."

She squeezed his hand. "I wish you still didn't know. I wish I didn't have to tell you. But you still care about the girl, don't you? So you need to know what's happened to her so that you can understand what she's going through. She's fragile in ways that you don't see. She might have mind-sight, but it's not sufficient protection against the monsters of this world and not enough to make up for the loss of her family. Her father, bad as he was, loved her, and she loved him. He was the support she could fall back on when things were too much for her. Who's going to offer her that support now?"

"I am," he said at once.

"Then you can't tell her you intend to leave her behind." Khyber's voice was fierce. "You can't make her safe that way, Pen. I know taking her is dangerous, but leaving her is worse."

They stared at each other in silence. In the background, the music and singing of the Troll revelers wafted through the darkness, rising above the firelight, echoing off the rock walls of the cliffs. Pen wanted to cry for what he was feeling, but no tears would come.

"I'll tell her she can come," he said finally. "I'll tell her I was wrong, that we need her."

She nodded. "Be careful what you say and how you say it. She wouldn't like it that I've told you what happened. She will probably want to tell you herself one day."

He nodded. "Thank you, Khyber. Thank you for telling me. Thank you for not letting me make a mistake I couldn't correct."

She got to her feet and stood looking at him. "I just did what I thought I had to do, Pen, but I have to tell you that it doesn't make me feel very good to have done it."

She turned and walked away.

Acting on whispered instructions from Shadea a'Ru, the Gnome Hunters removed the heavy mesh netting and bound and gagged Bek Ohmsford. He could have struggled or used magic to save himself, but he was terrified that if he did so, they would kill Rue. Bitter with disappointment and self-recrimination, he let them take him without a struggle.

"You aren't half so clever as you believe yourself to be," she said to him as the Gnomes carried him down into the cellars of the Keep. "I knew of your contact with your son the moment you made it. It was impossible to miss. I knew you were pretending at being ill earlier today, too, and that you would come back to the cold chamber to use the scrye waters again if you were given the chance. So I gave it to you."

She leaned over and tapped him lightly on the nose, a taunting gesture he couldn't fail to register. "You couldn't get a clear reading of where Penderrin was from your first contact; I saw that right away. So I knew you would have to come back and probe the scrye waters again when you thought we weren't around to see what you were searching for. Somehow, you found us out, didn't you? It was probably Traunt Rowan who gave us away. He lacks the finesse needed to fool someone as perceptive and experienced as you. Disappointing, if not entirely unexpected. At least I knew enough not to trust that you had been taken in by his explanation. I knew enough to read you the same way you must have read him."

She was silent for a time, staring straight ahead into the darkness, keeping pace with the guards who bore him. She took big, full strides that radiated power and determination. She looked taller and broader through the shoulders than he remembered, and there was a confidence about her that suggested she was equally comfortable with weapons or words. He did not know what his sister had done to antagonize her, but Shadea a'Ru was a formidable enemy.

"Your son has turned out to be a meddlesome boy, Bek,"

she continued after a while, "but no more so than Tagwen or the others who joined him to hunt for your sister. I took steps to put an end to their search, but until now they have managed to elude me. I tracked them all the way from Patch Run to the Elven village of Emberen and from there east to the Lazareen. Then, I lost them. But now, thanks to you, I know exactly where they are."

She smiled down at him, enjoying the dark look on his face. "Oh, you want to know how I know, since I wasn't in the cold chamber with you? Anticipating your nocturnal visit, I marked the scrye waters with a little magic of my own before you tampered with them. They will reveal to me exactly what they revealed to you. That should tell me everything I need to know about your son's whereabouts, I expect. Then I will find him and deal with him."

Bek listened with growing despair, aware of how completely he had been duped into doing just what Shadea had wanted him to do in the first place. Now he was a prisoner and unable to do anything to help either Pen or his sister. At least they were both alive. He could assume that much from what she had just told him. He could also assume she would try to change that.

They continued down until he smelled the damp and felt the cold of the deep underground. Somewhere not too far away, he heard water running. The heat of the Druid Fire was absent, as if that part of the Keep was far removed from the earth-warmed core.

Finally, they arrived at a corridor lined with heavy doors kept closed by iron bolts thrown through iron rings. His captors opened one of the doors and placed him in the tiny room beyond, a space barely larger than a closet. There was a wooden bed, straw, and a bucket. The floor, ceiling, and walls were rough and uneven and had been hollowed out of the bedrock.

They untied his arms and legs, but left his gag in place.

"Remove the gag when I am gone," Shadea said. "But first, listen to what I have to say. Behave yourself, and you might come out of this alive. I am locking your beloved wife up separately, in a place far away from you, somewhere you can't find her easily. I know stone walls and iron doors can't hold you, but they can hold her. If you try to escape, if your guards even *think* you are trying to escape, she will be killed at once. Do you understand?"

Pen nodded without speaking.

"Those guards will be stationed on each floor leading up, at each door, and they will communicate with each other regularly. If someone fails to answer, that will be the end of your chances of seeing your wife alive again. Behave yourself, and you and your family might still survive this."

She motioned the Gnome Hunters back into the corridor, followed them out, closed the door with a heavy thud, and threw the bolt.

Standing alone in the darkness and listening to their receding footsteps, Bek Ohmsford was certain of one thing. No matter what Shadea a'Ru said, if he didn't find a way to get out of there on his own, he wasn't getting out at all.

FOURTEEN

"I've been thinking about what I said to you yesterday," Pen said, sitting down beside Cinnaminson. It was midday, and he had been searching for her for almost an hour.

She kept her gaze directed straight ahead as her fingers worked the threads of the delicate scarf she was weaving on a tiny hand loom. How she could tell one color from the other was a mystery to him, but from the look of the completed portion, she was having no trouble doing so.

"I spoke without sufficient thought for what I was saying," he continued, watching her face for signs of a response. "You asked if I still cared about you, and I do. That was why I was so quick to tell you that you couldn't go with us. All I could think about was what it would mean to me if something more happened to you."

Still, she said nothing. They were seated high up in the bowl of the Gathering Place, the amphitheater used for elections when a Maturen was chosen, for presentations of music and song when there were celebrations and festivals,

and for meetings of the entire population when it was necessary to make determinations that might affect the whole
of the village. It sat well back against the cliffs and to the
south end of the village, ringed by stone walls and hardy
spruce, an oasis of calm in the otherwise bustling community.

It was deserted, save for the boy and the girl.

Pen sighed. "I want you to forget about what I said. You
saved our lives back on the Lazareen, when the *Galaphile*
was hunting us. You kept us from danger again in the Slags.
You proved your value then, and I don't have any right to
start questioning it now. I don't have any right to tell you
what to do. You can decide for yourself."

"Have you been talking with Khyber?" she asked quietly.

"I've been thinking about what she said," he answered,
avoiding the question. "She was so angry with me. It took
me a while to sort it out." He brushed at his red hair, knotting it in his fingers. "I didn't know why she was so angry
until I had thought about it for a while. I was presuming to
speak for you when I didn't have the right. You asked me
because you wanted my support. I should have realized
that, and I should have given it."

She continued her weaving, her fingers moving
smoothly and steadily, feeding in the colored threads and
pulling them through, using the shuttle to separate and
tighten down. He waited, not knowing what else to say,
afraid he had already said too much.

"Do I have your support now?" she asked him finally.

"Yes."

"Do you want me to come with you? You, personally?"

"Yes, I do."

"Why? Tell me, Penderrin. Why do you want me to come with you?"

He hesitated. "I don't want this to be about you and me."

"But it is about you and me. It has been from the first day we met. Don't you know that?"

He nodded. "I guess I do. I just don't want to use that as the reason for your coming. But it is the reason. I want you to come because I want you to be with me. I don't want you anywhere else but with me."

She went still, her fingers motionless, her entire body frozen. He saw her differently in that instant, as if she had been captured in an indelible image, a portrait of such exquisite beauty and depth that he would never imagine her any other way. It made his heart ache to see her so. It made him want to do anything for her.

Without looking at him, she reached for him with her right hand, laying it feather-light across his own. "Then I will come," she said.

She went back to her weaving, silent once more, her attention on her work, her hand gone from his. He stared at her for a moment, wanting to say something more, but deciding against it. Just then, things were better left as they were.

He rose. "I think I should see how the *Skatelow* looks, now that they've moved her off the plains. I'll find you later."

She nodded, and he went down off the risers to one of the passageways that exited from the amphitheater floor to the ring of stone walls and spruce trees outside. From there, he walked down through the village to the south gates and passed out onto the flats, then worked his way back toward the cliffs until he reached the shallow defile into which the *Skatelow* had been pulled to conceal her from view. He did that without really being aware of anything but Cinnaminson. Her face, her body, her voice, her words, her smell, the movement of her hands as she wove the delicate scarf.

He was still thinking about her two hours later, happily lost in a mix of dreams and memories that gave him the first real peace he had known in days, when the Troll watch sounded the alarm.

Khyber Elessedil was standing with Tagwen outside Kermadec's home, listening while the little man held forth on the peculiarities of Troll life, when the horns began to wail and the drums to boom. The sounds were so unexpected and so earth shattering that for a moment she stood staring at the Dwarf, who stood staring back.

"What is that?" she managed finally.

He shook his burly head, his blunt fingers tugging at his beard anxiously as he glanced around. "Don't know. A warning?"

Trolls had begun running everywhere, all sizes and shapes, men, women, and children, entire families and households, charging out of buildings and down roads and alleyways with a single-mindedness that suggested they understood the sounds perfectly. After a moment, Khyber was able to discern a pattern to their movements that suggested what was happening. The women and children were all retreating back through the village toward the cliffs, the biggest scooping up the smallest in squirming bundles. They took nothing else with them, not one single implement or piece of clothing. They went without the slightest hesitation or thought for what they were doing, moving swiftly without seeming to look rushed.

They have practiced this often, Khyber thought.

The men, meanwhile, were all moving in the other direction, down toward the front walls of the village, to the gates and ramparts that served as protection and fortification. Some wore chain mail and plate armor. All carried weapons. It didn't take a genius to figure out what was happening.

Khyber rushed back inside the house for her short sword. When she came out again, Kermadec was standing with Tagwen, huge and forbidding in a towering iron helmet and a chain-mail chest and shoulder guard.

"We're under attack," he advised, his words clipped and hard. She had not heard him sound like that before. All of the heartiness and openness was gone; his voice had gone tight and rough with anger and menace. "Airships fly in from the south bearing Druid insignia. We can assume the reason for their visit."

Khyber buckled on her sword, then felt for the reassuring presence of the Elfstones in her tunic pocket. She had no idea if she would be required to use them, but she intended to be ready. She glanced at Tagwen, who carried no weapons, then back at Kermadec. "How did they find us?"

The Rock Troll shook his big head. "No idea. The

Druids have ways of finding anyone, if they put their minds to it. I don't think they followed you. If they had done so, they would have been here sooner. I think they found you some other way."

He turned away from them to yell instructions to a squad of Troll warriors passing by, gesturing toward the south wall, separating out one and sending him in another direction. The village was alive with movement, swarming with Trolls. It felt like controlled chaos.

"We're preparing a welcome for our uninvited guests," he said, turning back to them, changing once more to the Dwarf language. "We won't attack them until we hear what they have to say. We'll let them talk first."

"Perhaps they're friends," Khyber suggested hopefully, cringing at the loud snort Tagwen gave in response.

"Too many ships for that," Kermadec advised. "If they were friends, they would come in one ship, not in a dozen. They would send a representative ahead to announce their intentions. No, this is an assault force, come for a specific purpose." He glanced around. "Where are young Penderrin and the girl?"

Khyber stared at Tagwen. The Dwarf shook his head. Neither one had a clue.

Kermadec glanced skyward. "Too late to search for them now. Come with me! Hurry!"

At the sound of the battle horns and drums, Pen dropped off the *Skatelow*'s decks to the ground and began to run. He needed no time to consider what he was doing or where he was going. He had left Cinnaminson inside the Gathering Place. She might still be there, alone and unprotected. She would not know what was happening. She would not know where to run.

He went through the south gates just as they were closing, bursting through the knot of Troll warriors bunched at the opening, huge armored shoulders and wide backs straining against the ironbound barriers and massive locks. Trolls were running everywhere, and the passageways of the village were all but completely blocked by Trolls hurrying toward the walls. Pen dodged past them, heading for the amphitheater and Cinnaminson. Shouts and cries rose all around him, their intensity and tone confirming what he already instinctively knew—the village was under attack. He would have liked to find Khyber and Tagwen to know more, but he would have to track them down later. First he had to reach Cinnaminson.

He gained a side street that was mostly deserted and led straight to his destination. He was running hard now, flushed with the heat of his efforts, a frantic warning sounding in his mind. *Don't lose her! Don't let anything happen to her!*

Ahead, the walls of the amphitheater loomed darkly through the ring of trees that surrounded the interior bowl. There was no movement at the entrance, no sign of life. Perhaps she had already gotten out. Perhaps one of the others had come to find her.

He glanced over his shoulder at the village walls, where Trolls were taking up positions all along the ramparts and at the gates. The central point of defense seemed to be the gates he had just passed through, the ones facing south down the broad corridor between the Razor Mountains west and the Charnals east. The reason for this became immediately apparent when he glanced skyward. A dozen black warships filled the horizon, flying down the gap directly toward Taupo Rough.

Shades!

He breathed the word in a whisper of fear as he burst into the tunnel leading into the amphitheater and nearly collided with Cinnaminson, who was trying to make her way out from the other end. She was careening from wall to wall, her hands clutching her ears to block out the sounds of the horns and drums.

"Cinnaminson!" he shouted as he reached her, grabbing her shoulders and pulling her against him.

"Pen!" she gasped in reply, burying her head in his shoulder. Her weaving materials and loom were gone, and he could feel her heart pounding. "I couldn't find my way out. The sounds disrupt my mind-sight. It was too much for me."

"It's all right," he said, stroking her hair. Her breath was coming in quick, frantic bursts. "I'll get you back to the others. They must have gone into the mountains to hide. The sky is full of Druid warships, right outside the walls. We have to go. Can you walk?"

She nodded into his shoulder, then lifted her face to his. "I knew you would come for me."

He kissed her impulsively. "I'll always come for you. Always. Come on. Run!"

They hurried back through the tunnel to the streets outside. But as they reached the far end, Pen drew up short and pulled her back against the passageway wall, keeping hidden in the shadows.

One of the Druid airships was hovering just outside the village wall and across from their hiding place. Any attempt at escape would require them to cross open ground, where they would quickly be seen.

Pen bit his lip in frustration. They were trapped.

Khyber Elessedil crouched with Tagwen on the roof of a building some fifty yards back from the south gates. Both wore dark robes drawn close and hoods pulled up. They hid behind a half-wall facade that rose in front of them, situated where they could see and hear what was about to happen.

Kermadec stood on the ramparts above the south gates, surrounded by a squad of huge Trolls wearing body armor and insignia-crested helmets. The Maturen was watching as the Druid airships—their flags clearly visible now—formed a line just beyond the outer wall, intimidating black hulks hanging over the village like birds of prey. There was an unmistakable arrogance to their positioning, as if they were disdainful of anything the villagers might try to do to harm them. No attempt was being made to suggest that this was a friendly visit. Kermadec had been right: The Druids had come to threaten.

After the foremost airship had dropped almost to the ground, a single Druid descended the rope ladder and walked forward. He was a big man, and as he approached, he lowered his hood to reveal his face, a gesture clearly meant to identify himself to the Trolls.

"Traunt Rowan," Tagwen whispered to Khyber. "One of Shadea's bunch."

She watched the Southlander come almost to the gates before stopping, his eyes fixing on the Trolls standing atop them.

"Kermadec?" he called, his voice clearly audible in the near silence.

"I'm here, Traunt Rowan," the Maturen called back.

"Open your gates to us."

"I don't think so."

"Then bring out the boy, Pen Ohmsford, and you do not need to. Just the boy. The others can remain, if you want them to."

"You are a bold man, coming into our country and making demands as if it were your own." Kermadec's voice had taken on a decided edge. "You might want to give some thought to where you stand before you say anything else."

"Is the boy here?"

"What boy?"

There was a measured silence. "You are a fool to challenge us, Kermadec."

"The only fool I see is the one who serves Shadea a'Ru. The only fool I see is the one who betrayed the Ard Rhys in a way so foul and indefensible that it will surely lead to his destruction. Don't threaten me, Traunt Rowan! Don't threaten the Trolls of Taupo Rough! We were the defenders of the Druids for almost twenty years, before this dark time in your history, and we will one day be defenders of the Druids again. We know enough about you to be able to challenge you, if that is what is required. Turn your ships around and fly out of here while you still can. Don't mistake where you are."

Traunt Rowan folded his arms. "We have the boy's parents, Kermadec. We know that Ahren Elessedil is dead. You have no one who will stand with you in this. You are alone."

Khyber and Tagwen exchanged a quick, shocked glance. The Druids had Bek Ohmsford and his wife? How had that happened?

"He's lying," Tagwen hissed.

"Alone?" Kermadec laughed. "The Trolls are always alone. It is a condition of life to which we are not only accustomed, but one that we prefer. Threats of the sort you seem intent on making don't frighten us. If you have the parents, you don't need the boy, do you? Can the parents not give you everything you need? What is it that you need, by the way? You haven't said. What is it that a boy can give you that his parents can't? You speak as if you know, but I think, in fact, you don't. Explain yourself, and maybe I can be persuaded to do as you say."

Traunt Rowan stood unmoving on the flats, dark and solitary, anger radiating off him like heat. "We are to raze your village and kill you all, Kermadec, if you resist us. Those are my orders. I have brought Gnome Hunters to carry out those orders. I have brought Mutens, as well. Do you wish your village and people destroyed? Is that your intent?"

Kermadec seemed to be thinking it over. "My intent, Traunt Rowan," he said finally, his rough voice so dark with menace that Khyber immediately tensed, "is to see you and your raiders and your airships consumed by the fires of the netherworld that spawned you."

His arm swept up. Instantly, a hail of fire-tipped arrows arced out of the village and fell all across the flats beyond. In the next instant the flats exploded in gouts of fire that spread quickly down concealed channels in a crisscross pattern that blanketed the earth for two hundred yards. The flames leapt so high that one of the airships caught fire and was consumed immediately, the fire spreading up the bottom of its hull to find added fuel in yards of light sheaths strapped to its gunwales. The ship heaved in response to the blaze that consumed it, tried futilely to rise into the sky, then shuddered, blew apart, and fell in ruins onto the flats.

The other airships were backing away by then, powered up in response to the threat and lifting swiftly beyond the reach of the flames. Traunt Rowan had gone into a protective crouch, hands moving, his Druid magic sweeping about him. Now he, too, backed away, avoiding the flames as best he could, shielded well enough that he didn't seem threatened. His black robes swirled about him in a wind generated by the sudden heat as he reached an open spot, caught hold of the rope ladder once more, and began to climb.

The Trolls of Taupo Rough were attacking the airships using catapults now. The wooden machines were mounted all along the ramparts, their cradles flinging huge rocks through the smoke-filled air with deadly precision. Several found their marks, smashing through the hulls and sails of the airships, leaving gaping holes and ragged tears in the wood and fabric. One brought down a mast, collapsing it onto the deck and sending the airship into a spin that took it out of the fight.

The Gnome Hunters aboard the ships fought back with crossbows and slings, filling the sky with a cloud of deadly missiles. But the arrows and stones fell harmlessly, bouncing off heavy armor and rock walls and doing little damage to the well-protected Trolls.

For a moment, it seemed as if the battle was over almost before it had begun. The entire south end of the flats was on fire, grasses and scrub and whatever was in those trenches and holes burning fiercely. The Druid airships were in retreat, those not already down vanishing beyond the flames and smoke. Traunt Rowan had disappeared with them, his flagship turned about with the others.

But already Kermadec was coming down off the ramparts and signaling to his men to do the same. In dark, bulky knots, they began to retreat through the village toward the cliffs. Khyber and Tagwen climbed down from their hiding place, casting anxious glances toward the flats, where fresh trouble would appear. They had just gotten to the ground when Kermadec came charging up to them.

"We have to find that boy!" he snapped, turning momentarily to yell something to the Trolls charging past. "If we lose him now, this will all have been for nothing! Where do we look?"

"He might have found his way to the cliffs," Tagwen suggested quickly. "He might not need finding."

"I would have heard, if he were there. I left word to be informed when he showed himself. No, Bristle Beard, he's still out here in the village somewhere."

As they tried frantically to come up with something that would help, Khyber threw off the heavy concealing cloak, which was now more hindrance than help. As she did so, her fingers brushed across the small bulk of the Elfstones. She jammed her hand into her pocket and yanked them out. Now that the Druids had located them, there was no reason not to call upon the magic.

"I know how to find him," she said, dumping the blue stones into her palm. "Stand away from me."

They did so at once, neither choosing to question her command. Eyes closed, she retreated into her calming center, reaching for the magic. Ahren had trained her in that approach, so the effort was almost second nature. Even the presence of the Elfstone magic was no longer entirely unfamiliar after the Slags, and she recognized the sudden flush of heat that rose in response to her summons. Tendrils of life pulsed from her hand through her body, then back again, gathering speed and power, building in intensity. The magic of the Stones filled her, a wash of power finding a welcome home. She let it happen, left herself open to its need.

The blue light burst from the Elfstones and shot through the village streets and buildings, through stone and timbers, power that solid materials could not contain. The vision formed and tightened, and the three who watched saw them appear in the haze, the boy and the Rover girl, crouched in the shadow of a darkened tunnel.

"The amphitheater!" Kermadec shouted, and despite the encumbering weight of his massive armor, he began to run.

Pen Ohmsford had waited just an instant too long to make his break from the tunnel. When the fighting started, he stayed where he was, Cinnaminson close beside him, as fire erupted from outside the village walls in huge gouts and then catapults began launching boulders and Gnome Hunters retaliated with slings and crossbows. A hail of missiles clattered against the stone of the walls and buildings outside their hiding place, and the boy did not dare chance a break without better protection.

Then, abruptly, the fighting stopped as clouds of dark smoke rolled across the flats and began to seep into the village as well. Still Pen hesitated, unsure. He counted off twenty seconds, then took Cinnaminson's hand and pulled her after him.

"Run!" he ordered, breaking for the open street.

But the instant he showed himself, the huge bulk of an airship hove into view, slicing through the screen of smoke and flames. Gnome Hunters crowded the gunwales, crossbows and slings firing at everything that moved. Out in the open and unprotected, the boy and the Rover girl were instant targets. A flurry of darts whipped past them, striking the stone walls in a cacophony of tiny, violent explosions. One sliced through Pen's ribs, spinning him around. Another struck him in the arm and sent him sprawling against the closest wall.

"Pen, what's happening?" Cinnaminson cried, crouching

on her hands and knees in the dirt, her face frantic with confusion and fear. Sling stones clattered all around her like hail.

"Get up!" he screamed, hauling her back to her feet, blood running down his arm and side. "Run!"

Searching for any sort of shelter that would deflect the deadly missiles, he tried to shield her as he pulled her after him. It seemed as if they were the only ones left in the village, the streets and buildings empty and the inhabitants all safely inside the tunnels and caves. But where were the tunnels? In what direction? Smoke obscured everything, and he had gotten turned around completely in his effort to escape.

A tiny alcove at the back of a building offered temporary shelter, and he shoved Cinnaminson inside, both of them gasping and bloodied.

I'm going to get us killed! he screamed at himself. *What am I supposed to do?*

Overhead, the Druid warship was swinging back around, searching for movement. They were safe for the moment, but trapped. Sooner or later, those Gnome Hunters would land and begin a search of the buildings. They couldn't stay where they were. They had to get out of there.

"Penderrin!" a familiar voice boomed, causing the boy to jump.

"Kermadec! We're here!"

He yanked Cinnaminson from their shelter and began to run toward the sound of the Rock Troll's voice, hugging the walls that best protected them as they went. Overhead, the smoke was building in thick black clouds, and the airship was a massive shadow wrapped in its haze. The Gnome Hunters were still firing blindly into the village, and the boy could feel bolts and arrows whistle past him as he ran.

Then Kermadec appeared in front of them, a huge armored behemoth. Without slowing, he snatched them up like children, tucking one under each arm. "Can't afford to lose you now," he said, pounding ahead like a great beast of burden. "Hold tight."

Gripped by one massive arm like a sack of grain, bouncing up and down with each footfall, Pen felt as if his eyes were going to be shaken loose from his head, but on balance he decided that was a small price to pay for being rescued. He closed his eyes to steady himself and waited patiently for the bouncing to stop.

FIFTEEN

When Kermadec set them down again, Pen and Cinnaminson were safely inside the caves that formed the Rock Troll fortress in the cliffs above the village. He had carried them in through an entrance concealed in the rocks, bundled them up a set of narrow stone steps to a door that opened after he'd manipulated various jagged outcroppings, then deposited them where they could spend a few moments regaining their equilibrium.

"We thought no one was coming," Cinnaminson offered, her face pale and her honey hair disheveled and coated with dust.

"Oh, it only took finding out where you were," the big Troll replied cheerfully. His strange, flat face glanced at her briefly. "You can thank the Elf girl for that. She had the magic, some blue gems that showed an image of you hiding in the tunnel of the Gathering Place."

The Elfstones, Pen thought. He had forgotten them entirely. *But of course she can use them now, when there is no longer any reason to guard against revealing our presence.*

"I remembered Cinnaminson and went back for her," Pen said. "But then after I found her, I got lost."

"Easy enough to do in our streets, young Penderrin. They were constructed to get you lost, if you weren't one of us. No need to say anything more about it. You're safe now, and that's what matters."

He released the locks on a concealed door and pulled it open to admit them to the safehold. Inside, it was controlled chaos of the same sort that Pen had experienced in the village on the approach of the Druid warships. Trolls bustled in all directions, each with a seemingly different task to accomplish. The chamber was huge, a monstrous cavern fully fifty feet high and more than a hundred across. Dozens of tunnels led away to places the boy could not see for the twists and turns in the corridors. But the openings to the left of where they stood formed a series of fortified redoubts in the cliff wall above Taupo Rough. Sunlight slanted through these overlooks in bright streamers, chasing back the shadows. Smaller cracks and crevices in the stone of the cliff wall admitted additional light. The combination of sunlit openings gave the chamber a peculiarly dappled look, but one that allowed the inhabitants to see clearly.

Kermadec refastened the locks on the concealed door, then added a pair of huge bars that slipped into iron cradles to further seal the entry. "That should keep out any unwanted visitors," he declared, brushing off his hands. He glanced around. "Come with me."

He led them to the left, to one of the redoubts, motioning the workers aside and moving to the edge of a thick protective wall of stone blocks that all but closed off the entry. He beckoned the boy and the girl forward and, when they were standing beside him at the fortifications, pointed outside. "I know you can't see what's out there, Rover girl, but young Penderrin can describe it to you in detail later. It's what's been sent to bring him back."

The Druid airships had repositioned just outside the walls of the village, hovering not far off the ground, but well back from the possibility of catapult attacks that might be launched from the cliffs. Dozens of Gnome Hunters were scurrying down rope ladders and up to the village walls, some carrying battering rams, some grappling hooks and ropes. They were already scaling the walls and forcing the gates. Behind them lumbered several dozen creatures that looked as if they had been fashioned from wet mud hardened by the sun, creatures that resembled Trolls but lacked the proper proportions and features, as if someone had concocted a batch of poor imitations.

"Mutens," Pen whispered.

"Our worst enemies. No brains, no feelings, no purpose. They are one step above rocks on the evolutionary ladder. Magic controls them easily. In the old days, it was the Warlock Lord who controlled them. Now it is our Druid adversaries. The Ard Rhys would weep."

He gestured toward the flats. "Those explosions earlier? We used oil culled from the darker regions of the Malg, capped in barrels and buried in the ground. Highly flammable. The Druids weren't expecting that. It gave us a chance to get safely away, once we knew that a fight was our only recourse. But that's all the advantage we get from down there. We fight now from up here, in our redoubt, for today at least."

He touched their shoulders and led them back into the cavern. "By tomorrow, we'll be gone from here. I need to make ready for our departure, and you need to rest." He searched the cavern for a moment, then shouted. "Atalan!"

A burly troll with the blackest eyes Pen had ever seen lumbered up to them. His dark gaze shifted from Kermadec to the boy and girl, then back again. "I have work to do."

"Now you have new work to do. Take young Penderrin and his friend and find their companions. Take them to one of the upper chambers. See that they all have something to eat and drink and a place to sleep. They will leave at first light. I'll select their escort."

The other Troll stepped closer. "What about me, Kermadec? Am I to go?"

His voice was rough and surly; he made it sound more like a demand than a request. Kermadec gave him a long, measured look. "I will give it some thought."

Then he turned back to Pen and Cinnaminson. "Atalan will see to it that you are made comfortable. The three of you should get along fine. You are all the same age, if not the same temperament."

He walked away without looking back, leaving the three staring after him. Atalan shook his head. "He treats me like a child. Who does he think he is?"

Neither Pen nor Cinnaminson was about to attempt an answer to that one, so they kept quiet. Pen was thinking they might have been better off if Kermadec had left them on their own. Atalan was still staring after the Maturen.

Then he seemed to remember his charges. He gave them a cursory look and shrugged. "Come with me."

He led them through the main chamber to a set of steps cut into the rock and from there upstairs to a new level. He didn't speak for a time, trudging ahead with the movements of one resigned to a fate he didn't deserve. When they reached the top of the stairs, he glanced back at them.

"Do you have a brother?" he asked Pen. The boy shook his head. "Well, if you did, I would hope he would treat you better than Kermadec treats me. He was born earlier, but not necessarily smarter. He is Maturen now, but I will be Maturen one day, too."

He broke off and turned away, leading them into a series of narrow tunnels that twisted and turned through the rock. Several times, they encountered Trolls coming from the other direction, but not once did Atalan give way, bulling past the oncoming Trolls with an insistence that bordered on rudeness. He seemed of such an entirely different temperament than Kermadec that Pen could not come to terms with the idea that they were really brothers.

"So you are the reason for all this madness," Atalan offered at one point. "What is it about you that attracts this kind of attention from the Druids?"

Pen shook his head. "The Ard Rhys is my aunt."

"Your aunt?" Atalan seemed impressed. "Missing for several weeks now, isn't she? Do they think you know where she is?"

"I don't know what they think. Except that they don't want me hunting for her."

Atalan nodded. "That would explain why they want you

so bad. It would explain why my brother is so intent on helping you, too. He thinks the Ard Rhys is the Word's own child. He thinks she can do no wrong. He forgets what she was before, a creature of darkness and murder. You know of this, don't you?"

Pen nodded. He was growing angry. "She was a creature of the Morgawr and not responsible for what she did," he answered in clipped tones.

Atalan glanced back once more. "If you say so."

They went on through the tunnels until they had reached a room far back in the cliff rock, where the light was dim and hazy and the noise of the activity taking place below was muted almost to silence.

The Rock Troll gestured. "Wait here."

He disappeared down another passageway, and when he was safely out of hearing, Pen said to Cinnaminson, "I don't think he likes us much."

She turned her milky gaze on him and smiled. "You don't like him, either. But this is mostly about his brother. You shouldn't take it personally."

He nodded, thinking it was easy to say, but hard to do. Especially when it was your family that was being attacked. But she was right, of course, so he put the matter aside. They sat together in the chamber, listening to the faraway sounds of the Trolls and waiting for something to happen.

When Atalan finally returned, he was carrying food and drink, which he deposited in front of them with barely a word before disappearing again. With nothing better to do, they began to eat. But it wasn't more than a few minutes later that Tagwen and Khyber appeared at the chamber entrance.

"Shades, Penderrin, can't you stay out of trouble for five minutes without someone keeping watch over you?" snapped the latter. "What happened to you out there? Are you all right, Cinnaminson?"

She rushed over to the Rover girl and embraced her warmly, giving Pen a dark look. Tagwen, standing at the entry with his arms folded over his burly chest, knit his brow in reproof and glared at him. Pen could tell already that nothing he said was going to make any difference.

Aboard the Druid flagship *Athabasca*, Traunt Rowan stood at the forward rail with Pyson Wence and watched the Gnome Hunters flood the abandoned Troll village. Already, the smell of smoke rising from fires and the sound of furniture being smashed had begun to reach them. Their orders, once it was determined that Kermadec intended to fight, were to destroy as much of Taupo Rough as possible and then lay siege to the cliffside redoubt. The Trolls might think themselves safe inside their rock fortress, but the Druid warships were equipped with catapults designed to breach such defenses. More to the point, the Trolls were outnumbered and constrained by the presence of their women and children. The Trolls might hold out for a day or even two, but in the end, they would be overrun.

"I don't like it that Shadea is so intent on finding this boy," Pyson Wence said quietly, his gimlet eyes shifting to find Rowan's dark face. "I don't like it that we're out here at all."

"Do you suspect that she wants us out of the way?" the

Southlander asked, keeping his attention focused on the progress of the Gnomes. Wence had brought them to Paranor from among his own people, but they were under Rowan's immediate command in this operation. Pyson Wence was adept at many things, but he was not a soldier.

"I think she would like to see what happened to Terek Molt happen to us. I don't trust her."

"If you did, you would be unique."

"It troubles me that we have lost both Molt and Iridia in the span of a week's time. One dead and one disappeared, and now here we are, the last two of Shadea's company, dispatched from Paranor to hunt this boy while she cuddles with Gerand Cera and schemes to make the position of Ard Rhys a lifetime appointment."

Shadea's infatuation with Cera bothered Traunt Rowan, as well, but he wasn't convinced yet that it was real. Shadea was far too self-centered to make a pairing of equals with another Druid. She was up to something, and on first hearing of her alliance with Cera, he had decided to wait her out. She wasn't yet so firmly entrenched that she could afford to discard her old allies. It was unfortunate about Molt and Iridia, but what had happened to them was not directly Shadea's doing.

Her obsession with finding Pen Ohmsford was more troubling. It was the parents who should concern them, he thought, particularly Bek Ohmsford, who had the use of the magic of the wishsong, which was Grianne Ohmsford's principal weapon. Yet even though Shadea had locked the senior Ohmsfords in the cellars of the Keep, she wasn't satisfied. Before imprisoning them, she had tricked them into

revealing their son's location so that she could continue to
hunt him down. She was merely being safe, she insisted,
but he thought it was something more.

Wheels within wheels. Games and more games. It was a
part of the Druid culture, but he had never been comfortable with it. He was better at confronting problems in an
open way, at meeting them head-on. It was one of the reasons he had gone to the Ard Rhys on that last night and
asked her quite bluntly to resign her office. She might have
been persuaded to do so, had he more time to convince her
and had Shadea not been so anxious to use the liquid night.
But Shadea was ambitious and manipulative; she was more
representative of the Druid order at large. Traunt Rowan
was more the exception. Oddly enough, it was one of the
reasons he believed himself less vulnerable to Shadea's
anger. She knew he was neither ambitious nor covetous;
she knew he was content to let her lead. His goal from the
beginning had been to remove Grianne Ohmsford as head
of the order; it had never been to take her place. In their
desire for advancement and acquisition of power, the others were more aggressive than he was. It put them in dangerous waters, while he stood safely on the shore.

He refocused his gaze on Taupo Rough. The Gnome attack force had reached the base of the cliff walls and was
forming up for an all-out assault. Scaling ladders and grappling hooks were being brought forward, and shield walls
were being prepared. When everything was in place, the
attack on the redoubt would begin.

"I want you to go down into the village with your
Hunters," he said suddenly to Pyson Wence. When the

other gaped at him in disbelief, he added, "So that they can see we are committed to their efforts. I don't need you to lead any charges, Pyson. I need you to provide reassurance."

"Then you go!" the Gnome snapped.

"I would, but I have to command the airships when we begin to launch the catapults. I would leave you to handle this if you had any idea at all how to use a catapult. But you don't, so your place is on the ground, keeping your Gnome Hunters in line."

The Gnome Druid gave him a withering stare. "You don't command me, Traunt Rowan. No one commands me."

"Aboard this ship and on this expedition, I do," he responded calmly. "I have been given the responsibility for bringing back the boy. You were sent to aid me. So you must do as I instruct you to do. As you agreed to do by coming with me, I might add."

Pyson Wence did not move. "If I do so, what is to prevent you from leaving me behind? What if that is what Shadea has asked of you?"

His voice was petulant and accusatory. Traunt Rowan held his gaze. "Look at me, Pyson. Look closely. Do you see treachery in my eyes or hear it in my voice? Since when have you ever worried that I would betray any of us in this business?"

Long moments passed, their measure a blink of an eye to both as they stared each other down. "All right," Pyson Wence said finally. His narrow face reflected displeasure and disgust. "I will do as you ask. I will go down with my people. I trust you, if not Shadea."

He went over to the ladder and began to descend to the flats, his black robes billowing out behind him in the breeze. Traunt Rowan watched him in silence, thinking that if Pyson Wence had ever trusted anyone, it was a miracle.

Within the caverns of the Troll redoubt, Pen was sleeping soundly when a rough hand shook his shoulder and an equally rough voice said, "Wake up! You're leaving!"

He jerked upright, groggy and lethargic, trying to figure out where he was. When he caught sight of Atalan moving over to Tagwen to wake the Dwarf, he remembered. He had no idea how long he had slept, but it didn't feel as if it had been more than a few minutes. He rubbed his eyes and climbed to his feet. Khyber and Cinnaminson were standing by the cavern entry, staring out into the corridor. Heavy booming shook the chamber, as if a giant were striking the cliff face with a huge hammer. From somewhere not too far away, shouts and cries rose, the sounds of a battle being joined.

Pen moved over to the girls. "What's going on? What's happened?"

"The Druids and their Gnome Hunters are attacking the Trolls," Khyber answered. "Hear that pounding? They're using catapults to launch huge boulders into the cliff walls to break down the Troll fortifications. Gnome Hunters are scaling the cliffs on ladders and ropes, trying to breach the redoubt."

"Which they will do, sooner than later," Kermadec de-

clared, appearing out of the corridor shadows. "They're determined about this, it seems. We have to get you out now,
before we lose the chance. All awake and ready to go?" He
swung around. "Atalan! Gather up their things. Distribute
them among the others. Hurry!"

Atalan hesitated. "Am I to go with you?"

"You are. Now join the others. Go!"

Black eyes glittering eagerly, Kermadec's brother
snatched up everything in sight belonging to the four companions and bolted from the room. It was clear that he had
taken on a new attitude.

Pen was less happy about the pending flight. "Kermadec," he said, drawing the big Troll's attention. "I'm
sorry about this. I shouldn't have let Tagwen talk me into
coming. Look what I've done."

To his surprise, Kermadec laughed. "Well, you can make
that argument, Penderrin. You can say that this is all your
fault. But the fact remains that we need to bring back the
Ard Rhys from where Shadea and those others have sent
her. Besides, what's happening now would have happened
sooner or later. There's no peace for the Trolls of Taupo
Rough while your aunt is lost to us. So don't blame yourself
for this. Blame her, if you want to blame anyone, for not listening to me or Bristle Beard when we warned her to be
more careful."

He beckoned Tagwen over and gathered all four around
him. "Now, listen. We haven't much time. Evacuation of
the women and children is already under way. All will be
spirited away through tunnels that open onto the other
side. The men will follow as soon as they are out. Then a

march will be undertaken to reach a new safehold. We've done this before, and we are practiced at it. Everyone will just disappear. There won't even be a trail left. The Druids and the Gnomes will never know what happened.

"But first, we have to get you out. I've selected a dozen Trolls to provide escort. That includes Atalan and myself. You'll be as well looked after as possible. But we have to move quickly in the beginning, because as soon as it is discovered we are gone, Traunt Rowan is going to realize what we have done and bring his warships over the peaks and down the other side to search for us. He'll have the advantage from the air because we must cross the Klu Mountains to reach the Inkrim. That's a journey of perhaps a week on foot. A long time to be out in the open, but we haven't any choice."

He looked at each of them in turn, measuring. "Are you up to it? Are you ready to try?"

All nodded, but the Troll shook his head. His blunt features were tight. "Don't be too quick to sign on. If any of you wants to stay behind, now is the time to tell me. It won't be held against you. Not by me or by any of those who go with me." He paused. "Cinnaminson?"

She stiffened. "Why do you choose to start with me? Is it because I am blind?"

Kermadec reached out with his huge hand and placed it gently on her shoulder. "No, girl. I start with you because you have less of a stake in all this than the others do. It would be easiest for you to walk away."

"Once, that was so." She shook her head slowly. "Not anymore. My decision is made. I am going."

Kermadec looked at the other three. "Pen, you haven't any choice, so there's no reason to ask you. And Tagwen will go because he doesn't trust me to get the job done alone. What of you, Khyber Elessedil?"

She gave him a fierce look. "I will go because my uncle would have gone if he had lived. I stand now in his shoes."

Kermadec nodded his approval. "Then we're a company." He wheeled away. "Come with me."

He led them back down the corridor they had come through earlier, toward the shouting of fighters and the thunder of siege weapons. Pen felt his temperature rise and his hands begin to sweat as the sounds of battle reverberated through the mountain catacombs. He remembered how it had felt to be chased through the streets of the village, dodging arrows and sling stones, trying to stay safe. He did not care to experience that again, and yet it seemed as if that was exactly what was going to happen. He wished they had an airship and could simply fly away. He wanted to be back in the skies, where he felt safe.

The main chamber of the redoubt was filled with Trolls charging in all directions. The men stood at the walls where the cliffs opened to the village below, crouching behind their fortifications as boulders smashed into the rock and arrows whizzed past their heads. The women and children were making their way in small groups toward the back part of the cavern, then filing down a series of tunnels into the torchlit dark. The women, distinctive by their smoother skin and slender bodies, herded the tiny children like puppies, urging them along, carrying those too small to walk. They seemed calm on the face of things, moving deliberately and with purpose, evidencing none of the panic that Pen felt. Their self-control impressed the boy, and he tightened his own resolve.

With Kermadec leading the way, they hurried after the women and children. Dust was falling from the cavern ceiling as the pounding of the catapult missiles against the rock walls grew more insistent, the resulting reverberations deep and threatening. It felt as if the mountain might come down about them, broken in two by the constant hammering. Pen ducked his head instinctively and reached over to take Cinnaminson's hand. He did so as much for himself as for her, and was grateful when she squeezed his fingers reassuringly.

They were mingling with the women and children now, the latter staring up at him with curious, anxious eyes. He tried not to read accusation in those stares; the children wouldn't know that their upheaval was his fault. He smiled at them as he hurried past. He didn't know how else to tell them that he wanted them to think better of him than he thought of himself.

"Stay together!" Kermadec called back.

Silt rained down on Pen in a sudden shower, and he tripped over one of the children. Releasing Cinnaminson's hand, he paused to pick the child up, brushing off its tiny head, handing it back to the closest of the women. The woman took the child and smiled at him, her strange black eyes and smooth features drawing him in. Something in the look she gave him reminded him of his mother, and suddenly he missed her so that it made him ache. The shock was like a physical blow, and it left him stunned and momentarily disoriented. His world compressed to a tightness about his heart, where the things he needed most felt the farthest away.

Still struggling with his feelings, he hurried after the others.

SIXTEEN

They fled through the tunnels, away from Taupo Rough and deep into the mountain rock. At first they followed the women and children, a part of their steady flow down the boltholes, and then they broke away to follow a different set of tunnels and did not see them again. Pen and the rest of their small group moved swiftly and purposefully, sliding through the darkness with torches to light the way and a sense of urgency to keep them focused. The din of the battle they had escaped was audible for a time, then dimmed and faded, and they were left with the soft scrape and rustle of their own movements in the ensuing silence.

No one spoke. All of their efforts were concentrated on moving through the tunnels, on getting clear of the pursuit that was sure to follow. It might be that the Druids and their Gnome Hunters couldn't track them through the rock corridors, but Pen knew that Kermadec and his Trolls would not rely on that. He held Cinnaminson's hand as they went, drawing on the strength he found there, reas-

suring himself that she was with him. He didn't even try to
tell himself that the contact was for her; he knew that she
was better able to navigate the dark than he was. It was to
keep his despair and loneliness at bay, for he was afraid that
otherwise, without the feel of her, he would give way to the
dark emotions that threatened to overwhelm his failing
sense of purpose and leave him drained of strength.

The eyes of those women and children haunted him,
burned into his memory, became ghosts in his mind. That
wouldn't have happened had he felt less guilt over their
fate. But he could not absolve himself of the responsibility
he felt, no matter what Kermadec might say. Too much of
what had transpired already on the journey was directly at-
tributable to him. Fortunes altered, plans shattered, and
lives given up—that was pretty much the story for everyone with whom he had come in contact since leaving Patch
Run. It might not be his fault and his involvement might
not matter anyway in the long run, but he could only see
what was, not what might be. His presence was the catalyst
for everything that had happened. So much depended on
him, and the weight of it was terrifying.

"Keep right," Kermadec called over his shoulder, motioning toward Pen and his companions. "Don't look
down."

They entered a cavern that dropped away on the left
into a black hole so vast that it looked as if it could swallow
whole villages. The trail became a narrow ledge that
hugged the wall of the cavern, and the company pressed
close to that wall as they edged forward. They were strung
out in single file, torches spaced along the ledge. Pen could

see for the first time the other Trolls who had joined them somewhere along the way, a line of burly, dark shadows in the flicker of the firelight. They wore no armor, only leather tunics and pants, closed-toe sandals, and heavy cloaks. All carried weapons strapped across their backs, along with packs of supplies. They moved ponderously, but with no visible effort or strain. They had the look of massive rocks into which faces had been carved.

On the far side of the cavern, a tunnel opened into the rock wall, and soon they were burrowing downward once more. They had been descending steadily since they had set out, and if Pen was judging right, they were below the level of the village of Taupo Rough by several hundred feet. He wanted to know where they were going, wanted to reach a place where he could ask, and wanted most of all to get out in the open air again, where he could breathe. The mountain and its darkness pressed down against him with suffocating force. He was a flier, born to the air, and he hated being closed away.

But the tunnels wound on, deep and dark passageways thick with stale air and tar smoke, dead feeling and tomb-like. Pen closed his mind to them after a while, a defense against his distaste and the hint of fear that lay behind it. He whispered now and again to Cinnaminson, just so that he could hear her voice. Each time, she squeezed his hand, as if sensing his need to make contact.

When they finally emerged from the tunnels, it was late afternoon and the sun had disappeared behind the peaks west, the light gone gray and misty. A narrow wedge of sky was visible overhead, distant and thick with clouds. They were deep in a valley where the shadows were so heavily layered that the trees carpeting the slopes surrounding them seemed already given over to night. Mountains rose all about them in sheer cliffs and jagged edges. Pen stood with the others, breathing the fresh, cold air and thinking that he had somehow tunneled down to the bottom of the world and must now climb back out again before he lost his way forever.

Kermadec was speaking in his deep, calm voice with one of the Trolls at the front of the line, but the conversation was being conducted in his own tongue so that Pen could not understand it. When they were finished, the other Troll disappeared into the trees, and Kermadec walked over to the boy and his companions.

"Barek will scout ahead to make sure the way is safe. We will follow in a few minutes." He gestured toward the dense line of peaks that lay east. "These are the Klu. Part of the Charnals, but their own range, as well. To the extent that it's possible to do so, we'll travel at night from here on." He paused. "Is everyone all right?"

They nodded, all of them, but with nothing that approached enthusiasm. Pen was somewhat relieved to find that his companions had seemingly fared no better than he had within the tunnels and the dark.

Kermadec nodded. "We'll go on in a few minutes. We have to cross the valley floor before nightfall to be certain we're safe enough to get some sleep. Drink plenty of water. The air is dry here. You won't notice it until you pass out."

Pen and his friends did as the big Troll instructed, casting uneasy glances back at the opening to the tunnels from which they had emerged, then at the sky overhead where searching airships might appear at any second.

"It will take them a day or two just to discover we're gone," Tagwen announced confidently.

"Only if they are exceedingly stupid," Atalan shot back, overhearing as he walked past. He gave a dismissive shrug. "The fortifications will have been abandoned by now and our people moved on. We're being hunted already, little man."

Tagwen scowled deeply, not at all happy with being addressed in such familiar terms by the young Troll. After Atalan had moved away, Pen said quietly to the Dwarf, "His name is Atalan. He claims he's Kermadec's brother."

Tagwen shook his head. "Kermadec never spoke of a brother. He never spoke about his family at all. Whoever this fellow is, he's in need of some manners."

"I don't think he's overly fond of Kermadec, from what he said earlier. I think he resents Kermadec's position as Maturen."

The Dwarf snorted. "Kermadec is a force to be reckoned with, make no mistake. If we're to complete this journey in one piece, he is the one who will make it possible. His brother, if that's what he is, ought to know as much."

At Kermadec's command, they began walking east through the trees. Because they were already on the valley floor, travel was smooth and steady. The Trolls set the pace and chose the way, finding paths where there didn't seem to be any, moving everyone along, keeping watch on all sides. Pen felt much better out in the open again, and his earlier discomfort subsided and eventually disappeared.

Things didn't seem so impossible when he didn't have an entire mountain pressing down on him. He gazed skyward and thought wistfully that if they could find an airship to convey them the rest of the way, things would be perfect.

But there would be no airships, of course. Kermadec had made it clear that airships were at risk in those mountains, and that travel afoot was much safer if their intent was to remain safely concealed from would-be pursuers. It was a choice that Pen might not have made, but they were in Kermadec's country, and the Rock Troll would know the best way to get to where they were going. Whatever else happened, Pen did not care to experience another encounter with the Druids who hunted him.

Ahead, the trees thinned as the valley floor opened up before them, and they crossed the central flats under a cover of clouds and mist and growing darkness. Diffuse and silvery, light from moon and stars began to filter through the haze, lending just enough brightness to enable the company to pick its way ahead without groping. Judging from the pace that Kermadec was setting, the Trolls knew the country well; there was no suggestion of hesitation as they progressed.

When they stopped to rest, just inside a thick stand of fir midway across the valley, Tagwen sat down next to Pen and leaned close.

"This is what you need to know about Kermadec, young Penderrin. It isn't the only story about him, but it is the one that I think says the most. Some years ago, when he was still a boy, he was taken on an outing with two dozen other young Trolls who were in the training stages of their wilderness survival education. All young Rock Trolls are given this instruction, boys and girls alike. Because they are a migratory people, it is presumed that at some point each of them will become separated from the tribe and be forced to find the way back alone, perhaps through dangerous country. Young Trolls are taken out twice a year beginning at the age of six or seven in order to learn what they need to know about doing so. The group in which Kermadec was included consisted of all ages and both sexes. For some, the littlest, it was the first time. It was autumn, and the green of summer was just changing to the bolder colors in the broad leaves. There was a bite to the night air."

His head lowered into shadow, Tagwen rubbed his beard. "Three handlers managed the two dozen, about average for a class of that size. They were hiking through the Razor Mountains across the valley from one of the villages several miles below the Lazareen. A two-week outing, give or take a few days—that was the intended duration. The country was familiar to them, mostly uninhabited, forested low mountains, some small lakes, streams, typical for the middle Northland and safely above the Skull Kingdom. Nothing too dangerous.

"Except that the unexpected happened. A band of renegade Forest Trolls, traditional enemies of the Rock Trolls and dangerous in their own right, stumbled across the group while it was descending a steep slope and recognized it for what it was. They began tracking it, deciding they would wait until their quarry was sleeping, kill the handlers, steal their supplies and weapons, and take the smallest children as slaves to sell to those who use children in that way. It wasn't much of a reason for such slaughter, but renegades don't usually need much of a reason to justify what they do."

He paused as Atalan stalked past, ignoring them as he had ignored them all day. Without a word of greeting, he moved over to talk with Kermadec. Tagwen glared at him balefully, then sighed. "I wish I could think better of him. I wish he would give me a reason."

He shook his head. "So, the Forest Trolls had their plan. But it failed because they weren't careful enough. The handlers spotted them and set about making an escape. That, too, failed. The Forest Trolls attacked, a dozen strong, and the two male handlers were killed along with one of the boys. Kermadec and the female handler managed to hide the rest of the children in a dense wood just as the sun was setting. The Forest Trolls spent all night hunting them, combing the wood in the dark. If they had been smarter, they might have thought better of the idea. But there were nine of them still alive after the battle with the handlers, and they thought there was safety in numbers. After all, these were only children they hunted."

He smiled. "I would have liked to have seen their faces when they found out otherwise. Kermadec was less a child than they thought, already big and strong, already as skilled as the adults. When he realized that the renegades weren't giving up, he slipped away from the other children and the woman handler, who was badly injured in the earlier skirmish, and began stalking the Forest Trolls. He caught them by surprise, and one by one, he killed four of them before the rest realized what was happening and backed off. But still they didn't give up. These were only children, after all. They waited until dawn, and they began to hunt again. A reasonable idea, but not when you're dealing with someone like Kermadec. He was waiting for them. He ambushed them and killed two more. This time, the rest fled for good.

"But that wasn't the end of it. Kermadec's little group was deep in the Razors, miles from their own tribe, and the woman handler was so weak she could no longer walk, let alone act as guide. So Kermadec led the rest of the children out of those mountains and back to the tribe. It took them four days. He carried the handler on his back the entire way, more than fifty miles. No one was left behind. All of them arrived home safe."

He paused. "Kermadec was fourteen years old when he did this." He arched one eyebrow at the boy. "That's the sort of man you've placed your trust in, should you be in any doubt about the matter."

They set out again shortly afterwards and walked the rest of the way across the valley into a deep wood that ran up the flank of the mountains and into the valleys and defiles in dark green fingers. The last of the light faded, and night drew in about them. By then, Kermadec had brought the Trolls and their charges to a grassy clearing by a stream that tumbled down out of the rocks into a high-banked pool that then spilled over to meander on across the valley west. They set camp, putting themselves safely within the cover of the fir and spruce and forgoing any sort of fire. They ate their dinner ration cold and rolled into their blankets to sleep without wasting further time.

But before they fell asleep, Khyber eased over next to Pen. Even in the darkness, he could see the troubled intensity of her dark eyes. "I've something to tell you, Pen. I'd forgotten earlier, in all the chaos, and when I remembered, I couldn't decide right away whether you should know. But I guess you should. I can't be sure if it's true, but Traunt Rowan told Kermadec that the Druids have made prisoners of your parents."

Her dark eyes studied him carefully. "I'm sorry. Especially if I made a mistake in telling you. Are you all right?"

He wasn't, of course. He wasn't anything close to all right. He felt hollowed out, drained of any good feelings he might have salvaged from their escape from Taupo Rough. It was bad enough that he carried the weight of his guilt from all of the others who had suffered on his behalf. He had thought his parents safe. The King of the Silver River had said he would warn them of the danger, that he would take steps to protect them. But perhaps that hadn't been enough and not even they were to be spared.

"It might have been a lie," she said. Her hand rested on his. "In fact, it probably is a lie. They would say anything to get to you. Even something as evil as that."

But it wasn't a lie. He knew it instinctively. It was the truth. Somehow, the Druids had lured his parents to Paranor and locked them away. What was expected of them, he couldn't be sure. But he was afraid for them because he thought that anyone connected with him, or with his aunt, was at risk. His impulse was to abandon the quest and go to them at once, to do anything that would help them. But of course, that was exactly what the Druids were hoping for, what they intended by giving out such information. He would not be helping his parents by giving in to his impulses. He could only help by finding his aunt and bringing her home again. She was the one who could save them all.

He remained awake long after the rest of them were asleep, trying to reassemble the shattered pieces of his confidence, trying to reassure himself that he wouldn't give way to what he was feeling.

They set out again at dawn, climbing out of the valley and into the jagged peaks of the Klu Mountains. The Klu were rugged, barren pinnacles that time and a shifting of the earth's crust had compressed as if they had been grasped by a giant's hand, the rock cracked and broken by the pressure, eroded by wind and water, and reshaped into strange formations that barely resembled the mountains they had once been. Narrow defiles and deep chasms split the rock at every turn, and passes were as likely to lead through stacked rocks and weather-carved fissures as along ledges or across slides. Nothing made sense about the Klu, which seemed to comprise an amalgam of every geological configuration that nature could devise.

As the day wore on and the air cooled at the higher elevations, the mist thickened about them. It did so slowly, but noticeably, so that Pen had time to realize that they would soon be climbing blindly into the rocks. It was not a pleasant prospect, given the treacherous terrain with its difficult and uncertain footing. But Kermadec pressed ahead, moving them along as quickly as conditions would allow, taking them off the flank of the mountains and into a series of defiles that twisted and wound through cliffs towering hundreds of feet above them.

The mist dissipated, but forward progress slowed. Loose stone littered the trail, and ice patches coated its surface. Wind howled overhead and down the gaps in the cliffs, buffeting them as they struggled to put one foot in front of the other without slipping. The path fell away to the left, the resulting cliff a sheer and unbroken drop that vanished into blackness.

Pen hugged the rock wall on his right, trying not to think of what would happen if he slipped, trying not to look down. He had managed to put his concern for his parents and his doubts about himself aside upon waking, but they nudged their way back into his thinking now, prompted by an increasing suspicion that their efforts on this day alone, their first day, were not going to be enough to get them to Stridegate. He watched Cinnaminson as she moved cautiously ahead of him, hands and feet finding the way. He would have taken her hand, done something to help her, but it was too dangerous on the narrow trail.

Then, abruptly, the mist gathered and settled down about them with such compacted heaviness that everything simply disappeared.

"Stay where you are!" Kermadec called back to them.

Pen froze on the trail, feeling the cold of the rock seep into him, listening to the wind die away to nothing, thinking that the worst had just happened. They were trapped, unable to go forward or back, exposed to the whim of the elements. It was probably close to midday. What would happen when it was night?

He reached out, groping, until he found Cinnaminson's hand and took it in his own, then edged forward until he was just behind her. "Can you see anything that we can't?" he asked.

Her face turned to his, her lips cold when they pressed against his ear. "I can see a little of what lies ahead, but I don't know which way to go. There are too many choices. It all looks the same."

Pen thought. "Could you guide us if Kermadec told you what to look for?"

She gripped his arm. "I don't know. Maybe."

She sounded scared, but no more scared than he felt. And she was their best hope. He called to Kermadec, then eased his way forward past the others, leading Cinnaminson by the hand. He moved carefully, taking his time, one foot in front of the other, body pressed to the cliff wall. The mist was getting worse, visibility dropping to where he couldn't see more than a few yards ahead, and no wind appeared to blow it all away.

When he reached the Maturen, he explained his idea. Once Kermadec understood what the Rover girl was able to do, he agreed to let her try. He had never seen fog so bad and didn't care to wait it out. Exposed as they were, it was too dangerous to remain on the cliff trails. They needed to find shelter.

So with Cinnaminson leading them, using her special sight to see beyond the layers of mist, they began inching forward. It was slow going; Cinnaminson stopped often to explain what she was seeing so that Kermadec could advise her on which way to go. A maze of similar paths and trails awaited his decision, most of them leading to sudden drops or blank walls and only a few leading out. Pen wondered how far they were from safe ground and an easier passage, but wasn't sure he wanted to know the answer.

The mist got worse, and their progress slowed even more. Pen felt Cinnaminson hesitate more often, as if even her sight could not penetrate the haze. He turned his face into the mist, and the feel of it made him shiver. There was something wrong with its dampness and color, something that sent a whisper of warning rushing through his chilled body.

"Kermadec!" he called back. "Why is it getting worse?"

"Because the mist is Druid-formed," Khyber answered, an invisible presence somewhere behind him. "Because it isn't real. We saw this before, Pen, when we crossed the Lazareen. The ones who track us now must have sent it through the peaks to trap us. They must know what we are trying to do!"

"Can you get rid of it, Elven girl?" Kermadec called back. "Can you counter their magic with your own?"

A long pause. "If I do, I will give us away. They will track my magic to where we are. I expect that is what they are hoping for."

There was a long silence in the aftermath of this pronouncement, a silence filled with heavy breathing and a shuffling of feet.

"We can't just stand out here!" Atalan snapped angrily.

"They'll find us anyway! Or the weather will. There's snow coming."

Cinnaminson leaned over to Pen and whispered in his ear. "I can't see anymore. My sight is gone. The Druid magic must be affecting it."

Pen leaned back against the rock, feeling the rough surface dig into his back. What could they do? If Cinnaminson couldn't find the way, they were trapped. But if Khyber used her magic to spring the trap, Traunt Rowan and his Gnome Hunters would be on them in minutes. They needed to find another way. But what way? A cave in which to hide? Even a deep crevice would be sufficient. Just something . . .

He turned his face into the rock, peering ahead, and felt something move against his cheek. He jerked away, looking back in surprise at a greenish gray patch on the stone.

Lichen.

But it had moved. He had felt it move. He hesitated, then placed his cheek against the patch again. Again, he felt it move. He wasn't sure if he was feeling it with his senses or his mind. It wasn't quite one or the other. He held his cheek against it and closed his eyes.

Warm.

The lichen was expressing what it felt, and his odd magic was reading its communication. He placed his cheek against it once more, feeling the faint movement of its tiny bristles, the expression of its tiny intelligence.

Warm.

He looked around quickly. Lichen grew all over these rocks in mottled greenish gray patches. He peered into the mist. Everything looked the same to him, but maybe not to the lichen. The lichen couldn't see, but it could feel. It was a plant. It sought the sun. That was what it was communicating to him. *Warm.* It was sensing the hidden sunlight.

Was there a way that he could use the lichen, a way that could help them get clear?

"Kermadec!" he said quickly, searching for the Maturen. The big man moved out of the haze past Cinnaminson. "What direction does the trail go, the one we need to follow?"

The big man bent down, his barked face as rugged as the mountains they were trapped in. "You look like you've seen a ghost."

"Just tell me. Which way?"

"Southeast. Why?"

"And the time? What time of day is it?"

"After noon by about an hour, I would guess. What are you asking, Penderrin?"

"Then north would be that way?" He pointed, and Kermadec nodded. "And south that way?" Again, the Rock Troll nodded. Pen took a deep breath. "Let me take the lead. I think I can get us out of here. If the trail leads down at some point, back to tree level, maybe we can get below this mist. Will you let me try?"

Kermadec eased him to the front of the line, and Pen began to move forward, running his hands along the patches of lichen that grew on the rock face. The afternoon sun would be south and west of them. He needed to lead them south and east to stay on the path. It was easy at first, because the trail only led in one direction and there were no choices to be made. But it quickly grew more difficult as the number of twists and turns increased and the path split, forcing him to read the lichen's response to his touch and then advance accordingly.

He couldn't be sure he was going the right way, not entirely, not while he was unable to see anything of his surroundings, the mist so thick and impenetrable it was like swimming underwater at night. But at least they were moving somewhere, rather than just standing out in the open with night coming on. It was better to take the chance, he told himself. It was better to do something than nothing.

Sometimes the lichen disappeared, and he was forced to continue on blindly until he found a new patch. Sometimes he found patches in places so cold and shadowy that they were locked down inside themselves and he could read nothing from them. Sometimes he was reduced to guessing at which way they should go, unable to be certain that he was interpreting the lichen's message clearly. It was slow, torturous work; the lichen's form of communication was much more subtle than that of a seagull or a deer. It wasn't a life-form of high intelligence, and what it gave to him was not much more than a tiny response to the environment that sustained it.

I can do this.

To their credit, the others in the little company left him alone. Once or twice, he thought he heard grumbling from somewhere behind, but it was always momentary and not directed at him. He never let it bother him, never let it break his concentration. Forgotten were the fears and doubts he had experienced the night before. He had something to do now, a purpose that was as much a lifeline as a duty. They were all here because of him, but now he was doing something to help. He wasn't just a charge to whom they were committed, to whom they must offer their protection. He was a member of the company, a part of the effort to find a way to their destination.

He ran his hands carefully over the lichen, feeling its tiny movement, its soft response. *Warm*. Reaching toward the sun, toward the light.

Deep and still, the mist continued to blanket them, and the light faded slowly with the passing of the day. Time was slipping away. He kept moving, kept his concentration focused. Cinnaminson hadn't spoken once since he had taken command. He understood. She couldn't do anything to help, her inner sight rendered useless by the onslaught of Druid magic. Like the others, she was relying on him.

I can do this.

It was nearing dark when at last they emerged from the mist and found the first sparse patches of grassy earth, uneven and rocky high meadows forming cradles of life among the barren peaks of the Klu. Slowly the mist began to dissipate as they continued downhill. Then all at once it was gone, and they were standing in scrub and twilight at the edge of an alpine forest, the air clear enough for them to see one another once more.

Kermadec came over to Pen at once and clapped him on the shoulder. "Well done, young Penderrin. We owe you a measurable debt for this day's work."

The other Trolls, even Atalan, nodded their agreement, dark eyes communicating what words did not. Khyber was smiling. Even Tagwen muttered grudgingly that Pen was to be congratulated.

Cinnaminson didn't bother with words. She simply walked up to him and hugged him so tightly that the breath left his body.

It was the best he had felt in a long time.

SEVENTEEN

When Grianne Ohmsford regained consciousness, she was surprised to discover that she was still alive. In attempting her escape from Kraal Reach, she had fully expected that if she failed, Tael Riverine would have her put to death. It was what she would have done if their positions were reversed and she were still the Ilse Witch. Lying on the stone floor of her cell in a wash of pain and despair, she found her earlier assessment of her situation reaffirmed: She was being kept alive because the demon needed her that way.

But that was a dangerous supposition, and she quickly abandoned it for a less pleasant conclusion: The Straken Lord intended to make an example of her. Some form of punishment was to be administered.

When she could sit up again, she made a quick assessment of her situation and found that not everything was as it had been. The conjure collar was in place, but now her hands were shackled behind her back and to her waist and ankles so that while she could shuffle about on her knees, she could not stand upright. She had been moved to a different cell, one in which the front wall had been replaced with iron bars so that a jailer could sit on a chair across from her and watch her every movement. She was still not gagged, but there was little risk in allowing that. She already knew the consequences of attempting to use the magic of the wishsong.

Nevertheless, she began thinking about doing so almost immediately because she knew what was going to happen otherwise.

Still, time passed, and nothing did happen. She was spoon-fed and given water by hand through the bars. At first, she resisted, but in the end, hunger and thirst won out. Besides, after her initial assumption regarding her fate failed to prove out, she grew increasingly curious to find out why this was so. She wasn't being kept alive for no reason; the Straken Lord didn't admire her pluck. Her escape was in defiance of the rules she had been instructed to obey and a challenge to the demon's authority. She didn't think it likely that it would forgive her for that.

But the hours passed, then the days, and neither Tael Riverine nor its underling, Hobstull, appeared. She saw no one but the guards, cloaked and hooded silhouettes in the faint light of the torches that burned in wall brackets across from where she lay. Now and then, one would rise from its sitting place to feed her or to clean the messes she made when she was forced to relieve herself, but otherwise they ignored her. She spent her time trying to get comfortable, to shift her position often enough to prevent cramping and sores. She was only partially successful. She slept fitfully and for short periods of time, and because she was locked in a windowless cell deep within the rock of Kraal Reach, she never knew for certain what time it was. After a while, it no longer mattered. Nothing did. She felt her hopes sliding away. She felt her courage failing. Her one real chance at escape had failed, and she did not expect she would get another. All that remained for her was to prepare herself for whatever fate the Straken Lord intended.

Then, when sufficient time had lapsed that she had lost all track of it, Hobstull appeared. One moment, the corridor was empty save for the guard, and the next, the Catcher was standing there, staring at her in that peculiar way, head cocked, eyes contemplative. He didn't say or do anything. She stared back at him, as still as he was, waiting him out. A small surge of expectation gave her new strength. Finally, something was going to happen.

When he had satisfied himself, the Catcher opened the cell door and came inside. A pair of wizened Goblins stood crook-legged to either side of him, crossbows armed and pointed at her. *Don't move*, the sharpened bolts advised wordlessly. She didn't. She waited while Hobstull bent down and released the chains from her waist and ankles, leaving them in place about her wrists until he had helped her to stand. Then he released those, as well, moved her hands in front of her, and refastened the chains about her wrists. He stepped back, waiting to see how she would react, his strange eyes fixed on hers, then nodded. Taking the loose end of the chain that bound her wrists, he led her from the cell.

They went down the shadowy corridor to a set of stairs

and began to climb, Hobstull leading, the Goblins trailing watchfully. Her mind raced. If they intended to kill her, she would have one final chance at escape when she got to where she was going. If they intended to punish her, she would have the same option. Perhaps she would live long enough to find out why they had kept her alive and left her alone for so long.

At the top of the stairs, she was taken down another corridor, then out through an entry warded by a heavy iron door and into a tiny courtyard walled in by buildings on four sides. The walls rose several dozen feet, leaving the courtyard bathed in cool shadows and resonant with the trapped echoes of voices that drifted in from more open places. She stood in the courtyard as Hobstull once again removed the chains from her wrists and this time left them off. The Catcher studied her in wordless appraisal, then went back through the door with the Goblins, leaving her alone.

She looked around. The walls were too smooth to be climbed. There were no doors save the one through which she had entered, and no windows at all. There were tiny slits that overlooked the courtyard from high above, too far to reach. Murder holes. She took a deep breath, walked over to one wall, and sat down against it. Overhead, clouds scudded through the gray sky like foam capping a rough sea, yellow-tinged and frothy. She saw a dark shape wing its way past, a Harpy perhaps. She smelled the decay of the land. Everything in this world felt ill used and tarnished. Everything felt as if it were dying.

Long minutes passed, and then the door to the courtyard opened again, and Tael Riverine appeared. It emerged into the pale courtyard light like a wraith risen from its midnight lair, so impenetrably black that its features were indistinguishable. It looked bigger than she remembered, but that might have been because its spikes were raised like the hackles on an angry dog, protruding everywhere in what felt to her like a warning. *Stay clear. Keep away.* It wore its weapons strapped on like body armor, studs and sharp edges glinting dully.

Its blue eyes fixed on her.

She climbed to her feet, unwilling to give even the appearance of weakness. It required noticeable effort to do so.

"You disobeyed me," it announced.

It gestured languidly, and instantly the familiar pain ripped through her, paralyzing her muscles and dropping her to her knees. She bent her head and clutched her body, trying to breathe.

"Disobedience is an unacceptable response to my commands," the demon continued, and gestured again.

This time, she collapsed altogether, her agony so excruciating she lay curled in a ball, sobbing. Her mind locked down and would not let her think of anything but the pain. She pressed her face in the dirt, feeling broken and helpless.

"Get on your knees," Tael Riverine ordered.

It took her a while to do so, but eventually she managed, still bent over at the waist, her arms wrapped protectively about her body.

"Look at me."

She did so, lifting her head from the veil of her dark hair, trying to hide the mix of fear and suffering that washed through her as she did so.

"Apologize for your disobedience."

"I am sorry, Master," she whispered.

The Straken Lord nodded, cold eyes glittering. "You are only sorry you were caught. I see it in your eyes. You do not respond well to discipline. It is not in your nature to choose obedience when you can avoid doing so."

It walked over to her, huge and forbidding, and reached down to haul her back to her feet, picking her up like a rag doll and propping her against the courtyard wall. She sagged slightly, but stayed upright, eyes locked on the demon's.

"I would have killed another for what you did," it said softly. "I would have taken my time doing so. I would have made the pain so unbearable that death would have come as a relief. Do you understand this?"

She swallowed. "Yes, Master."

"But you interest me."

It paused, and she waited for more, not yet understanding what that meant. Why would she be of any further interest? Other than the purpose she had already served in switching places with whatever creature the magic had set free from the Forbidding, what reason could the Straken Lord have for taking an interest in her?

"Do you know why you are here, inside the world of the Jarka Ruus?"

"No, Master."

The demon gestured angrily, and again the pain ratcheted through her, inducing a wave of nausea that caused her to wretch violently as she dropped to her knees. It was on her at once, hauling her upright and slamming her against the stone wall.

"Don't lie to me!" it hissed, fury etched on its flat features, rage mirrored in its strange eyes. "Do you think me such a fool? Speak!"

"I . . . won't lie again, Master," she gasped.

"You are intelligent. You are calculating. You are clever. You can pretend that you are not, but you will be disobeying me if you do and will be punished. Do you understand? Answer me."

"I understand, Master." Her stomach heaved, but she fought down the urge to empty it.

The Straken Lord nodded patiently. "Again, now. Do you know why you are here?"

"Yes, Master."

"Tell me."

"I was brought here so that something that lives in this world could be transported into my own."

"Very good. Do you know why I arranged for this?"

She took a deep, quieting breath. "No, Master."

The demon studied her carefully, then nodded. "Not yet, you don't. But you will, soon enough. You will understand everything, because that inquisitive mind of yours will mull it through until the answer surfaces. If not, I will tell you myself. If you stay alive long enough for me to do so."

If you stay alive. She closed her eyes and exhaled softly. What were the odds of that? She blinked, feeling the weight of his gaze on her, shifting from place to place, contemplative, curious. She was aware of how ragged and dirty she was, unwashed and uncombed, a used-up plaything. For an instant, she saw herself as worthless, of so little value that she deserved to be discarded without further consideration.

"You are a specimen," the Straken Lord said, as if reading her mind. "Hobstull finds you as interesting as I do. He makes more of a study of such things, so his opinion carries weight. He wishes to find out more about you, but I have forbidden him to use his knives just yet. Still, we both deserve an opportunity to see what sort of magic you wield. You do have magic, I know. It resides in you—a demon trait. His interest lies in that. He thinks you might be one of us."

She cringed at the idea. She was nothing like them. She was human. No matter what they thought or did to make her seem otherwise, she was human. But she said nothing, keeping what she was thinking hidden away inside.

"I intend to test you, Grianne Ohmsford, Ard-Rhys-that-was, my specimen of such promise." Its voice had turned oddly soft and soothing. "I intend to test you in a way that no one has ever been tested before. I want to see what you can do. I want to see how strong your survival instincts are."

As it spoke, its spikes lowered against its body, changing its look entirely. She stared in spite of herself, wondering what it was seeking from her that it didn't already have.

"This afternoon," it continued in the same compelling voice, "I will test you then. I will see how you respond."

Then it turned and disappeared through the door, leav-

ing her breathless and pressed hard against the courtyard
wall.

Hobstull returned with the Goblin guards moments
later, and she was taken back to her cell. Although the
chains were not put on again, three guards were stationed
across from her cell with crossbows pointed in her direction at all times. She sat quietly on the floor of her little
room and thought about what the Straken Lord had told
her. She would be tested. But what did that mean? Tested
how? She did not think the answer would please her. She
wished she could find some reassurance in still being alive,
but her instincts told her that she would be foolish to do so.

Hobstull reappeared after a while with a basin of hot
water, a clear indication that she was to clean herself up for
whatever was going to happen next. He deposited sandals
and a shift at her feet as well. She waited for him to leave,
then turned her back on the Goblin guards, stripped off her
rags, and used them to wash her aching body. Then she
dressed in the sandals and shift and sat back down again to
wait.

The wait was longer than she had expected. She had no
accurate way of measuring, but she thought afterwards that
it must have been several hours. When Hobstull led her
back up the stairs and out of the tower and into the light,
the day was edging rapidly toward nightfall, the gray of the
sky gone darker and the endless clouds and mist dropped
lower against the heights. The Catcher replaced the chains
about her wrists, and a phalanx of Goblins surrounded her.

She was taken across the courtyard through an outer wall to where a rolling cage similar to the one that had brought her to Kraal Reach was waiting. She was placed inside, and the chain that bound her was fastened to the bars. The Goblins formed ranks to either side of the cage, and Hobstull climbed onto the seat next to the driver. The driver snapped his whip over the heads of the massive horned creatures hitched up front, and the wheels began to roll.

They went out through a set of bigger, bulkier gates, heavy oak toughened with pitch and bound with iron plates. There demonwolves joined the procession, panting and slavering, yellow eyes shifting to find her, their muzzles drawing back. She felt their hatred for her, read the warning in their snarls.

Down through the buildings of the fortress they wound, heading east into the growing darkness, toward the mountains against which the keep was backed. The earlier crowds had thinned to a wary-eyed few, some of them Goblins, some of them Gormies and kobolds, and some of them creatures she could not identify. When they were outside the walls, they turned south, bending with the land toward a vast depression that dipped into the flats overlooking the countryside beyond. Scrubby and desolate, the depression was rippled by a maze of deep gullies and sharp ridges born out of massive erosion. They followed a cart path marked by wagon wheels and animal tracks, the dust rising in heavy clouds, the air hazy and gritty.

She sat quietly in the center of the cage, rocking back and forth to its uneven sway, one sleeve of her tunic held across her mouth to help keep the dust from her breathing passages. They had advanced far enough that when she looked back at the keep, its walls and towers had shrunk to the size of a child's toy. She watched as the image grew smaller and less distinct and finally vanished entirely.

As they arrived on the valley floor, the roadway straightened and the landscape opened up again. The denizens of Kraal Reach, absent before, were now clustered everywhere she looked, fingers pointing, eyes and faces bright and eager, their conversations animated as they watched her pass. They understood more about what was going to happen than she did; that much was clear from their behavior. It was not a stretch to think that most of the city had come out to watch.

An embankment rose in front of them, a wall of earth more than thirty feet high. A pair of tall gates opened through the wall, and when the cage reached the other side, she found that the embankment wrapped around a bowl of earth and rocks that was perhaps a quarter mile wide from end to end. Seated atop the embankment were thousands of Kraal Reach's denizens, sharp-faced and gimlet-eyed, hunched over in their robes as they cheered and gestured in greeting. It was not a comforting welcome; it was a welcome of dark expectation and impatience, the kind reserved for those who would provide a form of blood sport. Certain that her testing was to take the form of combat against a carefully chosen opponent, she did not like what she felt in that moment.

The wagon rolled to an unsteady stop in front of a set of tall risers formed of an iron framework and wooden slat seats. In the center of a group of unidentifiable creatures hidden within robes and hoods sat the Straken Lord. As the cage ceased its forward movement, the demon rose and walked down to greet Hobstull. Heads lowered and hackles raised, the wolves slunk away at his approach. The Goblin guards stepped back and bowed low. Only Hobstull made no overt movement of submission, his angular body unbent, his expressionless oval face lifted watchfully. The Straken Lord spoke softly to him, then nodded at Grianne.

She took a deep, steadying breath as the Catcher approached her, keys in hand. If she was going to attempt another escape, she would have to do so now.

But she fought down the urge, telling herself to wait, to be patient. A wrong move would mean the end of her. She stayed quite still while Hobstull opened the cage door and stepped inside, then walked over to unlock the chains that bound her wrists. He stepped back, beckoning her outside. She did as she was told, rising gingerly to exit the cage and stand on the floor of the arena, facing the Straken Lord.

"Bow to me," it ordered quietly.

She did so, deeply and slowly. It cost her nothing. She felt no respect for the creature, only a deep-seated wariness. She would do what was required of her until the time was right. She was good at waiting.

"Are you washed and rested?" the demon asked.

"Yes, Master."

"It is the time of your testing. Are you ready?"

"Yes, Master."

"The Jarka Ruus that are my subjects have come to watch. If you disappoint them by showing fear or cowardice, I will give you over to them to be killed. If you try to escape, I will kill you myself. You have only one choice. Complete the test successfully. Demonstrate that you are worthy of being kept alive."

She waited. She knew better than to speak without being spoken to, better than to ask questions. She held herself erect, her hands clasped before her, her fingers working slowly over her wrists, where the manacles had numbed the nerves.

The Straken Lord gestured, and the rolling cage was pulled away. With it went the Goblin guards and the demonwolves. Only Hobstull remained, bright eyes fixed on her. His specimen, awaiting her trial. She did not look at him. She would not give him the satisfaction.

"Walk out into the center of the arena," the Straken Lord ordered. The blue eyes glittered with an excitement she had not seen before. "There, you will find your opponent waiting. You may use any magic you possess to defeat it. You may call on any of your skills to protect yourself. So long as you do not attempt to escape this arena, the conjure collar will not be used against you. Your sole responsibility while you are here is to yourself. Your obligation is to survive. If you do, Ard-Rhys-that-was, your future is assured. There will be no need for further punishment. You will be given a place among us, one I shall choose for you, and it will be a place of honor. Now go."

She walked away at once, not daring to look at him another moment, afraid that the incredulity and disgust she was feeling would show through in spite of all that she was doing to hide it. What was the demon talking about? What could it think she would find to be honorable about life in this desolate prison world? All she wanted to do, all she lived for, was escape. The Straken Lord had an overblown opinion of what it could expect of her if it thought anything would change that, and she had no idea what fueled it.

She stared out into the flats as she walked, searching. There was nothing to see, no sign of movement in any quarter, no indication of any life. What sort of opponent had the demon chosen for her that an entire city would come out to see? What manner of creature was she expected to defeat in combat that would indicate she was worthy of keeping her life?

She glanced skyward momentarily, then out onto the horizon, thinking the attack might be coming from outside the arena. Nothing. She was aware that a hush had settled over the assembled denizens of Kraal Reach. They were waiting now, anticipating. All conversation had dropped to a barely audible whisper. Movement had stopped. All eyes were on her.

When the mewling sound began, soft and low, she had almost reached the center of the arena. She knew it for what it was immediately. A chill washed through her, causing her skin to shiver and the tiny hairs on the back of her neck to raise. She stopped at once, mouthing a single word voicelessly.

Furies.

She experienced an odd sense of calm. The uncertainty was gone, the waiting over. At least she could derive some small sense of satisfaction from knowing her opponent's identity. What better way to test her than with creatures like this? She breathed slowly, deeply, trying to steady herself. The mewling was rising steadily, building in intensity. She had only moments.

What shall I do?

Hers was the stronger weapon, her magic against their teeth and claws. Hers was the superior skill and cunning, her craft honed in a thousand battles. But the Furies were driven by instincts that did not value safety or self-preservation. A pack mentality ruled them when they found prey, and they would attack and keep attacking until either the enemy or they were destroyed. No quarter would be given and none asked. Furies knew only one way, and that way eschewed any identifiably rational behavior. She had been put into a den of madness, and the source of that madness was a legion of relentless, inexorable killers.

She tested the magic of the wishsong to see if the Straken Lord had told the truth about using it, thinking that if the demon had lied, she would be rendered unconscious fast enough that she wouldn't feel it when the Furies tore her to bits. But the magic blossomed at the end of her fingertips on command, gathering force, taking shape, waiting to be used, and the conjure collar gave no warning. Hope welled up within her at the realization that it would be an even battle. She would have her chance to survive.

A small chance.

She would have to kill all of them, if she was to walk away. Nothing short of that would save her. They would come at her in a rush, and they would keep coming until the life was bled out of them. Once, the task would have been a challenge she would have embraced, a struggle of dark magic against dark intent, the wellspring of the Ilse Witch's indomitable self-confidence. But she was no longer the Ilse Witch, and her desire for combat had fallen away with the identity she had shed.

Her strength must come from her life as the Ard Rhys.

What shall I do?

They began to appear, small shadows in the failing light, feline faces and slanted eyes, sinuous forms sliding from holes in the earth and from behind bits of scrub. Like ghosts, they materialized in the gloom, their mewling rising and falling in waves of expectation. They were all around her, perhaps a hundred of them. Too many for her to overcome, no matter how much magic she used, no matter how strong her determination. Like the ogre she had seen on her way to her confrontation with the shade of the Warlock Lord, she would fight with passion and fury, but in the end she would be pulled down.

Instantly, she began to rethink her strategy for surviving the confrontation. Strength alone would not be enough. Cunning was what would save her. Innovation and surprise. The unexpected might turn aside these little terrors. They were inching closer, some of them within twenty yards. She saw the madness glinting in their eyes. She felt the heat of their bloodlust. The longer she took to respond, the bolder they would grow. They were stalking her with a certain amount of caution now, but the testing would be finished all too soon, and then . . .

The testing.

Of who and what I am.

As swiftly as the thought was completed, she knew what

she had to do. She didn't pause to consider the consequences or weigh the risks; she just did it. She reabsorbed the magic gathered at her fingertips, pulled it back inside, changed its form, and redistributed it throughout her body. The effect was instantaneous and irreversible. She lost control almost immediately, swept away by the magic's implacable response. Gasping in shock, she dropped into a crouch, her appearance changing as she did so, her form altering. The magic burned within her, turning her feverish as it stripped away her look and smell, her thinking, her reasoning, her conscience. She began to mewl like those that stalked her. Like those she confronted. Like a Fury. She made the change in a heartbeat, the magic sweeping across her until Grianne Ohmsford, Ard Rhys of the Third Druid Council, simply vanished from the valley floor.

What appeared in her place was another Fury, this one larger and more dangerous than its brethren, but clearly a twin.

The transformation was so unexpected that the other Furies drew back in shock. One moment, their prey was standing helpless before them. The next, it was gone, replaced by another thing, a recognizable presence that somehow wasn't exactly what they were, but close enough that it gave them pause.

She moved forward swiftly, cat-smooth and challenging, all spiky fur and menacing sounds, her eyes sweeping across those smaller replicas of herself, her teeth and claws bared and threatening. She hissed and spit as she swung about in uncontrollable rage. Where was her prey? Where was the human? She went so deep into her assumed form that she could anticipate the taste of blood in her mouth. She was so removed from her human side that she wanted to rip and tear at something—anything—that came within reach. She mewled her need to her cat kind, mirrors of herself, and they hissed and spit in reply.

Down through their midst she stalked, lost to herself, turned killer demon, no visible, recognizable part of her human side in evidence. She was all Fury now, a part of the pack, at one with the madness. If there had been something to attack, she would have done so, shredding it with relish, satisfying her newly minted primal need. The other Furies rubbed against her as she passed, accepting her presence, her place among them. They circled and sniffed, taking in her smell, marking her as cats would. She responded in kind, moving through the landscape as if in a dream, afloat and not quite grounded by anything. She had a vague sense of things not being right, of seeming out of joint in place and time; she had a dim memory of having had another life that didn't square with this one. But her Fury self wouldn't give way to that other life, wouldn't let it intrude, and so she felt it slipping farther and farther away.

She cast frequent glances toward the embankment, where creatures she could eat if she could reach them buzzed and whispered among themselves, their voices raw sounding and enticing. She stalked toward them, drawn to them for a reason she couldn't identify. The other Furies ignored her, returning now to their dens, disappearing back into the earth like shadows in sunlight. The excitement was over, the chance for a kill gone. One by one they vanished, the happenings of earlier moments already forgotten.

She walked on, drawn by a craving she could neither understand nor resist. At first, it involved the creatures on the embankment, then only one of them, a singularly tall, dark, spiky being that was descending from its perch into the valley. Her ears pricked in expectation. Fresh prey. A meal. She eased forward, but the creature didn't turn aside or back away like her, it came on. She bared her teeth and flexed her claws. In a moment she would have it and then summon her brethren to the feast.

But all at once the spiky creature gestured at her, and pain ripped through her body, dropping her squirming and spitting on the earth. She tried to rise, and the pain returned, harsher and longer, flooding her with its razors and knives, stealing the last of her strength. She lay gasping as the black thing came over to her and stared down at her expressionlessly.

"Do you know me?" it demanded, blue eyes cold and brittle.

She did. It came back to her instantly, came back as the identity she had assumed fell away and her knowledge of who she was returned.

"Yes, Master," she whispered.

The Straken Lord nodded. "You have excelled in your testing. You have proved your worth. I am pleased."

The demon picked her up as if she were weightless and bore her from the arena to the thunderous roar of the assembled, to cheers and grunts and stamping of feet, to unmistakable acclaim. Yet she felt no euphoria; she felt only disgust and an appalling rage at what she had been forced to do. She had survived, as was her intention, but the cost could not be measured. It had taken more than she wanted to acknowledge, her emotional sanity compromised, her carefully constructed integrity destroyed. She had walked into the arena as the Ard Rhys, but she had emerged as something else. She had reverted to the monster she had once been. In the arena she had become the Ilse Witch again in everything but her heart, and that becoming could not be easily undone, if at all. She was blackened through and through by the change she had wrought in herself, by the adopting of the Fury persona.

She had made herself sick, and although it made her weep inside to acknowledge it, she did not think she would ever be well again.

EIGHTEEN

"Captain, he's calling for you."

Pied Sanderling, Captain of the Elven Home Guard, looked up from the maps he had been studying since rising early that morning and stared at the tent flap wordlessly. He had been expecting it, but he had hoped that somehow it might be avoided. He couldn't understand how the King could be so mistaken about something so obvious. But the King saw things differently, and perhaps that was why he was King, although Pied was inclined to think that being King was mostly an accident of birth.

Not that he had any room to talk. He was the King's first cousin, and that had played a significant part in his ascension through the ranks of the Home Guard and eventual selection as Captain. There had been Sanderlings standing with the Elessedil Kings for as long as anyone could remember. A Sanderling had stood beside Wren Elessedil when she had fought at the Valley of Rhenn and driven the

Federation and its allies back into the deep Southland more than 150 years ago.

"Pied, are you there?" Drumundoon pressed anxiously.

Sanderling could picture his aide's young, anxious face with its fringe of black beard, high forehead, swept-back hair, and deeply slanted Elven features. Drum was already anticipating the worst, imagining how it would be if it were left to him to face the King alone, unable to explain what had become of his trusted cousin. But that was Drumundoon, always seeing the goblet as being half empty, always missing the silver lining behind any dark cloud. If he wasn't so good at organizing and managing, wasn't so dependable, and wasn't so impossibly loyal . . .

But he was, of course.

"One minute," he called to his aide, alleviating the other's fears.

He rose, stretched to relieve cramped muscles, and stared down at the maps one final time. The whole of the Prekkendorran lay revealed in cartographic rendering, the positions of each army, Free-born and Federation, painstakingly delineated. It had taken someone a long time to do this, he thought. But it was a onetime job, since neither army had moved more than a few feet in over two years.

Until now, perhaps.

He reached for his weapons and began buckling them on. A brace of long knives went about his waist, and a short sword was strapped over one shoulder. He picked up his longbow as well, an unusual weapon for a member of the Home Guard. Their primary duty was to defend the King, which more often than not entailed hand-to-hand combat.

But Pied favored the longbow, a weapon both versatile and reliable. Like most members of the Elven army, he had done a tour of duty on the Prekkendorran, serving as an archer in the ranks for six months, then as the leader of a long-range scouting unit that spent the bulk of its time deep in enemy territory. Both assignments required extensive reliance on the longbow, and he had never felt comfortable without it since. It was his work on the Prekkendorran that had gotten him noticed and appointed to the Home Guard on his return. The longbow was his good-luck charm.

Besides, he was short and slight of build, and hand-to-hand combat with broadswords was never going to favor him. Skill and quickness were what he relied on, and the longbow was a weapon that utilized both.

He glanced around his quarters to see if anything else needed doing, decided it didn't, that he had stalled as long as he was able—though not nearly long enough to suit him—threw on his cloak, and went out through the tent flap.

Drumundoon came to attention, a habit he couldn't seem to break, even when only the two of them were present. Tall and lanky, he towered over the shorter Sanderling. "Good morning, Captain."

"Good morning, Drum." Pied led the way as they moved down through the Elven camp toward the King's tent. He brushed back his mop of sandy hair and squinted up at the cloudless sky. "So he's made up his mind." He shook his head. "I wish he'd wait."

"You don't know what he's decided," Drumundoon ventured hopefully. "He might have decided not to try it."

"No." Pied shook his head. "He had his mind made up last night when I left him, and he's not changed it. I know him. He goes with his first impression of a plan, and he liked this one right from the start. It doesn't matter what the risks are. It doesn't matter that the source is suspect. All that matters is that it's bold and it favors his nature. Like his father, all he lives for is to break the stalemate and drive the Federation down off the heights and south again. He's obsessed with it." He shook his head again. "I can't reason with him."

"You have to try."

"Of course, I have to try. I am being summoned to try. He likes it when he can win these arguments. He forgets that he wins them solely because he is King. But that is the way things are, and I can't change them."

They walked in silence, wending their way through the Home Guard units encamped about the King's pavilion tent, where brightly colored banners flew bravely in the midday breeze, marking the territories they had occupied for months or, in some cases, for years. Elven Hunters came and went with the beginnings and endings of their tours of duty, but the camps remained, like markers in a landscape that had been trampled and pummeled and fought over for so long that nothing recognizable was left. The desolation depressed Pied, the barren earth and broken rock, the colors all brown and gray. He missed the green of his Westland home. He missed the lushness of the trees, the cool breeze off the Rill Song, and the sound of birds singing. He wanted it all back again. Wanted it now. But he would have to wait. Even though he had been there almost two months, he knew it would be another two at least before the King lost interest and went home again.

Still, he knew the situation—had known it from the moment he had accepted his appointment. A Captain of the Home Guard was the King's right hand, and where the King went, he went, too. This King was not a stay-at-home King. This King was restless.

"You sent Acrolace and Parn to see what they could discover?" he asked finally.

Drumundoon nodded. "Last night. They haven't returned. Can you stall until they do?"

"Probably not." He hunched his shoulders defensively. "I wish this wasn't being rushed so. I would feel better about things if a little more thought were being given to the probable consequences of guessing wrong. It bothers me that we are so eager to charge into things."

"The King," Drumundoon pointed out.

"The King, indeed. What sort of advice is he getting? If someone besides me would speak up, we might be able to bring him to his senses."

"There is no one but you." His aide smiled cheerfully. "His advisers, Ministers and otherwise, are all back in Arborlon, safely out of harm's way. You know that. They want no part of this foolishness. Half of them want no part of this war at all. This was always an Elessedil war more than it was an Elven war. First, it was the King's father, after his grandfather's death, and now it is the King. All of them have viewed it in the same way—a chance to expand Elven influence into other territories, to reassert Elven control over the rest of the Four Lands, to place the Elven people at the forefront of development and expansion."

Pied Sanderling grunted. "We have Druids for that. Let them be the ones to spread their influence."

"Cheek by jowl with the Federation. They have no time for the Free-born. Not since the disappearance of the Ard Rhys. Not that it would make any difference while Kellen Elessedil is King, in any case. He hates the Ard Rhys and her Druids. He blames them as his father blamed them for all the bad things that have happened to the Elves. There's no reasoning with him on the subject. He sees our future as leader of the Free-born, and that's the end of it."

Pied glanced over at him. "You never cease to amaze me. Your political sense is as astute as . . ." He paused.

"As your own, Captain," the other interjected quickly. "Don't pretend otherwise."

Well, whatever political sense we possess, it isn't going to get us out of our current predicament, Pied thought. *We could analyze the situation all we want and still be helpless to do anything about it.*

Ahead, the King's tent rose above those of his retinue. Kellen Elessedil never traveled lightly, always with baggage consisting of a great deal more than the clothes he wore. On this occasion, he had brought his sons along as well, something Sanderling regarded as particularly dangerous. The King wanted them to learn early about the realities of his office—as he saw it. That meant coming to the Prekkendorran to witness firsthand what war with the Federation was like—if you could call this impossible stalemate a war. At fifteen and thirteen, they were old enough to understand, the King had insisted, in spite of his wife's and

Pied's pleas to the contrary. That he hadn't insisted Arling and the little girls come as well was the only true surprise of the whole business.

Sometimes, in his darker moments, Pied thought that the Elves had the wrong Elessedil as King. One of the others might have done a better job—say, the King's younger sister, Khyber. Headstrong and independent, she was forever sneaking around behind the King's back to visit her exiled uncle, which was a constant source of trouble. But she was true to her beliefs, chief of which was that Ahren Elessedil was the best of the lot and should never have been blamed for any of what had happened after the *Jerle Shannara* had returned.

Kellen thought otherwise, of course, as had his father. There was no reasoning with either one. There was no forgiveness in their hearts for perceived treachery, however misconstrued the judgment rendered.

"What can I say to him, Drum?" he asked quietly, their destination right in front of them now.

Drumundoon shook his head helplessly. He had no answer to that question. Pied marshaled his courage and resolve for what lay ahead, saluted the Home Guard on duty at the tent entry, nodded for Drum to wait, and entered.

Kellen Elessedil looked up from his own set of maps as his Captain of the Home Guard appeared through the tent opening, his young face eager and intense. Pied knew that look. It meant the King had decided on something and was impatient to act on it. It didn't take much thinking to know what would happen next.

"Good, you're here." The King's impatience was revealed

in his tone of voice. "The reports from the scouts are all in. Guess what they tell me, cousin?"

"That you should attack."

The King smiled. "The Rover mercenaries have all pulled out, the whole bunch of them. Boarded their airships and flown off. They're on their way home, back to the coast, off the Prekkendorran. We've confirmed it. This isn't a stunt. Either they've quit or they've been dismissed, but either way, they're gone. The best pilots, the best craft, the best of everything, gone. The Federation is on its own."

Pied nodded. "Any idea as to why this happened? Have we heard of a rift between the Federation and the Rovers? Anything out of the ordinary, I mean. Now and then, some of them quit anyway. But not all of them at once. Why now?"

"You're suspicious?"

"Aren't you?"

The King laughed. "No, cousin. You're suspicious enough for both of us. You always have been. It's worrisome."

Kellen Elessedil was not one to sit when he could move, rest when he could work. He was a big man, taller than Pied and broader through the shoulders. There was nothing soft about him, his muscular body hardened by hours of exercise and training, his devotion to physical perfection legendary. He was so different from his grandfather and father in this respect that it was hard to believe they had come out of the same family. When they were children playing together at Arborlon, Kellen had always been better at every sport, every game. The only way to beat him, Pied had discovered early on, was to out-think him.

Nothing had changed.

"Part of my role as your protector is to suspect everything and everyone of being something other than what appearances suggest. So, yes, I am suspicious of this Rover withdrawal. I am suspicious of the Federation leaving itself so obviously vulnerable, of inviting us into its lair like the spider does the fly."

"They still have their armies, and their armies are formidable," the King pointed out quickly. He pushed back his long dark hair and knotted his hands. "They may think these are enough to keep us at bay. They know we would never launch a frontal attack against their lines, because if we did, they would smash us to pieces." He paused. "Which is why an aerial attack is so perfect. Look at the opportunity they've given us! Their fleet is big, but unwieldy. Their airship Captains are no match for ours. One quick strike and we can set fire to them all. Think of what that would mean!"

Pied shook his head. "I know what it would mean."

"Complete and unchallenged superiority of the skies," the King continued, so caught up in his vision that he was no longer even listening to his cousin. "Control of everything that flies. Once we have that, their ground forces no longer matter. We can ravage them at will, from too far up for them to do any real damage, from too far away for them to do anything but cover up. We can break them, Pied! I know we can!"

His face was flushed with excitement, his blue eyes

bright and eager. Pied had seen him that way before. When they trained together with staffs and swords in hand-to-hand combat, it was the look he assumed when he believed he had gained the upper hand. What he had never learned was to distinguish the difference between when Pied really was in trouble and when he was only pretending at it in order to lure Kellen into making a mistake.

Nothing had changed about that, either.

Pied nodded agreeably, hiding his frustration. "You may be right. But just to be certain about all of this, I have sent two of my Home Guards into the Federation camp to see what they can learn. I would like to wait for their return before we act."

The King frowned. "How long might that be?"

"Today, I should think. Tomorrow, at the latest."

Kellen shook his head. "Today, perhaps. Tomorrow, no. That's too long. By then, reserves might be called up and the odds made too great for us to chance a strike. The time to act is now, while the Federation fleet is diminished, while we are clearly superior in numbers and experience. Waiting is dangerous."

"Acting out of haste is more dangerous still." Pied stepped in with both feet, his eyes locked on his cousin's, watching as the other's face darkened angrily. "I know you want to attack now, but something about all this doesn't feel right. Better to wait and chance losing this opportunity than to seize it and find we have been tricked."

"Tricked how, Captain?" His cousin's tone of voice had turned dark and accusatory. "What exactly is it you fear?"

Pied shook his head. "You know I don't have an answer

for that. I don't know enough about what the Federation's intentions might be. Which is why I want to wait—"

"No."

"—until we have a report—"

"No, cousin! No! There will be no waiting, no hesitation, no second-guessing what seems clear to everyone but you. None of my other advisers, commanders on the field and off, has voiced your concerns. Suppose you are correct. Suppose this is a trap. What risk do we take? We fly superior airships. We can outrun and outmaneuver our enemies at will. We cannot be hurt from the ground. At worst, we will find we were mistaken about the size of their fleet and be forced to retreat. We have done so before, and it has cost us nothing. Why would this time be any different?"

Because this time you are being invited *to act against them,* Pied wanted to say, but did not. He knew the argument was over and the matter settled. Kellen Elessedil was King of the Elves, and the King had the final word on everything.

"Cousin," the other soothed, stepping over to put his arm about him, "we have been friends a long time. I respect your opinion, which is why I asked you to come speak with me before I gave the command to proceed. I knew what you would say, but I wanted you to say it. I wanted you to question me, because frequently you are the only one who will. A King needs candid and reasoned advice from his advisers, and in most matters, no one gives better advice than you."

He gave Pied a small squeeze with his powerful arm. "That said, a King must listen to what his instincts tell him. He must not waver once his mind is made up. You know this."

He waited for Pied's response, so it was necessary to give it. "I know, my lord."

"I have made a commitment to turn the tide of this war once and for all, and now, at last, I have a way to do so. It would be cowardly of me to turn away a chance such as this merely because there are risks. It would be unforgivable."

"I know that, as well."

"Will you still come with me when we fly into battle?" The King stepped away, releasing his grip. "I won't ask it of you if you feel strongly about not going. Nor will I think less of you."

Pied arched one eyebrow at his cousin. "I am Captain of the Home Guard, my lord. Where you go, I must go, as well. That isn't open to debate. Don't make it seem as if it is."

The King's intense, considering gaze locked on him. "No, cousin, I guess it isn't. Not with someone as dedicated as you. And I wouldn't want it any other way." He paused. "I'll give this matter several hours more thought before acting. I had planned a late afternoon strike in any case, so that we can come at them from out of the twilight, out of the shadows. You may keep watch for your scouts until then. If they return in time, bring me whatever news you think matters. I promise I will listen. But if none comes, I will see you on the plains an hour before dusk."

Pied turned and started for the door. "One thing more," the King called after him. Pied turned. "I intend to take Kiris and Wencling with me." He must have seen the confusion in Pied's eyes. "Aboard the flagship, cousin. I want them to watch."

Pied stared. Kellen Elessedil was talking about his sons. About boys who were fifteen and thirteen. About taking them into the heart of an engagement with a dangerous enemy. "No," he said at once, before he could think better of it.

The King seemed unruffled. "They need to see what a battle is like, to understand what happens. They need to experience it for themselves, not just hear about it. They are future Kings, and this is a part of their training."

"They are too young for this, my lord. There will be other times, safer times, when the risk is not so great."

"The risk is always great in war, cousin," the King said, brushing his arguments aside.

Pied took a deep, steadying breath, picturing Arling's reaction once she found out what Kellen had done. "With any Elves-in-training, we expose them gradually to the dangers of war. We don't just throw them out on the battlefield—not unless we are desperate. We bring them along slowly. I think that is what is needed with Kiris and Wencling. Let them come on a few overflights first, ones in which combat is not a given."

Kellen Elessedil took a long moment to study him, as if seeing something he hadn't seen before, something he was not altogether pleased about. Then he said, softly, "I will think about it, cousin."

He motioned for Pied to go out, an odd gesture Pied had not seen before. But this was not the time for speculation. He departed quickly, happy to escape before Kellen could think of some further madness. Because he would, Pied knew. He was in that place where ideas came and went like silverfish, and each looked better than the one before, but never was.

Outside the tent, Drumundoon fell into step beside him, his tall form bent close as he said, "Did he listen to you?"

Pied nodded. "He listened. Then he ignored me. If I don't give him fresh reasons to call it off, the attack takes place at dusk. Worse, he intends to take his sons along for the ride."

Drumundoon exhaled sharply. "Has he lost his mind?"

"Arling would think so. I wish she were here to speak with him. She might have better luck than I."

Drumundoon shook his head. "I doubt it. He doesn't listen to her, either. Although he might, where those boys are concerned. What matters is that she left them in your charge. Yours, specifically. I was there when she did so. I heard the way she spoke to you. If anything happens to her sons, she will have your head."

Pied glanced at him. *Because I loved her once. Because I think she loved me, as well. You left that part out, Drum.*

He stalked off into the midday heat and tried not to think about it.

By late afternoon, Acrolace and Parn had still not returned. It worried Pied, but he had learned long ago to live with the guilt associated with sending his Home Guard to spy on an enemy. It was obvious in any case that Acrolace and Parn were not going to return in time to be of any help in dissuading Kellen Elessedil from his ill-advised foray. The attack on the Federation fleet was going to happen whether he wanted it to or not, and he was just going to have to make the best of it. That was sometimes a soldier's lot, even if you were Captain of the Home Guard and cousin to the King.

Dressed in his battle gear, his weapons strapped about him once more, he called Drumundoon to his tent, and with the sun creeping toward the horizon through a screen of thin clouds and the daylight becoming diffuse and weak, they set out for the airship field.

"No word of any sort, Drum?"

The aide shook his head. "Nothing. I hear that the Federation is massing soldiers along its lines, looking to shore up the weaknesses brought about by the departure of the Rovers. That's the King's reading of the situation, at least. It reinforces what he already believes, which makes it attractive. It supports the decision he favors. Word is, he sees this war over and done within a week."

"Celebrating his victory before he's even engaged his enemy. How very like him." Pied shook his head. "Something is going on that we don't know about. I can feel it in my bones. This attack is a mistake. I have to find a way to stop it."

Drumundoon pursed his lips. "I don't know this for a fact, but I am given to understand that the King hasn't advised our allies as yet of his plans."

Pied came to an abrupt halt, staring at him. "What?"

"He intends to inform them just before he sets out, I'm told. That way, they can't stop him." His aide cocked an eyebrow at him. "He doesn't want to risk anything or anyone getting in his way. He knows he isn't commander of the Free-born army, that he isn't even commander of the airship fleet. But he is King of the Elves, and the Elves make up the greater part of the airship command, so in his mind, that's sufficient justification for striking out on his own."

Drumundoon glanced around warily, making sure no one else was listening. "Captain, he doesn't intend to ask for support from any quarter in this business. He intends this victory to belong solely to the Elves. Dwarves, Trolls, and Bordermen can share in it afterwards, once it has been realized, but ultimately it is the Elves who will bring it about. That's what they say he's decided."

Pied fumed. How had he not seen that coming? For more than two months, Kellen Elessedil had camped on the Prekkendorran with his Elven Hunters, an inspiring presence and little more on the face of things. But Kellen Elessedil was nothing if not driven. You could see it in his impatience with the failure of the Free-born army to effect any noticeable change in the status quo. Always anxious to be in the thick of things, always looking to see how matters so long stalemated might be resolved, the King was pressing his fellow commanders at every opportunity. The war was more than thirty years old, and the Elves were sick to death of it. The King saw it as his moral imperative to bring it to a conclusion, and no one could fault him for his commitment to do so. What was wrong with his approach was his insistence on doing it his way, on finding a solution that did not necessarily involve his Free-born allies. What was mistaken in his thinking was that the solution existed in simple terms, that somehow the answer lay in a single brilliant military stroke, and that the finding of that answer had been left up to him.

Well, it was too late to try to explain it to him now, even supposing he would be willing to listen, which Pied was quite sure he would not.

He started walking again, more purposefully, a mix of irritation and concern flooding through him. King or not, Kellen Elessedil was overstepping his bounds, and it would come back to haunt them all. Drumundoon matched his strides to those of his Captain and kept his peace while he did so. Neither of them spoke. There had been enough talk already.

Pied surveyed the camp as they passed through it, taking careful note of what he saw. This section was mostly Elven; those farther on, east of where they walked, comprised Bordermen from the larger cities of Callahorn as well as Dwarves and Trolls, most of the latter mercenaries. The nominal leader of the army was an aged, though highly respected, Southlander named Droshen, but the real leader, the man who commanded the soldiers on the battlefield, was a Dwarf called Vaden Wick, a veteran of countless campaigns against the Gnome tribes before coming to the Prekkendorran. Just now, coordination of the various allied forces was loose, a condition brought about by the near inactivity of the armies on either side of the conflict over the past few years, an erosion of structure and discipline through constant changes in both ranks and command. The third generation of allies was fighting the war, and the toll was noticeable. It was assumed by most that the war would end only when the leaders finally grew so tired of it that they called it off by mutual agreement. No one thought it could be won on the battlefield. Not after so long. Not after so many failed attempts.

Except, of course, for a few who thought like Kellen Elessedil.

Pied was disconcerted by what he saw that evening. The obvious lack of discipline was worrisome. The looks on the faces of the men and women as they sat around their fires, playing games of chance and drinking ale, were more worrisome still. Disinterest and resignation were mirrored in those faces. That spoke to him clearly: No one believed in the war anymore. It said that everyone was sick of the fighting and dying. It said that keeping your head down and your mouth shut was all that would get you through. These men and women were waiting things out. They were waiting to go home.

He glanced around. No one drilled or trained. No one sharpened weapons or tightened straps on armor. There were Elven Hunters manning the walls at the front and there was a watch in place; that was enough. If something more was needed, it was somebody else's problem.

It was worse elsewhere, in the other armies, where discipline was even less in evidence. It wasn't that Bordermen, Dwarves, and Trolls weren't brave and capable; it was that they had no reason to think those attributes would be tested. The Federation army had squatted in place for almost two years without doing anything beyond sending out scouts and attempting an occasional foray into the Free-born lines. They were as indolent and disinterested in fighting as their enemies were. The mobilization of fresh forces along the Federation front in the wake of the departure of the Rover airships did not suggest to the Elves and their allies that their enemy's attitude had changed.

Pied glanced over at Drumundoon and gestured toward the encampment. "They don't seem to have much to do with their time, do they?"

Drum said nothing. There was nothing to say. He was of the same mind as his Captain. The Home Guard had a different approach to discipline than everyone else, but that was why they were Home Guard. The rest of the army regarded them as curiosities. They were a small unit assigned a single task—to protect the King. The way they conducted themselves, others believed, was mostly the result of the suspicion that the King was always watching them.

When they reached the heights, Pied paused. The front stretched along the plateau that comprised the Prekkendorran for more than two miles east and west through a series of broad flats segmented by twisting passes and ravines. At present, and for much of the past twenty years, the Free-born had occupied a pair of high bluffs bracketing a deep, wide pass that angled north all the way to the other side of the plateau before turning down through the foothills beyond. Elves occupied the smaller bluff on the west; a mix of Bordermen, Dwarves, and Trolls, the larger one on the east. By placing archers and slingmen on either side of the gap, where it narrowed, they were able to ward against penetration. The Federation's only choice was to come at the allies from the front or sides and to do so from a highly vulnerable position.

The Federation had penetrated deep into the flats early on in the war, but once the allies had found the bluffs on which to set their defenses, the attack had stalled. Because the Federation was the invading force, the allies could afford to sit back and wait. It was the invader who must come to them, and by now they had constructed defenses of stone and timber that were believed to be sufficiently strong that it would cost the lives of thousands of men to achieve a breakthrough. It was generally agreed by both sides that another way must be found, and as yet it had not.

Pied studied the Federation lines, situated on the flats not half a mile away. A mass of dark figures crowded behind fortifications similar to their own. In the two months he had been on the front, they had not emerged from behind those walls. The most excitement he had experienced was the result of a pair of rather haphazard airship attacks on the Dwarf lines a mile farther down the front, which had been quickly driven back.

Were there more Federation soldiers at those walls than there had been a week ago? A mottled stain of black-and-silver uniforms spread away behind those fortifications for better than a mile, clusters of men settled about cooking fires and stacks of weapons. There was no drilling or training in evidence, no suggestion of an impending attack. Everything looked as it always looked.

But that didn't mean it was.

He shook his head. He didn't like anything he was seeing on either side of the front. He had been a soldier all his life, and he had learned to trust his instincts. They were screaming at him, telling him that the possibility of disaster was enormous and close at hand.

"Drum, I can't let him do this," he said quietly.

"The King?" His aide shook his head. "You can't stop him, Captain. You've already tried, and he won't listen. If you can't tell him something he doesn't already know, you'll just make him more determined."

Pied walked on, saying nothing. There had to be a way to stall, something he could say or do to win a reprieve. He had always been able to out-think Kellen; he ought to be able to do so now.

Ahead, the airfield came into view, settled in a swale at the center of the encampment east, close to the draw that separated the allied armies. There was noticeable activity, even from a distance. Ships were being readied for liftoff, crews scurrying across the decks and atop the rigging, tightening draws and loosening sails. Railguns were already fitted in place, and missiles were stacked in boxes beside them. Two dozen airships were set to fly, the larger part of the fleet, the best of the warships it comprised. The King was determined that the attack would succeed, holding nothing back against the possibility that it wouldn't.

As he descended from the higher flat, Pied caught sight of the King grouped with his airship commanders in a tight circle by the flagship *Ellenroh*, talking. The discussion appeared heated, but all the heat was coming from the King. His Captains were doing little more than listening.

Then Pied caught sight of Kiris and Wencling, standing off to one side of their father, and his heart sank. The King had decided to take his sons with him, after all. In spite of Pied's reservations. In spite of his advice. His nephews were looking at their feet, trying not to draw attention to themselves, staring ill at ease and out of place, and he guessed they didn't like the idea of being there any better than he did.

Taking a deep breath, he walked across the airfield and up to the King.

"Captain," the King greeted on catching sight of him. He would never use Pied's name or refer to their familiar relationship in a situation like this. "We are ready to depart. No word, I gather, from your scouts? No? Then we have no further reason to delay."

"My lord, I wish you would reconsider," Pied said quickly. "I would feel better for your safety if we waited just one more day. My scouts should return—"

"My safety is in good hands with these men," the King interrupted, an edge to his voice. "I thought we had settled this earlier, Captain. Was there something I said that wasn't clear to you?"

There was no mistaking the anger in his voice. He did not care to be challenged in front of his airship Captains and his sons and particularly not about the coming attack. He was telling Pied he had gone as far as he was going to be allowed to go, and that he had better not try to go farther.

But Pied had no choice. Not if he was to keep his self-respect. "My lord, you made yourself perfectly clear. I respect your thinking. But I have been a soldier for a long time, and I have learned to trust my instincts. They tell me that something isn't right about what we're seeing— about the unexplained Rover departure and weakening of the Federation fleet. Nor do I feel right about the mobilization reported along the Federation front. I know it seems to be in response to the Rover departure, but I think it might be something else. If I could suggest an alternative plan, my lord, I would ask you to take an exploratory flight to see—"

"Enough, Captain!" the King snapped, cutting him short. There was a hushed silence. The King was seething. "More than enough. You are Captain of the Home Guard. Limit yourself to that and leave the decision making to me!"

"As Captain of the Home Guard, I am responsible for your safety and must do everything in my power to protect you!" Pied snapped back. "I can't do that if you won't let me!"

The silence turned as frosty as midwinter in the Charnals. Pied caught a glimpse of the shocked faces of the King's sons, who stared at him in disbelief—Kiris, tall and dark like his father, and Wencling, fair and small like his mother. No one talked that way to their father, certainly not outside the family and not in public. Pied had crossed the line, but his conscience refused to let him back down.

Kellen Elessedil turned away. "Captains," he addressed his airship commanders, "prepare to set out. Board everyone. Make certain they know what is expected of them."

He gestured to a messenger standing off to one side. "Carry the message I gave you to Commanders Droshen and Wick. Go quickly and tell them to take whatever precautions they feel necessary in case of a counterattack. Make certain they know that I have already left."

When everyone was gone but his sons, he turned back to Pied. "You have abused your position as Captain of the Home Guard. As a consequence, you will not be coming with me. I don't trust you anymore. You've lost your nerve. I don't want my life or the lives of my family and soldiers in your hands. You are relieved of your duties. My safety is no longer your responsibility. Perhaps others, more capable of understanding the nature of your office, will serve me better."

He paused. "Just because my wife still favors you, a kindness she would do well to reconsider, doesn't give you the right to question me as you have just done—in front of my sons and my officers."

He turned to his sons, beckoned for them to follow, and stalked angrily toward the *Ellenroh*. Pied watched them go, stunned. He should say something more, he knew. He should make another attempt to stop him or maybe just try to explain himself better. But he couldn't make himself move.

He was still standing there when the airships lifted off like huge hunting birds and swung south toward the Federation lines.

Drumundoon, who had waited patiently in the background until Pied's attention had shifted away from the departing vessels, came up to him.

"He will change his mind, Captain," the aide said quietly. "He will realize he acted out of haste."

"Perhaps." There was an awkward silence as they faced each other. "I couldn't think of anything else to say, Drum. I just stood there and let him walk away from me."

His aide nodded and gave a faint smile. "Maybe there weren't any words left to be said."

They walked back across the airfield and into the Elven encampment in silence. Now and again, Pied cast anxious glances toward the Federation lines, where the first torches were being lit with twilight's approach. He could still see the Elven warships, dark smudges pinned against the sky.

He searched for ground activity, but saw none. It was hard to tell, though, so far away and in poor light.

His thoughts drifted. He had grown up with Kellen Elessedil, and there were few men or women who knew him better. He should have been able to devise a more effective approach to dissuading him from making an ill-advised attack. He should have been able to avoid angering him so. Somehow things had gotten out of hand, and he was still struggling with the fact of it. He could see the faces of Kiris and Wencling in his mind, looking shocked and afraid, as if seeing what he hadn't seen, as if knowing secrets he should have known. He tried not to think what Arling would say once she discovered how badly he had let her down. If she would talk to him at all, he amended. She might not. She might dismiss him as swiftly as Kellen had.

"Captain," Drumundoon said suddenly, taking his arm.

A man was racing toward them from across the flats, one of his Home Guard. The man's name escaped him, though he knew it as well as his own. He struggled to remember it and failed.

"Phaile," Drum whispered, as if reading his mind.

Phaile reached them in a rush and saluted. "Acrolace has returned, Captain!" he exclaimed. His breath came in short, labored gasps. "She's badly injured! She says you are to come right away!"

They broke into a run, Phaile leading the way. Pied didn't bother questioning the man; Acrolace was the one he needed to see.

But the urgency of the summons frightened him.

They reached a cluster of Elves close to the edge of the bluff, just above the front of the Elven defensive line. Acrolace lay on the ground, the silver-and-black Federation tunic she had donned as a disguise stained and torn, her left arm ripped open all the way from shoulder to elbow. She was pale from loss of blood and rigid with pain. Her green eyes found his as he knelt beside her, and her fingers fastened on his wrist.

He bent close to hear her, his eyes never leaving hers. "What happened, Acrolace?" he whispered. "Where's Parn?"

She shook her head. "Dead." She swallowed thickly. "They have an airship . . ." She coughed, and blood bubbled on her lips. "Under heavy guard, no one allowed close. But . . . we got near enough . . ."

She trailed off, her eyes closing against pain or memory, he couldn't tell which. When she opened them again, he squeezed her hand. "What did you see?"

"A weapon mounted on the deck. Big. Something new." She inhaled sharply. "They're waiting for us, Captain. They know . . . we're coming. We heard them . . . say so."

She gave a long, slow sigh, and her hand released its grip on his. *A weapon*, he repeated silently.

"She's unconscious," one of the Healers said. "Better so."

Pied looked around quickly, trying not to panic. "Phaile," he said, spotting his Home Guard messenger. "Find Commander Fraxon. Tell him I said to expect a Federation attack. Tell him it will be massive, a push to break all the way through our lines. Tell him it will come at any time and to have his Elven Hunters ready. Hurry!"

He stood up. "Drum, call up all elements of the Home

Guard and place them on the airfield. They are to hold it at all costs. All costs, Drum. Until I tell them to stand down."

His aide nodded, his long face as pale as Acrolace's. "Where will you be? What will you do?"

Pied was already hurrying away, his determination etched on his lean features. "I'm going after the King," he called over his shoulder. "This time he will have to listen to me!"

TWENTY

§

Pied Sanderling sprinted the length of the Elven encampment, bumping aside anyone who got in his way, knocking over equipment and stores, leaving in his wake a string of angry shouts and curses. His mind was already far ahead of his body, thinking of what he must do and how he must do it, aware of how futile his efforts were likely to be. A terrible certainty gripped him. He was going to be too late. No matter how quick he was, he wasn't going to be quick enough. The disaster he had feared had come to pass, and all the failed warnings in the world would not be enough to persuade him it was not his fault.

Run faster!

He reached the airfield winded and flushed, and as he tore down the embankment toward the airships, he searched frantically for someone he recognized among the few who hadn't gone with Kellen Elessedil. He found only a lone commander of a railgun sloop, a grizzled veteran named Markenstall. He barely knew the man, knew more of his reputation than of him. A brave man, dependable in a fight, a solid presence in the pilot box—that would suffice.

"Captain!" he shouted, rushing up to the older man. "Is your sloop fitted and ready?" He glanced at her name, carved into the stern. *Asashiel.*

Markenstall stared at him with a mix of surprise and doubt. Gray whiskers stuck out from the sides of his jaw, deep lines furrowed his weathered face, and his ears were tattered and scarred. He had the look of a man who had been in more than a few fights.

"Answer me, Captain!" Pied shouted at him.

The older man started sharply. "Ready and fitted as she can be, Captain Sanderling," he growled.

"Good. We're taking her up. Cast off."

Markenstall hesitated. "Captain, I'm not authorized to—"

"Listen carefully to me," Pied interrupted. "The King flies into a trap. One of my Home Guard nearly lost her life getting that news to me; another lies dead somewhere beyond our lines. I'm not about to let that be for nothing! There isn't time to seek authorization of any sort. If you want to save the King and those who went with him, we must leave at once!"

He cast a quick glance south, where the sky had turned deep blue in the twilight haze and the airships his gaze had followed earlier had disappeared from view. The dusk was thickening, the last of the sunlight a dim glow below the horizon west, the first stars beginning to brighten in the sky north. East, the moon was a silvery crescent lifting out of the Lower Anar.

His eyes flicked back to Markenstall. "Captain, please!"

The veteran studied him a moment longer, then nodded. "Very well. Get aboard." He turned to a pair of sailors sitting nearby. "Pon! Cresck! Off your duffs and get aboard! Take in the lines and anchors! Prepare to cast off!"

The two crewmen and the grizzled Captain were skilled at making quick departures, and the *Asashiel* was airborne in minutes, swinging south with the wind, tacking swiftly out across the flats and beyond the Free-born lines. Pied stood in the pilot box with Markenstall while the crewmen manned the railguns to either side, breeches opened and loaded, triggers unlocked. No one mistook the foray for anything but what Pied was certain it was going to turn out to be.

"Mind if I ask what it is you intend to do with a sloop and two railguns?" Markenstall asked once they were winging out over the desolate front, a hint of sarcasm in his voice.

Pied shook his head. "Whatever I can."

Ahead, the Federation lines were so dark they were virtually indistinguishable from the surrounding land. Pied thought he heard shouting, the sounds of sudden activity, but it was hard to tell with the rush of the wind and the whine of the rigging in his ears.

Then lightning split the darkness, brilliant and piercing, the bolt a horizontal rope stretched low and taut against the horizon. The bolt struck something that exploded instantly into a fiery ball, burning fragments pinwheeling into the darkness to fall like tiny firebrands to the earth. For just an instant, a cluster of airships was silhouetted against the brightness, masts and hulls stark and black.

"Shades!" Markenstall hissed. "What was that?"

Pied swiftly amended his earlier conclusion. It wasn't lightning after all. Not riding that low and that straight.

Then it flashed again, and there was another explosion, this one more violent than the first, and again the airships were revealed, scattering in all directions now, angling away from the fireball like frightened animals. An earth-shattering boom reverberated through the night, the shock waves so powerful that Pied could feel them even through the deck of the sloop.

He knew then what it was. It was the weapon Acrolace and Parn had discovered in the Federation camp. The trap had been sprung; Kellen Elessedil's airships were being destroyed, one by one. Pied was too late to give warning. He was too late to do anything but witness the consequences of the King's ill-considered, rash behavior.

"Faster, Captain," he said, catching hold of Markenstall's wiry arm. "We have to try to help."

It was a faint hope at best. There was little one airship could do to help another in the best of situations, which this most assuredly wasn't, and his was likely the weakest airship aloft. But he had to get a closer look. He had to know what the Elves and their allies were up against. If the King didn't get safely back, if none of them managed to get back . . .

He forced the thought away, hating himself for allowing it to surface. But another firebolt erupted and another airship caught fire, the flames turning masts and rigging into torches that illuminated the whole of the night sky. Stricken, the airship wheeled away from the attack, trying to stay aloft, to seek cover. But there was no cover in the skies and no place to hide when you were burning. A second strike turned it into a massive fireball. It blazed brightly for a moment, then fell apart and disappeared into the dark.

"Shades!" Markenstall whispered again in shocked disbelief.

They were close enough by then that Pied could make out the vague shapes of the Elven airships as they wheeled this way and that to avoid the huge Federation airship that was in pursuit. Her name, emblazoned across her upswept bow, was the *Dechtera*. The terrible weapon was affixed to her decking; Pied could just make out its armored bulk. Even as the shape of it registered, the man-made lightning exploded out of it again, crackling with energy and power, a terrible bright lance through the enfolding night, burning everything in its path. It caught pieces of two ships this time, nicking the hull of one, boring holes through the sails of another. It was firing blindly, Pied saw, unable to distinguish its targets clearly in the darkness. The moon was behind a bank of clouds, and the starlight was still too thin.

The Elven airships might have a chance if they fled now, if they turned around, if they raced for the safety of their own lines.

Incredibly, they did not. Instead, they attacked. It was suicide, but it was exactly what Kellen Elessedil would do, refusing to quit a battle, ready to die first. *He will get his wish here,* Pied thought in horror. The Federation weapon was firing into the Elven airships as they drew near enough to distinguish, and they were exploding one after the other. The King was trying to ram the Federation ship, to damage it sufficiently that it could be forced down, perhaps even made to crash. He was intent on salvaging something out of this disaster, but he could not seem to recognize that it was already too late for that.

"What in the name of everything sane is he doing?" Markenstall whispered in disbelief, recognizing at once the futility of the effort.

Committing suicide, Pied thought. Trying to ram the bigger ship in the mistaken belief that by doing so he could still save his fleet. But he wasn't even going to get close. Already, the *Dechtera* was firing at the *Ellenroh,* a series of short, sharp bursts that set the Elven flagship on fire in several places and brought down the foremast. Still, Kellen came on, his railguns raking the enemy's decks. But the weapon that was destroying his fleet was protected behind heavy metal shields that the railguns could barely scratch. Another burst set the *Ellenroh's* mainsail afire, and now the airship was lurching badly, her sails gone and one or more of her parse tubes damaged or blown away.

"No, Kellen," Pied whispered. "Land her! Get her down now before she—"

A fresh burst from the Federation weapon rocked the big Elven flagship from bow to stern, striking with such force that it knocked her backwards. The *Ellenroh* shuddered and bucked, then exploded in a blinding ball of fire that consumed everything and everyone aboard.

In seconds she was gone.

Pied stared in stunned silence, unable to accept what he had witnessed. The King, gone. Kiris and Wencling, gone. The biggest warship in the Elven fleet together with every last one of the men and women who crewed her, vanished.

"Captain Sanderling," Markenstall hissed in his ear, and he jerked around in response. "What do we do?"

The *Dechtera* had turned her attention to what was left of the Elven fleet—a handful of airships only, three of which were already settling onto the flats. The plains were swarming with Federation soldiers marching toward the Elven lines, a dark stain that spread like ink on old parchment. Thousands, Pied judged. He watched the damaged airships fall into the mass of charging men. He watched the men swarm up the sides of the ships and onto the decks. Then he quit looking.

His eyes flicked back to the fleet, under attack once more from the Federation killing machine. The *Dechtera* was moving after them, overtaking them one at a time, burning them out of the sky the way an archer might shoot down a flock of trapped geese. She shouldn't have been able to do that, as big and cumbersome looking as she was. She must be powered by an abnormally high number of crystals, her stored energy capacity twice that of any other ship of the line. Some of the Elven ships were dropping toward the plains now, trying to use the enemy soldiers as cover so that they could not be fired upon from above. But the tactic wasn't working. The weapon aboard the big ship was too accurate to be deterred by the threat of what a miss would mean. It simply took its time, burning away the Elven ships whether they fled or tried to hide.

He looked at Markenstall. "We have to do something, Captain."

The older man nodded, but kept silent.

"Can you get behind that Federation ship? Can you come up at her from below?"

The veteran stared at him. "What do you intend to do?"

"Disable her steering. Use the railguns to damage her rudders and thrusters from underneath, where they can't do anything about it without breaking off their attack and setting her down." He paused. "We're small enough that they might not see us coming in from behind."

Markenstall thought a moment. "Maybe. But if they do see us, we won't have a chance. Railguns are only good from close in. From more than fifty yards, we'll be so much target practice."

Pied glanced quickly at the skyline. The moon remained covered by clouds, the light still something between dusk and full dark. Off to their left, the *Dechtera* was hunting its Elven quarry like a big cat, stealthy and sure, striking with bursts of white fire that filled the night air with blinding explosions and the pungent, raw smell of ash and smoke and death.

"We can't just sit here and let this slaughter continue," he said quietly.

Markenstall adjusted the controls without a word, swung the *Asashiel* toward the enemy camp, and sent her skimming over the heads of the advancing Federation soldiers, who fired up at them with bows and slings as they flew past. But they slipped through the darkness unhindered and undamaged, and soon they were behind their target, staying low so that they would not be silhouetted against the horizon, approaching in a gradual ascent that kept them carefully masked from view.

But suddenly new airships began to lift off from the Federation airfield, fresh reinforcements setting out to lend support to the ground attack on the Free-born camp, their dark shapes like hunting birds as they swung about to place the sloop directly in their path.

"Captain," Pied exclaimed with a sharp intake of breath.

Markenstall nodded. "I see them. Warn the men on the railguns."

Pied left the pilot box in a rush, scuttling across the deck to Pon and Cresck, his safety harness dragging behind him, and alerted each of the crewmen of this new danger. He found himself wishing they had something besides railguns with which to work, but there was nothing to be done about that.

Moments later, he was back beside Markenstall. The night had gone black again, the moon disappeared once more behind the clouds, and the air turned brisk and chilly. Pied shivered in spite of himself, wishing he had thought to throw on warmer clothing.

He glanced out at the cluster of rising Federation airships. At least half a dozen were advancing in their direction.

"They're gaining on us," Markenstall announced. "I don't think they see us yet, but they will soon enough.

We can't wait, Captain Sanderling. We have to take a chance."

"What do you mean?"

"We have to gain speed and altitude both, get above the heavier air and into the wind and closer to that ship." The other man paused. "We have to let them see us. If we don't, they're going to find us anyway. We don't have time to be clever or cautious about this."

Pied hesitated. He knew Markenstall was right, but he hated the thought of exposing the sloop when they had so few weapons with which to defend themselves. Once they were spotted, the other ships would be after them like cats after a mouse. That would give them only a single pass, barring a miracle, at their target.

"All right," he said. "Do your best. But find a way to get us close to that ship."

"Hold on," Markenstall said, and he pushed the thruster levers all the way forward.

The *Asashiel* bucked and shot ahead; the mouse was in flight. They rose swiftly into the sky, abandoning the comparative safety of the darkness for the revealing light of stars and moon—for the latter was emerging from behind the clouds. Fresh illumination bathed the Prekkendorran in brilliant white light, revealing the hordes of attackers surging toward the Elven defensive lines. Already they were flooding the gap between the twin bluffs occupied by the Elves and their allies, breaking down the Elven fortifications and scrambling onto the airfield, where the last of the Elven airships were frantically lifting off. All across the battlefield, the remains of the destroyed ships burned fiercely, signal fires for the advancing army, encouragement for its soldiers. Pied saw the *Ellenroh's* hull, a charred, smoking wreck at the center of everything.

You should have listened to me, Kellen, Pied thought. He closed his eyes. *I should have found a way to make you listen.*

They were approaching their target now. The *Dechtera* was right ahead of them, her bulk blocking out an entire section of the sky. She was huge, a flying platform supported by four sets of pontoons with cross-bracing running all along her underside. Three masts flew yards of light sheaths, radian draws feeding banks of parse tubes housing the diapson crystals that powered her, metal shields opening and closing in sudden bursts of converted energy as the ship maneuvered first this way and then that, bringing the deadly weapon mounted on the foredeck to bear. No one aboard seemed to realize yet that the *Asashiel* was tracking her, all eyes were directed forward to where another Elven ship was under attack, a rope of fire burning through her, sizzling and exploding wood and metal in a booming cough that rocked the sloop with concussive force. Burning bodies flew over the railings of the stricken airship, tumbling to the earth like stricken fireflies.

Pied made a quick, agonizing survey. Only three Elven airships remained aloft of the twelve or so that had started out. The fleet was decimated.

"Quick, Captain!" he hissed at Markenstall. "Before we lose any more!"

The *Asashiel* was right below the *Dechtera* now, and Markenstall angled her to the port side, away from the approaching vessels that by now had surely spied them, giving his crew a chance to position the railguns where they could do the most damage. He, too, knew they would only have one pass. The big ship was moving forward in a slow, steady line, a fresh target already in sight, still oblivious to them. They were going to have a clean shot at her underside. The men on the railguns had swung their weapons into position and were sighting down the long barrels, waiting patiently.

Pied glanced over his shoulder. Their pursuers were closing on them, and he could see the frantic efforts of some of the crew to give warning to the men on the *Dechtera*.

"Release!" Markenstall shouted.

Both railguns discharged in the same instant, sending a hail of metal shards into the underside of the Federation ship, the missiles striking with explosive impact. Pied had just enough time to see two of the parse tubes disintegrate entirely and the main rudder collapse, and then Markenstall was swinging the *Asashiel* away, speeding out from under the damaged enemy, a tiny gnat in flight from a giant bird. They emerged from beneath the warship's shadow into a sky awash with moonlight and were immediately exposed. The railguns on the decking of the enemy swung toward them, but Markenstall dropped the sloop below their angle of fire, skimming the flats once more, content to take his chances with the missiles fired from the foot soldiers.

But it wasn't over yet. A line of white fire sizzled past their mainmast, snapping off one of the spars, burning away wood and sail and knocking the *Asashiel* sideways.

"Brace!" Markenstall shouted automatically, grabbing onto the railing to keep upright. Reaching for the thruster levers, he jammed them all the way forward, then sent the sloop into a stomach-churning dive.

"We should have taken a shot at that weapon, too!" Pied snapped at the veteran.

The Captain righted their wounded vessel not fifty feet above the flats and lurched away from the deadly Federation weapon. Pied glanced over his shoulder. The *Dechtera* hung silhouetted against the moonlit sky. She was still moving forward, but he saw that her course was fixed and undeviating. At least one, and possibly both, shots from the sloop's railguns had done the job; the steering was damaged, and the vessel was unable to come about.

He exhaled sharply. The big ship was slowing down. The other Federation warships were coming up from behind, preparing to offer help. It occurred to him that now was the perfect time for that attack Kellen Elessedil had been so anxious to launch, the perfect opportunity to destroy that ship and the weapon she bore. But the bulk of the Elven fleet was in flames, and the ships of Callahorn were still on the ground somewhere east.

He looked down at the flats, swarming with Federation soldiers, then at the Elven defensive lines. He remembered the faces of the men and women he had seen earlier, weary and disinterested. He remembered the lack of discipline, evident everywhere. He was not encouraged. The Elven airfield had been overrun, the remainder of the fleet fled north. If their ground defenses held through the night, it would be a miracle. An impossible miracle, he amended, without help from the Free-born allies. And in the end, it might not matter anyway. By week's end, the *Dechtera* would be airborne again and would fly in support of the Federation attack, her terrible weapon primed and ready for use. What it had done to the Elven airships was nothing compared to what it would do to the Elven army.

The implications of his thinking did not escape him. The war on the Prekkendorran was about to take a disastrous turn, and he wasn't sure there was anything that could be done about it.

They were flying over the captured Elven airfield now, heading west toward the besieged Elven lines. "Captain," he called to Markenstall. The wind came up again in a sudden rush, tearing at his words. The veteran turned. "Can you fly us to where—"

He never finished. White fire lanced through the center of the airship in a searing rope of brightness that slammed the entire craft sideways with such force that Pied was thrown from the pilot box, catapulting over its railing. He caught a glimpse of the mast going up like a torch, the flames spurting skyward as the sails caught fire. Both rail-guns and crew disappeared into an explosion of sizzling light. The sloop lurched wildly, bucked, and began to drop.

"Markenstall!" he called weakly.

There was no response. His safety line was still attached to its ring inside the pilot box, but he was tangled so thoroughly in the rigging that he couldn't move. He tried to lift himself to see what was happening inside the box itself and failed. There was blood on his face, warm and sticky, running down his neck and arm. He had thought them safely

away from the Federation warship and her terrible weapon.
He had been mistaken. Its range must be enormous. Even
from the better part of a mile away, it had managed to fix
on them. Even now, after the fact, Pied could not imagine
it.

He felt the sloop plunge earthward with sickening
speed. He closed his eyes and waited for the impact.

TWENTY-ONE

It took Penderrin Ohmsford and his companions almost a week to navigate the maze of passes and defiles that wound through the Klu Mountains, although they did not again encounter the treacherous combination of mist and clouds that had very nearly prevented their initial escape from Taupo Rough. With Kermadec leading, steady and assured now in his choice of routes, they pressed on without needing to rely on Pen or Cinnaminson to find the way.

Nor did they see anything further of their Druid pursuers, although Tagwen was quick to point out, when the subject was raised, that not seeing them didn't mean they weren't out there. Once before they had thought themselves safe, only to discover how badly they were mistaken. If the Druids hunting them were doing so on orders from Shadea a'Ru, they were not likely to give up easily, the Dwarf insisted. But it was the use of the Elfstones that had brought Terek Molt and the *Galaphile* down on them in the Slags, Pen thought. As long as they were able to refrain from using the Stones, they should be able to keep Traunt Rowan and the *Ballindarroch* from finding them here. After all, he reasoned, if the Druid and his cohorts had magic that would enable them to find the little company, they certainly would have done so already. That they hadn't shown themselves even once suggested they were hunting blind.

Nevertheless, as the little company pressed on through the mountains, Pen found himself glancing skyward periodically to make certain he was not making a mistake.

It was late in the day, the sun already sinking into the jaws of the peaks west, when they climbed through a particularly nasty tangle of switchbacks to a ledge that overlooked the broadest, darkest valley Pen had ever encountered. It was difficult to judge exactly how big the valley was; from so high up there was no point of reference by which to measure accurately. Hundreds of square miles, perhaps? Even more? It sprawled in all directions, spilling out from its central cradle into passes and canyons like the fingers of a giant's spread hand. At its eastern end, farthest from where they stood, it simply disappeared into mist and twilight, so densely packed with trees and brush that its shadows overlapped to create the impression of a lake thick and black with deadwood and weeds.

Anything might live in a place that looks like this, Pen thought, and he shivered in spite of himself.

"The Inkrim," Kermadec announced, his voice flat and unemotional, a perfect match for his stolid Troll face. "Some say it is as old as the Races, and that the things that live there are older still. Some say there are things living down there that are as old as Faerie."

"Trees and dirt," Atalan muttered from behind Pen. "Nothing we haven't encountered before."

"And Urdas."

Atalan snorted. "Savages."

It seemed to Pen an odd comment coming from someone who looked vaguely like a walking tree stump, all bark and rough surfaces, as brutish and forbidding as anything that walked the Four Lands.

Kermadec must have thought the same. He looked at Atalan carefully. "Savages to us, but who are we to judge? In any event, I wouldn't be too quick to dismiss them. Urdas have lived in this valley since the destruction of the Old World. This is their ancestral home, and they regard it as sacred. Especially Stridegate. They will fight to protect it from outsiders. Like the Spider Gnomes on Toffer Ridge, they worship the creatures that share their abode, a symbiotic relationship, however one-sided, that influences their attitude toward intruders like us." He paused. "There are a lot of them down there, brother."

"Not enough to stop us, *brother*," Atalan replied, giving an edge to the last word that left no doubt about how he viewed the relationship. "We are the stronger force, no matter how few we are."

There was a hint of anger in Kermadec's eyes and a muttering among the other Rock Trolls. "You have never been down there," the Maturen said quietly. "I have. It isn't just trees and dirt. It isn't just Urdas, either. It is darkness of a different sort. Too many who thought as you do have disappeared into that darkness. If we are careless, we could end up the same way."

"Then we won't be careless, will we?" Atalan declared. His eyes flicked from his brother to Cinnaminson and Pen. "Lucky we have just the little people to help us. A blind girl who sees and a boy who speaks with lichen. What have we to fear?"

He shouldered his way forward and started down off the ledge, not bothering to see who might follow. Kermadec watched him go for a moment, then glanced back at the rest of the company and motioned them ahead.

The descent into the Inkrim was accomplished without incident. The trail down was not steep, though it was narrow and twisting, and at times even Pen, who was among the smallest, was forced to hug the cliff wall. The twilight deepened steadily all the while, and as it did so the valley came alive. Hushed before the change of light to dark, it began to hum and buzz with insect life. Night birds called out, their cries piercing and shrill as they took to the air in shadowy flocks, and Pen could hear grunts from ground animals, some recognizable, some not. He listened carefully as he walked and tried to sort them out. He searched for what sounded familiar amid the cacophony and failed.

At the bottom of the trail, the company made camp in a stand of fir. Even though they had reached the valley floor, they were still several thousand feet above sea level, cradled by the peaks of the Klu, and the air was clear and cold and the sky brilliant with stars and moonlight. As on past nights, Kermadec would not allow a fire. "Tomorrow," he promised. By then they would be deep enough into the territory of the Urdas that a fire would not draw Druid notice or, if spied, would not seem unusual to anyone searching for them. They would be risking discovery by the Urdas, of course, but that was a risk they were taking just by being there.

"The ruins of Stridegate lie much deeper in this valley, Pen," he told the boy later, when dinner had been consumed and they were sitting alone at the edge of the encampment. His blocky features were inscrutable, but his eyes were intense. "Two more days at least, and that's if we press ahead at a steady pace. I've been there, the one time I was in this valley before. I remember their look. It isn't a sight you are likely to forget."

"And the island?" Pen pressed. "The one that contains the tanequil?"

Overhearing their conversation, Khyber, Cinnaminson, and Tagwen had wandered over to join them. They sat down in a close circle, silent and attentive. Behind them, a pair of sentries had taken up positions just out of sight in the darkened trees. The rest of the Rock Trolls were settling in for the night, bulky forms lumbering through the darkness, the heavy clank and rasp of their weapons audible. Atalan was sitting not far away, hunched and unmoving, his back to his brother, his gaze directed into the forest dark.

"It is not an island of the sort you might imagine. It is surrounded not by water, but by a deep ravine choked with vines and trees. A single bridge spans its width, an ancient stone arch thousands of years old. It offers the only passage to the other side. But no one I know has ever crossed it."

"Why not?" Khyber asked at once.

Kermadec shook his head. "I am not superstitious in the

manner of the Urdas, but I know the nature of the things that live within the Inkrim and I respect the power they wield. A warding stone placed on the near side of the bridge forbids passage. I try to pay attention to such things, when I can."

He paused. "I was told that others did not. Some attempted to cross anyway. There were rumors of a great treasure. A few used the stone arch. A few went down into the ravine with the intention of climbing out the other side. None were ever seen again."

"Then how are we to cross?" Khyber sounded suspicious and didn't bother keeping it from her voice. "Why are we any different than these others who couldn't?"

Kermadec shrugged. "I don't know that we are. I only know that we have to find out." He nodded toward Pen. "It is what is needed if we are to save the Ard Rhys."

He rose and walked back toward his sleeping Trolls. As he passed Atalan, he reached down and touched his shoulder. His brother glanced up and said something. Kermadec kept walking. A moment later, Atalan rose and followed him.

Khyber glanced at Pen and Tagwen, her brow furrowed. "I don't remember the Elfstones showing us anything about a bridge. I don't remember being warned about not being able to cross one."

"They don't always show you everything, do they?" Pen asked.

"I just think it odd that we're hearing about this for the first time now." She looked angry. "Did the King of the Silver River say anything to you about this?"

Pen shook his head. "Nothing." He wasn't any happier than she was about the bridge and its warning. "He told me to find the tanequil and ask it for a limb from which to fashion the darkwand, then to take the darkwand back to Paranor and use it to cross over into the Forbidding." His lips compressed. "Nothing about a bridge that no one is supposed to cross."

"What are the Trolls doing?" Cinnaminson asked suddenly, her blind eyes directed toward the encampment.

The other three turned to look. The Trolls were gathered in a circle, all of them, including Kermadec and Atalan. They were down on one knee, their blocky heads lowered, their palms flat against the ground, murmuring what seemed to be a chant. Now and then, one of them lifted a hand momentarily to touch fingertips to his forehead or lips.

"They are speaking to the valley," Tagwen said, pulling absently at his beard. "They are asking that it protect them against the dark spirits that live within it. It is an old custom among the Trolls, to seek the protection of the land they pass through and might have to fight upon."

Then, one by one, starting with Kermadec, the Trolls rose and walked around the circle, touching each Troll atop his head before returning to his place and kneeling to be touched in turn.

"Now they are pledging their lives in support of each other, promising that they will stand together as brothers should the spirits bless them with their protection and guidance." He cleared his throat. "I don't believe in this nonsense myself, but it seems to make them feel better."

The ritual continued for several minutes more. Then the Trolls rose and moved off, the sentries to their posts, the rest to their beds. Only Kermadec and Atalan remained where they were, talking quietly.

"Guess they've made their peace." Tagwen stretched and yawned. "I'm going to bed. Good night to all of you."

He moved off, and seconds later Khyber went, too. Pen sat alone with Cinnaminson in the darkness, their shoulders touching as they listened to the forest sounds.

"This valley is filled with spirits," the Rover girl said to him suddenly. Her fingers reached up to brush the air. "I can sense them all around, watching." She paused. "I think they might have been waiting for us. I don't know why they would do that, but they are very purposeful in their movements, very deliberate."

"Maybe they are here because they were called just now by the Trolls." Pen glanced at her. "Maybe they have come in response."

The girl nodded. "They might be here to offer protection. I don't sense hostility." She touched his hand. "I have an idea, Pen. Use your magic to ask them. You can communicate with living things of all sorts. Spirits are alive. See if they will speak to you."

He looked off into the velvet darkness, into the massed trees toward the black wall of the Inkrim, and wondered how to go about it. It began, in most cases, with whoever or whatever he was trying to communicate with making a sound or movement that he could interpret. A hawk might reveal its hunger or its desire for a mate through its cries. A rabbit might convey its fear by the way it looked at him.

The way a small bird flew could reveal its urgency to reach its young. The brush of tree limbs or tall grasses against his face could tell him if they were in need of water. The movement of the wind told him of storms. He had once been warned of a wolf when a tiny ground squirrel darted through dried leaves.

But there was nothing to hear or see in this situation. Spirits did not always have a voice. They did not always take form. He would have to try something else.

He leaned forward and placed his hands against the earth, trying to read something from the feel of the ground. But after several minutes of patient concentration, there was still no response.

"No, Pen," Cinnaminson whispered suddenly, taking his hands and lifting them away. "These are spirits of the air. Reach up to them."

He did as she bid, holding up his hands with his fingers spread, as if to catch the feel of the wind. He held them steady, then moved them slowly about, groping for contact.

A moment later, he had it. Something brushed against his fingers ever so softly, just for a moment before it was gone. Then something else grazed his arm. He read purpose in those touchings; he found life. They were as gossamer as spider webbing and as ephemeral as birdsong, but they were old and therefore strong, too. They had lived a long time and seen a great deal. He could tell all that from a single touching, and it shocked him.

But they were gone as quickly as they had come, and they didn't return. After he told Cinnaminson what he had felt, he tried to reach for them several times more and could not find them.

"They are not ready for us to know them," the Rover girl said. "We must be patient. They will reveal themselves when they are ready."

Later, wrapped in his blanket, Pen thought for a long time before he drifted off to sleep about what form that revelation might take.

They set out at daybreak, moving into the heavy woods while the shadows still layered the earth in dark patches and the sunlight was a dim glow east through the canopy of the trees. The air was chilly and smelled of earth grown rich and fecund over time. The night sounds were gone, replaced by morning birdsong and the soft rustle of the wind through the leaves. The woods remained dark and deep, as impenetrable to sight as a midnight pond, looking exactly the same in all directions, the trees and grasses a wall against the outside world.

They traveled in single file, Kermadec leading, Atalan acting as rear guard, and Pen and his companions placed squarely in the center of the line. The boy walked with Cinnaminson, his eyes sweeping the forest, his senses alert. He searched the shadows and treetops for life, and more often than not, he found it. The Inkrim hummed with activity, its life-forms a surprise at every turn. The birds were often strange, colored and plumed in unfamiliar ways. There were small ground animals that reminded him of squirrels and chipmunks, but were something else. This valley and the creatures that lived within it were old, Kermadec had said, and that suggested that their origins could be found in the world that had existed before the Great Wars. Certainly nothing of the world Pen knew seemed to have a place here.

The day wore on and the sun lifted into the mountain sky, but little of its light penetrated to the forest floor. The night shadows remained thick and unbroken, and the air stayed cool and crisp. There was a twilight feel to the valley, a peculiar absence of real daylight and summer warmth. The woods produced their own climate, peculiarly suitable to this valley.

Now and then they would cross a trail. Narrow and poorly defined, the tracks meandered and ended abruptly, and there was little about them to suggest that they might lead to anything. Kermadec followed them when it was convenient to do so, but more often than not kept to the off-trail breaks in the trees that offered easiest passage and clearest vision of their surroundings. He did not seem particularly concerned about what might be hiding from them and spent no noticeable time searching the deep shadows. Perhaps his training and experience reassured him that he would sense any danger lying in wait. Perhaps it was his acceptance of the fact that in a place like this, ancient and secretive, there was only so much you could do to protect yourself.

Though he searched carefully at every turn, Pen did not see anything that day that seemed threatening. While at times the forest appeared dark and menacing, nothing dangerous ever materialized.

On the second day things changed.

They had enjoyed a fire and hot food the night before, the first of both in a week. They had drunk strong-flavored ale from skins the Trolls carried and slept undisturbed through the night. Rested and refreshed, they had set out again at dawn. This day looked very much like the first; the skies were more cloudy and the light paler, but the forests of the Inkrim seemed unchanged. Nevertheless, Pen felt a difference in things almost at once, a subtle distinction that at first lacked a source. It was only after he had been walking a while that he realized that the forest sounds were quieter, the wind softer, and the air warmer. Even these didn't seem to him to be the source of the problem, and he was plagued by a nagging certainty that he was missing something.

"Does everything seem all right to you?" he asked Cinnaminson finally.

"You sense them, too, don't you?" she replied at once. She was walking next to him, keeping close.

He stared at her, then glanced around quickly, scanning the forest shadows, the deep mottled black and green of the trunks and grasses, of the limbs and leaves. "Is someone there?"

"In the trees. Hiding. Watching. More than one."

He exhaled slowly. "I sensed them, but I didn't know what they were. How long have they been there?"

"Since we started out. They must have found us during the night." She brushed back loose strands of her honey-colored hair. "I thought they were the spirits of the air at first, the ones from last night. But these are creatures of flesh and blood." She paused. "They track us."

Pen took her hand and squeezed it. His eyes swept the trees. "Wait here. I'll tell Kermadec."

But Kermadec already knew. "Urdas," he advised, bending close to Pen to whisper the word. "Not many of them, but enough to keep us in sight without showing themselves. They're working in relays, small groups of them, each leapfrogging ahead of the others in turn to pick us up as we come past, bracketing us so that we don't get away."

Pen felt his heart quicken. "What do they want?"

The Maturen glanced over. His barklike features made him seem one with the trees. "They want to know what we are doing here. They will stay with us until they are sure."

Pen dropped back again, falling into step with Cinnaminson. "He says he knows about them. He says they are just watching us."

The Rover girl smiled. "Someone is watching them, too." Her blind eyes shifted to find his. "The spirits of the air didn't leave, after all. They are still out there."

The morning passed away, and the clouds massed and darkened overhead. A storm was blowing in, and it would bring a heavy rain. Kermadec began to look for shelter, but there were no caves or rocky overhangs to keep them dry. Instead, they crawled beneath the protective boughs of a huge fir, hunkering down when the cloudburst struck, staying put until the rains had slowed to a drizzle, then crawling out again, dampened and chilled, to begin walking once more.

That night, they camped in the lee of a lightning-split hardwood that had once risen hundreds of feet into the air and was now as dead as old cornstalks. Its leaves were gone and its limbs blackened and bare, charred bones on a skeleton. All around its shattered trunk, the ground was burned and denuded as well, and their fire cast its broken giant's shadow into the enfolding darkness. Kermadec doubled the watch, and Pen hardly slept at all. Overhead, clouds scudded across the stars and bats darted through the night like wraiths.

The third day dawned gray and damp, but the rains did not return. The company set out at daybreak, the Urdas tracking it from somewhere in the trees where Pen still could not see them, even if Kermadec could. Pen was tired and irritable from a restless night, and he was unnerved by the constant, unseen presence. His spirits lifted only marginally when Kermadec assured him that they were getting closer to their destination; seeing would be believing.

By midmorning, the look of the Inkrim had undergone a noticeable change. The trees had become massive and twisted, a forest of ancient behemoths that crowded out everything smaller and left the valley floor barren and stark. The gray light filtering through the clouds was diffused further by the canopy of leaves and branches. The forest was shadowy and gray at every turn, and the air had grown thin and stale. Birdsong and insect buzzing disappeared, and the ground animals faded away. There was a hushed quality to the landscape that reminded the boy of places where only dead things were found. He heard the sound of his own breathing as he walked. He could hear the beating of his heart.

"I don't like this place anymore," Cinnaminson whispered to him at one point, and took his hand in her own.

Sometime around midday, Pen saw the Urdas for the first time. They appeared all at once, coming out of the shadows, sliding from behind tree trunks, materializing out of nowhere. Even though he had never seen one before, he knew what they were immediately. They had a primitive, dangerous look to them. Physically, they appeared to be a cross between Trolls and Gnomes. Their bodies were small and wiry like those of the latter, but their skin was thick and barklike and their faces blunt and flat like the former. They were covered in a tangle of wiry hair, their Trollish features flat and expressionless. Short, muscular legs and long arms allowed them to move sideways in crab fashion as they shadowed the company on both sides through the ancient trees.

"Stay together," Kermadec called back over his shoulder. "Don't provoke them. They're only watching."

But more were appearing at every turn, gathering at the fringes of the hazy light in large clusters. Gradually, they began to surround the company. For the first time, Pen noticed the nature of the weapons they carried, a mix of short spears and odd-shaped flat objects that were hooked and sharpened on their ends and appeared to be designed for throwing.

"How far do we have to go?" Atalan called to his brother from his rear-guard position.

Kermadec glanced back and shook his head. "I'm not sure. It's been a long time. Another few miles, maybe. This forest runs all the way to the ruins of the city. Keep moving."

Moments later, more Urdas appeared directly in front of

them, narrowing the way forward even farther. They were beginning to close in, Pen realized. He did a quick count; more than a hundred were set to block the way. The flat, dark faces were expressionless, but the way they hefted their weapons and the deliberate stances they had assumed suggested the nature of their intentions.

"Khyber Elessedil!" Kermadec called out. He beckoned her forward. The rest of the company closed in behind them, sensing that things were about to change. "Can you work a little Druid magic to make them move back?" the Maturen asked.

She frowned. "I can. But if I do that—"

"Yes, it may give us away to the Druids," he cut her short. "But if you don't, the Urdas are going to try to take us prisoner. They have made up their minds that we intend to invade the ruins, and they won't allow it. There are too many to fight. Magic offers us our best chance of escaping, even if you use just a little of it. They are afraid of what they don't understand."

She glanced back at Pen, giving him a look that suggested this was all his fault. "All right," she agreed. "I can scare them. Then what happens?"

Kermadec shrugged. "Then, we run. If we can get to the ruins, they won't follow us in. The ruins are sacred ground, forbidden to them. They'll leave us to the spirits."

Of which we already know there are some, Pen thought. But he understood they hadn't any better choice.

"Stand ready," Khyber said, her hands already beginning to weave in small circles.

An instant later, the air was filled with bits of fire that

screamed and flew in all directions, a cloudburst of sound and light that sent the Urdas scrambling away in terror.

"Run!" Kermadec shouted.

The Trolls and their charges raced ahead through the trees and shadows. Kermadec led the way. As big as he was, he moved like a deer, leaping and bounding past scrambling Urdas and around ancient trunks with his war club swinging. Cinnaminson ran with Pen, holding his hand, letting him lead the way. The forest was open enough that she could do so, and he matched his pace to hers, quickly discovering she was almost as swift as he was.

Behind them, Tagwen lumbered mightily, his breath coming in short gasps, his stubby legs churning.

The whirlwind of fire darts lasted another few minutes, and then it faded, leaving a residue of smoke trails that lifted toward the canopy like tiny butterflies. It took a few minutes for the Urdas to collect themselves, and then they were in pursuit. They came through the trees in droves, small, wiry bodies leaping and scrambling, calling out in sudden, high shrieks that cut to the bone. Seconds later, their strange throwing weapons began to whiz through the air with deep humming sounds, slicing off small limbs and burying themselves in tree trunks. Had Pen and his companions been in the open and standing still, they would have been cut down in moments. Moving through the woods, they were less easy to hit. Nevertheless, Pen found himself running faster.

The chase wore on for a mile, then two. The Trolls were tireless, and Pen and his companions were driven by fear, so they managed to keep just ahead of the Urdas. When Tagwen faltered, one of the Trolls snatched him right off his feet, tucked him under one arm, and kept running. But the distance between hunter and hunted was closing fast. When Pen finally risked a quick glance over his shoulder, he found the Urdas right behind Atalan and the other two Trolls who were acting as rear guards. The throwing weapons mostly bounced off the Trolls like sticks, but Pen could see blood showing through rents in the leather tunics.

Then one of the Trolls running with Atalan caught a spear in the back of the neck above his protective vest, and he went down in a heap. Kermadec's brother turned instantly, shouted for help, and charged back into the pursuing Urdas with such ferocity that they were bowled over and scattered. Khyber wheeled around as well, words of magic tumbling from her lips, hands weaving. A fresh assault of fire darts flew at the Urdas, shrieking and burning. But this time the Urdas didn't flee. Ducking behind trees and flattening themselves to the ground, they simply waited out the barrage.

Atalan bent quickly over the fallen Troll. A moment later, he was back on his feet.

"Dead!" he snapped at no one in particular. Then, seeing Pen and Cinnaminson frozen in place and staring at him, he shouted, "Run, you fools!"

Everyone turned and began to race ahead once more. But the members of the company were winded, worn down by the chase and the never-ending number of pursuers. Already, more Urdas were after them, ignoring the fire darts, tearing through the trees and flinging their weapons with wild shrieks.

Then one of those weapons found Pen, catching him just behind the knees and toppling him in a wash of pain and blood.

It happened so fast that he was down on the ground almost before he realized what was happening. He had the presence of mind to let go of Cinnaminson as he was struck, so that she was not pulled down with him. But he tumbled hard, and when he tried to rise he found his legs would not work. Lying crippled on the ground, he would have died then if not for Atalan. The burly Rock Troll swept him up as he charged past, tucked him under his arm, pounded up to where Cinnaminson stood staring in petrified disbelief thinking she had lost Pen, and snatched her up as well.

"Can't be losing you now, little man," he hissed at Pen, racing after the others as missiles flew all around them. "Not after all the trouble you've caused us."

Somehow he eluded the Urda weapons flung at him, caught up to the others in the company, and matched their pace. Jounced and shaken in the crook of Atalan's arm, Pen was aware of how hard carrying him must be, how much strength it must require. But the Rock Troll didn't seem winded, just angry.

Ahead, more Urdas appeared, closing ranks in a line of dark, gnarled bodies. Beyond, the trees thinned, and the remains of rock walls and stone columns lifted against a backdrop of trees and mountains, their colors hazy in the grayish light. Kermadec yelled to his Trolls, and five of them joined him in a tight formation of armored bodies and heavy clubs and axes. The rest of the company, including

Atalan, fell into place behind him. There was no time to think about what they were doing; they were on top of the Urdas almost before Pen realized what they intended. The Trolls went through the Urda ranks as if they were made of paper. Weapons slashed and cut, but the Trolls fought past any resistance with ferocious purpose, and in seconds the entire company was through.

Again, the razor-sharp missiles flew after them, but this time they were thrown halfheartedly and to little effect. The effort to keep the intruders from the ruins had failed. Prevented by their beliefs from pursuing further, the Urdas clustered at the edge of the trees and screamed in fury. But by the time Kermadec and his Trolls had collapsed inside the first set of crumbling walls, putting Pen and his companions safely behind the protective stone barriers, the screaming had stopped.

In the ensuing silence, Pen Ohmsford listened to the pounding of his heart.

TWENTY-TWO

L ying on the ground beside a clearly winded Atalan, Pen managed to lift his head far enough to look back at his pursuers. A sea of staring eyes, the Urdas were hunkered down in knots all along the edge of the forest. The sudden silence was unnerving. It was as if they were waiting for something to happen, something they knew about that Pen and his companions did not. Pen looked over his shoulder into the ruins. Other than rubble, weeds, and a scattering of saplings that fronted the sprawl of walls of columns beyond, there was nothing to see.

"Savages," Atalan muttered.

Pen gave up on the Urdas and looked down at his legs. There was blood all over where the skin had been broken and the flesh gouged by Urda weapons. Cinnaminson moved over beside him, running her hands over his calves, exploring the wounds, her touch so gentle he could barely feel it. He marveled anew at how she could see so clearly what to do when she was unable to use her eyes. Her blind gaze found his face, as if she knew what he was thinking, and her sudden smile was so dazzling that it took his breath away.

"It doesn't feel as if the tendons have been severed or the bones broken," she said.

Beyond the walls of their shelter, the Urdas suddenly began to chant, breaking the momentary silence. The words of the chant were indistinguishable, but their purpose was clear.

"Look at them," Atalan growled. "Afraid to do anything more than stand out there and hope that by calling on their spirit guardians something bad will happen to us. Stupid."

"They do the only thing they know to do," Cinnaminson said quietly.

The Rock Troll glanced over at her, his gaze flat and unfriendly. "Don't make excuses for them, blind girl. They don't deserve it. They would have killed you."

"A blind girl understands something about the need for excuses," she replied, turning her empty eyes toward his face. "A blind girl perceives savagery differently than you do, I think."

Kermadec appeared and knelt down beside them. Without a word, he took out his hunting knife, cut off Pen's pant legs, and used the scraps of cloth to bind the wounds. "You can wash and dress this later, once we are deeper into the ruins and safely away from the Urdas."

Pen nodded. "I'll be all right."

Kermadec moved away again, and Pen looked over at Atalan. "I owe you my life," he said.

The burly Troll glanced at him, startled. His blunt

features tightened. "You don't owe me anything, little man," he replied.

Then he rose with a grunt and walked away.

Perplexed, Pen stared after him. "What is wrong with him? Why is he so unfriendly?"

"He isn't sure how he feels about what he has just done," Cinnaminson answered. "He doesn't know why he did it." She touched his shoulder. "This doesn't have to do with you, Pen. It has to do with his brother and himself. I think almost everything does."

Pen thought about that for a time, sitting with his back to the wall and listening to the Urdas chant, and decided she was probably right. Atalan's relationship with his brother was complex and disturbing, and he didn't think there was much point in trying to understand it without knowing a good deal more than he did. He glanced over at Khyber Elessedil, who was sitting by herself, looking off into the ruins, and then at Tagwen, who sat with his head between his legs, as if he was sick to his stomach. Pen didn't like it that the four outlanders had become so dependent on the Trolls. He couldn't put his finger on why that bothered him so, but he thought it had more than a little to do with his uncertainty about Kermadec and Atalan. Rock Trolls were strange enough in their own right without the unwelcome addition of sibling conflict; it only heightened his uneasiness to think that at some point their safety might depend on how well the brothers could manage to get along. He knew how highly Tagwen thought of Kermadec, but Kermadec was only one man. They would have to depend on the other Trolls, as well, and that included Atalan.

How much did Atalan care about what happened to them?

It was an unfair question, of course. Atalan had just saved his life. There was no reason for him to be suspicious.

Nevertheless, he was.

Kermadec allowed them a short rest, then gathered them together again. They knelt behind the wall at the edge of the ruins, listening as the Urda chant rose and fell in a steady, monotonous rhythm.

"We're going now," he said quietly, ignoring the wailing. "I want us to be at the bridge by nightfall. We will make camp there, then cross in the morning, when it is light and we can see clearly. I don't think the Urdas will come after us. They are afraid of the spirits and won't chance angering them, no matter how badly they want to get their hands on us. They will rely on the spirits to punish us for them."

He paused. "Still, I don't want to take anything for granted. So we will leave quietly and in secret, just two or three of us at a time."

At the mention of spirits, Pen glanced at Cinnaminson, but the Rover girl was staring straight ahead.

"Young Penderrin," Kermadec said, causing Pen to jump. "You and your Rover girl will go first. I want you to keep a sharp watch for anything moving once we start inside. I've been here only once, years ago, and I barely got past these walls. What I know, I've heard from others, and none of it is reliable. I know of the bridge and the island. I know of the thing that sleeps in the ravine. But there may be other dangers, and I depend on you, with your special talents, to warn us of them."

Pen nodded. He noticed that Khyber looked relieved. The onus of having to risk using her Druid magic again had been lifted for the moment. As Kermadec finished his instructions to Pen and Cinnaminson and turned his attention to his Trolls, Pen moved over to the Elven girl. "Well done, Khyber," he said. "That was a clever bit of magic back there. You saved us all."

She nodded. "At a cost I don't care to contemplate."

"You think you gave us away? You think we were detected?"

She shrugged. "I don't know. I didn't use much magic, and what I did use is not so different from what can already be found in this valley. Elemental magic, in its purest form. The Inkrim is known to the Druids as a place of such magic. Ahren told me of it on the way." She hesitated. "I might not have attracted any attention at all. But I can't be sure. I can't really be sure about anything."

She shook her head. "Ahren would know, if he were here. He would do better at this."

Pen leaned close. "Don't talk like that. I know you miss him. I miss him, too. I know it would be easier if he were still alive." He lowered his gaze quickly when she wheeled on him, her eyes hot and angry, but he kept talking. "He gave you the responsibility for what happens to all of us. He knew what he was doing. You've saved us twice now, Khyber. I know we have placed ourselves in the hands of these Trolls, but it's you we depend on. It's you who really keeps us safe."

He lifted his gaze again. She was still staring at him, but the anger had drained away. "Sometimes I think you are older than you look, Penderrin," she said.

Kermadec was motioning that it was time to go. Pen reached over and squeezed Khyber's hand. "We'll be all right."

The Maturen led Pen and Cinnaminson away from the rest of the company and into the ruins, creeping across the open spaces behind the crumbling wall to gain the concealment of the undergrowth and rubble beyond. The terrain was uneven and difficult to navigate, and it took them some time to make their way through the weeds and debris. Pen turned his attention to his surroundings, searching out any indication of danger. All he sensed were insects, ground birds, and small animals. Stands of trees rose from the piles of broken stone in sparse clumps, casting shadows across the open spaces like wooden fingers, marking the progress of the sun west. There weren't more than a couple of hours of daylight left, and it was already obvious to the boy that Stridegate was much bigger than he had assumed. He saw bits and pieces of it poking out of the hills farther in and to either side of where they walked. He found himself wondering how old the city was and who had inhabited it. Once, it must have been enormous.

He kept his questions to himself. There would be a better time to ask them. He looked over at Cinnaminson, noted the concentration etched on her face, glanced back the way they had come, saw nothing of the others, and turned to what lay ahead.

They walked for a long time, more than an hour by his estimation, and Stridegate's look never changed. At times, he thought he detected movement, but he was never able to pinpoint its source or its nature. He wanted to ask

Cinnaminson if she noticed anything, but he decided that if she did and if it was important, she would say something. The daylight was beginning to fade more rapidly by then, the shadows to lengthen and the sky to darken. Pen was growing hungry and wondered if they would be permitted a fire.

The others caught up with them shortly afterwards, appearing in small groups until the entire company had reformed. Atalan, bringing up the rear, reported that there was no indication of pursuit by the Urdas, who seemed content to remain outside the ruins. He started to say something more, then glanced at Cinnaminson and turned away.

They continued on, walking into the twilight, watching the shadows lengthen and feeling the air turn brisk as the mountain breezes increased. The Inkrim closed them away, yet they could still catch glimpses of the jagged peaks of the Klu through a cloak of mist and clouds that wrapped the tips of the mountains. Pen felt the enormity of those peaks, their immutability, their weight and age. They made him feel small and vulnerable, and he wished more than once he were somewhere else.

Then, all at once, it seemed as if he were. The ruins underwent a sudden and dramatic change that brought the entire company to a shocked halt. They had reached the entrance to a wall that, while ancient and worn, was almost whole. But beyond that wall, all evidence of time's passing vanished. Spread out before them were gardens of such incredible beauty that it seemed as if they belonged to another place entirely. Blankets of columbine tumbled from rock walls. Fields of mountain violets, lupine, shooting stars, and

paintbrush spread away in a dazzling mix of colors. Rhodo-
dendrons twenty feet high clustered against walls riddled
with ferns and tiny yellow blossoms Pen had never seen.
Clumps of pink-tipped heather grew everywhere.

There were fountains, ponds, and streams, too, their waters rippling and shimmering dark silver in the fading light.
There were walkways formed of crushed stone and tile, set
with benches of polished stone. There were shrines filled
with strange images and inset with precious metals. There
were columns of marble and granite. For as far as the eye
could see, that part of Stridegate looked to have been un-
touched by time.

"How can this be?" Tagwen whispered, coming up to
stand beside Pen. "Who could have done this?"

"Not those Urdas," Khyber whispered back.

Pen didn't hear them. He was listening to something
else, something the others couldn't hear. It was a voice,
deep and resonant. He couldn't locate its source, but he
could hear it clearly. It was speaking to him. It was calling
his name.

Kermadec and his Trolls were fanning out through the
gardens, searching for hidden dangers, suspicious of what
they were seeing. *As they should be*, Pen was thinking, still listening to the voice.

"Something lives here," Cinnaminson whispered, her
smooth face lifting toward the light. "Something waits."

Pen shook his head slowly. The voice that called his
name went silent. He was aware of something else then,
perhaps the same thing that had attracted Cinnaminson's
attention. It was close, but it was deep underground, he

thought. It was huge and ancient. It was not human. He was sensing it through his magic at every turn. He was reading it from the things that grew in the gardens, from the small rustlings and movements of the plants and flowers, vines and grasses. They whispered of it. They responded to it. Insects and birds and animals, they carried knowledge of it. They could not give it a name or a description; they could only give it a presence.

Pen took a deep breath. "I sense it, too," he whispered.

Cinnaminson was already moving ahead into the gardens, her sun-browned face intense and her blind eyes sweeping over everything as if seeing what no one else could. She moved swiftly and determinedly, passing by Kermadec, who turned at her approach but did not try to stop her. Instead he joined her and beckoned for the others to follow.

Khyber was already hurrying after them. Pen stood rooted in place, still hesitating.

"There is something wrong here," Tagwen said uneasily, standing beside him. "These gardens are beautiful, but there is something wrong about them."

Pen felt it, too, although he couldn't explain it. "We'd better go."

They followed the others, Pen casting wary glances left and right, still searching for the voice, for the presence, for anything that would explain what they were seeing. But nothing appeared, and the gardens stretched on in a profusion of brilliant colors and sweet smells. Even in the enfolding twilight, they shimmered with a vibrancy that seemed so foreign to everything that had gone before that it was as if the travelers had entered a dream world.

Pen stared about in wonder. How could it be possible?

They caught up to the rest of the company, which was still following Cinnaminson. The Rover girl was walking as if she knew exactly where she was going, her head lifted into the breeze, her path steady and undeviating. It seemed to Pen as if she were listening to something. He wondered suddenly if the spirits of the air had returned, if she was responding to their voices.

Was that who he had sensed, as well?

The group reached a set of broad stone stairs that led upward until they disappeared into the twilight haze. Cinnaminson never paused. She began to climb the steps as soon as she reached them, and the rest of them had no choice but to follow if they were to see where she was going. Pen and Tagwen still trailed the larger group. The boy was beginning to sense something again, a stirring or a whisper, it was hard to tell. He put out feelers, reaching for what was clearly there, but although he could sense it easily, he could not identify it. There was something confusing about what he was finding; it was almost as if he lacked a frame of reference with which to understand it.

At the top of the stairs, the little company came to a halt behind Cinnaminson, who had stopped finally and was pointing ahead. The Rover girl's face was intense and she was breathing hard. Kermadec was trying to talk to her, but she wasn't responding. Pen, seeing what was happening, abandoned Tagwen and hurried forward.

"Cinnaminson," he said, taking her by the shoulders and turning her to face him.

Her young face was flushed with excitement. "We have to go there. We have to follow them," she said.

He looked in the direction she was pointing. An ancient stone arch, pitted by weather and time, bridged from the grassy area on which they stood to a forest of massive trees that sat atop a pinnacle of rock, a forested island surrounded by a deep ravine that ringed it like a moat, stretching away for as far as his eyes could see in the rapidly dimming daylight. The trees on the pinnacle were tall and straight and unbroken, rising hundreds of feet against the skyline, their bark mottled by greenish gray patches of moss. Their branches were deeply intertwined, forming a canopy so thick that it shut away the sky, but their trunks were widely spaced and the ground beneath opened through, clear and uncluttered by undergrowth. The forest backed away from the edge of the ravine in front of them until it joined with the curtain of the encroaching night.

Cinnaminson lowered her head against his shoulder, as if all the strength had gone out of her. "Did you hear them, too, Pen? Did you hear their voices?"

He wrapped her in his arms and stroked her long hair. "The spirits of the air?" he guessed. "The ones from before?"

She nodded. "From the edge of the gardens. Did you hear them?"

"I sensed them, but they spoke only to you." *Something else spoke to me.*

"No. It wasn't speaking. They didn't use words. But I knew what they wanted. For us to follow them. For us to cross to the island."

Pen looked again at the narrow stone arch and the

forested pinnacle of rock beyond. The top of the pinnacle was mostly flat, though rock formations jutted from between the old growth and ravines split the forest floor. The interior of the woods was dark and shadowed in the failing light. It was difficult to tell how deep in it went.

"Is the tanequil in there?" he asked quietly. "Is this the place?"

She hesitated, then lifted her head to stare blindly at him. "Something is in there. Something is waiting."

Kermadec touched Pen on the shoulder and, when he turned, directed his attention to a flat-faced boulder into which symbols had been carved, the markings so worn they were almost unreadable.

"This is the warning of which I spoke," the Maturen advised. "Written in the Gnome language. Very old. It tells strangers that the place is forbidden. It warns that to cross the bridge is death." He looked at the boy. "We can't risk you going until we know. One of us will have to go first."

"No!" Cinnaminson said sharply. Her eyes were suddenly frantic. "No one is to cross but Pen and me. We alone are permitted entry. The spirits of the air insist!"

Atalan gave an audible snort and looked off into the trees. Tagwen began rubbing at his beard the way he did when he was anxious.

"They told you this?" Kermadec pressed her. "These spirits? You are not mistaken?"

"It doesn't matter," Khyber interrupted. "I'm going with them, whatever these spirits say. Ahren gave the responsibility of making this journey to me. He gave me the only real weapon we have. The Elfstones will protect us. And I have the use of Druid magic. Whatever threatens, I will be able to keep it at bay."

"No," Cinnaminson said again. She walked over to Khyber and embraced her. "Please, Khyber, no. The warning is clear. You cannot come with us. I wish you could. But whatever lies on the other side is for Pen alone."

"And for you, it seems," Khyber said quietly.

"And for me." Cinnaminson released her and stepped back. There were tears in her eyes. "I'm sorry. I don't understand why the spirits have chosen me. But my sense of what they want is very clear. Pen is to go and I am to go with him. But you cannot come. You must not."

"This could easily be a trap," Atalan pointed out, his flat face dark with suspicion as he swung back around again. "You are awfully trusting of invisible voices, Rover girl. If they have bad intentions, you will likely be dead before you know of them."

"He is right," Khyber agreed. "You are too trusting."

Cinnaminson shook her head. "They are not dangerous to us. They mean us no harm. I have felt them guiding us ever since we entered Stridegate. They are a presence meant to shelter us, not to cause us harm."

She turned to Kermadec. "Please. They have been waiting for us. They want something from us, but they won't tell us what it is until we cross the bridge." She hesitated. "What choice do we have but to do as they expect? Pen has come in search of the tanequil, and the Elfstones have shown it to be on this island. Doesn't he have to cross over and find out if it is really there?"

There was a long silence as the other members of the

company looked at one another uneasily. Even the Rock Trolls, who spoke little of her language, seemed to sense what was happening. Already on edge from their encounter with the Urdas, they were suspicious of everything in this strange place. Stridegate belonged to the past, to a time dead and gone. They had intruded on that past by going there, and they were anxious to do what was needed and be gone again. Most looked to Kermadec, waiting on his decision.

Cinnaminson turned to Pen, her blind eyes empty, but her face bright with expectation. "You understand, don't you, Pen? You know what we have to do. Will you cross with me?"

The boy nodded. "I will." He looked at Kermadec. "There is nothing to be gained by sending someone on ahead. It would be a pointless sacrifice that would tell us nothing. Cinnaminson and I are the ones who must test the warning."

He could tell that the big Troll was unhappy with the idea, the impassive face giving away just enough to reveal his displeasure. The Maturen glanced at Tagwen and then Khyber, shaking his head. "I don't like it, but his point is well taken. We won't know anything if we don't let them try. We will have come all this way for nothing."

Atalan walked to the edge of the ravine and peered down. "It's deep enough that I cannot make out the bottom. Maybe there isn't one." He looked back at them. "If you fall off that bridge, boy, we will have come all this way for nothing, anyway."

"Tie a rope around his waist," Khyber suggested suddenly. "Tie one to each of them. It couldn't hurt."

They did so, the trolls knotting the ropes in place and taking up positions on both sides of the bridge, ready to haul back should it be required. Pen felt foolish, trussed as he was. He thought the effort pointless. If the spirits of the air or whatever else dwelled in that place wanted them dead, they were not going to be able to save themselves anyway.

He looked at Cinnaminson and wished she weren't involved. It was bad enough risking his life. He didn't care to risk hers, as well. It wasn't her fight. It had nothing to do with her. She was here because of him, and that was unforgivable.

"Pen." Khyber came up to him. "I will stand at the edge of the ravine when you cross. If anything threatens—anything at all—I will use the Druid magic and the Elfstones to help you." Her lips tightened. "I won't fail you."

He nodded and smiled. "You haven't yet, Khyber."

Cinnaminson took hold of his hand. Pen looked around at those assembled, those who had come with him on the quest. The trolls stared back, blank-faced and imperturbable. Tagwen was tugging on his beard, but he managed an encouraging nod. Khyber was already at the edge of the ravine, the Elfstones gripped in her hand, her dark face alert and watchful.

Pen took a deep breath and exhaled slowly. With Cinnaminson's hand in his own, he began to walk toward the bridge.

TWENTY-THREE

As he approached, Pen was able to take a closer look at the bridge, and what he saw gave him pause. It was narrow, less than eight feet wide, and provided no handholds to protect against a fall. *You don't want to walk too close to the edge,* he thought. *You don't want to look down.*

But it was the nature of its construction that troubled him most. The bridge was formed of massive stone blocks cut and placed so precisely that the seams were barely noticeable. Each block was wedge shaped, with the narrow part pointed downward, the blocks carefully fitted and aligned so that the weight of each was buttressed by the others, the whole arranged to form the arch that spanned the ravine. There were no pins or supports or any kind. Stone abutments at each end wrapped the corners, serving as cradles to keep the stones tightly pressed together and immobile.

But the massive blocks each must have weighed thousands of pounds. How had they been shaped, carried, and placed across the ravine without underlying supports?

They could not have just hung in midair, each in turn, while the rest were fitted. Pen could not fathom it. Even using pulleys and a block and tackle it would have been impossible to suspend the first stones while waiting to set the others. They were too big, too heavy, and too cumbersome.

There was something else to consider, he saw. These stones were not as old as those of the ruins themselves. They were smooth and not yet worn and pitted by weather and time as were the walls behind which Pen and his companions had hidden earlier. Stridegate was thousands of years old. The bridge was much newer. It had been constructed long after the city was destroyed and its inhabitants dead.

The implications of his reasoning caused him to shiver; they made him want to turn around right then and there and go back.

It would have taken at least one giant to construct this bridge. It would have taken technology that no longer existed in his world.

Or it would have taken a very powerful magic.

He didn't care for any of those possibilities. All were beyond anything the group had ever encountered. It dwarfed them, reducing their tiny defenses to a handful of pebbles. Even Khyber, with the magic of the Elfstones to aid her, would not be able to stand against something that could accomplish what he saw before him.

He stopped abruptly, not five feet from the bridge, and stood staring at it. Sensing his discomfort, Cinnaminson whispered, "Pen? What's wrong?"

He didn't know what to say in reply, how to explain. He wasn't sure he should try. He couldn't turn back, couldn't give up. The Ard Rhys needed him to go forward if she was to have any chance at all of escaping the Forbidding. Those he had come with needed him to cross if they were to realize any success from their efforts to bring him there. All other considerations, no matter how daunting, had to be put aside.

He was just a boy, but he knew instinctively what he must do.

"Nothing's wrong," he said, squeezing her hand reassuringly. "Don't worry."

He started forward again, leading her onto the bridge, reaching out with his senses into the twilight shadows that now draped everything from the forested pinnacle to the ravine that surrounded it to the bridge that reached to it. He used his tiny magic, his strange gift, to seek anything that might be waiting. Whispers came back to him, small rustlings and little hissings. They came from unidentifiable sources, from the impenetrable dark, from the void. He heard them, but could not make sense of them. He sorted through them swiftly, seeking just one that he might recognize.

Nothing.

He glanced over the side of the bridge into the ravine, into the pooled darkness. His gaze tightened. Was something moving down there?

He slowed, caution once again taking hold.

—Cross—

A chorus of voices spoke, all sounding the same, all

whispering in perfect unison. They echoed in his mind, clear as the ringing of a bell. He started in shock, then glanced quickly at Cinnaminson.

"The spirits of the air," she said softly. "Can you can hear them, too?"

He nodded, surprised that he could, wondering why they were speaking to him, as well.

—Cross—

Fairy voices, soft and feminine. Telling him to come ahead, to do what they had brought him to do.

"Who are you?" he whispered.

—Aeriads. Spirits of the air—

"What is the matter?" Khyber called out to them, a disembodied voice from somewhere behind. "Are you all right?"

He waved back at her without looking.

—Cross—

The whispers urged him to obey, and he did so, not knowing why exactly, not understanding the nature of his readiness to do as they commanded, only knowing that he should. He moved slowly, one careful step at a time, climbing toward the apex of the stone arch, watching the island pinnacle draw steadily closer.

"Where do you come from?" he whispered, not really expecting an answer, but curious anyway.

—From our father and mother. From seedlings strewn far and wide. From wind and rain and time—

Surprised, Pen considered the words. He had no idea what they meant, but the word *seedlings* caught his attention.

"Are you children of the tanequil? Is the tree your father?"

—Our father and our mother. One lives in light; one dwells in dark. One has limbs; one has roots. They wait for you—

Pen shook his head. At the center of the bridge, at the apex of the stone arch, suspended above the dark void of the ravine, he was suddenly aware of something stirring down in the depths, down where he couldn't see. His senses warned him, but he could not trace that warning to anything specific. He just knew. He froze in response, feeling Cinnaminson do the same. She was aware of it, as well. It wasn't the rustle of grasses or the whisper of leaves. This was something much larger—like the heavy rub of a massive animal passing through brush or the drag of logs, cut and chained, through dry earth. But it wasn't localized like that, either. It was spread all through the ravine, twisting and turning along ruts and down sinkholes, oozing and burrowing through dirt and under loose stone.

Mirrored in the sharp glare of the setting sun, a vision flashed before his eyes. Out of that glare, a monstrous apparition took shape, vague and unformed, a thing of tentacles and feelers, of crushing strength and brutal response. He saw in its grip the bodies of humans and animals alike. He saw them break and bleed. He watched their struggles and heard their cries. He cringed from the vision, turning quickly away, closing his eyes to shut out the sights and sounds.

—Cross—

The ropes that had been bound about their waists fell

away as if severed by knives. Shouts and cries ensued from those left behind, but quickly faded.

—Cross—

The voices of the aeriads called to him once more, firm and insistent. Keeping tight hold of Cinnaminson, he moved swiftly ahead, no longer even glancing toward the ravine. The shadows had thickened with the twilight, and it seemed as if, sinewy and rapacious, they were trying to climb from the ravine, out of the darkness and into the light. Pen walked more quickly still, trying to ignore their presence, to block away his perception of the thing below, to ignore the possibility that it was attempting to find him.

Then he was across, safely off the bridge, standing on the solid rock of the pinnacle amid a fringe of trees and brush, just another of the twilight shadows. He no longer sensed the thing in the ravine. He no longer felt it coming for him. He breathed slowly and deeply, steadying himself, pushing back his fear. He was all right. He was safe.

He looked over at Cinnaminson, whose shadow-streaked face was pale and drawn, etched with lines of fear. He squeezed her hand. "We're across. It isn't coming anymore."

She nodded that she understood, but her tension would not be so easily dispelled.

—Come—

The aeriads had no time or interest in fear, it seemed. Pen and Cinnaminson started ahead once more, moving into the trees. Night descended, the moon and stars appeared, and the texture of the light changed. Slowly, their vision adjusted, and they were able to see well enough to know how to place their feet. The trees closed about them, towering old-growth giants, age-worn sentinels of that strange place. Pen could almost feel them watching, waiting to see what he and Cinnaminson would do. The forest was deep and still, and it was living. Pen stepped lightly, gingerly, thinking it made a difference where and how he walked. The earth was soft, carpeted with needles, damp and smelling of mulch and rot. He did not hear the sounds of night birds or small animals. He did not see anything move.

–Come–

The aeriads led them with whispered encouragement, leading them through the forest, between the massive old trees, down the ravines and across the ridges, over the rocky outcroppings and around the steep drops. The path was circuitous and unknowable, a thread that no one who hadn't traveled it many times before could hope to find. Pen could not explain it, but he had the curious feeling that it might not even be possible to travel the same path twice, that it might somehow be different each time. Even though composed of earth and rock, streams and trees—solid, knowable things—that place felt as if it were ephemeral and ever shifting. There was a changeling quality to it, a mutability that turned it from solid to liquid, from a terrain of the physical to a dreamscape of the mind. Pen had the feeling that it wasn't a place you could go to if you weren't a guest of its maker.

It was a place, he thought suddenly, in which the King of the Silver River would feel at home.

He began to hear humming then, soft and insistent. He

thought it was the wind at first, weaving through the branches of the trees, vibrating the leaves, but there didn't seem to be any wind. Then the humming changed to singing, the nature of the words indistinct but the sound clear and compelling.

"Cinnaminson?" he whispered.

She was smiling. "The aeriads are singing, Pen."

He listened to them, to the strange, echoing voices that seemed to come from both inside and outside his head, rising and falling in regular cadence, the sounds repeating, over and over.

"Can you understand them?" he asked, leaning close and speaking softly, afraid that his voice might do something to disturb the song, might break its spell.

She shook her head. "Isn't it beautiful? It makes me want to sing with them."

They continued on through the trees, deep into the forest, far away from the ravine and the thing that dwelled within it. Night had descended, and the world was a mix of tiny pieces of starlit sky glimpsed through breaks in the canopy. Pen could not be certain how far they had come, but it seemed much farther than should have been possible. The pinnacle, though large, was of a finite distance, certainly no more than a quarter of a mile across. Even allowing for all the climbing up and down and detours over rocky terrain, they shouldn't have been able to travel so far without reaching the opposite side.

But they walked on anyway, the time passing, the night settling in, silent and soft, the air warming, the light from moon and stars growing steadily brighter. After a time, Pen dropped Cinnaminson's hand, no longer afraid for her or himself, willing to believe that they had found a haven from the dangers that had tracked them for so many days. It was a conclusion based on a feeling, not rational cause. But it felt as real to him as the earth he walked and the trees he navigated, and that was enough.

Finally, long after the moon had risen and they had walked well beyond any distance it should have taken to cross the pinnacle, the aeriads, who had been singing all the while, went suddenly still.

—Wait—

Pen and Cinnaminson did so, taking hands again without looking at each other, an act of reassurance that had become as familiar and comforting to them as a childhood hug. All about them, the ancient forest had gone still, the silence deep and penetrating, a presence as real as the sky and earth.

Ahead, a sudden, unexpected brightness shone through the trees, as if the moon had broken through the thick forest canopy to light a place previously hidden from view.

—Come—

They went forward once more, drawn by the invisible presence of the aeriads, trusting to fate and their invisible guides. Pen felt a strange sense of calmness, a peace of mind he hadn't known since Patch Run. Everything would be all right, he knew. Whatever awaited, everything would be all right.

Then they stepped from the trees into a clearing awash with moonlight. The canopy of the trees had pulled back, opening to the heavens as if in deference to the ancient tree that sat at the very center. It was massive by any standard, its trunk thick and gnarled and its limbs twisted and broad, lending it an otherworldly, surreal look among even the largest and strangest of the old growth that surrounded it. The moonlight revealed it clearly, particularly the odd colors that infused its bark and leaves—the former a peculiar mix of mottled black and gray, the latter deepest green bordered in bright orange. Pen could see the colors clearly, even in the darkness. He could see the way they mingled with each other, forming a strange pattern that glimmered against the deep black backdrop of the starry sky.

He had found the tanequil.

He had seen it only once, in the flare of the vision revealed by the Elfstones weeks before, when Ahren Elessedil had used the magic in the Elven village of Emberen to make certain that finding the tree was an attainable goal. He had seen it then, but the vision was nothing compared to what he was seeing in front of him. No vision could adequately capture the size and majesty of that giant. No vision could reveal how it made him feel to stand before it, dwarfed by its size and the sum of its years.

Dwarfed, he thought suddenly, by its intelligence.

He blinked in shocked surprise. He could feel the tanequil watching him. He felt it considering him, deciding what it would do with him now that he was there. It was a wild, irrational conclusion, one couched in premonition. Nevertheless, he was convinced of it. The tanequil was watching.

"Pen, I have to go now," Cinnaminson said suddenly, releasing his hand and stepping away. Her milky eyes shifted blindly. "The aeriads say I must go."

"Go where?" He was suddenly afraid. He wasn't sure if he was afraid for her or for himself; he only knew that he didn't want to be separated from her. "Why do you have to go?"

"So that you can be alone. So that you can do what you came here to do." Her smile was quick and dazzling, lighting up her face in a way that rendered her instantly beautiful. "The aeriads are going to show me what they look like. They brought me here so that I could see them. I won't be long."

He stared at her helplessly. "I don't want you to leave."

Her eyes shifted again, searching the space between them, making it seem as if she were trying to find a way to reach him. "You came to find the tanequil, Pen. You have done so. Make something good come out of that. Find what you need to help your aunt."

She hesitated a moment longer, then turned away. "I am coming," she said to the air, to something only she could hear. Her head lifted slightly. "Good luck, Pen."

He watched her disappear into the trees, sylphlike, a shadow quickly lost in the changing mix of light and dark, swallowed whole.

"Good luck," he echoed back, and was alone.

He stood motionless in front of the tanequil for a long time, unsure of where or how to begin, of what to do. The tree would give him one of its branches, if he could find a

way to persuade it to do so. The branch could be shaped
into something called a darkwand, if he could figure out
how. The darkwand would give him access to the Forbidding and allow him to find and retrieve his imprisoned aunt
and bring her home again, if he could reach Paranor and
pass through the portal created by the potion called liquid
night.

If. That word was everywhere. It loomed all about him
like an impenetrable wall.

What should he do?

He waited some more, half hoping that the tree would
try to communicate with him, that it would take the initia-
tive and show him a way to speak with it. But after standing in front of it for what seemed an interminable amount
of time, he gave up hoping. The effort to communicate
would have to come from him. He was the supplicant; he
was the one who was going to have to find a way to break
through.

He had communicated with the aeriads just by speaking
aloud. Would that work with the tanequil, as well?

"My name is Penderrin Ohmsford," he said. "Can you
understand what I am saying?"

He felt foolish speaking that way, and he knew as soon
as the words were out that there wasn't going to be any response. The tanequil was different from the aeriads. He was
going to have to find a different way of speaking to it.

He walked up to the tree and placed his hands on its
bark, running them slowly over the hard, rough surface. He
was surprised at the warmth he found there, a pulsating
heat that radiated outward to spread through his own

body. He kept his hands in place as the heat entered him, thinking that might be the beginning of a way to connect.

But nothing more happened.

He took his hands away, staring upward into the thick nest of intertwined limbs. The orange-tipped leaves shimmered in the moonlight overhead, a rippling that reminded him of a sunset's glow on the surface of the Rainbow Lake. Rustling sounds emanated from that shimmer, soft and gentle, and he reached for them with his senses, drawing them in, trying to sort them out and make them into words.

But nothing revealed itself.

He moved back again, gaining some distance, hoping that by doing so he might also gain some perspective. But as he walked slowly around the tanequil, studying its shape, he began to doubt that such a thing was possible. From every angle, the tree appeared the same—ancient and huge, a knotted enigma a boy could never hope to untangle. It was a tree, and as such he understood some little bit about it. But it was a tree of such immensity—of size and shape and age and immutability, of innate intelligence and deep understanding—that it defied him. He recognized its power, but he could not begin to come to terms with it. The longer he tried to decide how it might be done, the more certain he became that it couldn't. The tanequil was too remote, too foreign, and too impenetrable for anyone possessed of less magic than a Druid.

Khyber, he thought, would be better suited for this. He wished suddenly that he had agreed to let her come.

But that was ridiculous. It wasn't Khyber who had been sent by the King of the Silver River. He was the one who had been told that he could find a way to communicate with the tree.

He sat down, crossing his legs before him, resting his chin in his hands, staring at its mottled trunk, and trying to think the problem through. There had to be a means for doing so. He might not know what it was yet, but he should be able to find it if he just thought about it long enough. Communication with living things came about in all sorts of unexpected ways. He had discovered that over the years; he knew it to be true. So there was a way to communicate with the tanequil too. There was a way to understand it and to make it understand him.

How do trees communicate?

He had no idea. Until then, he had never heard of one that did. Save for the legendary Ellcrys, when it spoke with the Chosen of the Elven people. But the Ellcrys was formed from a human who had willingly agreed to be transformed into a tree. So there was human nature buried somewhere deep within the Ellcrys. He wasn't sure the same could be said of the tanequil. He knew nothing of its history, nothing of how it had come into being. He could not presume that there was anything human about it.

He must find another way, then. It was a tree, and, as such, a plant. What did he know of plants and their relationship with the world? They were alive and took their nourishment from the soil. Some, like the tanequil, were very old, and because they could not move, they had to be very patient. They had endless amounts of time to think, and so they could reason in ways unknown to humans, who were never in one place long enough to give themselves over to reasoning as trees could.

He sighed, staring up into the branches. He was imbuing the tree with human characteristics. Should he be doing that? Did the tanequil think? Did it reason? Could it understand such concepts as patience? Did it do more than root and nourish as the eons passed and the world changed about it?

He thought for a time about the ways in which he understood other living things. Birds and animals he understood from their calls and cries, from the way they moved or didn't move. Insects communicated in much the same way, but without thought. Grasses and flowers possessed limited communicative skills, all in the form of instinctual responses to heat and cold, to wet and dry. Days earlier, in the Klu Mountains, he had read the responses of lichen to the sun's movement by touch . . .

He stopped himself. Would touch work here? He had tried placing his hands on the tanequil, but its bark was like an armor that protected it from the elements, designed specifically to shield it. It didn't take in nourishment or produce responses to the elements through its bark.

It did those things through its roots.

He stared at the tree. Was that the way to communicate with it—through its roots? How in the world was he supposed to do that, especially when those roots were buried dozens—perhaps hundreds—of feet underground? The prospect of digging down to find them seemed ridiculous. Surely that wasn't what he was intended to do if he wished to communicate with the tree.

If Cinnaminson were there, she might be able to offer a different perspective. In her blindness, sometimes she saw things more clearly than he did. He still didn't know why she had been ordered to leave him alone even though the aeriads had been so specific about her coming with him. Frustration and irritation warred with each other as he thought about it.

Suddenly, he was just tired. He didn't want to think anymore. He didn't want to do anything but rest. He couldn't remember how long it had been since he had slept.

He stretched out on the ground under the limbs of the ancient tree and closed his eyes. He needed only a few minutes, just long enough to clear his thinking, and then he would go back to work.

Overhead, the tanequil's branches formed a silvery green canopy in the moonlight, its strange webbing of orange lines shimmering softly. He had the distinct impression that time was slowing down, that his own breathing had become the measure of its passing. His tension and frustration drained out of him until nothing remained but the leaden ache of his body.

He closed his eyes and slept.

As he slept, he dreamed. His dream was of home and his parents. He was back in Patch Run, and his mother was telling him that magic wasn't important, that in some ways it was a burden. His father stood close by, using the wishsong to bring the buds of flowers into bloom. All around them, the sky was green and damp, and the air smelled of rain-soaked earth and leaves. Somewhere distant, an airship flew in silhouette against the sky, and he wished he were on it, safely aloft, safely away.

The scene changed, and he was hiding in a fortress, deep within its walls, down where only torchlight could penetrate the shadows and darkness. He crouched behind a wall, listening to sounds that came from the other side. He knew what was happening behind those walls, but he couldn't bring himself to look. His aunt, the Ard Rhys, was a prisoner of creatures so terrible that even to look at them was death. They were doing things to her best left to the imagination. Those things were meant to change her, to alter her mind, to make her something she didn't want to be. She was calling his name, begging him to help her, to save her from what was happening. Her cries were desperate, unbearable, filled with pain. She was all alone in that dark place, and he was the only one who could bring her back into the light.

But he couldn't move.

He could only sit there, listening . . .

He came awake again, eyes opening to a sunrise brightening through the heavy canopy of the tanequil in a flush of pink light. He stared at the limbs and the sky and the light, fighting back tears and a sense of desperation that threatened to overwhelm him. He lay without moving, waiting for both to pass, waiting to regain control of his emotions, to breathe easily again.

Something stroked the skin of his arms, soft and feathery. Little fingers were touching him, fairy hands or insect legs. They moved along the backs of his hands and wrists. But their movement was circular, a stroking that suggested an attempt to soothe or ease. He grew calm. His tears dried and his heartbeat slowed. He took deep, steadying breaths.

Without moving his hands or wrists, he raised himself carefully on his elbows.

Tiny roots sprouted from the ground all around him, little nests of them, some so slender they matched the hairs on his arm. They formed a bed, poking from the earth, weaving and touching, twisting and stroking. They were everywhere, though he felt them only where his skin was exposed. In front of him, the tanequil's limbs were swaying gently and its leaves shivering in time to the movement of the bed of roots that cradled him. He watched their undulation, watched the swaying of the tree, fascinated, mesmerized.

He lay back again and closed his eyes. The touching continued, and he lost himself in its hypnotic repetition. He reached out to it with his senses, embraced it, and made it a part of himself.

Then, deep within his consciousness, down where his heart beat and his life pulsed, he heard a deep, slow whisper, and even though it came from within himself, the voice wasn't his.

–Penderrin–

TWENTY-FOUR

§

A single word spoken. His name.

—Penderrin—

Only it wasn't spoken in the way that humans spoke. It didn't come from a mouth or even from an independent source. It came from the stroking of the tree roots against his skin, his magic extracting from that touch a communication meant solely for him.

—Penderrin—

The tanequil was speaking to him. He had been wrong about how communication with the tree would happen. It wasn't up to him to initiate contact; it was only up to him to be open to it. The tree would speak to him when it chose to. Trying to reach the tanequil on his terms was not going to work.

He lay against the earth, waiting for something more. But there were no further whispers, and he realized that the tiny fingerling roots were no longer stroking him. He rose to a sitting position and looked down. They were gone, all of them. He sat on a patch of sparse grass and bare earth from which no roots protruded and no sign of the ancient tree was in evidence.

He took a few moments to accept that the situation was not going to change, and then he rose and stood looking at the tree, trying to decide what to do next. Why had it stopped trying to communicate? Did it require something more from him? He couldn't think what else he could do that would help. To allow communication, he had opened himself up to the tree, reached out with his senses, engaged the magic that was his birthright, and it had happened. What more was there for him to do?

He circled the tree, squinting in the glare of the sunrise as the light fell across his face. The forest was silent and untroubled, a vast hall in which even the smallest sound could be heard. It was a sacred place, and he was a supplicant come in search of healing and direction. He stilled his mind and opened his thoughts, reaching to make a fresh connection, his eyes on the tree as he replayed in his mind the still-fresh whisper of his name.

Nothing happened.

After a time, he sat down again, taking up a new position on the other side of the tree, with his back to the sun. He watched the way the light played over the branches and leaves, illuminating fresh parts of the tree as the sun lifted out of the mountains into the sky. He tried speaking to the tree, tried engaging it with his magic, with his thinking, even by touching the earth in the hope that he might draw out the root tendrils. He did everything he could imagine that might stimulate the tree's consciousness.

Nothing worked.

Frustration washed through him. What had he done before that he was not doing now? Why wouldn't the tanequil continue their conversation? Perhaps, he thought, it was a question of patience. Trees had infinite amounts, and for them conversations might require a much longer period of time. Perhaps one word at a time was all that it could manage, and he must wait awhile for the next.

He didn't like that conclusion. He thought there must be a better one, a more sensible one. He went back to how things had begun, how he had been sleeping, dreaming of home, of the Ard Rhys . . .

He caught himself. Of the Ard Rhys, in danger, threatened because he could not help her, because he was incapable of acting. And then he had come awake in the sweat of his own fear and the roots of the tanequil had been reaching out to him. Responding, perhaps, to that fear, to his need to do something to help his aunt?

He lay down again on the earth, closed his eyes, and summoned pictures of his aunt in peril, jogging his memory, even though it was painful to do so, bringing to mind fresh images, fresh fears . . .

Almost immediately, the feathery touching begin again, a stroking of his skin that communicated a combination of reassurance and admonition. He remained still, giving himself over to the experience, but at the same time keeping his fears for his aunt at the forefront of his thoughts, the spark that he hoped would generate something more from the tree.

Hypnotically consuming, the stroking absorbed him. Lulled and calmed, he took a chance, speaking a single word in his mind.

–Tanequil–

–Penderrin. What do you require of me?–

The boy was so surprised by the response that he almost locked up, his mind going blank momentarily before he was able to construct an answer.

–A darkwand, so that I can reach my aunt, so that I can save her from the Forbidding–

–A darkwand formed of my body, of my limbs. What will you give me in exchange?–

Pen hesitated, surprised by the question. He had not thought to give the tanequil anything. The King of the Silver River had not mentioned anything about an exchange of gifts. Or was this something else? It might be that the tanequil was looking at a different sort of exchange entirely.

–What do you require?–

–What you ask of me. A part of yourself–

Pen took a deep, steadying breath, trying to stay focused on his aunt, on the Forbidding, on the journey he must make.

–What part of myself?–

As quickly as that, the stroking ended, the root tendrils withdrew, and the connection between them was broken once more. Pen lay where he was for a time, refocusing his thoughts on his aunt, stirring his emotions, and waiting for the words to come anew. They did not. He was left alone with his thoughts, his mind echoing with the words the tree had spoken and the silence that had replaced them.

Preoccupied with the crossing itself and with what waited, he had not thought to bring anything to eat with him when he crossed the bridge from Stridegate. He rose finally and went looking for food. He searched the forest about him, never moving too far from the tree, keeping the orange-tinged emerald canopy always in sight. But although he looked everywhere he could think to look, he found nothing save a tiny spill of water that trickled out of a fissure in a rock wall. He drank that, the water tasting of metal and earth.

He was about to return to the tanequil for another try at communicating with it when Cinnaminson appeared unexpectedly out of the trees, her face flushed with excitement as she rushed up to him.

"Penderrin," she gasped, "it was incredible!"

"Where have you been?" he asked, taking her by the shoulders. "I was worried about you."

She wrapped her arms around him and hugged him as if she had been gone for weeks, rather than hours. He could feel the soft hiss of her breath in his ear as she laughed. "Did you miss me?"

He nodded, confused by her strange excitement. "Are you all right?"

She pushed back from him so that they were face-to-face. Her smile reflected a child's wonder as she reached up to touch his cheek. "Pen, I saw everything. The aeriads showed me. I don't know how they managed it, but they let me see it all. They took shape and flew all around me, like tiny rainbow butterflies, changing colors and shimmering so brightly they seemed like pieces of the sun. It was so wonderful! Then they changed to become like me—girls, no older than I am! We danced and played! We laughed until I could hardly stand up! Do you know how long it has been since I laughed?"

He stared at her, shocked at the transformation. She had always been effusive, but she was alive now in a way he had never witnessed. It was as if she were being reborn into the world, made over by her encounter with the aeriads. He was surprised to find that he was vaguely jealous.

"Did you find out what they really are? Where they come from?"

She nodded. "They told me. They call themselves spirits of the air—aeriads—but they are much more. They call themselves seedlings, as well. They think of themselves as creatures of the tanequil, his children." She stopped herself. "Their children," she corrected. "I don't understand this part, but they think of the tanequil as both mother and father. The tree is both man and woman to them, able to be one or the other or both as needed." She shook her head. "I'm still learning."

Pen thought about the tanequil's voice in his head. Masculine, he reaffirmed, not feminine. Where was the mother side of the tree, then?

"Are you hungry?" she asked suddenly.

He nodded. "Starved. I've been looking for something to eat."

She took his hand. "Come with me."

She led the way through the trees, navigating the maze of ancient trunks as if her sight had miraculously been restored. There was no hesitation, no deviation. She seemed able to see even better than she had before, her strange gift enhanced perhaps by the magic of the place and its creatures.

She took him to a cluster of berry-laden bushes near a clear, spring-fed pool. The berries were rich and sweet, and he ate them hungrily, then drank the cool, clear water of the pool, which was nothing like the metallic trickle he had sampled earlier.

When they were finished, sitting next to each other on a grassy stretch by the pool, made lazy by the food and drink and the warmth of the sunlight through the trees, Pen asked, "How did you find this place? Did the aeriads show it to you?"

She nodded. "They seem to know what we need, Pen. They knew you were seeking the tanequil, and they led you to it. They knew that I needed to laugh again, and they made me. And they knew I needed to understand them, once they had revealed themselves, and they allowed me to do so. In part, at least." She paused, staring off into space. "They are so wonderful. I wish I could explain it better. They are free in a way I've never been. They can fly wherever they wish, be whatever they want, do whatever they choose. Sisters, of a sort—though I don't think they really are. They seem to have come from different places, at different times."

"But they sound the same," he pointed out.

"They have become one, become a part of a whole. They are different, each of them, but they are the same, too."

He puzzled over that one for a moment, thinking of the way a family worked, then of something more cohesive, like a flock or a herd. But that didn't seem right, either. Finally, he settled on a school of fish, all swimming together and then changing direction at once.

"What do they want with you?" he asked finally.

"I don't think they want anything, Pen."

"Then why are they so interested in you? Why did they bring you here in the first place? Why are they telling you so much about themselves?"

She laughed, as if the answer should be obvious. "I think they just want someone to talk to. I think they know I will listen because I am interested in them."

She reached over and squeezed his hand. "Tell me about the tanequil. What have you learned?"

Strands of loose hair fell across her face as she leaned toward him, and he reached out to brush them away. "I did miss you, Cinnaminson," he said. "I don't like it when you're gone."

She smiled. "I missed you, too." Her face brightened. "Now tell me about the tanequil. Did you speak with it?"

"I spoke with it," he said. "It took me a while, but I found a way."

He told her everything that had happened, how it had taken him all night just to make contact, how it had then withdrawn until he had realized that his connection was premised upon its sensing of his need to help his aunt. He couldn't explain that, didn't understand it at all. But it was clear that the tree knew why he had come and what he had come for, and if he wanted to see the quest through, he was going to have to keep the needs of his aunt and his concerns for her safety foremost in his thoughts.

"But it was what it said last that bothers me most," he finished. "It said that if I wanted to take a part of it—a limb from which to fashion the darkwand—then I must give it a part of myself in return. When I asked what part it wanted, it quit talking to me."

Cinnaminson thought about it. "Perhaps it was just testing you. Or perhaps it was speaking about something else. Maybe it wants a part of you that's emotional or spiritual." She paused. "It can't be talking about an arm or leg."

Pen wasn't so sure. The entire business was strange enough that he wasn't willing to rule out anything.

He looked off in the direction of the tree. "I should go back and try to find out. This is taking longer than I thought it would."

"It is taking as long as it must," she corrected him gently. "Don't be impatient. Don't let yourself become frustrated."

He nodded, shifting his gaze to study her. "What will you do? Will you go back to the aeriads?"

"For now. I already know I can't be with you. You have to be alone to speak with the tanequil. I will come looking for you tonight."

She leaned over and kissed him lightly on the cheek, then on the mouth. He kissed her back, not wanting to sever the connection, not wanting her to go.

But when she rose and waved good-bye, her face still flushed with excitement and expectation, he didn't try to stop her.

He returned to the tanequil in the warm hush of midday, the sun spilling in faint, thin streamers through the thick canopy of the old growth. Clouds scudded overhead in billowing white clusters, throwing shadows to the earth, and the skies were so blue they hurt his eyes. A breeze blew through the trees, and the air was scented by leaves and grasses sweet with summer warmth. It was the sort of day when you felt that anything was possible.

He sat down in the space he had occupied the night before, where the tree had first spoken to him, studied it for a time, then lay down beneath it and closed his eyes. He gave himself time to relax, then turned his thoughts to his aunt, to the Ard Rhys and her imprisonment inside the Forbidding, embracing the fear such thoughts automatically generated.

And waited.

—Penderrin—

—Tanequil—

—You must have what you came for. You must take what you need—

—What of giving you a part of myself? What of that?—

—You must do so—

He couldn't help himself. —Will I be crippled?—

—You will be enhanced—

—A part of me will be missing?—

—A part of you will be found—

There was no way to make sense of what he was being told. Pen could not decide if he was about to make a good or a bad decision. He could not read the consequences clearly.

—Are you afraid?—

—Yes—

—Fear for yourself has no place in what you would do. Your fear must be for your aunt if you are to save her. A darkwand is born of fear for another's safety. A darkwand responds to selfless need. Do you wish to save your aunt?—

He swallowed hard. —I do—

—Then no sacrifice is too great, even that of your own life—

—Is that what is required?—

—What is required should not matter. Do you wish to proceed?—

He took a deep, steadying breath. Did he? How great a risk was he taking? Things weren't working out the way he had expected. The King of the Silver River had told him he must persuade the tanequil to his cause. But the tanequil didn't seem interested in being persuaded to anything. It seemed to have already made its decision, and what mattered now was how far Pen was willing to go to allow that decision to be implemented.

It was like being trapped in a cave with no light and having to find his way in darkness. There might be pits into which he could fall, and he had no way of knowing where they were.

—Do you wish me to give you what you came for, Penderrin?—

He closed his eyes. —I do—

—Then rise and come to me. Walk to me and place your hands on my body—

He opened his eyes and saw that the tiny roots had withdrawn once more, then rose and moved over to stand before the tree. Gingerly, he pressed his palms against its massive, rough trunk.

—Climb up into me—

He found handholds in the bark and began to climb. It was easier than he would have expected. The bark was strong and did not break off. The effort was considerable, but eventually he reached the lower branches and from there was able to continue on up through the sprawl of limbs as if climbing a ladder. He wasn't sure how high he was supposed to go, and so kept looking for some indication of where he was to stop. But he was deep within the canopy of the tree, its leaves forming a thick curtain about him, before it spoke to him again.

–Stop–

He stopped climbing and looked around. He was at a junction of branches where deep fissures had split the tree's trunk, forming crevices and boles in which birds or small animals might nest. The fissures were old, and in the wounds that had healed the skin had grown back over the soft heartwood, the bark wrapped about the openings anew.

–Look up–

He did so, turning his gaze skyward to the sea of limbs and leaves that spread away overhead.

–Reach up–

He did this, too, and his hand touched a limb that extended some six feet from the trunk, a limb that seemed too small and straight, that lacked twigs or even leaves. Heat radiated from the branch, sudden and unexpected, and Pen jerked away in surprise.

–Take hold–

Pen gripped the branch tentatively, feeling the heat course through his fingers and down his arm. The branch was vibrating, humming deeply as it did so, a strange, mournful sound.

Then the entire tree shook, and its trunk split apart where the branch sprouted, a sharp rending that sent pieces of bark and splinters of wood flying in all directions. Pen ducked his head and closed his eyes, keeping tight hold of the branch, rocking unsteadily with the tanequil's quaking. There was a deep, audible groan of darkest protest, and abruptly the branch came away in Pen's hands. The boy caught himself against the trunk and stared in shock. The tree had cracked wide open where the branch had broken off, and sap was leaking out in a steady stream. The sap was red and viscous and looked like blood. It ran down the trunk in thick rivulets. It dripped from the branch onto his arm.

He was studying it, his left hand braced against the tree for support, his fingers gripping one of the older splits, when the tree groaned again, deep and menacing, and the split closed over his fingers. He screamed in agony and jerked away, feeling flesh and bone tear free as he did so. He reacted at once, but was still too slow. When he stared down at his hand, he saw that his middle two fingers had been severed at the first knuckle. Blood dripped from the ragged wounds and ran down his hand. His finger bones shone white and raw.

Still clutching the tanequil's severed limb, Pen collapsed into a crook in the branches of the tree, pressing his injured hand against his chest, staining his clothing with his blood. For a moment, frozen by pain and shock, he couldn't move. Then, realizing the danger as his blood continued to well

up, he tore free one sleeve of his tunic and wrapped the
cloth about the stubs, compressing it into the wounds.

—A part of you for a part of me—

Pen nodded miserably. He didn't need to be reminded.
The pain ratcheting through his hand and arm was reminder enough.

—Take my limb in your hand—

Holding his shirtsleeve-wrapped fingers tightly against
his chest, he reached down with his right hand and took
the tanequil's limb from his lap, where he had dropped it
moments before. To his surprise, it was still warm and pulsating, as if it retained life, even though it had been severed
from the tree.

—The wood of this limb comes from deep inside me,
where my life is formed. The limb must be forced to the
surface from the soft heartwood and forcibly severed. Such
a sacrifice is necessary if a darkwand is to be shaped to the
use you require. But you must give back what you are given
if the sacrifice is to have value. A piece of your body. A
piece of your heart. Remember this—

Pen closed his eyes and exhaled slowly. The loss of his
fingers in exchange for the loss of the tanequil's limb. He
wasn't likely to forget.

—Climb down from me. Carry my limb with you—

Pen cautiously made his way down from the tree, protecting his injured hand as he did so, cradling the limb in
the crook of his arm. It was a long, tedious descent, and
when he was still ten feet from the ground, he slipped and
fell, striking the earth with force and jarring his hand. Fresh
pain caused him to cry out. He was sweating heavily as he

dragged himself to his feet and leaned back against the ancient trunk. His fingers throbbed, and the fabric wrapping them was soaked with his blood. He felt nauseous and weak.

—Move away from me and sit—

He lurched from the tree and found the patch of ground he had occupied before. He dropped heavily, crossed his legs before him, and bent his head to the earth as he felt everything begin to spin. He glimpsed the tanequil's root tendrils as they reemerged and began to stroke his clothing and boots. He pulled back his pant legs so that the roots could find his skin, so that the tree could make contact with him. He reached out with his own hand to touch them.

—Unwrap your fingers. Take the sap from the end of my limb and place it on your wounds—

Pen hesitated, then unwound the soiled cloth. The stubs of his fingers were red and inflamed, and blood was still leaking from them. He used his good hand to gather sap still oozing from the end of the tanequil's limb, and he rubbed it gingerly into his wounds. Almost instantly, they began to close, the bleeding to stop, and the flesh to heal. The pain, so intense only moments earlier, faded to a dull ache. He stared at his fingers in disbelief.

—Take your knife from your belt—

He did so, frightened anew of what would be asked of him.

—Close your eyes—

Again, he did so.

—You must shape the darkwand now, while the life of the wood is still strong—

He waited. He could not begin to carve the wood until

he could see how to do so. He must be permitted to open
his eyes. But no command to open them came. Instead, the
nature of the touching changed, and communication that
had come in the form of words now came in the form of images. He saw in his mind what he was meant to do, a clear
and unmistakable direction.

Then something odd happened. He felt another hand
on his, covering it, guiding it, and his own began to move
in response. By feel alone, he began the cutting that would
shape the limb into the darkwand. He should have been
terrified that he would make a mistake. The cuts were often
tiny and intricate. They were impossibly time-consuming.
But the images were so clear and his sense of what was
needed so strong that he never wavered in his efforts. And
time did not seem to matter. It was as if time had stopped
and he could use it in whatever manner or measure he
deemed necessary to accomplish his task.

He worked through the remainder of the day and into
the night. He did not eat or drink. He did not move from
where he sat. His concentration was complete as he responded to the tree's steady, calm commands. Nothing distracted him; not the tiny itch of an insect's wings or the
cool whisper of a breeze against his skin. He was in another
world, another time, another life.

It was night when he finished, the moon risen and the
stars come out, their light falling through the forest canopy
in pale, thin streamers, the darkness about him deep and
pervasive. The images stopped, the roots withdrew back
into the earth, and he was alone in the silence. He opened
his eyes and looked down at his lap.

The darkwand lay cradled in his hands, its six-foot length a rich mottled gray and black, the same colors as the tanequil's trunk, gleaming and smooth in a way that should have been impossible for newly carved wood. An intricate pattern of runes wrapped its surface, strange markings that Pen did not recognize and could not interpret. When they were turned to the moonlight, they gleamed as if lit by an inner fire. Pen could still feel unmistakable warmth emanating from the wood, the tanequil's life force firm and strong.

The boy unfolded his legs, which were cramped and sore. His mouth was so dry he could barely open it. He took a few minutes to gather his strength, then got to his feet and began hobbling toward the pool that Cinnaminson had showed him earlier. He carried the darkwand with him; he knew he would carry it everywhere from then on. Slowly, his legs regained their feeling and the cramps disappeared. He listened for signs of life as he walked, but there were none. Even as long as he had been sitting beneath the tree, he was still alone.

He wondered suddenly what had happened to Cinnaminson. She had told him she would come back to him at nightfall. She had promised.

He found the pool and dropped down on his hands and knees to drink. The water was cool and sweet, and he got back a little of his strength. When he had drunk his fill, he stood up again and looked around.

Where was Cinnaminson?

He exhaled in frustration. He didn't like it that she was still gone. He never liked it when she was gone. Losing her was worse than losing his fingers . . .

He stopped himself, remembering suddenly the sensation of another's hand guiding his as he shaped the tanequil's limb into the darkwand, one that allowed him to work blindly, his eyes closed, his reliance on touch alone.

A piece of your body. A piece of your heart.

A terrible certainty swept through him, harsh and implacable, so traumatizing that he could not give voice to it, but only whisper it in the silence of his mind. He thought he had understood. He hadn't. He assumed that the loss of his fingers was enough to balance the scales. It wasn't.

Something more was required.

Cinnaminson.

TWENTY-FIVE

Shadea a'Ru stood at the window of her sleeping chambers and looked out from Paranor's towers over the forested sweep of the land beyond. The sun was rising, a soft golden glow in the east that silhouetted the jagged peaks of the Dragon's Teeth against its bright backdrop and gave promise to the coming of a warm, languorous summer day.

Her lips compressed into a tight, angry line. It would not be such a good day for her. And less so for some others.

She glanced down at the note she held in her hand, at the words written on it, then looked away again. *Idiots!* She brushed absently at her short, spiky blond hair and flexed her shoulders. Her muscles were stiff and tight. She missed the training and fighting that had been so central to her life when she had been a soldier in the Federation army. She missed the discipline and the routine. She had never thought she would feel that way, but after weeks of struggling as Ard Rhys of the Third Druid Order, she was ready to abandon it all for a chance to go back to a time when things were less complicated and more direct.

Her gaze drifted back to the note. It had arrived during the night, while she slept, and she had found it on waking, tied to the leg of the arrow swift. The bird's dark, fierce face had peered out at her from its enclosure, almost daring her to reach inside. But it was her bird, one of the many she had appropriated and trained to carry her messages from her co-conspirators and servants in the plot against Grianne Ohmsford. Its countenance only mirrored the intensity that could be found in her own.

She knew the bird. *Split* was its name, chosen for the strange wedge in its tail feathers, an accident of birth. The arrow swift was one of those assigned to Traunt Rowan on his departure to the Northland; it had been sent by him.

She had reached inside for the message, untied it from Split's leg, withdrawn it from the cage, opened it, and her face had gone dark with rage immediately.

THE BOY AND HIS COMPANIONS ESCAPED FROM TAUPO ROUGH.

HAVE FOLLOWED THEM INTO THE KLU.

And lost them there, of course, though the writer had been careful not to say so.

She looked back at the message again, still furious with its contents and its incompetent sender. She had expected better of Traunt Rowen. She had expected better of Pyson Wence, as well, and better still of the two of them working together to track that boy!

She gritted her teeth. Why was it so difficult for anyone to find and hold him? The effort had cost Terek Molt his life. It had cost Aphasia Wye her respect, a respect she had thought nothing could diminish. What would it cost her this time? The lives of two more of her allies, men whose support she could scarcely afford to lose, even if they were proving less competent than she had imagined possible? Her respect for them had long since vanished, so there was no danger of losing that.

She crumpled the note in her hand, then set it in a small bowl on her desk, fired it with magic, and scattered the ashes out the window. She watched the breeze carry the ashes away and wished her anger and disappointment could be made to vanish as easily.

What was she going to have to do to finish this business?

For a moment, for just an instant, she toyed with the idea of breaking off the hunt entirely. It was requiring much more time and effort than she cared to spend and netting no favorable results at all. She had the boy's parents safely locked away in her dungeons. Couldn't she just wait for him to come for them? He would surely do so, once he found out where they were, and it would be easy enough to make him aware.

Her frustration building toward a headache, she rubbed at her temples with her fingers. The trouble with ignoring him was that she was almost certain she knew what he was doing. He was trying to find a way to reach his aunt. She had no idea how he planned to do that and believed it beyond his or anyone else's capability. But she could not chance being wrong. If he had found a way into the Forbidding, if he had discovered an avenue about which she knew nothing, then she had to stop him from using it. Because if he managed the impossible and actually reached Grianne Ohmsford from Paranor's side of the wall, he might find a way to guide her back again.

If that happened, Shadea knew she was finished. They were all finished, all who had conspired with her.

The chance of that happening was so small that it was scarcely measurable, but she knew better than to put anything past the Ohmsfords. Their history spoke for itself. They had survived impossible situations before, several generations of them. They were imbued with both magic and luck, and the combination had kept them from harm more times than anyone could count.

She could not afford to allow that to happen again.

So she would leave things as they were. She would allow Traunt Rowan and Pyson Wence to continue to hunt down the boy. Perhaps Aphasia Wye still tracked him as well, even though she had heard nothing from her assassin in days. One never knew about that creature. One could never predict.

The ashes of the burned note were gone, turned to dust and blown away. She breathed in the morning air, calming herself, reassuring herself that everything was going to be all right. In the next few days, she would journey to Arishaig to meet with Sen Dunsidan. The Prime Minister was seeking her support for a sustained assault on the Freeborn, a course of action on which they had already tacitly agreed but had yet to act. The Federation required the backing of the Druids if they were to succeed in their plans

to break the stalemate on the Prekkendorran and advance
into Callahorn. The Prime Minister needed to know that
Shadea, as head of the Druid order, would not act to stop
him. She, in turn, needed to know that he would continue
to support her as Ard Rhys.

She was less concerned about his backing than she had
been at the beginning, when her support was so small and
her position as acting Ard Rhys so tenuous. But things had
changed. Once she'd bedded Gerand Cera and made him
her consort, she began working to gain the support of his
followers as well. One by one, using promises and threats,
she had subverted them. Even though Cera still thought of
himself as leader of his own faction, she had long since replaced him in that position.

She glanced at the rumpled bed to one side and grimaced. She had played at that game long enough. She had
allowed him enough liberties. It was time to put an end to
it. It was time to toss him from her bed and from her life.

Intent on going out to confer with a handful of those on
whom she believed she could depend, she threw off her
nightclothes and dressed in her Druid robes. Matters would
get rough before the day was out, and she must know who
would stand with her when they did. She knew better than
to leave such things to chance.

Wrapped in her black garments, her chain of office hung
about her neck, she was moving toward the chamber door
when it burst open and Gerand Cera strode through, his
hatchet face dark with anger.

"We have been betrayed, Shadea," he announced without preamble. He flung off his robe and threw himself

down in one of the cushioned chairs. "By the very ally you were so confident would not dare to do so."

She stared at him. "Sen Dunsidan?"

A sneer twisted his lean face. "Sen Dunsidan. Last night, the Elves launched an airship strike against his army. The strike failed because the Federation forces knew about it in advance and were waiting. They have invented a weapon that produces a light beam of such intensity and power that it can burn an airship right out of the sky. It did so in response to the attack, destroying virtually the entire Elven fleet before the Federation airship that bore it was damaged and had to set down."

He leaned forward. "But that was just the beginning. During the airship battle, the Federation army attacked the Elven defensive lines and broke through. The Elves were driven right off the Prekkendorran. They might still be running, for all I know. Their allies are trying to hang on, but they're surrounded. I wouldn't give them much chance."

He shook his head in disgust. "So tell me, Shadea. What do you think of your precious Prime Minister now?" His sharp eyes fixed on her. "You didn't know about this attack beforehand, did you? I would hate to think you were keeping things from me."

She hadn't known a thing about it, of course. She was as surprised by the news as he was. But there was no reason for her to tell him so. Better that he thought her one step ahead of him.

"There was some discussion about it. I hadn't thought he intended to act so quickly."

"It would have been nice if you had told me."

She shrugged. "We both keep some things to ourselves, Gerand. Don't pretend otherwise. As I said, I hadn't thought he was going to do this until later. Apparently an opportunity presented itself that he couldn't afford to pass up. We can hardly begrudge him that."

Gerand Cera frowned. "I don't like it that he's acted without seeking our approval. It will look to everyone as if he no longer cares whether we stand with him or against him. It will look as if he considers our support irrelevant."

Just so, she was thinking. Sen Dunsidan would have to be called to account once she was able to confront him. It might be that it was time for her to end their relationship in a way that left no doubt as to who was the real power in the Four Lands.

"This weapon," she said, changing the subject. "It doesn't sound like anything I have ever heard of. It sounds as if it employs a form of magic."

Gerand Cera shook his head in disagreement. "The Prime Minister doesn't have the use of magic."

"Perhaps he has acquired the aid of someone who does." Her eyes locked on his. "One of us."

He snorted. "Who? Who would want to give aid to Sen Dunsidan, knowing that you would view it as a—" He stopped himself. "Are you thinking of Iridia?"

"Do we know where she is? Did we ever find out where she went after she left here?"

Cera shook his head slowly. "No. But she wouldn't dare to betray us. She knows what would happen if she did."

She cringed at his use of the word *us*, at the implication that he was somehow a part of the decision-making process, when in fact he was little more than another obstacle. She glanced away to hide her disgust, then turned and walked to the window. She stood there for a moment, thinking.

"What do you intend to do?" he asked, rising and coming over to put his hands on her shoulders.

She felt the strength of those hands as they gripped her. They were possessive and commanding as they turned her about to face him. They suggested in no uncertain terms that he was the one in control. She smiled agreeably as he leaned down and kissed her mouth. She kissed him back, waited for the kiss to end, then broke away.

"I intend to drink my morning cup of tea before speaking with those in the order who will keep an eye on things in our absence."

He stared after her. "Our absence? Are we going somewhere?"

"To confront Sen Dunsidan, of course."

She had told him nothing of her plans to visit Arishaig before this. The reason was simple. She had not intended for him to go. She still didn't, but it was best to let him think she did.

"To confront him? In his own home, his own city, surrounded by his own people?" Gerand Cera considered the prospect. "A bold course of action, Shadea. How safe can we expect to be?"

She shrugged, pouring tea into cups, slipping into his the tiny pill she had been saving for that moment and watching it dissolve instantly. "We are Druids, Gerand. We can't afford to worry about being safe. We can't afford to be seen to be afraid."

She handed him his tea, stood in front of him as she sipped from her own, and watched with satisfaction as he drank.

"Sit with me on the bed." She took his arm and moved over. She pulled him down next to her. "Perhaps we needn't go down right away. The tea is making me warm all over. I need to find a way to cool off."

She smiled and sipped again. "Come, Gerand. Finish your tea. Don't keep me waiting."

He drank it in a single gulp and reached for her. His appetites were so pathetic, so predictable. She eased away playfully. He was still grinning when the drug took effect. An abrupt change came over his hatchet features. His face went slack and empty, and he lurched forward, falling onto his side.

That was quick, she thought. She rose and looked down at him, at the way his eyes rolled frantically from side to side as he tried to understand what was happening to him. She eased a pillow under his head, then reached for his legs and lifted them onto the bed so that he was lying stretched out along its length.

"Comfortable, Gerand? Much better to rest while this is happening." Knowing he could no longer reach for her, could no longer move at all for that matter, she bent over him. His lungs and his heart still worked, but not very efficiently. He barely had the strength of a baby.

"I've given you a drug," she explained, sitting next to him. "It saps the strength from your muscles and leaves you paralyzed. It only lasts a little while. There is no trace of its presence afterwards. Unlike poison, for example, which I considered using but decided against. After all, I can't afford to be seen as a murderess."

She leaned close. "You see what is to happen, I expect. Your eyes tell me you know. So now you no longer love me. Now, you despise me. Love is like that. It only lasts for as long as both parties require it, and then it becomes a burden, which is one reason I do not permit myself to love anyone too much. You should have learned that lesson a long time ago. I am surprised you didn't. Now you must learn it the hard way."

He was staring fixedly at her, and she read the hatred in his eyes. In contrast, his face was empty of expression, and it seemed as if the eyes must belong to someone else. Yet the eyes were really all that was left of him. Everything else had been stripped away by the drug.

She leaned down and kissed him lightly on the forehead. "Try not to think too harshly of me, Gerand. You would have done the same, if you had paid closer attention to how I looked at you."

Then she took the pillow from under his head, placed it firmly over his face, and pressed down on it with all of her considerable strength until he stopped breathing.

When the cell door closed and the locking bolts were thrown, Bek Ohmsford was engulfed in blackness. He sat down, waiting for his eyes to adjust, and after a time they did. A sliver of light crept under the door and through the seams on the latch side, permitting him just enough illumination to find his way around. The cell was tiny, and it didn't take him long to explore it. He found nothing that would help. The walls, floor, and ceiling were hewn from bedrock, and the only exit was through the barred door. The room contained only the bed, straw, and bucket he had seen upon being brought in. There were no implements that might be used for tunneling or prying. There were no fissures or seams on which to employ such a tool in any event. And there was nothing he could use for a weapon.

He sat on the bed and thought about his situation for a long time. If Shadea was to be believed—and he had no reason to assume she wasn't—there was a guard stationed on the other side of the door, watching for any attempt at escape. Down the hall and up the stairs, there would be others. A relay was in place to send word faster than he could run, should he attempt to break free. He couldn't know all the particulars, but he had to assume the guards had a form of communication that would allow them to know if one or more of their number had been overpowered.

Time passed, and eventually the door opened far enough to permit a Gnome Hunter to slide a tray of food inside before the locks were thrown anew. Accustomed by then to the dark, Bek was blinded by the sudden glare of torchlight and barely caught a glimpse of what was happening before the door was closed again. He took that into account as he continued to make his plans, sitting on the floor of his cell and eating his meal. The food, he found, was reasonable; apparently, Shadea didn't intend to do away with him through starvation. But he hadn't

changed his mind that she intended to do away with him
in some manner.

He waited through three more meals, measuring the
time it took the Gnome to pull back the lock bolt, open the
cell door, slide the food tray inside, close the door, and
throw the bolt again. It was clear to him that any escape
would have to come then. It would not be possible to escape if he had to break down or lever open the door. The
noise such an effort would require, even if time and opportunity allowed for it, would alert the Gnome Hunters immediately, and any chance of surprise would be lost.

Even then, once he was through, what would he find on
the other side? At least one Gnome Hunter, but how many
more would be keeping him company? If he were Shadea,
he would insist on at least two, possibly more, being present anytime the cell door was opened. That would eliminate the chance that he could successfully overpower one
guard without alerting the others.

He began positioning himself so that he could see something of the hallway outside when the cell door was
cracked, and through two further meals, he tried to catch a
glimpse of what was out there. But it was impossible to see
more than a little of what lay beyond, never enough to be
certain. He did catch sight of movement once, a shadow
thrown by torchlight that indicated the presence of another man. But it was clear that he would have to make his
break into the hallway without knowing how many
Gnomes he would find.

How could he do that and still make certain they could
not sound the alarm?

He puzzled it through with an increasing sense of desperation; he needed to find a solution quickly, because time was slipping away and with it his chances of freeing Rue and warning Penderrin. In spite of what Shadea had learned of Taupo Rough, he had to assume that his son was still free and his exact whereabouts still undiscovered. But that could change in a hurry.

He decided in the end that what he must do was use the wishsong in a blanket assault, stunning everyone within hearing distance and giving him a chance to get up the steps to confront whomever he had missed. It was a long shot at best, one he did not much care to take. But sitting in his cell and waiting for the inevitable was madness. He hated putting Rue at risk, but he knew that she would want him to if it meant giving them a chance, however slim, of reaching Pen.

He decided to try for one more look, using the next feeding as a trial run for determining exactly where he should stand to get through the door to the guards. He waited patiently, using his time to run repeated rehearsals of what he would do, working and reworking his timing, his movements, everything that would be required of him.

When the door finally opened, he was standing just to the open side, watching the movements of the Gnome Hunter as he knelt to slide the food tray inside, counting the seconds from the time the door opened until it closed again. It took twelve seconds. He would have to act quickly. He would have to summon the wishsong and hold it within himself until the locks were thrown. Then he would have to sprint through the door, directing the

magic down the hallway as he emerged, a quick and certain strike.

He sat in the darkness and thought about how little
chance he had of making this plan work. Wasn't there a
better one? Wasn't there something else he could do?

He was just finishing his meal when a piece of paper was
slid under the door. He stared at it for a moment, then
reached down to retrieve it. Bent close to the bottom of the
door, where the thin light gave just enough illumination to
allow him to make out the words, he read:

HELP IS COMING.

Bek recognized the writing immediately. It was the same
hand that had penned the note he and Rue had received on
their arrival at Paranor, the one that had warned them not
to trust anyone. He had never discovered the identity of
the writer, and in truth, he had forgotten all about the note
until that moment.

Lying on the floor next to the crack beneath the cell
door, he read it again. Could he believe it? Could he trust
that the writer would be able to find a way to free him?
How long could he afford to wait to find out?

He stared blindly into the darkness of his prison, searching for the answers.

TWENTY-SIX

H e heard the voices first, soft and insistent, joined
as one, humming and then singing, the words in-
decipherable, but their sound sharp and clear and
compelling.

–Penderrin– she whispered from out of the confluence.
–I've come back–

But it wasn't her voice, and he knew that when he
looked, it wouldn't be her. It wouldn't be anybody at all.

–I said I would come back. I promised, didn't I–

He lay where he had fallen asleep near dawn, exhausted
from searching for her after realizing where she might be
and what she might have done. Frantic with worry, he had
torn through the ancient forest like a madman, plunging
through the dark trunks and layered shadows, calling her
name until he was too tired to continue. Then, heartsick
and drained of hope, he had collapsed. It couldn't be true,
he kept telling himself. His suspicions were unfounded and
fueled by his weariness and the shock of losing his fingers.
It was all a lie of the mind, born of his misinterpretation of

the tanequil's words, of the fears raised by the tree's dark reminder that its gift of the darkwand required a like gift from
him.

Of the body. Of the heart.

—Penderrin, wake up. Open your eyes—

But he kept his eyes closed, wrapped in the comforting
darkness that not seeing her afforded, unwilling to let that
last shred of hope fall away. He moved his damaged hand
beneath him, feeling with his good fingers for the ones that
were missing, finding the stumps healed over and the pain
gone. It wasn't so bad, he supposed, losing parts of two fingers. Not for what he had been given in turn. Not for what
it meant to his efforts at finding his aunt. Not for what it
meant to the future of the Four Lands. It wasn't so bad.

But losing Cinnaminson was.

"Why did you do it?" he asked finally, his voice so soft
that he could barely hear his own words.

Silence greeted his query, a long and empty sweep of
time in which the voices grew quiet and the sounds of the
forest slowly filled the void their departure created.

"Why, Cinnaminson?"

Still no answer. Suddenly fearful that he had lost her
completely, he lifted his head and looked around. He was
alone, sprawled on the grassy patch on which he had fallen
asleep the night before, the darkwand resting on the
ground beside him, its glossy length shimmering, its carved
runes dark and mysterious.

"Cinnaminson?" he called.

—It was a chance for me to be something I couldn't otherwise be— She spoke to him from out of the air. —I am free

from my body, Pen. Free from my blindness. Free in a way
I could never be otherwise. I can fly everywhere. I can see
what I could never see before. Not in the way I do now. I
am not alone anymore. I have found a family. I have sisters.
I have a mother and father—

He didn't know what to say. She sounded so happy, but
her happiness made him feel miserable. He hated himself
for his reaction, but he couldn't find a way to change it.

"It was your choice to do this?" he demanded, his words
sounding woeful and plaintive, even to him.

—Of course, Penderrin. Did you think I was forced to become one of them? It was my choice to shed my body—

"But you knew I wouldn't be given the tanequil's branch
any other way, didn't you?"

—I knew it was the right thing to do. Just as you did,
when you agreed to come here to find the tree and to seek
help in freeing your aunt—

"But you knew," he persisted, desperate to wring from
her one small concession. "You knew that becoming an
aeriad would help me. You knew that giving yourself to the
tanequil was what it would take for the tanequil to give me
its limb."

Her hesitation was momentary. —I knew—

She was moving all around him, a part of the ether, a disembodied voice buttressed by the soft singing and humming of her sister aeriads, her new family, her new life. He
tried to see her in the sound of her voice, but he could not
quite manage it. His memory of her was strong, but his efforts to form a picture from her voice alone were insuffi-
cient. He didn't want her back in still life; he wanted her

back as a living, breathing human being, and the images he managed to conjure failed to capture her that way.

He sank back wearily. "When did you decide to do this?" His voice broke as despair threatened to overwhelm him. "Why didn't you tell me? Why didn't you talk to me about it?"

The singing rose and fell like a wave of emotion born on a shift in the wind. —What would I have said to you? That I love you so much that I cannot imagine life without you, but that I am old enough to understand that loving someone that much isn't always the only measuring stick for making a life with them? That choosing love should never be selfish—

"If you loved me that much . . ."

—I *love* you that much, Penderrin. Nothing has changed. I love you still. But you were sent here for another reason, one too important to sacrifice for anything—even for me. I know this. I knew it from the moment that I heard the aeriads speaking to me. They were telling me what was needed—not directly, not in so many words, but in the way they sang to me, in the sound of their voices. I knew—

He shook his head. "I don't think I can do this without you. I can't even think straight. I can barely move."

Matched by the voices of her sisters, soothing as a breeze on a hot summer day, her voice trilled with soft laughter. —Oh, Pen, it will pass! You will go on to do what you were sent to do! You will find your aunt and bring her home again. I am already a memory, already fading away—

He stared into space, into the place from where she

spoke to him, trying to make himself accept what she was telling him, and failing.

The voices sighed and hummed and sighed some more. –Do not be sad, Penderrin– she whispered. –I am not sad. I am happy. You can hear it in my voice, can't you? I made a choice. The aeriads asked me to join them, to help you and myself. While you slept, I went with them from the surface of the earth to the Downbelow. From the sunlight and air world of Father Tanequil to the darkness and earth world of Mother Tanequil. She roots deep, Pen, to provide for her children, to give them life, to allow them the freedom she can never have. I saw the truth of what she is. Of what they both are. Joined as one—Father, the limbs; Mother, the roots. One lives aboveground, but the other must forever live below. She gets lonely. She needs company. I was a gift to her from Father Tanequil. But it was what I wanted. Perhaps he knew that when he sent me to her. Perhaps he knows us both better than we know ourselves. They are very old spirits, Pen. They were here when the world was born, when the Word was still young and the Faerie creatures newly made. We are children in their eyes–

"We are Men!" he snapped. "And they don't know what's right for us! They don't know anything about us because they aren't like us! Don't you see? We were manipulated! We were tricked!"

A long silence punctuated his angry words. –No, Pen. We did what we thought was best. Both of us. I don't regret it. I won't. We have the lives we have chosen, whether fate or the tanequil or something larger pushed us to that choice–

He took a long slow breath to calm himself. She was wrong; he knew she was wrong. But there was nothing he could do about it. It was over and done with. He would have to live with it, although he couldn't imagine how he would ever do that.

"Did it hurt at all?" he asked quietly. "Your transformation? Was there any pain?"

–None, Pen–

"But what of your body? Did it just . . . ?"

He couldn't finish the thought, unable to bear the image it conjured—an image of her turning to dust, disintegrating.

Laughter greeted his failure, gentle and soothing. –Kept safe and unchanging in her arms, I sleep with Mother Tanequil, Pen, down within the earth, in the darkness and quiet, where she takes root. She nourishes me, so that I can live. If I were to die, I would cease to exist, even as an aeriad–

She is down in the ravine, he thought suddenly. He was finally beginning to understand. The tanequil was both male and female, mother and father to the aeriads, a trunk joining limbs at one end to roots at the other. Cinnaminson was in the keeping of the latter, down in the shadowy depths they had crossed over on the bridge. Down where something huge had stirred awake on their passing.

But still whole, she was telling him. Still alive in human form.

"Cinnaminson," he said, an idea coming to sudden life, a plan to implement it taking shape. "I need to see you again before I go. I need to say good-bye. It isn't enough just to hear your voice. It doesn't feel real to me. Can you take me to where you sleep?"

There was a long pause. —You cannot have me back, Pen. Mother Tanequil will not let me go. Not even if you beg—

She recognized his intentions all too well, but his mind was already made up. He was terrified of what he might find if he did it, half certain that she was already reduced to bones and dust, that her vision of herself as still being whole was a subterfuge fostered by the tree. But he couldn't leave without knowing, no matter how devastating the truth. If there was a way to set her free again, to take her with him . . .

"I won't do anything but make sure that you are safe," he lied. "I just need to see you one last time."

—This is a mistake— she trilled, her voice rising amid those of her sisters, sharp with rebuke. —You shouldn't ask it of me—

He took a deep breath. "But I am asking." He waited a moment. "Please, Cinnaminson."

The voices of the aeriads hummed, a long sustained chord that matched the sound of wind whispering through the leaves of trees, soft and resilient. He forced himself to keep silent, to say nothing more, to wait.

—I am afraid for you, Pen— she said finally.

"I am afraid for myself," he admitted.

A pause followed, and the humming died away.

—Come with me, then, if you must. If you can remember my warning—

He exhaled softly. He was not likely to forget.

* * *

On the far side of the ravine, Khyber Elessedil stood at the foot of the stone bridge, listening to the soft moan of the wind. She had been standing there for the better part of an hour, using her admittedly unskilled Druid senses to scan the forest for sign of Pen and Cinnaminson. It wasn't the first time she had done so, but the results were the same. She might as well have been casting about the Blue Divide for a sailor lost at sea, for all the good it was doing her.

One hand clutched the Elfstones. She kept them close on the theory that they might at some point prove useful in her search. They were doing her about as much good as her Druid skills.

Frustrated, she turned away. She hated feeling so helpless. Ever since the safety lines tied to Pen and Cinnaminson had dropped away as if severed by an invisible blade, she had known that the fate of her friends was out of her hands. More than once she had considered trying to cross over herself—and she wasn't afraid to try, in spite of the warning on the stone—but she didn't want to do anything that would jeopardize Pen's efforts to secure the darkwand.

She looked back into the gardens, her dazzlingly colorful prison. Trapped in all that beauty and unable to enjoy it, her concentration on Pen and on the island and on the Druids tracking them and on time running out—thinking about it all made her want to scream. But there was nothing she could do.

Nothing but wait.

She stalked over to where Kermadec sat talking with Tagwen, trading stories of the old days, when Grianne

Ohmsford was new to the position of Ard Rhys and they were just beginning in her service.

"Do you think there might be another way across?" she asked abruptly, kneeling next to them, her voice urgent. "Another bridge or a narrows we might vault?" She exhaled sharply. "I don't think I can stand waiting another minute without doing something."

Kermadec stared at her impassively. "There might be. If you want to take a look, you can. I can send Atalan or Barek with you."

She shook her head. "I can manage alone. I just need to do something besides stand around."

Tagwen frowned into his beard, but didn't say anything.

"You won't lose your way, will you, Elven girl?" the Maturen pressed. "I wouldn't want to have to come looking for you."

"I can find my way."

"If you discover anything, you will come back and tell us?" Tagwen pressed suddenly.

"Yes, yes!" she snapped. "I'm not going to do anything rash or foolish!" Her irritation got the better of her for a moment, and she took a deep breath. "I just want to see if that ravine goes all the way around or if there are other places to cross. I won't attempt anything on my own."

She didn't know if they believed her or not, but if they did, they ought to be less trusting. She fully intended to attempt a crossing if a place to make one could be found. She should have gone with Pen and Cinnaminson in the first place, but she had allowed her instincts to be overruled.

She stood up, giving them a bright smile. "I don't expect

to be gone long. I probably won't get much beyond what we can see from standing right here, but it will make me feel better to have tried."

Their eyes fixed on her, as if searching for the truth behind her words, neither replied. She turned away quickly and started off, choosing to go south, where the gardens opened out toward a thinning woods and a set of hills. She could see the ravine as it snaked its way into those hills, disappearing finally into the horizon. In truth, she didn't have much hope that she would succeed in her quest. She mostly hoped that the distraction would help with the waiting.

She was so intent on her efforts to get clear of the others that she failed to detect with her normally reliable Druid training the shadowy form lying in wait directly ahead. She missed it entirely as it slipped away at her approach and circled back around toward the bridge.

Pen Ohmsford followed the low, vibrant humming of the aeriads as they led him on through the trees and back toward the dark cut of the ravine. The light casting his shadow before him as he walked, he could measure the direction they were taking from the slant of the sun's thin rays through the heavy canopy. He tried to hear Cinnaminson in the mix of aeriad voices, but he could not detect a noticeable difference in any of them. She was being assimilated into their order, and he could not stop himself from thinking that if he did not reach her soon, there would be no way to separate her from the others, even if her body was still intact.

Thinking of her body at rest beneath the earth in the cradle of the tanequil's roots made him wonder about the condition of the bodies of the other aeriads. For their spirits to survive in aeriad form, their bodies must be kept whole, as well. But how was that accomplished? He was feeling less and less certain about what it was he was going to find. He was starting to think that his request was a mistake.

Yet he kept on, drawn by the humming, by the promise it offered that he might still find a way to bring Cinnaminson back to him. Both hands gripped the polished length of the darkwand, the only weapon he possessed aside from his long knife. The darkwand was a talisman of magic meant to be used to breach the wall of the Forbidding. But it had come from the wood of the tree. Could it be used to penetrate the tangle of the tanequil's roots? Could it be employed in some way to free the Rover girl?

It was wishful thinking, seductive and empty of promise. There was nothing to suggest the darkwand would do him the slightest bit of good in his effort to bring Cinnaminson out of the ravine. But it was all he had to rely on, and so even in the face of the patent improbability of it helping him, he held out hope that it would.

Time slipped away. He was beginning to lose his sense of direction as the tree limbs tightened overhead and the light faded to a dull wash. But the voices stayed strong, the humming steady, and so he persevered, his determination unshaken. Now and again, he thought to call out to Cinnaminson, to reassure himself that she was still there, but he restrained himself from doing so, knowing that it

suggested a weakness in himself he did not want to acknowledge.

Eventually, the ground began to slope, then to drop
sharply, and the dark crease of the ravine loomed ahead
through the trees. As the trilling of the aeriads intensified,
Pen felt his hopes sink further; there was unmistakable joy
and expectation in those voices. Tightening his grip on the
darkwand, he followed the singing to a narrow trail that led
downward. The brush and trees a concealing wall, the trail
was invisible from anywhere but where he stood. He descended slowly, tracking the trail's switchbacks, keeping
close to the ravine wall so he would not slip. One glance
down revealed that if he was to do so, he could fall a long
way.

As he went deeper, the light grew ever more faint, until
everything was shrouded in gloom. Spots of iridescence
given off by organisms growing on the plant life began to
shimmer softly in the enfolding darkness. The ravine had
the feel of a maw, its dark, wet earth sprouting jagged rocks
that jutted like teeth.

I am a fool to come here, he thought.

Yet he continued, unwilling to accept that the danger he
faced might be too great or the consequences of his effort
too terrible. Would Cinnaminson lead him to his doom,
even in her newly adopted form? He could not make himself believe so. No, he decided after considering the possibility. She would keep him safe. She would take him to
Mother Tanequil. She would do as he had asked, and he
would have his chance to free her.

Then the trail ended, and he was at the bottom of the

ravine. A vast tangle of roots stretched away before him. The smallest of them were closest, some no larger than strands of human hair. The largest were farther back, barely visible through the enfolding darkness and the pale wash of diffused sunlight, and many were thicker than his body. They lay in twisted heaps, loose and coiled, half-emerged from the earth in which they had buried themselves.

Pen drew to a halt, uncertain about what to do next. All around him now and no longer moving forward, the aeriads hummed and sang. He glanced about for help, but there was no help to be found. He had gotten as far as he was going to get without doing something on his own, and he had no idea what that something should be.

"Cinnaminson?" he called softly.

Ahead, the tree roots shifted, and in their slow grating and scraping he heard the sound of his own death. Like snakes, they were coiling and uncoiling in anticipation of wrapping about him, of squeezing him until there was no breath left in his body. He felt himself begin to shake as the image eroded his courage, and he tightened his grip once more on the darkwand.

"Cinnaminson!" he called again, louder.

As if in response to his cry, the tree roots parted where their wall was thickest, and he saw revealed in the pale trickle of sunlight and tiny flashes of iridescence the bodies of dozens of young girls. Thousands of tiny roots wrapped about them, cradling them in nests of dark, earth-fed fiber, their ends attached to the exposed skin where clothing had rotted and fallen away. Their eyes and mouths were closed, and they appeared to be deep in sleep, locked in dreams that he could only imagine. They must have been breathing, but he was too far away to be certain.

Then he saw Cinnaminson. She was off to one side in an area in which the tendrils had not yet grown so thick, and her body was still mostly exposed and unfettered. She slept the sleep of the others, and most probably dreamed their dreams. But her place among them was newer, her coming clearly more recent.

He didn't stop to think about what he should do. He simply started toward her, compelled by his determination to get close enough to touch her and, by doing so, to wake her and then to free her. He didn't know how he would manage it or even if he could. He only knew he had to try.

—Pen, no— Cinnaminson cried out, her voice separating suddenly from those of the other aeriads.

Instantly, the tanequil's roots began to shift, the rasp and scrape of fiber on earth and stone so menacing that Pen froze in midstride and brought the darkwand up like a shield. The wall had re-formed in front of him, barring him from getting any closer, telling him in no uncertain terms that he had transgressed. Tendrils stroked the exposed skin of his hands as the tree roots closest to him lifted out of the earth. In his mind, he could hear a hiss of warning, a sound so soft it was like the rustle of sand on old wood.

—Don't come any closer— It was the sound of a serpent's tongue sliding from a scaly mouth. —Go back to where you came from—

—Please, Pen— he heard Cinnaminson whisper. —Please, go away. Leave me where I am—

He wanted to ignore the warning, to go to her, to reach

out to what was still real and substantive about her, to free her of that nightmare. The tanequil had given her the boundless world of an unfettered spirit, of the aeriads for whom it provided such freedom, but it was feeding on her, as well. He could tell that much just from looking. Did she realize that? Did she understand what was happening to her?

But he sensed, even as he asked these questions, that it didn't matter what she knew or how she might respond to knowing. What mattered was that she was content. She was the tree's captive, a slave to the roots that formed its feminine half, and they were not about to let her go for any reason. If he tried to take her, he would be killed. Then no one would know what had happened to her and no one would ever come to set her free.

He closed his eyes against what he was thinking, against his feelings of frustration and helplessness. He should do something, but there was nothing he could do. He had lost her all over again.

–Good-bye, Penderrin– he heard her say to him.

Her voice rose and fell to blend with the voices of the other aeriads before finally disappearing into them completely. Then the voices faded entirely, and she was gone.

Cinnaminson.

Aware of the sudden silence, he stood staring into space. Even the tree roots had gone still. Their tangled lengths lay limp and unmoving before him, a wall that he must breach. But he lacked the means to do so. He looked down at the darkwand, wondering anew if it might provide him the magic that was needed. But the purpose of the talisman was to help him gain access to Grianne Ohmsford, not to Cinnaminson. The darkwand could breach the wall of the Forbidding, but not the wall of the tanequil's roots. Nothing had happened to suggest otherwise. No magic had surfaced when his passage through the roots had been denied. No magic had emerged to help him.

His throat tightened as he realized that there was nothing more he could do. He would have to abandon his hopes of freeing her. He would have to leave her where she was. He would have to take the darkwand and travel to Paranor. He would have to attempt to cross over into the Forbidding and rescue the Ard Rhys. Cinnaminson had given herself to the tanequil so that he might do so. What was the point of her sacrifice if he failed to take advantage of it?

But it meant risking the possibility that he might never have a chance to come back for her.

He closed his eyes and took a deep breath. "Good-bye," he said softly to the darkness.

Then he turned away, walked back to the trail that had brought him down into the ravine, and began to climb.

TWENTY-SEVEN §

The hand shook him gently awake, and Drumundoon's familiar voice whispered, "Captain, they're coming." The Federation army. Preparing to attack.

Pied Sanderling opened his eyes to dawn's faint glow on the eastern horizon, scanned the maze of hills and ravines that surrounded him, and waited for the buzzing in his ears to quiet. Every muscle and joint in his body ached, but he couldn't very well complain. He was lucky to be alive at all.

He closed his eyes again, remembering. The explosion of fire, rocking the *Asashiel*, sweeping away railguns and deck crew. The plummet of the craft toward the earth as he clung to his safety line and called in vain for Markenstall. The impact of the airship as it slammed into a grove of wide-limbed conifers, breaking them apart, leaving him hanging from their shattered boughs. Miraculously, in one piece. No broken bones or severed limbs and no cuts or slashes deep enough to bleed him dry while he waited to be found.

And found he had been, almost at once, by Elven Home
Guard in retreat from the airfield, who had watched his
vessel fall out of the sky. His own troops, who had recognized him instantly and cut him down, pleading with him
not to die, begging him to hold on until they could get
help. He had been half-delirious then, burned and
shocked, fighting demons that he imagined still flew overhead and hunted him as a hawk would a mouse seeking
refuge where there was none to be found.

He had come around eventually, sometime during the
long nighttime retreat through the cut to the hills north of
the Prekkendorran, getting his first good look at the ragtag
condition of his valiant Home Guard. Obedient to his orders, abandoned by Elven army regulars, they had stood
alone against the hordes of Federation attackers that had
swept across the airfield. The Home Guard had tried to
hold their position, a hopeless task that, in the end, had
failed. He had learned this much from Drumundoon, who
had found him somehow during the night and stayed with
him. He had learned, as well, that the Elven sector of the
Prekkendorran was lost and that the Free-born allies, besieged on three sides, were in danger of being overrun. The
battle was still being fought, a mix of Bordermen, Dwarves,
and mercenaries fighting under the command of the charis-
matic Dwarf Vaden Wick. But disheartened by the death of
their King, broken by the swiftness of their defeat, the
Elves had abandoned the field.

"We need you, Captain," Drum had hissed at him, bent
close so that only Pied could hear. "We need you desperately."

Pied could not quite understand why his aide was saying that. There was no longer anything he could do. He was a Captain of the Home Guard relieved of his command, reprimanded and humiliated by his King in a way that left no doubt about his future. Nothing could change that, especially with Kellen Elessedil dead and the Elven army scattered to the four winds.

But that was just the point, Drum had said. Kellen Elessedil *was* dead, and so was everyone who had heard him dismiss Pied as Captain of the Home Guard. The whole incident might never have happened, and in truth it would be best if everyone thought it hadn't. Look at how matters stood. Stow Fraxon, who commanded the Elven army regulars, was dead, killed in the Federation assault during the night. All of the airship commanders were dead. Most of the other commanders were scattered or lost. Of all Elven army units assigned to the Prekkendorran, only the Home Guard was still intact, and only Pied Sanderling was still with his command.

"We have Elven Hunters coming in from all over, Captain," Drum whispered. "They think you are their only hope, the only commander of the only unit still making a stand. Think about it. If they can't depend on you, who *can* they depend on? You still command, no matter what Kellen Elessedil might have said. Besides, a dead King can't do anything to save us from his mess. Only a live Captain of the Home Guard can do that."

Pied slept for a time, too tired to argue the point. When he woke, it was midday, and the Home Guard was deep in the tangle of hills north of the flats, pulling together the strays and the lost, linking up with other units that still looked to stand and fight somewhere, in spite of what had happened the night before. Most were in shock, but word had spread that Pied Sanderling had led a successful counterattack against the Federation and damaged the airship and weapon that had destroyed their fleet. While others had run, the Captain of the Home Guard had stood his ground. If there was any hope for the Elves, it lay with him.

Pied heard the talk, even though the words were whispered and the looks cast his way furtive. Drum hadn't exaggerated—everyone was depending on him. He might have been an ex-Captain of the Home Guard twenty-four hours earlier, but he was back in harness, like it or not. He could choose to set the record straight, but what good would that do? The Elven army needed confidence and determination; he knew better than most how to provide that, and he was in a position to do so. To forgo that responsibility would be to commit a violation of trust worse than anything Kellen Elessedil had ever imagined.

So he had called together his subcommanders and Lieutenants and devised a plan that would give them a chance to stall the Federation advance. In these hills, the Elves were a less visible target than on the flats or in the skies. Here, they could be more elusive as the terrain better suited their style of fighting. The Federation army was advancing on them with the intention of crushing any final resistance they might offer, then flanking and surrounding their Free-born allies. Putting a stop to their effort might very well determine the outcome of the entire war.

With a plan in place and the army regrouped, Drum had

persuaded Pied to go back to sleep. He was still battered from his tumble out of the sky, still exhausted enough that he needed to rest. Nothing he could do now was more important than what he would do when the Federation found them.

And now, he thought, opening his eyes once more to stare up into the still-darkened sky, *it has.*

He looked at Drumundoon. "Any sign of their airships?" He pushed himself up on one elbow with a grunt. The resulting aches and pains gave evidence of the time and distance he must travel still before he healed. "What about that big ship that was carrying their weapon?"

"No airships in sight at all," his aide responded, reaching down to pull him all the way up and handing him the chain-mail vest he always wore in battle.

Pied stared in disbelief. "How in the world did you find this?"

"I never let go of it, Captain," the other man advised, giving him a wry smile. "I knew you'd be needing it when you came back."

That he believed Pied *would* come back spoke volumes about his faith in his commander. Pied pulled on the vest, buckled on the leather greaves and arm guards that Drum had also somehow salvaged, strapped on a short sword and long knife, and slung his bow and arrows across his back.

He shook his head. "You never cease to amaze me, Drum." He stretched, adjusted the armor and weapons, and nodded. "All right. Lead the way."

They went down through the camp to cheers and waves from the Elven Hunters and Home Guard. The ranks of the previous day had swelled to double and, in some cases, triple what they had been, units that had been broken and scattered re-formed and made whole again overnight. The day was clear and the sky cloudless, but the light was pale and silvery on the horizon, the sun still down behind the hills. When it lifted into view, it would blind those walking into it.

Accordingly, Pied had set his defensive line on a low rise that placed the Elves with their backs to the sun and required their enemies to come at them from out of a wide draw that was flanked by high hills on either side. The draw led out of a ten-mile-long cut that twisted through the twin plateaus of the Prekkendorran, a natural passage that seemed to those marching north to be the beginning of a clear opening to the land beyond. But the look was deceptive; after entering the draw, it became apparent that navigating a series of narrow defiles was then necessary to reach open terrain.

Pied was hoping that whoever was leading the Federation pursuit force did not realize that. It was a realistic hope, given the fact that no Federation force had penetrated that far north in almost fifty years. Airships scouting the Prekkendorran might have noticed the lay of the land, but surveys so far north would have been deemed unimportant or, even if made, long since forgotten or lost.

He put his archers on the flanking heights and his Home Guard and regulars within the draw in two ranks, splitting each into a series of triangles that could attack or retreat in sequence. He was counting on a shifting, three-sided Elven counterthrust to slow the expected full-frontal assault by the larger Federation force. He was counting on being able to turn the attacker's left flank into its main body. He was counting on the resulting confusion and the blinding sunrise to allow the Elves to inflict enough damage to force a retreat. The Federation, he believed, would be relying on superior numbers and brute strength to break the back of the Elven defense. Its perception would be that Elven morale was low after the previous night's debacle and that not much would be needed to put an end to whatever resistance remained.

In truth, Pied was not entirely certain that that wasn't exactly what would happen. He believed the Elves had recovered their pride and sense of purpose, but he also remembered his own assessment of two days earlier, when he had judged them ill prepared and poorly motivated. He had to hope that things had changed, that their defeat on the Prekkendorran, rather than disheartening them, had given them fresh courage.

But it was only in the heat of battle that he would discover which way the tide was running. By then, the die would be cast.

Sen Dunsidan stalked the perimeter of the cordoned-off shipyard where Federation workers were crawling all over the *Dechtera* in an effort to get her back in the skies. She had suffered damage to her steering mechanisms and several of her parse tubes, and he did not want to risk taking her up again until he was certain she was not in danger of going down behind Free-born lines, where his enemies could get their hands on his precious weapon. Nor did he want to risk the possibility of further damage if there was a way to protect against it. So he was impatiently biding his time while the airship engineers worked on repairs and improvements, all of them aware of what would happen if they failed in their efforts.

Sometimes he wished he were sufficiently skilled and knowledgeable to solve all of his problems himself, knowing that the job would get done quickly and efficiently. He hated relying on others, hated waiting to discover if they would succeed or fail, and hated the fact that members of the Coalition Council and the public alike would attribute their failures to him and their successes to anyone but.

Still, what was the point of being Prime Minister if you couldn't delegate and command the services of those you led?

He stopped his pacing and stared north. He could take considerable pleasure in what his leadership had accomplished so far. The trap he had set to snare the Elven warships had been more successful than even he had believed possible. In a single night, he had destroyed the bulk of the enemy fleet and killed the King and his sons in the process. The latter was an incredible stroke of good fortune, for it left the Elves not only without a fleet but without their titular leader and his chosen successors, as well. He couldn't imagine what had possessed Kellen Elessedil to do something so foolhardy, but he was grateful for the unexpected gift. Like his father before him, Kellen was given to rash acts. That his last had come when it could be capitalized on so completely was a sign to Sen Dunsidan that his fortunes were about to turn.

But not if he failed to finish the job. Not if he failed to destroy what remained of the Elven army so that he could surround and annihilate its allies. Not if he failed to get the *Dechtera* back into the skies.

He caught sight of Etan Orek scurrying across the platform that housed the weapon he had invented, checking fittings and surfaces, making certain that everything was sound. He had brought the little engineer out to the battlefield with him when he flew the *Dechtera* from the shipyards in Arishaig, deciding that he should be close by in case anything went wrong with the weapon once it was put into use.

A needless concern, as it turned out, but how was he to know? The prototype had performed as expected—better than expected, really, given the destruction it had wreaked on the Elves. It was the *Dechtera* that had fallen short of her goal. Still, a delay was not so costly at this point. The Federation army had penetrated the Free-born lines, taking command of the west plateau and sweeping all the way north into the hills in which the remnants of the Elven Hunters hid. The Free-born allies still held the east plateau, but they were surrounded on three sides. More to the point, they were confused and hesitant to counterattack. Having witnessed the destruction of the Elven fleet, they were terrified for the safety of their own. *As well they should be*, he thought. Because once the *Dechtera* was airborne again, it would be a simple matter to burn the allied vessels to cinders while they sat on the ground and cut apart the

Free-born defensive lines to allow the Federation army passage through.

He was impatient for that. He wanted it to be over and done with. He wanted his victory in hand.

Beware, Sen Dunsidan, he cautioned himself as the adrenaline sent a fresh surge of heady, euphoric anticipation rushing through him. *Don't overstep. Don't overreact. Don't rush to your own doom.*

He had been a politician too long to indulge in rash behavior. Mistakes of that sort were for less experienced men and women, for the likes of those whose life spans he had cut short on more occasions than he cared to remember. Being a survivor meant being wary of premature celebration and incautious optimism. Being a survivor meant never taking anything for granted, never accepting anything at face value.

"Are your thoughts deep ones, Prime Minister?"

He whirled at the sound of Iridia Eleri's voice, surprised to find her standing right next to him. It frightened him that she could get so close without him hearing her approach. It angered him that she had been doing so repeatedly since he had agreed to accept her offer to act as his private adviser, as if their arrangement invited such intrusion. Worst of all, it reminded him of the way the Ilse Witch used to materialize in his bedchamber, a memory he would just as soon forget.

"My thoughts are my own, Iridia," he replied. "They are neither deep nor shallow, only practical. Have you something to offer, or are you just looking for new ways to stop my heart?"

If she was offended by his irritation, she kept it to herself. "I have something to offer, if you seek a way to end this war much more quickly than it will be ended otherwise."

He stared at her, transfixed by more than the possibility her words suggested. She was so pale in the moonlight that she seemed almost transparent, the cast of her skin as white as death, the darkness of her eyes in such sharp contrast they seemed opaque. She was dressed in a black robe, her slender body completely shrouded and her head hooded. Her face, peering from the hood's shadows, and her hands, clutching loosely at the robe's edges, gave disconcerting evidence that he was in the presence of a ghost.

It was not the first time he had experienced that feeling. There had been a look to Iridia of late that was so chillingly otherworldly, he had trouble at times believing she wasn't something less than human.

He pursed his lips at her. "I will end it quickly enough on my own, once the *Dechtera* is airborne again. My weapon will burn what remains of the Free-born fleet to cinders. I already hunt the remnants of the Elven army and will find them within the week, as well. Aren't you better off worrying about Shadea and her Druids than matters of war? Isn't that the task which you were assigned?"

It was a stinging rebuke, delivered as much out of distaste for her unwanted intervention as dismay over her lack of sophistication in battle tactics. But she seemed unmoved by his words, her expression empty of feeling.

"My task is to save you from yourself, Prime Minister. The Free-born have lost their ships on the Prekkendorran, but they can obtain others. Their army might be scattered and in momentary disarray, but it will regroup. You will not win this war through a single victory. You should know as much without my having to tell you."

Her words were so dismissive that he flushed in spite of himself. She was talking to him as if he were a child.

"This war has lasted fifty years," she continued, seemingly oblivious to his reaction. "It will not be ended on the Prekkendorran. It will not be won on any Southland battlefield. It will be won in the Westland. It will be won when you break the spirit of the Elves, because it is the Elves who are the backbone of the Free-born struggle. Break their spirit, and those who fight with them will be quick to seek peace."

He frowned. "I would have thought that the loss of their fleet and their King had accomplished that. Obviously, you don't agree. Have you something else in mind, a more persuasive way to bring them into line?"

"Much more persuasive."

He felt his patience ebb as he waited in vain for her to continue. "Am I expected to guess at what it is, or will you save me the trouble and simply tell me?"

She looked away from him, out over the shipyard to where the *Dechtera* sat dark and menacing in the moonlight, to where the shipyard workers continued to repair her. She was looking in that direction, but he had the feeling that she was looking at something else altogether, something hidden from him. He was struck again by the distant feel of her, the sense that she was not entirely where she appeared to be.

"You are not averse to killing, are you, Prime Minister?" she asked suddenly.

It was the way she asked the question that made him think she intended to trap him with his own words. He had developed a sixth sense about the use of such tactics over his years, and it had saved him from disaster more than once.

"Are you afraid to answer me?" she pressed.

"You know I am not afraid of killing."

"I know you believe that the ends justify the means. I know you believe that accomplishing your goals entitles you to take whatever steps are required. I know that you are the architect of the deaths of your predecessor and those who would have succeeded him. I know that you have participated in blood games of all sorts."

"Then speak your mind and quit playing games with me. My patience with you grows thin."

Her bloodless face lifted out of the hood's concealing shadows so that her dark eyes locked on his. "Listen closely, then. You waste needless time killing soldiers on the Prekkendorran. Killing soldiers means nothing to those who send them forth. If you want to break the spirit of the Elves, if you want to put an end to their resistance, you have to kill those whom the soldiers protect. You have to kill their women and children. You have to kill their old people and their infirm. You have to take the war from the battlefield into their homes."

Her voice was a hiss. "You have the weapon to do so, Prime Minister. Fly the *Dechtera* to Arborlon and use it. Burn their precious city and its people to ashes. Make them afraid to think of doing anything other than begging for your mercy."

She said it dispassionately, but her words transfixed him.

He went hot and cold in turn, cowed at first by the prospect of such savagery, then excited by it. He was already perceived to be a monster, so there was little reason to pretend he wasn't. He did not care in the slightest about preserving the lives of those who opposed him, and the Elves had been a thorn in his side for twenty years. Why not cull their numbers sufficiently that they would not threaten again in his lifetime?

"But you are an Elf yourself," he said. "Why are you so willing to kill your own people?"

She made a sound that might have been meant as laughter. "I am *not* an Elf! I am a Druid! Just as you are a Prime Minister and not a Southlander. It is the power we wield that commands our loyalty, Sen Dunsidan, not some accident of birth."

She was right, of course. His nationality and Race meant nothing to him beyond the opportunities they provided for advancement.

"As a Druid, then," he snapped, "you must know that Shadea will not approve of this. She will be here to confer with me in two days. She is already distressed that I attacked the Free-born without first advising her. Once she discovers my new intention, she will put a stop to it. In appearances, at least, the Druids must seem impartial. She might back the Federation in its bid to reclaim the Borderlands, but she will never countenance genocide."

"Tell her nothing, then. Let her respond when it is over, after she has already openly declared her support of the Federation. Will anyone listen to her, no matter how loudly she protests?"

"In which case she will come looking for me, and not to offer congratulations."

The pale face looked away. "I will deal with her when she does."

He thought to question such boldness, for in the time he had known Iridia he had never once believed that she was a match for Shadea a'Ru. But perhaps things had changed. She sounded very sure of herself, and the steely resolve she brought to their alliance had given him reason to suspect she had grown more powerful.

"What is your decision, Prime Minister?" she pressed.

He was certain of one thing only. If he chose to pursue Iridia's course of action, questions of ethics were pointless. If he failed, questions of ethics would be the least of his problems. And if he succeeded, such questions would be whispered in private, because he would then have become the most powerful figure in the Four Lands. Not even the Druids would dare to challenge his authority.

It should have been an easy decision. Where power and influence were at stake, he had never hesitated in making his choice. Yet he hesitated here. Something felt wrong about this, perhaps a consequence he had not considered or a possibility he had overlooked. But whatever it was, it was definitely there, nagging at him. He could feel it deep inside where such things could not be ignored.

"Prime Minister?"

He gave the doubt another few seconds, and then he dismissed it. There was never gain without risk, and risk always raised doubts. He knew his own mind well enough to embrace what he must do. Without Grianne Ohmsford to worry about, he could afford to take chances he might not otherwise take. The loss of a few thousand lives was not worrying enough to deter him. There was more at stake than lives.

"We will fly to Arborlon," he said.

Dawn broke in a flare of brightness as the sun crested the rim of the hills and began to lift into the sky. The Elves were settled in, most hidden from view behind hummocks and rocks and in the shadows of the defiles, ranks formed and weapons at the ready. Already, they could hear the sound of the Federation army marching to the attack, the pounding of boots and the thumping of spears and swords against shields steady and rhythmic and unnerving. Flashes of light reflected off the flat surfaces of blades as the Federation soldiers wound through the cut and began the long, twisting trek across the flats to where their quarry waited.

Pied, standing with his Home Guard, scanned his ranks for movement and found none. The Elves had disappeared as only the Elves could. They would not be spied out by the Federation until it was too late. He wished he had the services of cavalry to ride at the Federation flanks, but foot soldiers would have to do. He wished he had the use of catapults and fire launchers, but slings and arrows would have to do. He would be outnumbered, perhaps by as much as five to one. He lacked practical experience commanding on a battlefield; he was Captain of the Home Guard, not a Commander of the Elven army. He was the highest-rank-ing officer present, and he had never been in a battle of such size.

There's a first time for everything, the old saying went. He just wished there wasn't so much at stake.

He looked down the ranks of those closest and found Drumundoon standing almost next to him, tall and gangly and looking oddly out of place in his battle gear. Drum wasn't meant to fight on the line; he was meant to serve behind it. Yet there was determination in his young face, and when he caught Pied looking at him, he winked.

Reason enough to believe in him, Pied thought. *Reason enough to believe in them all.*

He tightened his grip on his sword and settled deeper into the shadows.

TWENTY-EIGHT

Grianne Ohmsford lay with her face pressed against the stone floor of her cell, her eyes closed. She was trying to escape, even though there was nowhere to run. Torchlight from the hallway beyond intruded on the darkness in which she wished to hide. Low voices and the soft shuffling of boots nudged her out of her hiding places. Water dripped and the earth rumbled deep within its core, reminders of where she was. Like hungry predators from the black holes into which she had tried to banish them, memories emerged and made her skin crawl.

But it was the mewling cries of the Furies, triggers to a mix of horror and madness from which there was no escape, that chased her down and found her out no matter how far inside herself she retreated. She cringed from them, drawing up into a ball, becoming as small and still as possible, willing herself to disappear. But nothing helped. She had used her magic to become one of them, and she could not change back again. She mewled with them. She hissed and snarled with them. She spit with poisonous intent. She flexed her claws and drew back her muzzle. She rose to greet them, responding to their summoning, a response she loathed but could not prevent.

She squeezed her eyes so tightly shut they hurt. She would have cried had there been tears to do so. Her world was a room six feet by ten feet, but it might as well have been the size of a coffin.

They had returned her to her cell from the arena in the same way they had brought her, in a cage and in chains, Goblins and demonwolves surrounding her, Hobstull directing them. Back through the crowds and the blasted countryside. Back through the gloom and mist. Time had stopped, and her sense of herself and her place had disappeared. She was a captured beast. She was a lifetime removed from her role as Ard Rhys, and the Druids and Paranor were a dim memory. All the way back, she fought to regain her identity, but the rolling and the jouncing seemed only to exacerbate her confusion. It was easier to disappear into the role she had adopted than to try to follow the threads that might lead her out. It was simpler to embrace the primal creature she had awakened than to cast it aside.

They stripped and bathed her on her return, and she did not try to stop them. She stood naked and exposed and uncaring, gone so deep inside herself that she felt nothing of what they did to her. Cat sounds issued from her lips and her fingers flexed, but she did not see the way her captors drew back. She did not see them at all. She did not know they were there.

I am lost, she thought at one point. *I am destroyed, and I have done it to myself.*

Time passed, but little seemed to change. Guards came and went, the light dimmed and brightened as torches sputtered and were replaced, food was delivered and taken away uneaten, and the demons that haunted her kept edging closer. She wanted to break their spell, to banish them along with the hissing and mewling of her Fury memories, but she could not gather together the will to do so.

One time only did she sleep. She did not know for how long, only that she did, and that when her dreams took the shape of her memories, she woke screaming.

The Straken Lord did not reappear. Hobstull stayed away. She did not know what they intended, but the longer she was left alone, the more certain she became that they had lost interest in her entirely. There was no use for such as her, for a woman who was willing to take the form of a monster, to assume the persona of a raver. There was no place, even in the world of demons, for something that lacked any moral center or recognizable purpose. She saw herself as they did, a damaged and conflicted creature, a chameleon that could not distinguish between reality and fantasy, able to be either or both, but unable to tell the difference.

She felt herself sliding over the edge of sanity. It was happening gradually, just a few inches at a time, but there was no mistaking it. Each day, she felt her Ard Rhys self fall just a little farther away and her Fury self close about her just a little bit tighter. It grew easier to embrace the latter and reject the former. It grew more attractive to see herself as inhuman. If she was no better than one of the Furies, her life became less complicated. The madness seemed to ease and the conflict to diminish. As a Fury, she did not have to worry about where she was or how she had gotten there. She did not need to concern herself with the increasingly fuzzy distinctions between different worlds and lives. As a Fury, the world flattened and smoothed, and there was only killing and food and the lure of life with her cat kind.

She began seeing herself as an imprisoned animal. She began making cat sounds all the time, finding comfort in the soft mewling. She flexed her fingers and arched her back. She bit her cheek and tasted her own blood.

But she did not rise or eat. She did not move from where she lay. She refused to come out of the dark refuge of her delusions. She stayed safe and protected in her mind.

Then, as if from a dream, she heard someone calling to her. At first she thought she must have imagined it. No one would call to her, not here or anywhere else. No one would want to have anything to do with someone as terrible as she was.

But she heard the voice again, hushed and insistent. She heard it speak her name. Surprised, she stirred from her self-induced lethargy to listen for it, and heard it again.

"Grianne of the trees! Can you hear me? Why do you make those cat noises? Do you dream? Wake up!"

Her mind sharpened and her concentration coalesced, until the words became distinct and the voice recognizable. She knew the one who called to her, remembered him from another time and place. She felt the pull of that familiarity, as if she were coming back from a long journey to someone she had left behind.

"Wake up, Straken! Stop squirming! What is wrong with you? Don't you hear me?"

Her breathing quickened, and a bit of the sluggishness fell away. She knew that voice. She knew it well. Something about it gave her fresh energy and a sense of renewed possibility. She tried to speak, choked on words that wouldn't come, and made unintelligible sounds instead.

"What are you doing, little cat thing? Have I wasted my time coming here? Are you not able to speak? Look at me!"

She did so, opening her eyes for the first time in days, breaking the crust of tears that had dried and sealed her lids, squinting against the unfamiliar brightness, reaching up to rub away the sleep and confusion. She stirred slowly, raised herself on one elbow, and looked toward the light that spilled from the hallway into her cell.

A Goblin sentry stood pressed against the cell bars, peering in at her. The torchlight cast his shadow across her like a shroud. She stared in confusion, feeling the lethargy and hopelessness return almost at once. This was no one. She was deceived. Her head lowered once more, and her eyes began to close.

"No! What are you doing? Straken! It's me!"

She looked up in time to see the Goblin pushing back the hood of his cloak to reveal his face. She peered at it out of a fog of exhaustion and uncertainty, watched it take shape, and struggled to make sense of what she was seeing.

"Weka Dart," she whispered.

She stared at him, not quite believing he was actually there. She had all but forgotten about the little Ulk Bog. Once he had abandoned her and she had fallen into the hands of the Straken Lord, she had not expected ever to see him again. That he was standing there was almost incomprehensible.

"You should have listened to me!" he hissed. "Didn't I tell you? Didn't I warn you not to go on without me?"

His sharp features were scrunched into a knot, giving him the look of a demented beast. His hair was standing straight out from his head and neck, bristling and stiff. His sharp teeth flashed from behind his lips as he tried to smile and failed, and his fingers knotted on the bars.

Her mind cleared a bit further, and she pushed back against the urge to mewl and spit. "How did you find me?"

He stared at her as if she were mad. "You still don't know anything, do you? What kind of Straken are you?"

She shook her head. "The worst kind."

"You certainly look it." Weka Dart laughed. "I found you by paying attention to the world around me, something you seem to have failed to master. But this isn't your world, is it? This isn't even remotely like it. So maybe you aren't to blame for anything more than bad judgment."

He was telling her something, but she couldn't make sense of it. "Was it good judgment that brought you here, then?"

The Ulk Bog spit. "I am not sure what it was. I heard in my travels what had happened to you, and I admit that I thought it best to leave you to your fate. But then chance and inspiration intervened, so here I am."

"Chance and inspiration?"

"I was crossing the Pashanon on my way to Huka Flats, the route I had chosen for myself and advised you to take as well. As I traveled, word reached me of your capture. Such things do not go unreported in this land, and I keep my eyes and ears open. It was easy enough to determine what had happened to you. The difficulty was in deciding what I should do about it."

He puffed out his chest. "I will admit that at first I thought it best simply to go on. You had dismissed me, after all. What did it matter what became of you? You were rude to me. You insulted me. In the end, you ignored my good advice and brought disaster on yourself. I owed you nothing. No one could fault me if I chose to leave you to your fate.

"But then, I reconsidered. After all, it wasn't your fault that you were a stranger to this country, one lacking in good judgment and common sense. You were to be pitied. I felt an obligation toward you. I thought it over and made up my mind. I would come find you. I would see how you were. If you were nice to me, I would decide whether you deserved a second chance."

Even in her confused and debilitated state, of being not all of one thing or the other, she recognized that his words were lies. She could hear it in the way he spoke; she could see it in the rapid shifting of his eyes and body. As always, he was after something, but she had no idea what it was.

"How did you get down here?" she asked.

He gave a casual shrug. "I have my ways."

"Ways that allow you to get past the demonwolves and the Goblins that serve the Straken Lord?"

He sniffed. "I am not without skills."

She pulled herself into a sitting position and became

aware for the first time in days how stiff and sore she was. She looked down at herself, first at the bruises and cuts on her arms and legs, then at the white shift she wore. She was much better dressed than when she had been taken to the arena. She glanced around. Her cell was cleaner, too.

Her focus narrowed sharply. Was she mistaken about the intentions of the Straken Lord? What was going on?

She looked at Weka Dart. "If you don't stop lying to me and tell me the truth," she said softly, "I might have to use my Straken magic on you, Ulk Bog."

He grinned, showing all his sharp teeth. "That might be a little difficult, since you wear a conjure collar."

He seemed to realize his mistake almost immediately, a change coming into his eyes and the self-satisfied look fading as his lips compressed in silent reprimand. "Conjure collars are not unknown to me," he said quickly. "I've seen them before."

In truth, she had forgotten about the collar until he reminded her of it, but he didn't know that and she wasn't about to tell him so. She held herself very still and continued to stare at him.

"I don't know who you are or what you want, Weka Dart," she said finally, "but you haven't told me one word of truth since we met. This has all been a game for you, a game in which you seem to know all the rules while I know none. If you know what a conjure collar is, you know too much to be just a simple village creature traveling to a new part of the country. If you know how to bypass the Straken Lord's guards, you have skills and knowledge that suggest you are something more than you pretend. I have had enough of you. Either tell me the truth or leave me here to rot."

She held up one finger as he started to speak. "Be careful. If you are about to tell me another lie, think twice. I don't have much left to call my own, but I do have my sense of what is true and what isn't. You don't want to try to take that from me."

The Ulk Bog stared at her. Wary eyes studied her uncertainly; deep creases etched his wizened face.

He shook his head. "I don't know how much I should tell you," he said finally.

She sighed. "Why not tell me everything? What possible difference can it make now?"

"More than you think. Difference enough that I must consider carefully. You are right about me. You are right about my story. But you are in a stronger position than you believe. You have something I want. All I have to offer in exchange is the truth—and perhaps a way out of here. I can give you the one for the other. But I am afraid you will refuse me when you hear what I have to say. I am afraid you will hate me."

He spoke with such sincerity that for the first time since she had met him she was inclined to believe what he said. She did not understand how all that could be, but it didn't matter. What mattered was that he had said he might be able to help her escape. At that point, she would do anything; make any bargain, agree to any conditions to gain her freedom. Because if she remained where she was, she knew she was lost.

But she couldn't let him know that. She couldn't let him

see her desperation. Giving Weka Dart that sort of power over her was too dangerous. He would take advantage of her as quickly as Tael Riverine had.

She took a deep breath. "Listen to me. You came here with the intention of trading or you wouldn't have come here at all. My word is good, Weka Dart. I keep my promises. So I will give you one now. If you tell me the truth about yourself, I will tell you if I can forgive you for your lies. Then you can decide if you still think it's worth it to try to trade what you want for my freedom."

She hauled herself to her feet and with some effort stumbled over to where he stood. "What's it to be, little Ulk Bog? A bargain or a good-bye? I don't really care anymore."

He stared at her some more, his yellow eyes flicking left and right, up and down, scanning the whole of her face, but never settling on any one part. She could see a glimmer of doubt and fear mirrored there. But she could also see hope.

He nodded. "Very well, Grianne of the many promises. I will tell you, even though I think all Strakens lie." He spit again and shook his head. "I know who you are and where you come from. I always did. I know because I was Catcher for Tael Riverine before Hobstull was. I would be Catcher still if the Straken Lord hadn't decided I had lost my skills. He was wrong, but there is no arguing with a Straken. So he replaced me. But not before he humiliated me in ways I will never discuss, so don't ask it of me."

He swallowed hard. "He took me in when I was driven from my tribe for eating my young. He cared nothing for any of that, only for what I could do for him. He recognized my skills and offered me a place at Kraal Reach as his

Catcher. He knew that I would accept, that I had to because I could not survive alone and unprotected in the world of the Jarka Ruus. He gave me what I needed, but then he took everything back when he cast me out. So I vowed that I would take everything from him in turn."

His voice grew fierce. "The plans to bring you here have been in place for some time. Tael Riverine would swap you for his changeling creature, the Moric. Easy enough for a Straken of his power. I decided to disrupt his plans by getting to you first, which I did. I intended to take you away from him, to steal you out from under his nose. I intended to embarrass Hobstull and reveal him to the Straken Lord as a failure! Then I would produce you and regain my rightful place!"

He was breathing hard, his eyes become narrow slits, his throat working rapidly as he sought to gauge her reaction. She gave him nothing, listening blank-faced and empty-eyed, her talent as the Ilse Witch resurfacing from where she had kept it buried for twenty years. *So easy to call it up again*, she thought. *So easy to go back to being what I was.*

"My plan failed when you refused to come with me," Weka Dart continued. "Failed completely. I tried everything. But you were so insistent on going your own way! And I couldn't change your mind without giving myself away!" He shook his head. "So I let you go. I said, *If that is what she wants, then give it to her! See how well she does without you! Walk away from the Straken and nothing is lost!* I wasn't going to risk my life following after you when I knew what would happen. Hobstull was looking, and it was only a matter of time until he found you. He didn't know exactly where you would appear, only that you would. But I knew! I knew, because I have always been better able to read the signs of such things! I have always been the better Catcher!"

He spit the words out and flung himself away from the cell bars, dropping to the floor in a crouch, refusing to look at her. She watched him for a moment, her mind working through the choices his revelations had given her.

"Weka Dart," she said.

He stayed where he was.

"Look at me."

He refused, turned away, and hunched down.

"Look at me. Tell me what you see in my eyes."

Finally, he turned just enough to glance over his shoulder and make momentary eye contact, then looked away again.

"I am not angry with you," she said. "You did what I would have done if our positions had been reversed. In fact, once upon a time, when I was a different person living a different life, I did things much worse to others than what you have done to me."

He looked back at her once more.

"I don't hate you," she told him.

"You should." His teeth clicked as his jaws snapped shut.

"My hate is reserved for others more deserving and less forthcoming about their efforts to see me dead and gone." She gestured for him to come back. "Tell me the rest of what you know."

He stayed where he was a moment longer, then sighed, rose, and came back to stand in front of her. "You don't hate me? If you were free, you wouldn't try to kill me?"

She shook her head. "I don't hate you. Even if I had the chance to do so, I wouldn't try to kill you. Now tell me the rest. Do you know the Straken Lord's plans?"

The Ulk Bog nodded. "I was here at Kraal Reach when he was making them." He looked closely at her. "You still don't know what he intends? You haven't seen the way he looks at you?"

She went cold all the way to her bones, the little man's words conjuring up an image that froze her blood. "Tell me."

"He has been testing you to see if you are a suitable vessel to bear his children. He wishes to mate with you."

For the first time, she was really afraid. The demon was anathema to her. She could think of no worse fate than to be the mother of its children, the mother of demonkind, a bearer of monsters. She had never considered the possibility. She had never recognized that the Straken Lord had any interest in her beyond keeping her imprisoned and alive until its creature, the Moric, could do whatever it had been sent to do in her own world.

"This was the reason for bringing me here?" she managed to ask, working hard to keep her voice steady.

Weka Dart shook his head, his gimlet eyes glittering. "No. The idea must have occurred to him after you were his prisoner. His plans are much grander than that."

"How much grander?"

The Ulk Bog leaned close. "He has been searching for a way to send the Moric into your world for some time. But for that to happen, it was necessary to find someone in your world willing to help. He found those people, and he used them as his tool. Whoever they were had no idea what the Straken Lord intended, but were only interested in disposing of you. That was what your betrayer knew—that using the magic would banish you to the world of the Jarka Ruus. That, and nothing more. Your betrayers knew nothing of the exchange, nothing of the way the magic really worked, nothing of the trade that was necessary to bring you here. The Straken Lord was careful to keep that secret hidden."

As well it should have been, she thought. But she wasn't sure that knowing a trade was required would have stopped whoever was desperate enough to send her into the Forbidding.

"But why was I brought here if not to mate with Tael Riverine?" she pressed.

"You miss the point, Straken!" Weka Dart snapped. "Bringing you here was never what mattered! What mattered was sending the Moric into your world!"

She shook her head. "Why?"

"So that it could destroy the barrier that keeps us locked away! So that it could free the Jarka Ruus!"

Now she understood. The Moric had been sent to complete the task that the Dagda Mor had failed to accomplish more than five hundred years earlier—to break down the walls of the prison behind which the dark things of Faerie had been shut since before the dawn of Man.

Her mind raced. To do that, it would have to destroy the Ellcrys, the magic-born Elven tree that had been created to ward the Forbidding. How would it manage that, when the tree was always so closely guarded?

More important, how could she stop it from happening?

"Does the Moric have a way to destroy the barrier?" she asked Weka Dart.

He shook his head. "It was to find one once it crossed over into your world. It is very talented and very smart. It will have done so by now."

She ignored the fear that rushed through her at the thought that the Ulk Bog might be right. "Do you have a way to get me out of here?" she asked quickly.

On the landing above them, at the top of the stairway, a door opened and closed with a thud. Footsteps sounded on the stone steps, coming down.

"On the floor!" he hissed at her, and darted away.

She threw herself back down, sprawling in the same position in which he had found her, her heart pounding, her muscles tensed. *Don't move,* she told herself. *Don't do anything.*

The steps approached her cell and came to a stop. A silence settled in like morning mist.

Eyes closed, body still, she waited.

TWENTY-NINE

Pen Ohmsford's ascent from the ravine was an endless slog. Burdened with self-recrimination and despair, it was all he could do to place one foot in front of the other. He kept thinking he should go back, should attempt one final time to free Cinnaminson, make one more plea or take one last stand. But he knew it was pointless even to think about doing so. Nothing would change until he had some better means of succeeding. Yet he couldn't stop thinking about it. He couldn't stop himself from feeling that he should have done more.

Lead-footed, he climbed through the hazy darkness, working his way up the narrow switchback trail, ducking under vines and brushing past brambles and scrub, leaning on his staff for support, his thoughts scattered all over the place. His grip about the rune-carved handle of the dark-wand helped to center him, a reassurance that he had accomplished something in the midst of all the failures. Lives had been lost and hopes blown away like dried leaves in a strong wind, and he blamed himself for most of it. He should have done better, he kept telling himself, even though he could not think what more he might have done or exactly what he might have changed. Hindsight suggested possibilities, but hindsight was deceptive, sifted through a filter of distance and reason. Things were never so easy as they seemed later. They were mostly wild and confused and emotionally charged. Hindsight pretended otherwise.

But knowing so didn't make him feel any better. Knowing so only made him work harder to find a reason to believe he had failed.

He took some comfort in the fact that he had gotten to Stridegate at all, that he had confronted the tanequil and found a way to communicate with it, that he had secured the limb he needed and shaped it into the darkwand. He had gotten much farther with his quest than he had ever believed he would. He had never spoken of it, but he had always thought in the back of his mind that what the King of the Silver River had sent him to do was impossible. He had always thought that he was the wrong choice, a boy with little experience and few skills, a boy asked to do something that most grown men would not even attempt. He did not know what had persuaded him to try. He guessed it was the expectations of those who had accompanied him. He guessed it was his own need to prove himself.

These and other equally troubling thoughts roiled through his brain as he climbed, working along the tunnels of his conscience like worms, probing and sifting for explanations that would satisfy them. He tried to lay them to rest, but he only managed to settle with a few. The rest continued on, digging away, finding fresh food in his doubts and fears and frustrations, growing and fattening and taking up all the space his emotional well-being would allow.

He rested at one point, dropping down on his haunches with his back against the wall of the ravine, feeling the cold and damp of the earth seep through his clothing and enter his body, too tired to care. He leaned on the darkwand for support as he lowered his head and cried soundlessly, unable to help himself. He was not the hero and adventurer he had envisioned himself to be. He was just a boy who wanted to go home.

But he knew that wasn't something that was going to happen anytime soon, and it wasn't helping him to think that it might, so he quit crying, stood up, and began climbing once more. Overhead, the daylight was beginning to fail, a graying of the sky that signaled the onset of twilight. He needed to reach the top of the ravine so that he could cross the bridge before it was dark. It never occurred to him that he would have any trouble doing so; the tanequil would let him pass unmolested. It had taken from him already what it wanted.

The slope broadened and the trail cut away from the bridge into a thicket of scrub and grasses that quickly melded into the beginnings of the island forest. The way forward grew more difficult and the light continued to dim steadily. He continued on, eyes forward as he resisted the urge to look back, knowing he would see nothing if he did, that she was too far away from him now. His memories of her were firmly etched in his mind, and that was as much as he could hope for.

He was thirsty and wished he had something to drink, but that would have to wait. He was hungry, too. He hadn't eaten anything since . . . He tried to remember and couldn't. More than a day, he thought. Much more. His stomach rumbled and his head felt light from the ascent, but there was no help for it.

He rested again, pausing in the dark concealment of a stand of saplings to let the dizziness pass, and it was then that he realized he wasn't alone. It happened all at once. A mix of things warned him of his danger—things not so much external as internal, a sensing through his magic that the world about him wasn't quite right. He stood listening to the silence, took notice of the way the light shifted with the passing of clouds west across the sunset, caught the feel of the wind through the trees. His awareness was born of those mundane, ordinary observations, though he couldn't explain why. Something was there that hadn't been there earlier. Something he knew.

Or someone.

He felt a chill creep up his spine as he waited, trying to decide what he should do. His instincts told him that he was in danger, but they did not yet tell him what that danger was. If he moved, he might give himself away. If he stayed where he was, he might be found out anyway.

Finally, unable to think of anything else to do, he started forward, very slowly, a few steps at a time. Then he stopped and waited again, listening. Nothing. He took a deep breath and exhaled silently. If something was there, it was probably deeper in. His better choice was to skirt the rim of the island, above the ravine, until he reached the bridge and could then cross.

It occurred to him suddenly that he might be sensing someone from his own party, Khyber perhaps, grown impatient with his delay. But he didn't think Khyber would elicit the sort of response he was having; he wouldn't be made so uneasy by her presence. His reaction was surprising in any case, given the nature of his magic. Usually, he required contact with animals or birds or plants for such sensations to happen. Yet his response hadn't been triggered by any of those. It was coming from somewhere else entirely.

Move, he told himself silently, mouthing the word.

He started ahead, angling back toward the ravine. He could just make it out through the screen of the trees, the earth split wide and deep, a maw as black as night. An image formed, unbidden. *Cinnaminson*. He cast the troubling image aside angrily. *Move!*

To his left, farther into the trees and away from the ravine, something shifted. He saw it out of the corner of his eye and froze instantly. Leaves and grasses shivered, and the air stilled. Twilight had fallen in a gray mantle that blended shadows into strange patterns that gave everything the look of being alive.

He was aware suddenly that he was silhouetted against the horizon, easily identifiable by any eye. He thought to drop flat, but movement of that sort would give him away instantly. He stayed where he was, a statue, waiting.

In the trees, there was fresh movement. He saw it

clearly this time, shadows separating and taking shape, the outline of a cloaked figure revealing itself. The figure crept through the maze of dark trunks and layered shadows like an animal, crouched down and moving on all fours.

Spiderlike.

He recognized it from their previous encounters. It was the thing that had chased him when he fled the seaport of Anatcherae to cross the Lazareen. It was the monster that had killed Gar Hatch and his crew and taken Cinnaminson.

It had tracked him all the way.

His heart sank. It was moving away from him, which meant it did not yet know exactly where he was. But it would find him soon enough, and when it did, he would have to face it. He wasn't going to have any choice. He knew it with a certainty that defied argument. He might try to run, to reach the bridge and cross to where his companions waited, but he would never make it. Flight wasn't going to save him. Not from this.

His fingers tightened on the darkwand, and he wondered again if it might possess a magic that could save him.

Then he wondered if anything could.

Khyber Elessedil had walked for the better part of two hours, following the dark line of the ravine through the trees, searching without success for a way across. At times, the gap narrowed, but never enough to suggest that trying to jump it or bridge it with a tree was going to work. Unchanging in its look as it twisted and turned and disappeared into the horizon, it angled on ahead of her as she stopped to consider whether to continue.

She glanced west, where the sun was dropping toward the jagged peaks of the Klu. No more than an hour or two of daylight remained. She sighed in exasperation. She did not want to give up, but she did not want to get caught out there alone in the dark, either. She looked ahead once more, then reluctantly turned around and started back. There was no help for it. Tomorrow, if Pen and Cinnaminson hadn't reappeared, she would consider going the other way, following the ravine north.

Or perhaps she would simply cross the bridge and find them, her promise to wait notwithstanding.

Perhaps enough was enough.

She trooped back through the trees and grasses, muttering to herself and thinking that they had all been ill served in the venture, starting with the questionable decision by the King of the Silver River to entrust the rescue of the Ard Rhys to Pen. Not that she doubted Pen's courage, but he was only a boy, much younger even than she and totally lacking in skills or magic. That he was still alive at all after what had happened to them was something of a miracle. Look how many of their company had died instead, including the most talented and experienced of them all.

But it didn't do her any good to think that way—to suggest that in some way Ahren Elessedil had died without reason—and she put the matter aside. Her doubts and fears could not be placed at the feet of others. If she was worried or afraid, she would have to find another way of dealing with it.

She thought it odd how things had changed since she had left Emberen. There, her chief concern had been in determining how and when to reveal to Ahren her theft of the Elfstones so that he wouldn't take them back until she had learned to use them. Now that the Elfstones were hers to keep for as long as she chose, she wanted nothing more than to be able to give them back.

Thinking she might as well wish she could fly for all the good it would do her, she kicked at the earth as she walked. She was in until the end, which meant at least until Pen had returned to Paranor and gone into the Forbidding to find his aunt. Even then, she would not be free to go home again until Pen reappeared safely. Probably, she should go with him. After all, they only had the word of the King of the Silver River that she couldn't, and there was good reason to question anything the Faerie creature had told them.

The sun slid down into the peaks, coloring the horizon in the wake of its passing, leaving the depthless bowl of the sky dark with night's approach. She cast wary glances left and right as she walked, using her Druid skills to make certain she was not being tracked by anything unfriendly. The Urdas might have chosen to come around the walls at the front of the ruins in an effort to get at them from the sides.

It was because her senses were pricked and her magic deployed that she found Pen. It happened unexpectedly, when she was nearing the bridge, her attention focused mostly on her return to her companions. She caught a whiff of his presence and slowed at once, casting all about. He wasn't immediately visible, but she could tell that he was still on the far side of the ravine, back in the trees. He was moving slowly and cautiously, as if wary of something.

When he appeared at the ravine's edge, her impression was confirmed. He was advancing in a crouch through a thin screen of trees, stopping frequently to look back into the deeper part of the forest. Each time he did so, he cocked his head as if listening for something. Or *to* something. She couldn't tell.

She thought to call out to him, but she was afraid that if she did so, she would give him away to whatever he was trying to avoid. So she waited, tracking his movements. She noticed a dark staff he was carrying, something new. Was it the darkwand? A rush of expectation surged through her. It must be. He had found what he had come for and was heading back.

She wondered suddenly what had become of Cinnaminson. Pen would never leave her behind, at least not without good reason. Perhaps he was trying to lead whatever pursued him away from the Rover girl. That sounded right.

As he edged ahead, she went with him, keeping low in the scrub and grasses, aware that the darkness was deepening and her ability to see lessening. There was no sign of the moon, and there were few stars in a clouded sky. Soon she wouldn't be able to see him at all.

Then a black shape appeared out of the trees behind the boy, a cloaked and hooded form that she knew immediately. It was the monster from Anatcherae. It had tracked them all that way, and now it was over there with Pen and had him alone. Her scalp crawled, and she felt a moment of panic. All she wanted to do was to rush to his rescue.

But she couldn't reach him. No one could.

Her fingers fumbled wildly for the Elfstones, but even as they closed about the talismans, she hesitated. There was no reason to think their magic would work against the creature. And there was no time to test it. She needed something else, something more reliable.

Her mind raced in search of a solution as the black thing crept closer to her friend.

Pen was still trying to decide what to do, still frozen by fear and indecision, when he heard the voices. At first he was certain that his hearing was playing tricks on him, that he was imagining things, that the loss of Cinnaminson had affected his mind. He cocked his head in response, trying to understand why the wind would sound as it did and why it would do so now.

–Follow–

The chorus whispered softly to him from out of the twilight before dancing away in a fading echo. The aeriads, and no mistake about it. Not Cinnaminson alone, but the entire chorus, a blend of identical voices as they called to him.

He stared into space, hesitant and confused.

–Follow. It comes–

He understood. They were speaking of the black thing back in the trees, the creature that was hunting him. They were trying to help him get away from it.

He began moving, obedient to the voices, thinking that in some way Cinnaminson was reaching out to him from her prison, giving him one more gift. He slipped silently through the trees and grasses, casting quick glances toward where he had last seen his pursuer. He could feel its presence. He could sense it as it tracked him. It had found his trail and was following him, but it did not yet realize how close Pen was. Once it cut across his most recent tracks, the ones leading out of the ravine, it would be on him in seconds.

How far, he wondered suddenly, was he from the bridge?

He looked for it in the fading light, but could not find it. He was right at the edge of the ravine then, skirting its rim as the voices beckoned him on. He peered down into its darkness, but nothing could be seen. He glanced across its span, as well, but there was nothing to see there, either. The voices whispered more urgently, redirecting his concentration. They were humming now, but he could detect in the rise and fall of their music the need they were trying to communicate to him. *Don't slow down*, they were saying. *Don't hesitate.*

He gripped the darkwand in both hands, moving ahead in a crouch, the twilight deepening swiftly toward nightfall. If he failed to reach the bridge quickly, he would be left in darkness. What chance would he have against his pursuer then?

He felt a sudden rush of panic, sweat forming on his brow and trickling down his spine, soaking through his tunic.

—Follow—

He did so, focusing his attention on the sound of the

voices, the direction of their humming becoming his com-
pass. He must trust in them. He must believe that it was
Cinnaminson who guided him, the controlling voice
among the many, no different now than before, when she
had led him down into the ravine to find Mother Tanequil.
She was watching out for him still. She was protecting him.

Behind him, he heard movement, a sudden rustling, and
he turned to look. A shadow moved slowly through the
trees, bent low, scrabbling on all fours, head close to the
ground. An animal, tracking. It was moving slantwise to
where he crouched at the edge of the ravine, not yet seeing
him, but sensing his presence, realizing he was close. He
froze, watching it creep through the grasses, appearing and
disappearing. He felt his throat tighten and his mouth go
dry. He had never been so afraid.

–Follow–

Mechanically, he started moving ahead again, his
thoughts scattered, his mind on the consequences he
would face if his pursuer caught up to him. He saw Bandit
stretched lifeless on the grassy flats near Taupo Rough. He
saw the desiccated bodies of Gar Hatch and his crew hanging from the spars of the *Skatelow*. He felt Cinnaminson
shiver against him as she told him some of what she had endured as a captive. He felt his skin crawl as he imagined
what it would be like for him if he were caught.

–Quickly–

No longer pretending that there was any time left, that
he could afford to rely on stealth and caution to see him
through, he began to run in a low crouch. His only chance
was to reach the bridge and his companions. Surely Ker-

madec was a match for that monster. Surely Khyber could call on the Elfstones to stop it.

Please, please, someone must be able to help!

Then he heard the sudden, explosive sound of his pursuer coming fast, tearing through the trees, heedless of caution. He wheeled back to see the shadowy form bounding toward him, the glint of its strange weapon flashing in the darkness in small bursts of silver fire. Pen backed toward the ravine's edge, lifting the darkwand to defend himself, a pitiful weapon employed in a hopeless effort.

–Stop. Do not move. Trust us–

What choice did he have? There was nowhere left to go. He waited helplessly, staff lifted, body tensed, not knowing what he was going to do, no longer able to think clearly, watching as his pursuer drew closer, grew larger, turned darker than the night about him. He could see its cloak and hood. He could see that they were shredded and blackened with blood, the result of its encounter with the moor cat days earlier. It looked ragged and wild, something left over from the netherworld. It came at him in a frenzy, screaming, the sound so chilling that the boy very nearly broke and ran in spite of the admonition of his protectors.

–Stand. Be strong–

Help me, he thought.

Then the monster was on top of him.

On the far side of the ravine, Khyber Elessedil watched Pen stop suddenly and turn back toward his pursuer, as if realizing that he had been discovered. Then the black-cloaked hunter leapt from cover and closed on the boy in a reckless, maddened rush. She was shocked by its ragged look, its clothing torn and crusted with muck, pieces of its cloak trailing behind it in long black streamers. It had clearly gone through some bad times to get there, but now, having arrived, its course of action was settled. Even from as far away as she was, she could see the flash of its knife as it attacked.

She had only a moment and only one thing she could think of to do. She threw up her hands, the Druid magic gathering in a sudden rush at her fingertips. *I know so little*, she was thinking. She needed more time, she needed better preparation, she needed Ahren to act for her, she needed so much and she wasn't going to be given any of it. She wasn't even going to be given a second chance if she failed with the first.

She braced herself against the earth, legs spread for balance, arms extended.

It felt to Pen as if a giant's hand had struck him, the force of the blow knocking him completely off his feet as his attacker leapt at him, knife sweeping through the space he had just vacated. But the back side of the giant's hand caught the attacker as well, flinging him away in an audible rush of wind that scattered dust and debris in all directions and ripped up clots of scrub and grass. Out flew the black-cloaked form toward the dark drop of the ravine, arms and legs flailing wildly. The hood fell away, and Pen saw his pursuer's face for the first time—a blasted, torn visage that was only barely human and reflected an unfathomable madness.

A fresh shriek ripped from its twisted mouth, one born not of fear or anguish, but of fury and a promise of terrible retribution. Still trying to escape, Pen scrambled backwards on all fours. His attacker's abnormally long limbs grappled for the roots that grew along the edge of the ravine, fingers catching hold, toes digging in. It caught itself and hung there, scrambling to find purchase, to get back atop the slope, its crazed eyes fixed on Pen.

Then a dirt-encrusted root snaked out of the ravine like a sea leviathan's tentacle and wrapped about the leg of the dangling creature, fastening tight. The black-cloaked form twisted and struggled as its grip was loosened. Another yank, and Pen's attacker was falling into the abyss, down into the blackness. It struck with an audible thud, and then the roots of Mother Tanequil were moving, sliding against each other in rough scrapings. Pen heard the sounds of flesh tearing, bones breaking, and blood exploding out of ruptured limbs.

A final shriek rose out of the ravine's depths.

And then there was only silence.

THIRTY

Pen sat facing the ravine, breathing so hard he thought his heart would give out. He stared down into the void, half expecting the hooded creature to reemerge, even knowing that this time it was dead and gone and never coming back. Stunned by the suddenness of its demise, not quite certain that he could trust what he had seen, he waited anyway.

When he lifted his gaze, he saw Khyber. She was standing on the other side of the ravine, arms extended, body braced. Her posture and the shocked look on her face revealed her part in what had happened. It was her Druid magic that had knocked him aside. She had used it there, as she had weeks earlier aboard the *Skatelow* in Anatcherae to sweep their hunter from the decks of the airship and into the waters of the Lazareen. Both times, she had saved his life.

He stared at her in disbelief and gratitude, then lifted his hand in a small wave. She straightened and waved back. They stayed where they were for a moment, looking at each other across the ravine, but from a greater distance, too, one measured by hardships endured and deadly encounters survived. Suddenly it made him feel close to her, enough so that he wanted to call out and tell her so. But the darkness was a curtain between them, and the night seemed poised to steal away his words, so he stayed silent.

She waved once more, pointed in the direction of the ruins, and started off into the darkness.

He watched her go, then gathered his strength, stood, and walked to the edge of the drop. He didn't want to look down, but he did so anyway. He peered into the blackness, telling himself that it was all right, that he didn't need to be afraid anymore, that the thing that had hunted him for so long was really dead. He stayed where he was for a long time, waiting for the bad memories and troubling emotions to settle, to lose their edge, to find a resting place inside.

When he had satisfied himself, he exhaled slowly and deliberately and turned away. He wondered if Cinnaminson was at peace with what had happened, as well, asleep in the arms of Mother Tanequil. He hoped she was.

He followed the rim of the ravine once more, stepping carefully along its border through the deepening night, the clouds drifting overhead in tattered dark strips, the stars a sprinkle of silver dust in the firmament. He had no idea what time it was. He scanned the horizon for the moon, hoping to use it to judge the hour, but he failed to find it. He couldn't seem to remember if it was waxing or waning, full or new. He couldn't remember when he had seen it last. He was tired, he knew. Too tired to think.

His thoughts scattered, and he found himself wondering

if the aeriads had known that Khyber was across the ravine and ready to act to save him. He wondered if Cinnaminson was responsible, and if, being linked to the tanequil, she had asked the tree to aid him, too. Then it occurred to him that for the black-cloaked creature to reach the island to begin hunting him in the first place, the tanequil would have had to let it cross the bridge, thereby inviting it to its own doom.

He looked down at the darkwand. Having given up its limb in exchange for his fingers and Cinnaminson, had the tree become linked to him in a way he did not yet fully understand? It seemed clear that he was being kept safe at least until he was back across the bridge. It was no accident that he had been rescued that night. Khyber had not found him by chance. The aeriads had not led him to the edge of the ravine without knowing that Mother Tanequil was waiting.

How far did the protection of the tree reach?

He stopped and looked back into the darkness of the island forest. He wanted to know so much more than he did. He wanted to return to the tree to ask for the answers to his questions. But there was no point. His road lay ahead, on the other side of the ravine, back in the world of the Druids and Paranor.

And beyond, in the world of the Forbidding.

He began walking again, a steady march. The bridge was not far ahead. He saw a glow in the distance, fires lit within Stridegate's ruins. Kermadec and his Trolls were waiting. Khyber would be back. He was anxious suddenly to see them. He was tired of being alone. He needed their companionship; he needed the reassurance their numbers would provide.

He pushed through the screen of saplings fronting the bridge supports and stopped short.

Three huge warships hung anchored above the ruins, their massive black hulls reflecting dully in the light of bonfires lit all through Stridegate's flowered gardens. Shadows cast by the flames danced across through the carpeted beds and vine-covered walls, a swarm of shimmering black moths. Kermadec and his Rock Trolls sat weaponless and ringed by Gnome Hunters, their impassive faces lowered, their huge hands clenched about their knees as they faced away from their captors. Tagwen was crouched in their midst.

Directly across from Pen, on the far side of the bridge, stood a singular figure cloaked and hooded in black. At his appearance, the figure turned to face him.

Pen felt his heart sink and his euphoria fade.

The Druids had found them once more.